Another Glass of Tea

Katherine Ward (signature)

KATHERINE WARD

FriesenPress

One Printers Way
Altona, MB R0G 0B0
Canada

www.friesenpress.com

Copyright © 2022 by Katherine Ward
First Edition — 2022

ISBN
978-1-03-914561-0 (Hardcover)
978-1-03-914560-3 (Paperback)
978-1-03-914562-7 (eBook)

1. FICTION, ROMANCE, MULTICULTURAL & INTERRACIAL

Distributed to the trade by The Ingram Book Company

To the important people in my own exchange year — it was life-changing, in ways you may never understand.

And to those in the years afterwards who held my hand, held me up, and filled my life with joy.

And finally, to my SEA creatures, who've put up with far too many of my own İstanbul stories over the years.

Hepinizi çok seviyorum / I love you all.

INTRODUCTION

There's a Turkish expression: *Çaysız sohbet, aysız gökyüzü gibidir* that means conversations without tea are like a night sky without the moon. Anyone who has spent any time in Turkey will be familiar with the red-and-white-striped saucer that holds a delicate tulip-shaped glass filled to the brim with piping hot tea. Whether you stir in a sugar cube or two is up to you, but milk is never added. Tea is everywhere and punctuates every moment. Westerners tend to equate Turkey with Turkish coffee but tea is far more popular. Turks drink more tea per capita than any other country in the world at almost seven pounds per person per year, according to a 2016 Statista report. Compare that with the UK at a little more than four and a quarter or Canada at just a little over one pound.

Tea is part of daily rituals that begin with breakfast and finish at the end of a long day. The tiny glasses of goodness force you to slow down. In fact, it's impolite to refuse a glass of tea even if you've had your fill. Some Turks drink upwards of thirty glasses a day. Super strong tea is brewed in the top of a double-decker teapot called a *çaydanlık*; the bottom is filled with boiling water. This lets everyone have tea to the strength they prefer, whether *acık* (open) or *koyu* (dark).

Although I spent almost a year living in İstanbul, this story is not mine, nor are any of the characters real people. They are in part, composites of some of the best people I've known in my life, mixed with a healthy dose of pure imagination. Some of my memories, both faded and enhanced by time, make an appearance from time to time, but just to move the story along.

Like tea, you will find Turkish words woven through this book where it felt right; the guide on the next page will help you with some of the pronunciations of several Turkish letters. Errors (and I'm sure there are many) are purely mine.

It would be impossible to write a story that is set even partially in Turkey without tea. So please pour yourself a mug or a glass and enjoy the story.

TURKISH LETTERS

Turkish uses a modified Latin alphabet, containing twenty-nine letters. There is no Q, W, or X in Turkish, but there are seven additional letters (Ç, ğ, I, İ, Ö, Ş, and Ü). Below is a guide to help with the pronunciation of Turkish words.

A: as *a* in *father*

C: as the *j* in *jam*

Ç: as *ch* in *church*

E: as *e* in *den*

ğ: no English equivalent. Think of it as silent, but lengthening the preceding vowel. No Turkish word begins with this letter.

I ı (dotless i): as *i* in *cousin*

İ i (dotted i): as *i* in *it*

J: as *j* in *j'adore*. Used mostly to spell words borrowed from French.

O: as *o* in *order*

Ö: as *u* in *measure*

Ş: as *sh* in *shirt*

U: as *oo* in *room*

Ü: as *u* in the French *tu*

Prologue

Hayley stepped out of her Sultanahmet hotel in İstanbul into the bustling streets. The *müezzin* had begun the evening call to prayer and observant Muslim men were hurrying to their local mosques. Hayley was excited to be back in this city, and thinking back thirty years ago to her exchange year, she smiled. There had been many loves that year. She wondered what had become of those boys, and whether she'd recognize them when she saw them in a few days.

Looking around, she shook her head to clear it after the long flight from the US, trying to get her bearings. Everything was the same, but different. Including her, she thought wryly, as she considered her waistline.

One thing that had remained the same, it seemed, was the countless red carts selling food. She approached one, her stomach growling, confused as to whether it was dinnertime or not.

"*Bir simit, lütfen,*" she said hesitantly to the street vendor, in very rusty Turkish. But he understood, and the wizened old man gave her the ring-shaped bread. After holding out a few lira — she wasn't sure she'd understood how much it cost — and letting the man make change, Hayley wandered over and sat down on the benches in front of the Blue Mosque, looking at it with renewed reverence. Enjoying her first bite, she once again said a silent thanks that her friend Fiona had taken the lead to reconnect everyone and then suggest this journey down memory lane.

Yeşim looked up from her computer, where she'd just finished preparing her next lecture. Notebooks beside her, she reached her arms overhead and stretched her back before taking a sip of strong *çay* from the delicate tulip-shaped glass in front of her. An assistant professor, Yeşim spent a lot of time honing her plans in the study of their Beşiktaş home. But just now, she turned her attention to her eighteen-year-old son, Kaan, who was explaining why he'd be home late that night.

"*Tamam anneciğim?*" he asked, seeking her permission.

"*Tamam oğulum,*" she answered, okaying Kaan's social plans. He ran away with a smile, leaving Yeşim to sigh as she returned her attention to her computer. Her schedule had been so busy recently, and she'd been looking forward to a family evening with her husband and with Kaan and his sister, Melek. But that would have to wait, and at least now she could spend some time finalizing reunion plans of their graduating class. Sunday was only two days away and there was still lots to do. Putting on her reading glasses again, she picked up the photos beside her keyboard. As she pulled out the pencil that had been anchoring her hair on top of her head, it tumbled down in waves down her back. It had been longer back then, she thought, as she leafed through the stack. The three musketeers had become five that final year. And soon they'd finally be back together again. Turning back to the computer, she opened up her reunion planning file.

Nazlı shut off the lights and turned her key in the lock of her Cihangir yoga studio, after another great class. She was so proud of the success she'd had in the past few years since opening the studio, and loved bringing calm and peace to her students through her teaching.

"Görüşürüz!"

She waved goodbye to her other yogis, who had gathered for *çay* on the terrace of a tiny rundown café next door to the studio. Tonight, she wouldn't be joining them. Nazlı had dinner plans with former colleagues at the engineering firm where she'd worked before her radical career change.

Walking up the steep cobblestone street from the studio toward Taksim Square, she thought about how fun the reunion would be. Twenty-five years had gone by in a flash. Of course she saw Yeşim regularly, but there were many classmates she hadn't seen in years. She'd enjoyed getting to know Fiona again during her visits over the last few years and was looking forward to seeing Hayley too. Her brow furrowed as she suddenly worried her English might not be strong enough anymore — she had little need to use it at the studio.

Halfway around the world, **Aylin** was thinking about the reunion too. But she was anxious. She kept picking at the hangnail on her thumb, and wondering again if she was doing the right thing by going to this reunion. She did miss her old friends. She had been the self-acknowledged leader of the group, although she certainly didn't feel like it now. Despite being well regarded in her profession in Australia, nervousness of returning to her homeland was battling her eagerness to reconnect with those from a simpler time in her life, before everything had changed. All week long, she'd been putting clothes into her suitcase and taking them out again, having alternately convinced herself that going was either a good or bad idea.

Finally, filling the suitcase again, she steeled her nerves and turned off the lights. Taking a deep breath, she took one last look in the mirror. The woman she was today was not the girl she had been then. She looked older, but she was pleased to see she still looked confident. It helped to know that nobody could see the turmoil within.

Raking her hands through her unruly curly silver hair, Aylin grabbed her purse and her bag, and stepped out the door. For good or for ill, she was going home.

"*Sağol, abi.*" **Fiona** tossed the words of thanks over her shoulder to the local *bakkal* owner, giving him a broad smile as she left his shop with the makings of that night's dinner. Fiona loved it when her schedule allowed her to spend a few weeks back in İstanbul, enjoying all it had to offer and spending time with her exchange-year friends. Successfully self-employed, Fiona could work from anywhere, and she'd visited the city several times over the past few years. This time she was spending a month in a charming little flat on the Asian side of the city, close to where they'd gone to school that year. Her first week in İstanbul had been filled with a mixture of work, socializing, and exploring — exactly how she liked it.

With a huge pair of sunglasses protecting her grey eyes from the bright sun, the petite redhead walked down the hill toward her flat, catching glimpses of the Bosphorus between the buildings. She knew Haley had arrived today and was on the other side, behind the minarets of the Blue Mosque. The women had reconnected a few years earlier and messaged each other from time to time, keeping in touch and sharing stories of their children.

Haley's boys were teenagers, about the same age as Yeşim's pair, but Fiona's four were grown and on their own now. A widow — how she hated that word — of more than fifteen years now, Fiona had raised them on her own. But this weekend was for them, not their children, and Fiona couldn't wait until all five women were together again for the first time. It was going to be a wonderful reunion.

Reaching her home away from home, Fiona climbed the stairs to her flat. She put the groceries in her small kitchen and poured herself a glass of white wine before wandering into her glass-fronted living room in her stockinged feet. She smiled at the sight. The sun was just starting to set and the sky across the Bosphorus was a brilliant orange. Seagulls followed the ferries hoping for bits of bread to be thrown to them and small fishing boats zigzagged across the water. Sea tankers waited their turn at the mouth of the Sea of Marmara to enter the narrow channel on their way to the Black Sea.

The slim body of water separated Europe from Asia and sometimes Fiona couldn't believe that she'd crossed back and forth at least once a week that year. As she gazed out the window, memories flooded back and she could almost hear the giddy laughter of five teenage girls, gossiping about boys and making plans as they nibbled on snacks and drank glass after glass of piping hot tea. Taking another sip of wine as the call to prayer began, Fiona wondered, as she did every time she returned to İstanbul, if this would be the time she'd see Metin.

Part 1

Chapter 1

"Geldim!" Aylin bounded up the street breathlessly announcing her arrival, to meet with her two best friends at their favourite ice cream shop in Moda, a trendy neighbourhood in residential Asian İstanbul.

Aylin, Nazlı, and Yeşim had been fast friends since they met on the first day of primary school, standing in line together in their crisp black school uniforms with white collars and their hair tied back into tightly controlled ponytails and braids. When they got the results of their high school entrance exams, the girls were thrilled to learn they had all gained entrance to the same prestigious *lise* with its uniform of plaid skirts, powder-blue shirts, and cerulean-blue sweaters. They boys wore grey pants, navy blazers, and blue ties that matched the girls' sweaters. Students were proud to wear this uniform.

There was a strong English focus at this *lise*, which they all believed would be important in the future, especially if they wanted to travel or work abroad. English and Turkish shared very little in common and was structured very differently. It was no wonder many people struggled with it. Aylin and Yeşim, more outgoing by nature, took to it with relative ease. Nazlı, who was quieter and less apt to put up her hand to answer, had the mechanics, but putting it into practice was harder for her. Three years passed quickly and the girls remained steadfast friends, and could often be found walking down the road, arms linked, in fits of giggles.

Now, it was just two weeks until their final year began and Aylin had gathered them together for an afternoon of shopping. But first, ice cream. The girls chose their favourite combination of flavours — two small scoops each, and savoured the fresh sweet and tart combinations of chocolate and sour cherry, vanilla and pomegranate, and strawberry and lemon.

This was an important year for them. The nationwide exam they would write in the spring would determine which university they would attend for the next four years. There would be a lot of studying this year as they would need excellent grades to get into their universities of choice. But in this last week of freedom before school began, they were still carefree and had all the time in the world.

With the last of the *dondurma* licked off their fingers, the girls spent the afternoon wandering through the streets looking for clothes and makeup they could wear after school or on weekends, and buying new notebooks and paper to cover their textbooks with. Finally, laden with packages, they stopped to rest and to have a glass of *çay* and savoury biscuits.

"Do you know anything about this year's exchange students?" asked Nazlı curiously, stirring a sugar cube into her tea. While justifiably confident in her math and science skills, she was irrationally nervous about her English. With foreigners joining the senior class she knew she'd be called on to use the language in an everyday context, not just academically. Exchange students were a regular occurrence at their school, and they'd watched older students make friends with kids from England, the Netherlands,

America, and Mexico, to name a few. This year, it was their turn to host the foreigners, and Nazlı's curiosity was tempered with a little bit of insecurity.

"I've heard there are only two this year," offered Yeşim, blowing on her *çay* to cool it. Her family was involved peripherally in the exchange program, so she often had inside information. "An American and our first Canadian — both girls." She sipped from the tulip-shaped glass and then put it back in its red-striped saucer.

"I wonder if they'll be alike," mused Aylin. Americans and British girls were quite different, she knew, but they didn't know anything about Canada. Her fingers hovered over the pastries, as she decided which to choose.

Going back to Nazlı's concerns, Yeşim reassured her. "Nazlı, you'll be fine. Your English is stronger than you think, and I'm sure they'll learn at least some Turkish while they're here."

"Do you remember those boys who were here during our second year?" Nazlı asked. "None of them could speak Turkish at all, even at the end of their year."

"But that was only once," said Aylin. "I'm sure these girls will make an effort. Most others have." She popped the last biscuit in her mouth.

Nazlı picked at the crumbs left on her plate. "*Inşallah*," she murmured, looking at the other girls through long eyelashes, her lack of confidence continuing to show.

"Oh, my God, what have I done?" Fiona O'Reilly asked herself that same afternoon, as she hauled two heavy suitcases off the carousel at Atatürk International Airport. She might be small, but she was strong. Her bags were easy to find, with straps of the iconic red maple leaf around them to distinguish hers from the hundreds of other suitcases being spit out one at a time from the belly of the plane. Fiona had splashed water on her face to try and shake off the long journey once she'd passed through customs and immigration. It hadn't helped much. It had been a long trip, beginning with a three-hour bus ride the day before from her small central-Ontario town and followed by flights from Toronto to Frankfurt and then on to İstanbul. They'd flown through a storm and there had been some turbulence on the overseas flight, which had added to Fiona's anxiety of the reality of what she'd signed up for.

In just minutes, she would meet people who would be her family for this year. They were waiting for her just outside the doors. All she had to do was muster up the courage to go through them.

Taking a deep breath, she walked through the big glass doors, pulling her suitcases behind her, and looking around for someone — anyone — who looked like they were waiting for her. She'd received a brief letter from her host parents with a photo of them and their daughters. Now, she scanned the crowd to see if she could recognize anyone.

Finally she saw — well, she didn't quite know what to call them. A kind-looking woman in her mid-forties and a handsome man with a greying mustache, perhaps a few years older, held up a sign with her name on it. She smiled tentatively and started toward them, pulling her bags behind her.

"*Merhaba*," she greeted them nervously, with one of the three words of Turkish she had learned. Before she knew it, Fiona was pulled into the woman's arms and greeted with a kiss on each cheek.

"*Hoş geldin, kızım*," she said and then repeated in heavily accented English, "Welcome to you, our new daughter." And just like that, Fiona knew she was home.

Home, however, turned out to be nothing like she expected. Back in Canada, Fiona was an only child in a comfortably middle-class family. Her father was an electrician and her mother a teacher, both active in the community. Fiona's lakefront home had huge rooms and sat on several acres of land. They were surrounded by nature, but could walk to the nearest village in about twenty minutes. The nearest town — and traffic light — was forty kilometres further away.

Fiona had visited Toronto on many occasions and thought she was prepared for a big city, but the sheer size and density of İstanbul was hard for her to take in. She knew she'd be living with a relatively well-to-do family, so when they pulled up to an apartment building after a long drive, she had to hide her surprise. Nilüfer — Fiona had been told she should call her *anne*, which meant mother — walked up the stairs while Hasan — *baba*, she corrected herself in her head — crammed her luggage into the tiniest elevator she'd ever seen, for the short five-story journey to an apartment with tiny little bedrooms. There was just enough space in Fiona's room for a bed, a desk, and a small wardrobe. Her two new sisters helped her settle in. Ceylan — *abla* — she was to call her older sister — was finishing her last year at university and Defne was just entering high school. Ceylan *abla* could provide some very basic translation, but in general, the family spoke very little English, so there was a lot of pantomiming as they communicated in those first hours.

Fiona's new *baba* helped her dial the international codes to call her parents before dinner to let them know she had arrived.

"They seem very nice, but it's all so different," she said, swallowing hard. "I'm going to have to learn Turkish quickly."

She handed the phone to Ceylan, who haltingly spoke to Fiona's father. "I am Ceylan. I am oldest daughter. My *baba* want me say you we take good care of Fiona. You no worry."

"You're sure you're going to be all right?" Fiona's father asked her when his daughter was back on the line.

"I just need some sleep, I think," she assured him. "Tomorrow I'll have to hit the books."

"Call us whenever you need to," he said. "We love you, Fiona. You're going to have a great year."

"Love you too." Fiona hung up the phone and took a deep breath, looking a little lost.

"Fiona *abla*, *sofra hazır*. We eat now." Defne was calling her to the table for supper, where Fiona had her first vocabulary lesson. By dessert, she was smiling again, proud that she could at least name her knife, fork, spoon, and glass as well as several of the delicious dishes on the table. When she tumbled into bed that night, exhausted after the long day, she thought she might be all right after all.

As Fiona settled into her new family, she learned that she should answer the welcoming *hoş geldin* with the corresponding *hoş bulduk*. She learned *gün aydın* meant good morning and that it was used as a greeting until noon. After that it was *iyi günler* until dinnertime, and then *iyi akşamlar* until the end of the night when she wished her new family *iyi geceler* as she turned in for the night. She managed *lütfen* easily for please, but *teşekkür ederim* for thank you was a mouthful and *Allaha ısmarladık* for goodbye tied her tongue in knots.

She learned that breakfast would not be toast or cereal and milk, but fresh bread, that someone got from the local bakery every day, cheese, tomatoes, cucumbers, and olives. She quickly learned those words. And she learned that tea — *çay* — was everywhere, all day long. Tiny little glasses of incredibly hot, almost red, tea. No matter where they went, *çay* was offered, and was not to be declined.

Fiona's *baba* sat down with her every night when he returned from work to give her a short lesson. She learned that the alphabet had several extra letters and was missing one or two in English. She memorized words for bed, door, book, and skirt and learned to conjugate verbs. Fiona felt like a toddler, frustrated she couldn't put the words together into sentences or understand anything other than one or two words at a time. But it was a beginning.

Her family took her on outings during these last days before school began. They took a ferry to Adalar, a small grouping of islands off the coast, and spent the day among the most trees Fiona had seen since she arrived, and drove up to a beach on the Black Sea on Saturday. As the family settled on beach loungers, she slathered sunblock onto her pale, freckled skin, adding sunglasses and a sunhat over her copper-coloured hair. The girls all swam in the sea and Fiona read for a time under an umbrella while the others baked in the sun. Her lake was home to powerboats and even the occasional small tour boat, so she was in awe of the big ocean liners she saw on the sea, faraway from where they swam.

One morning, toward the end of her second week, Fiona's *anne* took her shopping. Consulting the school list, they chose two regulation plaid skirts and three powder-blue blouses. A blue cardigan sweater and crew-neck sweater rounded out the mix. Fiona's own shoes and socks would be fine. They added a couple of lined notebooks, some pens and pencils, and Fiona was ready. They sorted out the school minibus, and then finally, it was the first day of school.

A few days after Fiona arrived in İstanbul, Hayley Jones flew in from Cincinnati. She'd had an easy journey, making friends with a nice young man from İstanbul on her last flight who spoke good English and they'd promised to meet up. He gave her his phone number and she gave him the number of her host family.

Like Fiona, she was nervous, but she'd spoken on the phone with her new *anne* and *baba* before leaving Ohio, so she knew they spoke good English. She adjusted her very full backpack and with her two big suitcases strode confidently through the big glass doors and found her new family. They were enthusiastic to meet her, and she melted into warm embraces of her host parents. Their son, Can, was waiting at home. He was a university student, who had spent his own exchange year in Michigan three years earlier. He quickly took Hayley under his wing.

15

Like Fiona, Hayley was surprised to learn she would be living in an apartment. She was from a reasonably sized American city, but İstanbul was still overwhelming. Can chatted comfortably with Hayley, showing her around the neighbourhood and taking her to good places for *çay* and snacks. In the evenings, they watched TV and Hayley strained to hear words she had learned that day.

The last weekend before school, the family went to the historic peninsula to show Hayley the Blue Mosque and Saint Sophia. She was mesmerized by both and awestruck by the years of work that had gone into building them. Hayley was particularly drawn by the architecture and the artistry of the interior finishes and decoration. She'd seen nothing like it before and didn't yet have the words to describe how it made her feel.

Chapter 2

"*Gün aydın*," called Nazlı as she caught up with Aylin and Yeşim on the crowded blacktop on the far side of the schoolyard, wishing them a good morning. In their uniforms, with their faces freshly scrubbed and their hair pulled back, the girls looked younger than the young ladies who had shopped together two weeks earlier. They were excited to begin their final year of high school and eager to learn who their teachers would be.

On the other side of the schoolyard with their host families, Fiona and Hayley sized each other up for the first time. They looked quite smart in their identical uniforms — the only thing that was different was their running shoes. That and their height. Fiona was quite petite at only five feet tall, and Hayley, seven inches taller, towered over her. Both were nervous about today — their first day away from the safety net of their new families, and they were more than a little anxious about what school would be like.

"I'm a little scared," admitted Hayley. "Can told me a little bit about what to expect, but . . ." She trailed off, her slim fingers playing with the hem of her blue cardigan.

"I know what you mean," Fiona agreed, as she took in what looked like complete chaos in the schoolyard. "It's all a little overwhelming, isn't it?"

They laughed nervously. "A blonde and a redhead. We don't stick out at all, do we?" Hayley mused.

Fiona smiled in amusement. But she'd always stood out, even at home. It was the same here, although she'd been surprised to discover not all Turks had dark hair and eyes. Hayley was every inch the all-American girl with her blue eyes and dark blonde hair, so standing out would be new for her. At least the uniforms helped them blend in a bit, and they'd both tied their hair back like the other girls. Hayley's pin-straight hair was just long enough to make a short ponytail, and Fiona had tamed her waves into a long thick braid that hung down her back.

Before they had time to learn much about each other, a bell rang and suddenly, from chaos emerged pattern, as students quickly moved from their groups into long orderly lines, each one seeming to represent a class. A serious looking man — the principal, they were told — stood on a platform tapping the microphone in front of him to make sure it worked.

After a short speech, the orderly lines of students started moving into the school building one class at a time. Fiona and Hayley went with their host parents to the main office and were given their own class assignments. A sparse room, with little decor except for the omnipresent picture of Atatürk and a flag, Ayşe *hanım*'s office bore little resemblance to a vice-principal's office in either of their home countries. And then suddenly it was time to wish reluctant goodbyes to their families.

"Welcome to our school," said Ayşe *hanım* tersely, as she ushered them down the empty corridor, her sensible shoes echoing with every step. They would be together it turned out.

"I wonder where we put our stuff," Hayley whispered to Fiona, who shrugged. Neither saw signs of lockers anywhere.

Ayşe *hanım* was the very definition of a traditional school official, with greying hair pulled back into a severe bun and a pair of wire-rimmed glasses perched on her nose.

"I hope you will like it here," she said as the heels of her sensible shoes clicked on the floor as she continued down the long corridor. Reaching the classroom, Ayşe *hanım* opened the windowed door and nodded to the teacher at the front of the class, who was clearly expecting them.

As they stood in the doorway, Fiona and Hayley took in the view. This was not the kind of classroom they were used to. Instead of the single desks and chairs of their high schools at home, Fiona and Hayley were surprised to see many rows of wide wooden desks, with students sitting together in pairs on benches. The windows had deep sills, but no curtains. Grey paint coloured the bottom half of the walls, and white the top. And the no lockers mystery was solved. The students had their bookbags with them on the floor beside their seats. The teacher at the front of the class gestured enthusiastically for the girls to come in and introduced herself. Demet *hoca* smiled as she welcomed the exchange students to 6J.

She raised her voice. "*Arkadaşlar*," she announced, clapping her hands to get the attention of the class, before continuing in English. "Please welcome Hayley from America and Fiona from Canada. They will be our guests this year. Fiona, you will share with Nazlı, and Hayley, you will be with Yeşim," she added, as she showed them to their seats.

Yeşim smiled broadly as Hayley made her way down the aisle. "Come and sit," she said, patting the seat beside her. Hayley returned the smile, taking in the dark-haired beauty with whom she would share a seat. Even without makeup, the blue-eyed girl with olive skin and a wavy high ponytail was very pretty. And she seemed friendly.

"Hi," Hayley whispered as put her bag down and settled herself down on the bench.

The next row over, and one desk ahead, Nazlı gave Fiona a timid smile. "Welcome," she said, self-conscious about her poor pronunciation of the word's first letter and worried that she was making a bad first impression. She fiddled with the end of her long dark braid nervously. It was even longer than Fiona's.

"*Memnum oldum*," Fiona replied tentatively, having practised with Defne that morning. Her reasonable attempt at a Turkish "pleased to meet you" brought a relieved smile to Nazlı's face, and the two girls settled in for the first lesson, both feeling that it would be all right.

The morning passed quickly, with classes in both English and Turkish. Fiona and Hayley quickly learned that teachers — not students — moved between rooms and that the class stood up at attention whenever a teacher entered the room.

As soon as the lunch bell rang, Aylin flew down the aisle from her seat near the front of the class, wild corkscrew tendrils around her hairline already escaping, as usual, from her ponytail, to join Yeşim and Nazlı, and the foreign girls.

"I am so glad you are in our lessons," she said enthusiastically, staking her claim as well to their friendship. "Nazlı and Yeşim and I are best friends and we welcome you. I know we will have together a very good year."

Over lunch from the canteen, the tight-knit group of three morphed into five as the girls learned where each other lived, and a little more about each other. The exchange students were happy to have found friends so quickly.

Chapter 3

With every day that passed, the girls became closer and soon spent almost every day after school together before heading home. Fiona was working hard to learn Turkish, and was picking up new words each day, scribbling them down in a little notebook she kept in her school bag. Soon, she could string a few together and could ask and answer simple questions with some confidence. Her French knowledge helped with pronunciation, but the grammar was still very much a challenge. Nazlı was a tremendous help, explaining and translating for Fiona, but using simple Turkish whenever she thought Fiona could follow it.

The gestures were as confusing as the grammar. A click of the tongue against the roof of your mouth meant "no." Shaking your head back and forth didn't mean "no," it meant you didn't understand and the hand gesture Fiona knew for "go away" meant "come"

Where Fiona was making progress, Hayley was struggling. She found herself taking advantage of her chatty seatmate, and her fluently bilingual host family. She found the new sounds really hard to imitate, even when Yeşim repeated them for her. The grammar was so difficult and the word order was almost backwards to English. It made her want to throw up her hands. Besides, she justified it to herself, everyone around her spoke English better than she'd ever speak Turkish, so maybe it wasn't important that she try so hard.

CRUIO

Within a few weeks, both Hayley and Fiona's host parents became comfortable that the girls could make their way home, so they had given them a little bit of freedom with their new friends. Sometimes Yeşim's boyfriend, Mehmet, would join them for after-school conversation and a snack, but as often as not, the girls were on their own, and the conversation turned, as it does with teenagers, to boys.

A few weeks into the school term, just before lunch, a boy's smiling face appeared at the window of the classroom door. Fiona had been concentrating on the lesson, so didn't see him immediately, but when she looked up, she saw him waving frantically, trying to get someone's attention.

"*Kim o?* Who's that?" she asked Nazlı.

"*O Metin.* That's Metin. Metin is . . . he is like you."

At that moment, the teacher walked past their desk, and Fiona didn't get a chance to ask more. When the lunch bell rang, Metin rushed in and was instantly surrounded by the boys in the class. He was clearly very popular.

"*Tamam,* okay, now I can explain. Last year, Metin was exchange student to America," Nazlı said. "Actually, he passed from the American school so now he . . ." she trailed off, searching for the right words.

"Ah, *anladım.* I understand," said Fiona, grasping the issue. "He graduated there so doesn't need to finish *lise* here, right?"

"*Aynen öyle* — exactly."

Two days later, Metin turned up again. This time, Fiona noticed his sparkling green eyes, infectious smile, and dark curly hair. Broad shouldered, at a smidge more than six feet tall, Metin was taller than most of her classmates. He'd heard about this year's exchange students, and when he glanced their way, he smiled, giving them a wave before turning his attention back to his friends.

Both girls were looking forward to meeting Metin properly and learning about his exchange year. By now, they'd heard from their classmates that he'd lived in North Carolina, and that he'd been back in İstanbul for just a few weeks. But Metin's focus today was on arranging *futbol* matches with friends, so the hoped-for introduction was delayed.

Metin became a frequent visitor. Because he didn't have school to attend in what amounted to a gap year between high school and university, he would pop in regularly at lunch, or toward the end of the day to see his friends or to make plans for the weekend. Those plans often involved soccer or basketball. Fiona got used to seeing his face on the other side of the door, and catching his eye from time to time, but the boys kept him occupied and she was busy with her own friends too.

While they still hadn't met this particular boy yet, boys were a regular topic of conversation among the girls. If Hayley and Fiona had thought that Turkish girls their age wouldn't have boyfriends, they were soon corrected. There were a number of girls and boys coupled up at their school, although some were more secretive than others.

Nazlı's parents, for instance, didn't know about her boyfriend. She was always making up plans with one friend or another so she could see him without them knowing. Ozan was already at university — an older man — and Nazlı felt very grown up on the arm of her philosophy major boyfriend.

Yeşim's boyfriend, Mehmet, on the other hand, was not a secret. Their families were close and the two young people had grown up together. Mehmet was very protective of Yeşim and sometimes a little jealous of the amount of time she spent with her girlfriends. Still, Nazlı was envious of the openness of their relationship.

Hayley was thrilled to learn that romance wasn't off limits for this year. She had been flirting with Barış from their class during breaks and she'd also spoken on the phone a few times with the boy she'd met on the plane. Hayley was hoping to meet him after school one day soon. And then there was Tuncay from the class down the hall, whose curly hair and chocolate-brown eyes made her swoon, and the tall, dark, and handsome Cetin from the class across from theirs, who was the tallest boy at the school. Fiona couldn't keep up with all of Hayley's love interests. And the boys were more than happy to flirt back with the pretty American.

On a clear and still summery day in early October, with classes finished for the week, Fiona packed her books and pens into her bag and followed everyone out of the school, squinting in the bright sunshine and shading her eyes quickly. Her nose twitched and she suddenly sneezed quietly. And quickly sneezed again. And then again.

"*Çok yasa*," she heard from behind her.

"*Sen de gör*," she responded out of newfound habit, giving the appropriate reply to the Turkish "bless you" that had been called out. She'd learned this verbal repartee early on. Sudden bright light had made her sneeze since she was young. It happened whenever she went outdoors on a sunny day, or sometimes when she looked at a very bright lamp. Her Turkish family had found it amusing, and they'd taught her these words in her first week with them.

"*Hasta mısın?*" asked the concerned deep voice, a little closer now. Fiona turned to realize that it was Metin asking about her health.

"No, no, I'm not sick," she assured him. "The sun just makes me sneeze."

"That's weird."

"It's hereditary — and annoying."

"Well, I'm glad you're all right," he said. "I wanted to ask if you'd like to come and play American football with us this weekend? I'm going to teach the guys and you could help, if you like."

Fiona hesitated.

"We've invited lots of people — including Hayley and your three musketeers," he assured her, making sure she knew that there would be a group of girls there as well.

"Is that what you call them?" Fiona laughed. "I supposed it's probably an appropriate name."

"What about the football?"

"Well," she appeared to consider the offer. "You know, we play Canadian football where I'm from — and I'm not sure I really understand the rules of that game, let alone the American version," she teased. But when she saw disappointment register on Metin's face, she smiled and hastily added, "But it sounds like fun. I'm sure you and Hayley can teach me too."

Saturday rolled round and Fiona walked over to Hayley's apartment to pick her up for the football game.

"*Merhaba,* Can," she greeted Hayley's *abi* when he answered the door. "Hayley *hazır mı?*" Hayley was, in fact, ready and came running. She was a big football fan, often watching a game on TV with her father and brothers on a Sunday afternoon. Hayley was excited to see if Metin could teach it quickly to everyone. And she was curious to see her classmates in "regular" clothes. This would be the first time they'd been together that wasn't directly after school. She and Fiona hooked arms and walked together down Bağdat Street toward school.

About twenty minutes later, they arrived to find about a dozen boys and another half a dozen girls, all ready to toss around the old pigskin. Everyone looked so different, especially the girls. Wearing makeup and jewellery, jeans and sweatshirts, the girls looked older, and more sophisticated. They could have been in the US or Canada or anywhere else. The boxy school uniforms had been hiding youthful figures of different shapes and sizes. Out of their jackets and ties, you could see the boys' personalities too, in their choices of clothes.

Metin bounded up to say hello, wearing his prized St. Louis Cardinals emblazoned sweatshirt.

"Hey, that's my dad's team," Hayley told him with a big grin. "Great choice!"

"Cool," Metin said, "It was my host family's favourite too. You should be on my team. Come on with me, we're just about to start choosing sides."

She tucked her hair behind her ears and Metin grabbed her hand. Metin and Mehmet started making choices, and the teams were quickly formed. Yeşim joined Hayley and Metin while Aylin, Nazlı, and Fiona joined Mehmet's team.

An afternoon of hilarity followed, as they all tried to make sense of the game, learn how to throw the ball, and how to block and tackle. They didn't really keep score, and after a couple of hours, they called it a day. Nazlı and Aylin had to leave, but others formed smaller groups, some moving on to play basketball, some talking *futbol*, and others discussing the weekend's homework. Hayley was holding court on one side of the school yard with Barış and three other boys. The shapely blue-eyed blonde who could play football had their attention, and she was soaking it all in.

Another Glass of Tea

Yeşim and Fiona joined Mehmet and Metin at the bottom of the garden and over the next little while, Fiona finally got to know a little bit about Metin's exchange year in Charlotte. His American classmates quickly started calling him Matt, which made Fiona giggle. Metin talked about his host family — he'd had an older brother and sister to show him the way — and why he wasn't in school this year. He was waiting to write university exams next spring. Until then, he was tutoring and trying to keep busy.

At some point, Mehmet and Yeşim slipped away, leaving Metin and Fiona sitting on the garden's back wall looking at the sea, still engrossed in conversation. She asked about his family. Metin was the middle child in a spread-out family. He had a twelve-year-old sister and a twenty-two-year-old brother who was doing his compulsory military service this year. They lived not far up the road from Fiona's family, it turned out. Fiona was surprised to discover that Metin's family had no telephone.

"We're not the only ones, you know," Metin enlightened her. "Most of my friends do, but not all of them."

"How do you make plans?" Fiona asked him, a puzzled look on her face.

He smiled. "Well, first, we don't plan in such detail. Things are more spontaneous here." Fiona nodded. She'd definitely noticed that. "Someone might run a message, and if we have to, there's always the PTT." Turkey's post office also held yellow telephones and you could buy *jeton* to operate them. Fiona already kept one in her purse just in case, but she still couldn't imagine a house without a phone.

As the sun started to descend in the sky, Metin realized he'd done most of the talking and hadn't learned much about Fiona yet. He asked if he could walk her back home. Fiona glanced across the schoolyard and realized that apart from the two of them, Hayley and Barış were the only ones left. She walked over to them.

"Hayley, Metin and I are going to head out, okay?"

27

"No problem. I'm sure Barış will take me if it gets dark," she said, rolling her eyes at the need.

It had taken the girls a few weeks to get used to the idea that they were expected to be escorted home in the evenings. Both of them shook their heads at the absurdity of it, but their host parents found it important, and boys seemed to expect to do it. Fiona had been walked home by her friends' older brothers more than once already and she was getting used to it. Hayley was chafing more at the restriction. As the nights started getting darker earlier, she was frustrated at the limitation. She was used to more freedom and she gritted her teeth when her *abi* was overprotective with her. It seemed that her *anne* and *baba* thought it was just fine that her older host brother could order her not to go out without his protection. It had been the cause of more than one disagreement at her house. She had complained bitterly to Fiona about it just the day before. Today, however, she was having fun with Barış.

As Metin and Fiona left the school, they continued their conversation. "I've never met anyone from Canada before," admitted Metin. "All I really know is that there are moose, and winter is cold."

Fiona laughed. "There's a little more to it than that!" Walking along Yoğurtçu Park, she told Metin about her little town and her dreams of writing. She was an only child, she explained, and was very close to her parents. She knew that her being away this year was difficult for them, but they were always supportive of her dreams. Fiona explained how she used to take a notebook up into the tree fort her father had built her and write stories. It was all she had ever wanted, and she was hoping to go study marketing when her exchange year was over. She told him about her Turkish family and how much she was enjoying her year so far. "But I'm just so frustrated at how long it's taking to learn Turkish," she complained. "I've been here close to two months and I don't feel like I've learned anywhere enough yet. It's hard, and everyone wants to speak English with me. It feels rude to insist, but if I want to learn, I have to."

Metin stopped and looked at her directly. He switched to his native language, asking slowly and clearly if she'd like him to speak Turkish with her sometimes. He knew plenty of exchange students to Turkey who hadn't been all that motivated to learn the language when they realized their classmates and host parents spoke at least reasonable, and sometimes fluent, English. There was something about Fiona that intrigued him greatly, and the fact that she was taking language seriously set her apart from others. He wanted to spend more time with her and hoped she'd say yes to his offer.

She broke out into a grin and so did he, knowing she'd understood. She nodded. "*Evet, konuşalım.* Yes, let's do that."

Chapter 4

"Hayley, *mektuplar var,*" called her *anne* when she arrived home from school on a grey and rainy day.

As soon as Hayley changed out of her uniform she grabbed the letters from home and curled up to read them. Maybe they would help make this day better. Demet *hoca* had spoken sharply to her about something in the morning but she hadn't understood the teacher properly. She'd joined Fiona and the girls at lunch break, but she found it hard to follow along even when they slowed down for her. Hayley knew that Fiona was getting closer to everyone and she was starting to feel like she was on the outside. It was so frustrating. Then, her latest flirtation had ended at afternoon break when Tuncay told her he needed to concentrate more on his studies. And to top it all off, she'd forgotten her umbrella and was dripping wet when she got home. Alone in her bedroom, hair still damp, Hayley quickly scanned a postcard from her friend and then tore open the thick letter from her mother, soaking up all the news from back home and fighting back tears of homesickness.

There had been a letter awaiting Fiona that day as well, full of cheerful chatter. Fiona's mother told to her about the new students in her grade six class and explained that her father was volunteering again for the town's fall fair. Fiona was sad to miss it, but everything in İstanbul was so new and exciting. Except grammar. Today she had promised herself she would open her grammar book after school to try and master a past tense that didn't have an English equivalent. She was having trouble figuring out when to use it. She was just beginning to understand how to use it when the doorbell rang and her *anne* came to tell her Haley was there.

"Come in, come in. What are you doing here?" Fiona was surprised to see her friend. They hadn't made plans. Her surprise quickly turned into concern when she saw Haley's face.

"I just needed to talk to someone without having to slow down and use simple words all the time."

"Come into my room. Let's talk." Fiona led Hayley by the hand and they sat down on her bed. Hayley looked like she was going to cry. "*Ah canım,*" Fiona started, not even realizing she'd begun with a Turkish term of endearment. "What's wrong?"

Slowly it came out. First Hayley told her about Tuncay. "I really liked him and I thought he liked me. I don't understand why he can't study and spend time with me. Is it because I can't figure out Turkish? It's so hard! Or is there something wrong with me?" Fiona opened her mouth to reassure her friend, but Hayley was on a roll. "And then I got a letter from my mom today and she told me all about my sister's homecoming. She's a freshman and so it was her first one and I missed it." She sniffed and then continued quietly. "I didn't realize that last year would be my last one." Fiona put her arm around her friend as she started to cry. "I just miss everybody so much."

Fiona had experienced homesickness from time to time as well, so she could sympathize with Hayley. "I'm sorry about Tuncay. He doesn't know what he's missing. Let's go out after school tomorrow to cheer you up. I'll talk to Aylin and the others and we'll make plans, okay?" They sat together quietly for a while. "Do you want to improve your Turkish?" Fiona asked gently. She hadn't noticed Hayley making much effort recently. "It's so much harder than I thought it would be. I don't know if I can."

"It is difficult, but if you study, and make people speak it with you you'll get better, I promise. But you have to insist. Maybe start by asking Can first."

Hayley nodded, but she seemed noncommittal and Fiona didn't know what else to tell her friend.

Metin had made good on his offer and spoke in Turkish with Fiona for a while every time he came to school, introducing new words, more complicated phrases, and more recently, starting to pick up the tempo. He was a good teacher. Others had noticed their exchanges and joined in. Between that and her dedication to working through the dreaded Turkish grammar book, her language skills were improving in leaps and bounds.

Metin appeared at school almost every day now. Some days he spent time with Fiona, but many days, he came to be with his friends. But even when he was busy talking with them, he kept glancing over at Fiona and flashing his smile. And her eyes lit up whenever he did. The girls noticed.

"Fiona*cığım*, do you like Metin?" asked Yeşim. "He's very cute, and I think he likes you."

Fiona blushed. "Maybe," she said. "He is handsome and he's being very kind to me. I'd definitely like to get to know him better."

Yeşim smiled. She thought she'd seen sparks at the football game so she was pleased to know she was right. And when she saw Fiona's face turn the same colour as her hair, she was sure her friend liked Metin far more than she had said. She decided to give them some help.

The next day, she and Mehmet invited them both to join them after school. The four walked from school down to Bahariye where they sat and drank glass after glass of *çay* to ward off the chill and nibbled on salty biscuits. The hot *çay* was nice on the damp afternoon, and Fiona enjoyed the warmth as it was replenished often as they chatted.

Eventually, Yeşim and Mehmet needed to head home to tackle their homework. Fiona shivered as she and Metin slowly walked up Bağdat Caddesi. He took the lightweight moss-green scarf that made his eyes pop and wrapped it around her neck. She caught the scent of his cologne on it — she'd smelled it before when he'd kissed her cheeks in welcome or when leaving.

"*Sağol,*" she said in thanks. "It's chilly today."

At her apartment door, Metin unwound his scarf from her neck. "Thank you again," Fiona said. "It was really kind of you to lend it to me."

"*Sorun değil,*" he said with a smile. "No problem." And he leaned down to kiss her on the cheeks, leaving her to think about how much she liked the woodsy scent he wore.

A week later, Nazlı was next to extend an invitation. She and Ozan wanted to go to the symphony at the Atatürk Cultural Centre in Taksim Square on the weekend. This way, she could tell her parents that she and Fiona were going together. Nazlı didn't want to lie to them, and this way she wouldn't have to. She just wouldn't tell them the whole truth.

The afternoon of the concert, Fiona waited at the ferry dock for Metin to join her. He wanted to show her a new neighbourhood before they met Ozan and Nazlı there. She checked her watch. Metin had said four thirty and it was already fifteen minutes past that. With a sigh, Fiona leaned against the railing. She couldn't get used to the elastic concept of time that was so prevalent here.

It frustrated her to no end. But nobody seemed to mind, and the idea of phoning to say you'd be late wasn't common. She shook her head. Without a phone, Metin couldn't even do that. So she gritted her teeth and smiled when he finally arrived after another ten minutes.

Fiona thoroughly enjoyed the concert and had been pleasantly surprised at how inexpensive the student tickets were. Afterwards the group discussed the music before piling into a *dolmuş* back to the Asian side of the city. Fiona always smiled when she saw a *dolmuş* in the street. And they were everywhere. Great big 1950s American cars, they travelled a set route picking up and dropping off passengers along the way. She supposed that the cars lasted so long because there would be no salt on a winter street in İstanbul to rust holes through the frame. Their name meant "stuffed" and they were stuffed — with people. A *dolmuş* would let you off wherever you wanted, and pick you up if there was room, almost like a bus. But unlike a bus, when it reached the end of its route, it wouldn't set out again until it was full. Fiona had learned how to send her money up to the driver if she was in the back, and how to pass back change, if there was a new passenger in the back row. It was an amazing system.

Metin and Fiona walked the final kilometre back to her apartment and she told him all about the university application she had to fill out soon. At the door, instead of the usual double cheek kiss, Metin gave Fiona a hug and then leaned down and gave her a gentle kiss on the lips.

It was electrifying. Fiona had, of course, been kissed before. She'd had boyfriends in high school, but this kiss was different. In spite of its gentleness, it made her toes and fingertips tingle and every hair on her head stand up. She hadn't been expecting it, but it was thrilling and she liked it very much. Fiona kissed him back, and in that instant, Metin felt the same shock waves. He pulled back and looked deep into her eyes. Having assured himself that

Fiona had enjoyed the kiss just as much as he had, he pressed his lips against hers again. He was rewarded with a soft sigh.

"Metin," she said, when she caught her breath. "*Gitmem lazım.* I have to go. Thank you for a nice time. Good night. *İyi geceler.*" And she slipped in the door to her apartment, and leaned against the other side of it, her heart pounding, thankful her *anne* and *baba* were already asleep.

Metin found himself whistling as he headed further up the road home. He was happier than he'd ever been before.

Metin was surprised by the depth of feelings he was developing for Fiona. When he first met her, he thought that it would be nice to have a girlfriend to help pass the time until he wrote the university entrance exam. She was fun to be with and pretty to look at. But with every day that they were together, he found himself liking her more and more. He was touched that she was serious about learning Turkish and the local customs. She was respectful of tradition while still pushing the envelope just slightly. She liked to slip her arm in his when they were walking down the street. He felt a jolt every time their hands touched, and when she laughed, her big grey eyes lit up like stars and he couldn't help but smile too. He tried to get to school to see her often, and he loved showing her his favourite places.

Metin realized he was talking about her a lot when his mother suggested he bring her by the house for tea the next day. He agreed, thinking it might be nice if they could meet at his house sometimes to talk or listen to music. She might even keep him company when he studied. But for that to happen, it would be important for his mother to like her.

"Tomorrow?" Fiona was startled by the sudden invitation when Metin came to the school at the end of the day.

"Yes, tomorrow," Metin confirmed. His eyes glittered and he grinned as he continued. "I thought you'd like that I'd planned that far ahead." Fiona laughed nervously. Meeting Metin's mother was a big stop. Still, she took a deep breath and nervously agreed. Tomorrow came quickly, and they were both jumpy as they approached his apartment building.

"*Memnum oldum*, Özlem *hanım*" Fiona very formally greeted his mother, who welcomed her son's girlfriend with kisses on both cheeks and immediately told her to call her the more familiar *teyze*. Metin reached for her hand and squeezed it. She'd passed the first test.

They were just sitting down in the living room with glasses of *çay* as Safiye burst in the door from her middle school. She couldn't wait to meet Fiona and was preparing to tease her brother mercilessly after she left.

Safiye and her mother were delighted when they realized Fiona didn't need continual translation from Metin. Özlem *teyze* seemed particularly interested in what Fiona thought of İstanbul, and about how different the city was from her hometown. Her eyes widened when Fiona explained that yes, her little town only had only six hundred people. Fiona was getting used to people trying to convince her that she must have not learned her numbers properly and surely she meant six million.

Safiye asked Fiona about Canada. She thought that if she went on an exchange in a few years like her *abi* she might try to go to there instead of America. In response, Fiona asked her about her school and what subjects she liked.

Özlem *teyze* asked her about the university application her son had told her about, and Fiona explained that it was *çok zor* — very difficult. She was starting to run out of vocabulary, so was very relieved when Metin's mother suggested that he take Fiona to his room so they could listen to music while she worked in the kitchen.

"I think that went well, didn't it?" she asked him, as he turned up the volume.

Metin turned around with a huge grin on his face. "Really well. She liked you a lot. And Safiye too, not that that matters so much."

"Your sister's really sweet."

Metin rolled his eyes. "She's a real pain, but I guess she's okay."

Fiona admired the number of books on his bookshelf. Metin had an old loveseat in his room and he loved to lounge on it, leafing through volumes of literature. The fabric was fraying, but it was covered in afghans his mother and grandmother had made.

"Do you have pictures from Charlotte?" she asked, pulling her legs up under her on the loveseat. She was glad there was somewhere to sit other than his bed. Nodding, Metin pulled out an album. He sat beside her and they leafed through it. Metin pointed out his host family, some of his schoolmates, and some of the places he'd travelled to while he was there. "Who's she?" Fiona asked, pointing to a photo of a pretty girl who had her arms around Metin.

"That's, well, that's . . ." Metin was flustered.

"A girlfriend?" Fiona offered.

"Well, yes. I dated a couple of girls while I was there." He looked nervously at Fiona, trying to gauge her reaction.

Fiona was nonplussed. "Was it hard when you came home?"

Metin breathed a sigh of relief. Fiona didn't seem to mind. "No, we broke up a couple of months before I left. Wasn't meant to be, I guess." He squeezed her hand. "Nothing for you to worry about."

"Oh, I wasn't worried," she assured him. "Just curious whether you'd stayed in touch with her, or actually with anyone." Fiona was already determined not to lose touch with her new Turkish friends.

When it was time to go home, she goodbye to Safiye and then to Metin's mother, who assured her she was welcome any time. "*Seni bekliyoruz.*"

࿐

One Sunday afternoon, the girls were sprawled over Yeşim's bed and on the floor, munching away on cookies Hayley had made, and listening to a new album by a popular Turkish group. Aylin, who'd been last to arrive, was sitting at Yeşim's desk, writing out lyrics in purple pen for Fiona, who really liked their music.

Suddenly, Hayley sat up on the bed. "Tell me about your last names."

"What do you mean, Hayley?" Fiona asked, puzzled by the request. Hayley's *abi* had recently explained many Turks had stories about their surnames. In fact, the girls said that their grandparents had all chosen surnames for their families after Atatürk's reforms in 1934.

"I'll start," said Yeşim. "I remember when I was little, my *dede* used to tell us this story all the time. He was very proud of the name he chose and he wanted to make sure we all knew why and he made us promise to tell our own children and grandchildren the story. You know my last name is Çalışkan. Do you know what it means?"

Hayley shook her head. "Something about working?" guessed Fiona, recognizing the verb root.

"You're right. It means hard-working. *Dede* had a small textile company and he wanted customers to know that if they hired his company, he would work hard for them. Actually, he also thought that if his employees knew he was a hard worker that they would work hard for him too. And he wanted to make sure that his children — my *baba* and his brothers and sisters — knew that working hard was important to success. I guess it worked. My *baba* and my uncles have made the company very successful and you know my *abi* is at the new *üniversite* to study business. He wants to join them as soon as he can. My grandfather thought very hard about our name."

"Not everybody did, though," interrupted Aylin, putting her pen down for a moment. "The story of my name isn't as interesting but it is a bit funny. The meaning is easy to figure out. Karabulut."

"Black something?" asked Hayley tentatively.

"Black cloud. *Bulut* is cloud," Fiona filled in the blank for her friend. "But why, Aylin?"

Aylin laughed. "My grandfather told us he couldn't decide. It was a big responsibility to choose the name for his descendants. A lot of pressure. He considered lots of names, but finally, when the day came that he had to write it down, he still didn't know. Then he looked up at the sky. It was a stormy day in Adana where he lived. He saw black clouds, so that's what my *dede* wrote on the form. My mother says she almost didn't marry my father because she was worried it was a bad omen. But I guess it worked out."

Nazlı was next. "Mine is easy too, I guess. My *dede* was not so creative either, but it's a good name. You know lots of names end in 'oğlu', right?"

Hayley and Fiona nodded.

"It means son. My *dede* was son of a *yazıcı* — a printer. His *baba* made books. So he chose for his name Yazıcıoğlu. The printer's son." She shrugged her shoulders. "*İşte böyle.* That's it." She looked at their new friends curiously. "Do you know stories about your names?"

Hayley shook her head. "Jones is a really boring, really common name. I have no idea what it means or where it comes from. And honestly, I never thought to ask."

"Mine is Irish," said Fiona. "As if you couldn't guess by my hair. The O part is like *oğlu*. So I guess O'Reilly the son of Reilly. But we don't know when our family came to Canada from Ireland, or who Reilly was." Her ears pricked as the next song started. "Oh, I really like this one," she said, and the girls all started to sing along to the song about having given up on love. Fiona loved the line about talking to the stars and sleeping on the pier. It sounded so romantic. "Yeşim, *bunu da yazabilir misin, lütfen?*" she asked, and Aylin nodded. Of course she'd write out the words for her friend.

Fiona was frustrated. She had spent most of the weekend poring over her university application. She needed to get it just right, so she could get into the program she wanted, but she'd put it away because she and Metin were going to go for a walk together on the European side of the city. She was waiting for him at Altıyol, where six streets came together, giving the location its name, and where they often agreed to meet. But she'd been waiting for half an hour in the cold. It wasn't the first time that plans had fallen through with Metin. Or with other friends, she acknowledged. It wasn't just him. The fluidity in plans, she'd learned, meant that an agreement to do something in the future didn't hold the same certainty it did at home. She was learning to live with it, but it didn't mean she liked it. Because Metin had no telephone, he had no way to tell her if he would be delayed, or if something urgent had come up. She thought about her friends back home. They never would have been that late without letting someone know.

Another five minutes passed and Fiona shivered as she let out a breath of annoyance. She'd really been looking forward to relaxing with her boyfriend, but looked like it wasn't going to happen. She bought a small bag of chestnuts to warm herself and started back home, stewing about the inconvenience. She was still in a black mood when she arrived.

"You're back soon," said Ceylan, surprised to see Fiona already. She shook her head. "*Gelmedi.* He didn't show up."

"Don't worry about it. I'm sure there is a good reason," assured her host sister. "Come and have some *çay.*" Ceylan had a boyfriend who had graduated university the previous year, and so the two girls commiserated about the imagined flaws of their beaus.

Instead of returning to her application, Fiona settled down to read a book. Just as she was getting into the plot, the doorbell rang. "It's for you, *abla*," called Defne. "*Metin geldi.*" Metin stood just inside the front door waiting for her.

Fiona grabbed her coat. "*Neredeydin sen?* Where were you?" she demanded angrily when they started out onto the street. "I waited a long time."

"Let me explain," Metin started.

But Fiona lashed out with red-headed temper. "You stood me up. Again. I'm starting to think I'm not important to you at all."

"Fiona*cığım*, listen to me." Metin tried to grab her hand, but she wrenched it away.

"No. I'm tired of listening. Why do you tell me you'll come? Why do we bother making plans if you aren't going to come? I have other things to do." Fiona had worked herself up into a frenzy and her grey eyes were flashing.

"I wanted to come, *canım*."

"It's just so frustrating when you don't tell me when things change. I wasted so much time that I could have been spending on my university application. That's my future and it feels like you don't respect that."

"I'm sorry," Metin tried to explain. "My *baba* asked me to help him and my uncle. I had no choice."

Fiona stopped dead on the street and put her hands on her hips. "Oh, you had a choice, all right," she all but hissed. "You have a choice every time. And you don't choose me."

Metin took her hands. He realized this was about more than just today. "Let's sit and have *çay*." He led her into a little tea garden. "Come and sit down." A waiter quickly materialized with two glasses of hot tea. "I'm so sorry about today. I came as soon as I could. You know how important family is and I didn't have a choice." He took a sip of tea. "But I could have tried harder to let you know."

All of Fiona's anger deflated when he reminded her of family responsibility, so strong here, and she put her head in her hands. "I'm sorry too," she said. "I'm being unreasonable. I'm just so stressed about university and sometimes it's hard being away from home." She looked up at Metin. "I'm taking it all out on you."

"It's okay, *canım*. I remember what it's like." He grinned. "But at least there were telephones in America!"

⌒⌣⌒

"It's strange, isn't it?" Hayley asked out of nowhere just a week later while she and Fiona sat in a café drinking cherry juice and eating chocolate pudding. "Christmas is just around the corner and there's no sign it anywhere. I mean I know they don't celebrate it, but I thought we might see something. Maybe a Santa Claus, or some lights. But nothing." They'd already missed Thanksgiving and Hallowe'en.

"Does it bother you?" Fiona asked.

"No, I guess not, but I'm ready for some Christmas songs."

"And what about snow?" Fiona added with a grin. "Somehow it doesn't feel like December without some snow."

As the girls tried to figure out where they might get their hands on some Christmas cassette tapes, or even a Christmas movie on videotape, Metin was busy scheming with Yeşim and Mehmet. Not only was Christmas coming, but Fiona's birthday was the next day and he needed help with a special plan for her.

The day dawned clear and bright after days of dull grey weather. Defne and Ceylan brought out some birthday balloons and with their *anne* and *baba,* the girls gave Fiona some small gifts at breakfast. She loved her new wallet and little jewellery box. *Anne* promised her cake at dinner and Fiona hurried off to school to see what surprises awaited her there. She'd heard some whispering, so she thought there might be something special planned.

Fiona's classmates were full of birthday greetings, but it was at lunch that the real fun began. Mehmet pulled a small cassette player out of his bag and Yeşim was putting a tape in when Fiona felt cold hands reach from behind her and cover her eyes.

"Guess who!"

"Metin! What are you doing?"

"Keep them closed, Fiona. Yeşim, hit play. OK, now open your eyes!"

As the sound of "Jingle Bell Rock" started to fill the room, Fiona opened her eyes and Metin, Mehmet, and Yeşim were dancing in front of her wearing Santa hats. She clasped her hands with glee.

"I thought you might be missing Christmas," Metin said. "And for your birthday too, I thought you might like this." He put his hands out for her to join him. Hayley looked around for Berkin, who she'd been flirting with most recently, and grabbed his hands too. She and Fiona started singing the words and Aylin and Nazlı joined in the dancing.

A little later on the cassette, some more traditional songs came on and Fiona found herself with an audience, as she sang the familiar songs in her rich mezzo-soprano voice. When the tape stopped, she flung her arms around Metin's neck. "Thank you for my wonderful birthday present," she whispered in his ear. Out loud, she thanked him again, and his co-conspirators. "I think this is exactly what Hayley and I needed."

"I'll be back later," Metin told her. "I have one more gift for you. And my *anne* wants you to come. Yeşim told me there's a test in last period today, so expect me then." Fiona nodded and Metin disappeared into a crowd of his friends as they headed to the canteen.

The girls gathered around her, chattering up a storm. Yeşim admitted she'd had almost as much fun preparing the surprise as Fiona had in receiving it.

"We knew you'd like the songs too," she said in English, turning to Hayley, who was failing miserably in keeping up with the conversation.

Hayley smiled. "It was a lot of fun," she agreed. She turned her attention to her lunch as the conversation switched back to Turkish.

"That was so romantic," Nazlı sighed, linking arms with Fiona as they headed back to the classroom after lunch. "Aylin and Yeşim and I have something for you, but if it's okay, we'll save it until later this week. We want to take you and Hayley out to celebrate your Christmas."

True to his word, Metin was back a couple of hours later and they walked up the road, arm in arm, to his apartment. His mother had baked a cake and they sang "Happy Birthday" to Fiona before giving her a beautiful soft mauve scarf she could wear all winter. The icing on the cake for her was a pair of dainty silver hoop earrings from Metin. She put them in right away.

Her parents called that evening from Canada and Fiona told them how well everything was going and how spoiled she'd been. The package they had sent hadn't arrived yet, but Fiona assured them it would likely come soon. She spoke to her parents once a month, but they said they'd call again in five days. They missed her and couldn't imagine Christmas Day without at least speaking with their only child.

With help from her family, Fiona found a church with a late-night English service, and she were planning to go with Hayley, her *abi*, and Metin. It promised to be a special evening, even if there was no snow. But before that, their Turkish girlfriends were taking them out after school.

"*Nereye?*" asked Fiona. "Where are we going?" She had thought they would go to one of their usual places but Aylin was pushing them further up the road to a fancy bistro Fiona had seen before but never been in. Aylin took care of ordering, and soon they had two types of cake and a plate of profiteroles in front of them along with their tea. Five forks appeared and between bites of the delicate vanilla and raspberry cakes and cream puffs, Hayley and Fiona were spoiled with bracelets and the sweetest little Turkish socks Fiona had seen. Doll-sized, they were strung together almost like children's mittens. The girls had put their money together and bought Fiona a necklace as well, that matched her new bracelet. She was overwhelmed. "*Sizi çok seviyorum!*" she exclaimed. "I love you all so much!"

Later that evening, sitting with Hayley, Can, and Metin in the chapel and waiting for the service to start, they were all quiet. Metin and Can were remembering the Christmases of their own exchange years and Hayley was pining for home. Fiona looked over and squeezed her hand.

The service was lovely, with carols that Hayley and Fiona sang all enthusiastically. After exchanging Christmas greetings with the minister, the four young people piled into a taxi. Getting out at Can and Hayley's house, Fiona gave Hayley a huge hug.

"I'll see you tomorrow," she whispered and then she and Metin waved goodbye, leaving for the ten-minute walk down the street to her apartment. She was happy for her new scarf to keep her neck warm, and she noticed Metin had a new one as well, in a deeper green that matched his eyes.

"What a wonderful day," she sighed.

"Will you be okay tomorrow?"

"I'll be fine," Fiona assured him. "Hayley and I aren't going to school so I'm going to go over to her apartment and we'll sing songs all day and just be together. I think she needs it more than me, but it will be good to be with each other."

"You're a good friend." Metin thought for a moment before continuing delicately, "I think you've settled better here than she has."

"They warn us, when we're getting ready to come, that not every exchange year turns out the way you expect," Fiona admitted. "But you probably heard the same thing." Metin nodded as she continued. "I wouldn't say hers isn't good, but you're right, I don't think she's as happy as I am. Mind you," Fiona continued, looking up at her handsome boyfriend as he opened the door to her building, "I have a few more reasons to be invested."

Closing the door behind him, Metin kissed her in the dark stairwell. "I'm glad you feel that way." He unwound her scarf and kissed her neck. "Do you like this?" He moved to her clavicle. "And this?" Fiona did and she stroked his cheek. She used her fingers to lift his chin so his lips brushed hers.

"I should really go in," she said. "But I don't want to." She kissed him again and Metin groaned. She tasted sweet and the smell of her perfume was making him crazy. He brought his lips down harder on hers, and she made a purring noise deep in her throat that made his world spin. He wanted more.

"I think you should go in too," he said hoarsely, finding it hard to stop. He dug deep and looked at his watch. "Look, it's Christmas. Merry Christmas, *sevgilim*." It was the first time he'd called her sweetheart.

"Merry Christmas, Metin." And she slipped behind the door.

Chapter 5

"*Ah, kar karıyor,*" Fiona exclaimed as she looked out the window when school resumed after the New Year break. She'd spotted a few small white flakes of snow falling from the sky. Nazlı and Yeşim broke into fits of giggles.

Fiona was confused. Months ago, she learned the construction for "it's raining." It was literally "rain rains — *yağmur yağıyor.*" She knew *kar* was the word for snow, and because she'd learned that even in its difficulty, Turkish was very logical, so she extrapolated: if rain rained, snow must snow.

"What's so funny," demanded Aylin, joining them from the front of the classroom.

"She said '*kar karıyor!*'" Yeşim finally managed to get out, tears rolling down her cheeks, she'd been laughing so hard. Aylin laughed along with them.

Nazlı was first to pull herself together. "Fiona'*çığım, kar yağıyor.*"

"But that doesn't make any sense," she said. "The snow rains?"

"Maybe not, *canım,* but that's how we say it." Fiona didn't think she needed to write that one in her notebook.

Of course the snow didn't stay, and turned into rain later in the day, so the friends shook the drops off their coats before they went into Aylin's apartment after school. She had new music they wanted to listen to.

Music had bonded the girls early in the year and they listened to their favourite American and Turkish artists together whenever they could. Neither Hayley nor Aylin cared much for classical music, but the others did, so often the couples — Fiona and Metin, Nazlı and Ozan, and Yeşim and Mehmet — went to the Atatürk Cultural Centre together for concerts, opera, or ballet. Fiona loved those times. They didn't have to get dressed up, but she liked to pull on her nice black pants instead of jeans and wear a little bit of a heeled shoe or boot. She was so much shorter than Metin that every little bit helped. They usually went to matinees so they could have dinner afterwards, but occasionally she and Metin went together to evening performances without the others. Fiona was enjoying soaking up all the culture that the big city offered.

Modern music was more Aylin and Hayley's style so they were excited when there was a chance to see Barış Manço in concert. The long-haired rock star was very popular and he had just released a new album that Aylin, Yeşim, and Nazlı were all wild for. All five girls bought tickets. The theatre was full and the crowd was on their feet from start to finish. Hayley and Fiona could hardly hear the amplified voice of the singer over the noise. They stopped for a quick dinner after the concert, and the Turkish girls sang the songs again in the little restaurant while they waited for their order, while Fiona and Hayley watched and laughed.

"Here we go," said Metin, opening the door to İstanbul's main post office. Fiona's Christmas package had finally arrived and she was practically vibrating with excitement. It was almost February and she'd been waiting a long time, but Metin was afraid she might have underestimated the bureaucracy involved in this process. "*Canım*, we could be here for a while," he cautioned, as she walked through the door.

Together, they climbed the massive central staircase of Büyük Postane. Fiona's jaw dropped when she saw the number of people waiting. Metin pulled a number from the dispenser. It wasn't too bad, she thought. There were only thirty people ahead of them. She'd have her package soon.

Her turn came, and they approached the wicket. "*Paketim gelmiş*," she told the man confidently handing him the form that had come to her apartment. "My package has arrived."

He looked at her identification, stamped the form with a loud thump, and thrust it back to her. "*Dördüncü kat*," he said gruffly.

Fiona looked at Metin bewilderedly as he exchanged rapid-fire Turkish with the official. "Fourth floor? Why didn't he just give me the package?" she asked as he led her up the stairs.

"His job is to confirm that the package is here and that you have the right identification to collect it," Metin told her. "There are a few more steps yet. You'll have to be patient."

On the fourth floor, they lined up again. This time, when Fiona told the postal worker that her package had arrived, he not only stamped her paper, but gave her another one. This one told her how much she needed to pay to pick it up. She started to pull the paper bills from her purse, when he stopped her. He spoke to Metin and then turned back to her.

"*Üçüncü kat*."

"Really?" Fiona asked Metin. "We have to go to the third floor to pay?"

"I'm afraid so," he told her and they headed down.

After another wait, Fiona paid the fee, and expected her package would be brought out for her. But instead, the man handed her a receipt and turned to Metin to give the instructions. She shook her head in amazement. She didn't understand it all, but she did know there was one more stop to make.

They went down the stairs to the second floor and took another number. Metin looked at it and sighed.

"We should find a seat. It's a long wait," he advised Fiona.

"This is crazy," she whispered to him, sneaking a peak at her watch. "I didn't believe you, but we've been here for almost two hours already."

"I warned you," he teased. "Bureaucracy is an artform in Turkey!"

Finally, after another forty-five minutes of cooling their heels, their number was called. Fiona handed over her receipt and the old man took it and disappeared behind a grey door. He returned a few minutes later with a battered box tied up with string. Fiona's face fell. She hoped nothing had been damaged. Metin spoke to the man and Fiona gave into the feeling of frustration with the system. It had beaten her.

"Merry Christmas?" Metin said tentatively, trying to cheer her up.

Fiona smiled and tried to feel positive. "Absolutely. Now let's go home so I can find out what's in here!"

Metin carried the heavy box as they walked back down the hill to the ferry. Back on the Asian side of the city they rode a *dolmuş* to her apartment. Racing up the stairs, they stole a breathless kiss in the hallway before opening the door. Everyone was out, so they sat at the dining room table as Fiona finally had her Christmas. Fortunately her mother hadn't packed anything breakable, and there was even a small fruitcake at the bottom.

"No wonder it was so heavy," she joked. Nevertheless, she cut them small slices that they nibbled on with their *çay*, and she thought she had the best of both worlds.

Metin had made plans for Valentine's Day, but was keeping them secret. He'd convinced Fiona not to go to school that day which in itself felt a bit exciting to her. The only thing he'd told her was to wear good walking shoes and to meet him at the Besiktas pier.

The day was wet and miserable, like most had been recently. Fiona sometimes felt like she'd never get warm. It wasn't really that cold, but it was damp. She kept her purple scarf wrapped firmly around her neck whenever she was outdoors. Today was going to be another one of those days. Fiona looked around when she reached the pier, but Metin hadn't arrived yet. She shouldn't have been surprised. Even this many months later, to her, nine o'clock still meant nine o'clock and she found Turkish people's sense of fluidity around time frustrating. Metin teased her as she needed to let go of her need to plan, she needed to relax. So Fiona resigned herself to waiting and pulled her scarf tighter around her neck. At least it had stopped raining.

She had a small gift for Metin, a book of poetry she'd found at the old book bazaar. She liked to go there sometimes on the weekend to see what she could find. It wasn't much, but it was poems by a writer he'd mentioned before. She had it tucked in her purse and she hoped he would like it. It was too wet from the rain to sit on a bench, but Fiona leaned against the railing at the shore and pulled out her notebook. She was doing her best to recreate the ambiance of the day in words when Metin arrived. He watched her for a few minutes as she tucked a few strands of hair back behind her ear and returned to writing. Maybe it was the day, but watching her made his heart do flip-flops.

"*Gün aydın, sevgilim,*" he said, coming up behind her.

"Good morning to you too," she said, turning around and giving him a hug. "*Mutlu Sevgiler Günü.* Happy Valentine's Day." The pier was almost deserted with rush hour over, so he leaned down and gave her a big kiss. "Not here, Metin," she demurred, embarrassed to be kissed out in the open in broad daylight.

"Okay, okay," he grumbled affectionately. "But do I have a day planned for us! First the ferry." He grabbed Fiona's arm and pulled her to the wicket where he purchased two tickets to Adalar, where Fiona had gone with her host family in her first days in Turkey.

The ferry was almost empty, so they had a corner of the large ship to themselves for the ninety-minute voyage. Metin bought *sahlep* — a hot milky orchid-root drink — to warm them up and put his arm around Fiona's shoulder, pulling her close. "Do you know how much I love you?" he asked.

"Tell me."

"I want to be with you all the time. When I'm supposed to be studying, I'm thinking about you. When I go to bed at night, I dream about you. I've even written to my *abi* about you, did you know that?"

Fiona blushed. "What did he say?"

"He thinks I'm crazy, but I'm ignoring him. He's never even met you!" Metin reached over and kissed Fiona. "What does he know? This is for real."

"I love you too, Metin. You make me so happy. I think about you all the time too. I get lost in your eyes, and when you kiss me, it's like the world stands still. I never imagined I'd find someone like you here."

It was Metin's turn to feel self-conscious. Wanting to lighten things up, he pulled his scarf off and put it on top of Fiona's purple one.

"What are you doing?" she laughed.

"Well, speaking of eyes," he started, "yours are still a mystery to me." He pulled his scarf off her neck and then took hers off as well. "When you wear your scarf, they're definitely blue. But when you put mine on, they look green. And when you don't have either on, they're grey again. How is that possible?" He kept switching out scarves, watching her eyes take on the reflection of the colours near her face. "You have magic eyes, my love."

She kissed him then, a long, slow, deep kiss that he felt down to his toes. "It's okay to kiss here," he teased, "but not on the pier?" His humour was rewarded by a playful swat. "Oh no, you don't," he growled, kissing her back with equal ardour.

As the ferry docked, the sun broke through the clouds. They jumped off the ferry ready to explore the second biggest of this small chain of islands in the Sea of Marmara. Bypassing the horse-drawn carriages, they headed off down the dirt road hand in hand. "Listen," Metin said. "Listen to the quiet." There were no cars on any of the islands and the sound of silence was deafening. Fiona forgot, sometimes, how noisy the city was. They spent the day wandering through nature and visiting some of the island's attractions. By lunchtime, their stomachs were rumbling so they bought fresh *balık ekmek* to eat. As the wooden boats rocked in the water, fishermen set up little hibachis on the wharf and cooked the fish sandwiches up right there and then. Metin bought *lokma* for dessert and took it all back to the now dry picnic tables in a forest clearing to eat.

Fiona licked her fingers when she was done. The little balls of sweet deep-fried dough reminded her of the tiny doughnuts that were a staple at big fall fairs back home. She leaned up against an old pine tree as Metin threw the cardboard container in the trash. He came back and kissed her gently. "You taste like *lokma*," he laughed. There was nobody around, so he pressed her against the tree and kissed her more ardently, sliding his hands underneath her blouse. She wrapped her arms around him and they stayed there until the sounds of horses clopping along the road started to grow louder. They pulled apart, hearts racing. "I love you, Fiona," Metin said, cupping her face with hand.

"I love you too," she replied breathlessly.

Hayley and Fiona had been navigating Turkish cuisine fairly well since they arrived seven months ago, but it had taken some time. Hayley loved yogurt in the US, using a spoon to mix in the sugary fruit on the bottom of each single-serving. But here, yogurt wasn't sweet and it came in huge containers. Her family heaped it on their rice at dinner and even made soup out of it. She had gotten used to the taste and quite enjoyed it now.

Fiona still couldn't stomach olives for breakfast, but generally had embraced all the new tastes she'd been exposed to. Sometimes she feared her waistline showed it, but she still fit into her clothes. The amount of walking she did here — including all the hills — must be helping.

Hayley and Fiona had made cookies for their classmates and their families several times now, with chocolate chips that were sent from home. Fiona made French toast for her host family one weekend. She'd served it drizzled liberally with maple syrup that tasted a little bit like home to her. Her family had been polite about it, but she didn't think they'd be repeating the dish anytime soon. Fiona wanted to learn how to cook some Turkish dishes, so she jumped at the chance when Metin's mother asked if she'd like help make *mantı*. And that was how Fiona found herself sitting at the kitchen table with Safiye as Özlem *teyze* mixed flour, water, eggs, and salt to make the dough for the tiny meat-filled dumplings that Fiona loved so much. Metin had been sent with his father to run a long list of errands, so that afternoon Fiona was on her own with the women of the house for the first time.

Safiye rummaged through a kitchen drawer and brought her mother an *oklava* to start rolling out the dough. To Fiona, the unusual-looking item bore no resemblance to the rolling pin she was expecting to see. It looked like a long wooden dowel, but slightly tapered at each end. She was amazed at how it let Özlem *teyze* roll the dough so thin. Safiye took a turn too. She didn't get it quite as thin as her mother, but her efforts put Fiona's to shame.

They cut he dough into two-inch squares with a knife and then put a tiny bit of a ground beef mixture into the middle of each square. Özlem *teyze* taught Fiona how to bring all four corners of these little squares together and pinch them into tiny pockets of goodness. Fiona was very much at home in this kitchen and had the sense that making food was very much a communal event. It reminded her of the canning and preserve parties the women of her small town held in the late summer.

Several hours after he'd left, Metin returned home with his *baba*, the checklist completed. Metin was slightly anxious to find out how the afternoon had gone. He needn't have worried. As he leaned on the door frame, he realized the kitchen was full of laughter as his mother shared stories of his childhood misadventures while washing the *çay* glasses and keeping an eye on the activity. He grinned. Fiona had a dusting of flour on her cheek, and was stirring together the yogurt and garlic as Safiye gently placed the *mantı* in a pot of boiling water. A warm feeling came over him as he watched these three women in his life working together in harmony. Then the smell of red pepper paste and mint filled his nose and his stomach growled. They were going to eat well tonight.

Pushing his chair back from the table after dinner, Metin's father looked at Fiona, his wife, and his daughter and gruffly said, "*Ellerinize sağlık*," literally wishing health to all the hands that had made the meal. Fiona joined them in the set response, "*Afiyet olsun*."

After the dishes were done and more *çay* had been drunk, Metin waited with Fiona for her bus to come. "The *mantı* was really good," he said. "I guess you'll be able to make it for me when we're together." Fiona looked up at him as he turned red, embarrassed to be caught thinking out into the future.

"Yes," she said. "Yes, I guess I can."

Chapter 6

The day came when Fiona finally put her pen down and decided she was done with her university application. All that was left was to send it by registered mail, something she was determined to do herself on this day when school ended at noon, so she waved off offers of help from Metin. She was going to beat the bureaucracy today. However, she couldn't shake Aylin.

"I need to run an errand for my *anne* just around the corner from Büyük Postane anyway," she told Fiona. "She wants olives."

"Olives?" Fiona was surprised.

"She says her favourite ones come from a shop just outside Mısır Çarşısı," Aylin explained, referring to the Spice Bazaar in Eminönü.

"Fine," Fiona agreed. "But only if you let me do my own talking." Aylin smiled and nodded. But she'd still be there just in case the Turkish bureaucracy became too much.

"You'll have to come here and get Turkish coffee to take home before you go," Aylin told her, pointing out the famous *kurukahveci* in Eminönü where Turks lined up for freshly ground coffee beans.

Fiona felt a sudden lump in her throat and her fingers brushed against the envelope in her pocket. Despite the job at hand today, she wasn't ready to think about going home just yet.

"Oh, here we are," Aylin exclaimed, oblivious to Fiona's internal conflict. She pulled her friend into the little shop and proceeded to buy three different kinds of olives for her mother.

Errand complete, they headed up the street to Büyük Postane.

"*İyi günler*," Fiona started out, confidently greeting the clerk who she expected would only be the first of many she would have to talk with today. Slowly, she explained she had a thick envelope she wanted to send to Canada by registered mail. Speaking quickly, he handed her a form and directed her to a colleague on another floor. When it was her turn, she patiently explained again what she wanted to do.

"*Kimlik*," the man demanded brusquely, and Fiona replied that she didn't have a Turkish identify card and showed her passport instead.

"You don't have a one?" he asked. "*İmkansız o zaman*. It's impossible then." He started to write on her form.

This was not a response Fiona had expected. "*Anlamıyorum*. I don't understand. Why is it impossible?"

"You need a *kimlik* to send registered mail."

"But I don't have one."

"Then you must send by regular mail."

"But I need to know it arrived." Fiona started to get concerned. This envelope represented her future and she needed to know when it reached its destination.

"But . . ." she began, her earlier confidence having melted away, and now finding it hard to find words. Her voice raised in in volume and pitch. "But it's very important. There must be a way."

The post office official looked at her and spoke very slowly. "*Türk kimliğinize ihtiyacınız var*. You need a Turkish identity card." He took a very official-looking stamp and thumped it over her form. As tears welled in her eyes, he thrust the form back at her and told her to go over to the other side of the building to speak with someone else.

"*Lütfen.* Please," she begged, as she angrily wiped away the tear that had fallen.

He shook his head and waved her away, dismissing her and asking for the next customer.

Fiona turned and headed over to the benches where Aylin was sitting.

"Were you successful?" Aylin asked, glancing up from the book she'd been reading. True to her promise, she had let her friend do this on her own. But her face changed when she saw Fiona standing in front of her, tears now freely flowing down her face. "What happened?" she asked with alarm.

It was as if all the stress over completing the applications and the anticipation of seeing them sent had multiplied and completely overwhelmed Fiona. She opened her mouth, but found she couldn't speak. She collapsed on the bench and sobbed as Aylin watched helplessly. She put her arm around Fiona's shoulder and left it there as Fiona struggled to get control.

Finally Aylin felt Fiona's breathing return to normal. "Tell me what happened," she asked gently, as her friend wiped tears away with embarrassment.

"He said it's impossible without a *kimlik.* I don't know what to do, Aylin." Fiona's face crumpled. "I have to get into this program. I just have to." Tears welled up again. "What am I going to do?"

"You're going to let me help."

Fiona sniffed and nodded. She'd been beaten again. "Thank you," she whispered.

It took an hour, but Aylin's determination finally broke through the system and she found someone who knew how let Fiona send the precious envelope by registered mail using her passport. It cost more than either of them expected, but it was done.

"I'm so glad you were here." Fiona gave Aylin a hug as they left the post office with a receipt and instructions to return in two weeks to get the confirmation of receipt by the university. "I couldn't have done this without you. You may have just saved my whole future!"

"That's what friends are for," Aylin demurred. "You would help me too."

"You know I would. Friends forever, right?"

Metin had been out of school for almost a year, so when he and Fiona weren't exploring the city parks and finding quiet corners for sharing stories, talking about the future, holding hands, and kissing away from prying eyes, he started to hit the books, preparing for the dreaded university entrance exam. Fiona spent a lot of time at his house reading and writing while he studied. Behind the closed door of his room, they made the most of his study breaks. Sometimes they read poetry to each other, holding hands and kissing gently. Sometimes they shared their deepest secrets. And sometimes, if was nobody was home, their teenage hormones get the better of them. They always managed to pull things back before they went too far. But it was getting harder.

When the calendar turned to April, the last of the winter cold and damp seemed to disappear along with it. No longer were the skies grey and gloomy. The sun returned, and with it, the entire city seemed to be in a better mood. The only fly in the ointment was that exam. The closer it got, the higher tensions rose. Everyone was on edge. Turkish students across the country were studying hard in the evenings and weekends, so they had little time for fun as they memorized facts and figures and stuffed their heads full of theories they thought might be on the exam. Fiona and Hayley were tense too. Fiona had received confirmation that her application had been received and Hayley's parents had submitted her applications for her. Both were now waiting to hear news.

To keep her mind off university, Fiona broached the topic of romance with Yeşim. "How do I know if Metin is serious about us? I mean, we're having a really good time, and it feels real, but one day, I have to go home."

Yeşim could see Fiona was conflicted. "Fiona, please be careful," she started frankly. "I've known Metin a long time. I can see that he loves you. And I know that you love him too. But I'm worried that you're both going to have your hearts broken in a few months. Have fun. Have lots of fun. But be realistic." Fiona looked annoyed. She didn't want anyone raining on this parade. "*Canım arkadaşım.* My dear friend, I don't want to hurt you," she continued, "but I also don't want you to get carried away. Maybe it can last, and maybe you two will be able to beat the odds, but you need to think about what's more likely."

Nazlı was more hopeful when Fiona asked her the same question at lunch the next day. "I think love always wins," she said confidently. "If it's meant to be, love will find a way somehow. Look at Ozan and me. Even though my parents don't know about him, we find ways to be together. And next year when I'm at university, it will be even easier, especially if I'm at the same school as him. Trust your love. You and Metin will find a way."

The day before the exam, pretending to concentrate on the geography lesson, Fiona was writing in her notebook when Metin's face appeared at the classroom door. Nazlı poked her and Fiona looked up to see him wave. Seeing his face made everything feel better. Fiona wished everyone good luck on the exam and the couple headed out to a favourite *çay bahçe* that looked out over the Bosphorus.

The girls had all conferred at lunch and were planning to go to Emirgan Park on Sunday to relax after the exam and enjoy the beauty of all the tulips. Aylin's father had told her they were almost at their peak and that she shouldn't miss the opportunity to share it with her foreign friends. Fiona was tired, so she was explaining this in English over a glass of *çay* when he surprised her by saying, "I approve. You can go."

She was taken aback. "You what?"

"I approve."

"You approve." He suddenly sounded like Can, who was forever telling Hayley what she could and couldn't do. Fiona was flabbergasted and something snapped inside her. "I didn't ask for your approval. And I certainly don't need it. I think I know my own mind and I can take care of myself. I'm not your property, you know."

"I didn't mean . . ."

"I'm not sure I care what you meant. What you said was disrespectful, misogynistic, and I don't like it. Maybe I should go now." Fiona stood up and began to walk away.

"Fiona, wait!" Metin ran after her. "Fiona, please! Listen to me." She whirled around so quickly that her braid flew over her shoulder. "Fine," she huffed indignantly. "Explain."

"Blame my bad English," he apologized, eyes downcast. "I'm tired too, Fiona, and stressed about the exam. What I should have said was that it is a great idea and that you should go with your friends. You'll have fun."

That took the wind out of Fiona's indignation. "Oh," she said. "I guess we're all on edge. I'm sorry I took it the wrong way." People were bumping them as they passed by. There was no way to apologize properly.

Metin pulled Fiona onto a side street. There, on the steps of an abandoned house, out of the way, he put his arms around her and hugged her tight. "I'm so sorry," they both said at the same time. It was the best they could do where they were but both were reassured that everything was all right.

Fiona wished him good luck on his exam before she headed home on her bus. But his reaction to her plans continued to niggle in the back of her mind.

The girls met up at Sarıyer to walk up to Emirgan Park. "So, how did it go?" Hayley asked curiously.

"It was hard, but I think I did well," volunteered Nazlı. The others agreed. "Now all we have to do is wait."

There was a man with a wagon full of strawberries at the bottom of the hill, so Aylin bought some to go along with the picnic lunch. Fiona had been so nervous for everyone yesterday that she'd passed the time making more chocolate chip cookies. Nazlı and Yeşim had *börek* and *dolma* and Hayley bought fresh cheese-stuffed *poğaça* on her way to meet everyone. They would have a feast.

Fiona was astonished when they reached the top of the hill. There, as far as the eye could see, were tulips in bloom. Thousands upon thousands of tulips. Thankful she'd brought her camera, Fiona took photos of them all among the flowers, and they asked a stranger to take a few so they could all be in them together.

"Has Metin told you how he thinks he did?" Yeşim asked her as they walked back down to the sea. "I saw him with Mehmet when we were done, but I didn't get a chance to talk to him."

"I haven't heard from him yet," she sighed. "I guess I'll learn tomorrow."

"He's smarter than all the rest of us," Yeşim said to reassure her. "I'm sure he did really well. And you two have that trip to look forward to!" Then she linked her arm through Fiona's and they ran the rest of the way down the hill, laughing all the way.

Metin was still in touch with the organizers of his exchange year and he had worked with them to organize a trip to Marmaris shortly after the exam. İstanbul was just starting to warm up, but the south was perfect. Because it was an officially sanctioned trip, Fiona's family allowed her to go with the group of close to twenty young people. They didn't need to know that some creative assignments had been unofficially sorted to let girlfriends and boyfriends share rooms.

In the quiet of Metin's house when everyone was gone, Fiona and Metin had taken the physical part of their relationship as far as they dared. Hayley, who wasn't going on this trip, but was going on a similar one a few weeks later with the same creative rooming assignments, pulled her aside the day before the trip. "Be careful, Fiona," she warned.

"I will — and you be careful too." She was pretty sure Hayley was thinking of sleeping with Cetin on that trip. They'd been dating for a couple of months now.

The group endured an uncomfortable, bumpy overnight bus ride to get to Marmaris, but it was worth it to shake off the damp greyness of the İstanbul winter.

After a short nap, Metin and Fiona got ready to explore. Fiona applied sunscreen liberally, slapped a straw hat on her head, and added oversized sunglasses before they headed out. "If I don't, I'll burn to a crisp," she explained. Metin barely had to look at the sun and his skin turned a gorgeous bronze tone.

After dinner, the students all went to the disco to dance the night away. Drinks were plentiful and the music was great. Fiona enjoyed meeting and sharing stories with other foreign students who were spending the year in other cities in Turkey, and Metin chatted with those from his year, and comparing notes on how they'd settled back into their lives.

Eventually, the band turned its attention to slow songs, and Metin held out his hand to Fiona. She took it and he led her back to the dance floor, where his arms encircled her waist. The difference in height between them meant that when she leaned into him, her head nestled into his chest. Metin rested his cheek on the top of her head and he breathed in the scent of her lavender shampoo. Soon Fiona was dizzy with the woodsy smell of his cologne. She wanted to remember that smell forever.

They got back to their room at midnight, giggling from the wine. Fiona slipped into the bathroom to put on her nightgown before giving Metin his turn. A soft blue jersey fabric, it had cream lace trim and delicate narrow shoulder straps. Metin came out wearing just his pajama pants and pulled the mosquito netting tightly around the bed. Fiona reached out her hands to his and drew him close. Metin kissed her hungrily and she responded, wrapping her arms around his neck. Gently pushing down the thin straps of her nightgown out of the way, he kissed her shoulders and the tops of her small breasts. She sighed with delight, and in the moonlight the young lovers discovered each other's bodies.

The next morning when they awoke, almost at the same time, Metin was curled around Fiona with one arm over her protectively.

"*Gün aydın*," she said sleepily.

"Good morning to you too, my love," he answered.

She rolled over to give him a kiss. "Last night was amazing. I don't ever want to leave this place." She sighed. "It's magic."

"I know," he agreed, propping himself up on his arm. "I don't know how we'll do it, but we'll have to find some magic back home too." He kissed her freckled shoulders and drew her close again.

That day, the group spent the day on a *gulet* — a large wooden sailboat — exploring the many coves lining the shore. They cruised and swam and cruised some more before the captain took them to a small beach for lunch. Fiona was diligent in reapplying sunscreen often and keeping her hat on. In the bright afternoon sun, she pulled a lightweight linen shirt over her shoulders. Metin teased her, but she knew better. By the end of the day, she was one of a few who wasn't feeling the effects of the sun. Even Metin's shoulders were a little red and she gently applied cream to them that evening. The cool felt refreshing, and the touch of her hands as they fluttered across his back was arousing. It wasn't long before he turned around and kissed her, starting another night of love-making. They were drinking in every moment they had together.

They had just half a day left to explore the old city before the bus took them back to reality. As a memory of this special time, Metin bought Fiona a necklace with a seagull pendant. Seagulls symbolized freedom, and that's what he wanted more than any-thing — for them to be free to be together, no matter what.

Shortly after they returned from Marmaris, Fiona joined Metin's family for his birthday and presented him with one of her last pewter and granite Canada goose paperweights. The pink granite stone that was the base came from near her home. He put it in a place of honour on his desk, after giving her a big hug and kiss — right in front of his parents. Fiona blushed beet red, but it seemed to be okay. Özlem *teyze* called Fiona *yavrum* that evening, a term of endearment that she took to be a good sign. She helped with the dishes and left Metin to have a conversation with his father in the living room.

After the *mantı*-making afternoon, Fiona had become much more comfortable around Metin's mother. She often helped out in the kitchen when she was there and had learned how to make *börek* and a delicious poppy-seed roll while drinking seemingly gallons of tea. They talked about what Fiona liked about Turkey and what she missed from home. Fiona confided in her that she was nervous about her university application and hoped she would get in. She borrowed a needle and thread to fix the hem on her school skirt one day, and much to Metin's horror, helped once or twice with the ironing when she was there on washing day. Metin pretended to sulk, saying she only visited to see his mother now.

One day, while they washed dishes together, and Metin read in his room, Özlem *teyze* looked at Fiona strangely. "You'll have to learn to make *aşure* if you're going to be our bride," she said quietly. Fiona tried to stammer an appropriate answer, knowing that was Metin's favourite dessert.

When she went home that afternoon, Fiona knocked on Ceylan's bedroom door. "*Abla*, can I talk to you?" she asked timidly. Fiona had met Ceylan's boyfriend, Mert, several times, and she knew they were serious about each other. Her *abla* was exactly the right person to ask.

"Come in. What's up?"

"*Abla*, what does it mean when your boyfriend's mother talks about you becoming their bride? I mean, I think she was teasing me, but I'm not sure."

"Really? She said that? Turkish mothers don't joke around about things like that." Ceylan gave Fiona a big hug. "It means that she accepts you like part of the family. And that she thinks it would be good if you come back to İstanbul to marry Metin."

Nobody that Fiona knew fasted for *Ramazan*, so the holy month passed almost unnoticed. But when *Şeker Bayramı*, the holiday that followed, came, she couldn't miss it. Ceylan and Defne had tried to warn her what to expect but nothing could have prepared Fiona for the three-day orgy of sweet, sugary food. It seemed everyone was out visiting everyone else and there was an expectation that you ate everywhere. Of course, hospitality was over the top for the exchange student experiencing her first ever *Bayram*.

Fiona kept track on the first day, and discovered she and her family visited eleven different homes. She'd held her cupped hands out for the inevitable offering of *kolonya*, and Fiona thought her hands might always smell the lemon-scented alcohol-based refresher. The night before, Ceylan had taught her how to kiss a hand and touch it to her forehead. It was expected that she, along with her host sisters, perform this honour to any elderly person they visited. She'd been offered, and had eaten, something at every home along with a glass of tea. Fiona thought she might fall into a sugar-induced coma when they got home, but Ceylan reminded her it was their turn to host the next day. It wasn't quite as busy, but they still opened their doors to half a dozen separate visitors, with all the ritual and tradition of the day before.

Fortunately, on the third day, everyone simply stayed at home, and recovered from the overindulging. Fiona called Hayley that afternoon. "Did you eat as much as I did?" she asked. "I think I gained ten kilos!"

"Tell me about it," groaned Hayley. "I think that was Hallowe'en, Thanksgiving, and Christmas all rolled into one."

With exams out of the way and *Ramazan* over, the last few weeks of the school year had a lighter feel.

"*Kızlar!*" shouted Aylin, as they all raced from the school gates toward the shore one early June afternoon. "Hey, girls!" she repeated in English for Hayley's benefit, "*Beni bekle!*"

Fiona, Nazlı, Yeşim, and Hayley slowed down to wait for their friend. Heads together, Aylin suggested, they stop in at their favourite spot for *lahmacun* to celebrate Fiona's news before heading their separate ways.

Fiona's father had called from Canada the night before. A big fat envelope had arrived in the mail. She'd been accepted into the program she'd so desperately wanted. Hayley had received a similar phone call about college during Bayram so now it was just

67

the Turkish students who were waiting on news. They all had their hopes pinned on different universities. Aylin desperately wanted to get into a school in Ankara, but Nazlı and Yeşim were hoping to stay in İstanbul.

As they piled parsley and onions onto their *lahmacun* and squeezed lemon juice over it before rolling up the thin flatbread that was topped with ground meat, they nervously joked about how funny it would be if they all ended up at each other's first pick. Fiona was just so happy she knew where she was going now. Ottawa wasn't too big or too far from home, but as Canada's capital city, it had the advantage of cultural activities she might not have got elsewhere. İstanbul had spoiled her.

Snack finished and *çay* drunk, the girls all got up from the table and kissed each other on both cheeks. Parting shouts of "*İyi akşamlar*" and "*Yarın görüşürüz*" filled the air as they went their separate ways.

Fiona and Hayley walked together along Bağdat Caddesi, talking about what the next few weeks would bring and how strange it would be to leave this city. Hayley was going to a travel agent on the weekend to book her flight home. She'd been dating Ömer from the plane way back when she arrived for the past couple of months, but they'd just broken up and she was almost ready to go home. Fiona didn't even want to think about it.

Metin asked Fiona to meet him at the Beşiktaş pier one afternoon. She met the ferry and they walked arm in arm up the Bosphorus. When they reached Ortaköy, they stopped for tea. Metin had a serious expression on his face. "Would you be able to live here?" he asked. "I mean, after university, if I asked you to?"

Fiona was taken aback and took a moment to think. She thought she knew where this was going. "I'm not sure," she answered honestly. She continued quietly, looking at her hands, "It's a long way from my family. I love İstanbul, but it's so different from home."

They sat quietly beside each other for several minutes before Fiona looked up. She saw a pained look in Metin's eyes.

"That wasn't what you wanted to hear, was it," she said quietly.

Metin shook his head. He swallowed. "I love you, Fiona," he said, when he finally trusted his voice not to wobble.

"I love you too, and I want to be with you," Fiona reassured him. "I suppose if I knew I would be able visit every so often . . ." Her voice trailed off, unsure what to say next.

"I need to stay for my family," Metin said, leaving her no doubt where he stood. "I know you need to go home for university. But maybe later? Maybe then?"

Fiona nodded. Now it was she who didn't trust her voice. "Yes," she finally whispered. "Yes, maybe then."

Metin banged his fist on the table in frustration. "I wish we were older. I wish I had a job. I wish . . . Fiona, will you spend the rest of your life with me?"

As much as she wanted to say yes and throw her arms around him, Fiona's practical side won. "Metin'*ciğim*, I love that you asked me. And you know I want to. But will you ask me again later? I promise, when the time is right, I'll say yes."

He looked crestfallen, but he knew she was right. He was just nineteen years old and she was still eighteen. They would both go to university and then he'd ask her again. He could wait.

As Hayley counted down the days until the end of school and then her plane ride home to Ohio, Fiona was feeling torn. This magic year was coming to an end too quickly for her, and she could hardly believe she was heading home for her own university experience. How had the year slipped away this quickly? Hadn't it only just started? Things were going so well. Nazlı told her she hardly needed to ever use her "terrible English" anymore with her, and her relationship with her host sisters was loving. Things were great with Metin and her friends were amazing.

Aylin's parents let her throw a big end-of-year party after graduation. Fiona and Hayley had gone to the ceremony in the afternoon and had their pictures taken with so many students and teachers. There were tears shed because they knew that they'd never see some of these people ever again. Later, at Aylin's party, they danced and danced to the stereo in her living room until the wee small hours of the morning. There was wine to drink, *meze* to eat, and balloons all around the room. Yeşim, Nazlı, Hayley, and Fiona all spent the night and there were tears again the next morning with hugs and whispered promises to keep in touch. Hayley was leaving in two days.

Fiona hadn't made her arrangements yet, but knew she couldn't put it off much longer. Walking home from Aylin's, she decided to go to a travel agent the following day to book a flight home to Canada in two weeks. She'd try and get a summer job and earn some money before university. But when she got back to her apartment, the family was in a frenzy of excitement. Now that Ceylan had graduated from university, the family had learned that Mert was planning to propose and they wanted Fiona to stay for the wedding in early August. Fiona couldn't say no, so quickly clearing it with her parents back home, she put aside thoughts of booking her ticket and got swept up in wedding planning.

Chapter 7

Hayley woke up in her sun-filled bedroom and stretched out, enjoying the extra room in her double bed. Wait. Where was she? Home. She'd been home for a week. It was almost like İstanbul was a dream.

It felt good to be home. Hayley had loved her exchange year and wouldn't have traded it for the world, but she was glad to be back. It felt good to not feel she needed to look down when she walked along the street. It felt good not to be stared at just because she was a tall blonde girl. It felt good to have all her favourite foods. It felt good to have hot water every day. And it felt so good to understand every conversation around her. Hayley was going to enjoy being home for a couple of months before beginning college.

But she was surprised by some of the small things that tripped her up. She hadn't expected culture shock coming home. Hayley felt strange not kissing her friends on both cheeks when they met at the mall. Even having a mall to go to seemed odd. She missed *çay*. She missed Fiona and her Turkish friends. And the Ohio River was no match for the Bosphorus.

CRwe

Metin had been thrilled when he learned that Fiona was staying longer. His stomach had been in knots, making him almost physically ill, when he thought of her leaving. Thanks to Ceylan and Mert, he'd been given an extra six weeks with the girl he was sure was the love of his life. When she told him about staying for the engagement and wedding, he had picked her up and whirled her around and around and around until they were both dizzy. He started making plans for them now that school was over. There was so much of İstanbul he still hadn't shown her. There were exhibits to see, museums to visit, concerts to go to. And now he had six more weeks.

Fiona's whole family was excited for the engagement. She went shopping with her *anne* and sisters for fancy dresses for the event. On the day the engagement was to happen, Ceylan went to the hairdresser and had her chestnut hair piled on top of her head. The rest of the family put on their best clothes and got ready for the groom's family to visit.

They had explained all of this to Fiona, but it still felt very strange to her. Even though everyone knew the couple was going to get married, there was this elaborate ceremony to make the engagement official.

Finally, in the evening, Mert came to the door with his mother and father, and his siblings. He had a box of chocolates in one hand and a huge bouquet of flowers in the other. Everyone sat around in the living room making nervous chit-chat.

Eventually Fiona's *anne* told Ceylan to help her in the kitchen. Defne gestured for Fiona to join them. Tradition said that Ceylan had to prove her worth as a bride by making Turkish coffee. But at the last minute, following a custom as old as the hills, she would put salt in Mert's coffee, making it all but undrinkable.

Mert would have to drink it, proving he would overlook all flaws to make the marriage a success. Giggling, Defne watched Ceylan add the salt before she took the tray into the living room. She offered each guest their cup, making sure Mert got the special one. As most soon-to-be grooms do, he choked a bit on the drink, but gamely drank it all.

Only then did the official discussions begin. Mert's father asked their *baba* for Ceylan's hand in marriage for his son. After the appropriate amount of discussion, *baba* said yes and suddenly the tension was gone and everyone was ready to celebrate.

Ceylan and Mert put on rings tied together by a red ribbon. The ribbon was cut and they were engaged! The couple honoured the parents by kissing their hands and putting them to their foreheads.

The wedding would follow more quickly than usual because Mert had received an unexpected promotion at work that meant a quick move to Ankara. He and Ceylan would start married life together there and Fiona's *anne* would go up to Ankara with them to help get the couple settled.

While the family was busy with frantic wedding planning, given the short engagement, the university matches were published. Fiona rushed to meet up with all her friends to learn the news. Metin and Mehmet joined them too. That morning, with their parents, Turkish students across the country had pored over the paper looking for their number to find out what university they would attend and which programs they would study.

It was good news for Fiona's friends and she could hear the sounds of congratulations as she arrived in front of the school gates. There were smiles all around. Almost everyone would be attending their first choice university in the fall. Only Mehmet would have to go to his second choice, but it was still a very good school in İstanbul, so he wasn't disappointed. "I got in!" Metin whispered ecstatically in Fiona's ear as he hugged her. Fiona only had a momentary twinge of sadness thinking that their futures were going in different directions before she was caught up in the celebrations.

A few nights before the wedding, they held Ceylan *abla*'s *kına gecesi*. Fiona was expecting a bridal shower but was in for a surprise as she learned the occasion was for the bride's female family and friends to come together dressed in their finest and celebrate the upcoming nuptials. The women ate and danced for hours and then Ceylan disappeared along with several of her friends. The lights dimmed, and they emerged, but now the bride-to-be was wearing a beautiful embroidered red veil that matched her red dress. Ceylan's friends led her to a chair in the centre of the room. Fiona watched, entranced, as they walked in a circle around her, candles in their hands, singing traditional folk songs. She couldn't make out all the words but she was surprised that they seemed like sad songs about leaving home. Ceylan looked upset.

Worried, she asked Defne if their *abla* was all right. "She's fine," Defne assured her. "It's tradition that the bride should cry because years ago, it was the first time she would leave her parents' house. We sing sad songs to help make her cry." Sure enough, a few tears soon rolled down Ceylan's face. Mert's mother put a coin in each of her hands, and then her own mother put henna on top and then eased each hand into gauzy red bags and tied them around her wrists.

With the formal part of the evening out of the way, the dancing began again until everyone was ready to drop.

There had been much debate as to whether to include the traditional *gelin alma* as part of the wedding. At the end of the day, modernity had ruled the day. Ceylan explained to Fiona that some weddings started in the morning with the groom hiring a drummer and at least one horn player and showing up at the bride's house to collect her from her family. The musicians would play and the groom's family would dance in the street to announce their arrival. The bride might cry again, sad to be leaving her childhood home and family. But the groom would bring her into the street to dance with her new family. After some time, they would drive away to prepare for the ceremony. Fiona thought it sounded lovely, but Ceylan wrinkled up her nose and said it was too traditional and not something she wanted.

Ceylan did keep at least one traditional element in her wedding. She wrote the names of her single friends on the soles of her wedding shoes. "I'll write your name here," she said to Fiona, pointing to a part of the shoe that would get a lot of wear during the day. "Maybe it will bring you luck with Metin." She explained that if Fiona's name was worn off by the end of the night, she would be married soon.

The actual wedding ceremony was very efficient. Mert and Ceylan sat at a long table in front of all their guests and were asked if they agreed to the marriage. After they both answered yes, all that was left was for the couple and their witnesses to sign their names in an official government book. Five minutes, and it was over! Ceylan held their red marriage booklet high proudly as relatives snapped photos of the happy couple. She looked beautiful in her white wedding gown.

And then the party began. The newlyweds danced together first and then they were joined by their family and friends. Fiona had so much fun. Defne dragged Fiona onto the dance floor for some of the traditional dances and they laughed so much as she tried to copy the movements. It was a wonderful mix of old and new. Just as she thought she wouldn't be able to dance any longer, the cake was cut and a receiving line formed where the guests had a chance to congratulate the couple, giving gold coins or pinning money to red ribbons around their necks. Afterwards, some of the older guests left, and the younger generation danced until dawn.

Shortly after the wedding, the dreaded day arrived — Fiona's last day in İstanbul. It was an emotional one as she said goodbye to people who had been such an important part of the last year. She had tissues in her purse and she knew she'd need them.

After some final gift shopping, she met with Nazlı, Yeşim, and Aylin for lunch. There were tears and laughter, as they remembered some of their adventures. They talked about Fiona's first day at school, the concerts and movies they went to, and the many Saturday afternoons spent in each others' bedrooms where they listened and sang to music with Yeşim or Aylin writing out lyrics to help Fiona learn the songs. And at the end of the meal, the girls presented her with a box of baklava to take home and they all promised to write to each other frequently, pledging their lifelong friendship.

"Promise me you'll write," pleaded Fiona.

"Of course, we will," said Aylin, wiping tears away. "Friends forever, right?"

"Just don't forget us," Yeşim demanded.

"Never," Fiona assured her. She was determined that these wonderful girls would always be in her life.

"Come back and visit us, Fiona," whispered Nazlı. She was going to miss her seatmate and couldn't believe how nervous she'd been to meet her all those months ago. "There is always a place for you here."

"Of course, I will, Nazlı. And you can come and visit me too." She flung her arms around her friends.

After tearful goodbyes, Fiona headed to Metin's house. Özlem *teyze* answered the door and bundled Fiona up in her arms. "*Seni çok özleyeceğiz, kızım,*" she said sadly, telling Fiona they would miss her.

Fiona felt tears welling up in her eyes again. "*Ben de.* Me too," she whispered.

Özlem *teyze* had made a special cake that afternoon and they ate it with glasses of *çay* as Fiona handed out gifts for the family.

She pressed a small inukshuk into Metin's hands. "It's an Inuit symbol," she explained. "They mark directions on a journey so people don't get lost." With tears threatening to fall, she whispered to him that she hoped it would help them always find their way back together.

Dinner at home was equally emotional. Of course, Ceylan was gone now, but Defne cried enough for both of them. The house would be too quiet without her two *ablas*. Even *baba* had to clear his throat several times as he told Fiona to keep her house key. That way she would always be able to come home to them. Fiona cried herself to sleep. She did not want tomorrow to come.

Just after the sun rose Fiona's family all came downstairs to see her off in a taxi. She didn't want them to come to the airport. She hugged and kissed them, promising to write soon, and there were tears all over again. *Baba* helped get her luggage in the taxi and everyone wished her a good journey home with an "*iyi yolculuklar.*"

Fiona told the driver to go to Bağdat Caddesi first, where they found Metin waiting. He got in the car with the saddest eyes Fiona had ever seen. They held hands and cried in the taxi on the way to the airport. Neither of them was ready for this to end. Metin went as far as he could with her, but finally they were at security. Fiona clung to him, feeling safe and loved wrapped up in his arms. She felt like this was where she was meant to be. Finally, she pulled away and looked up into his eyes.

"I don't want to go," she said through her tears. "I'll call your neighbour in two days to let you know I got home safe. And I'll write to you every day. I love you so much." She flung her arms around Metin one more time.

Metin reached down and cupped her face in his hands. "Fiona. *Bir tanem. Sevgilim.* I love you," he said, being strong for both of them. "I'll wait for you. We'll wait for each other. But you need to go home to your family now." He kissed her. "Go, my dear, and whatever you do, don't look back."

Fiona nodded. "*Seni özleyeceğim*," she whispered.

Metin smiled. "*Ben de*. I'll miss you too," he answered.

Taking a deep breath and drying her eyes, Fiona squared her shoulders, picked up her carry-on bag, and headed through security. Just before she was out of sight, she looked back and saw Metin standing all alone in the hall, hands in his pockets, tears streaming down his face.

Part 2

Chapter 8

Fiona felt like a fish out of water at home. She had been prepared for culture shock going to Turkey, but like Hayley, she had not expected it coming home. Everything felt foreign and she felt out of place. Fiona kept expecting people to kiss her on the cheeks and she missed the sound of the call to prayer. She was astonished at how much space there was, but she had forgotten that she'd need to drive to get anywhere. And of course she missed Metin terribly. She had called him at his neighbour's house when she first got home as they'd organized, and she cried again when they had to hang up. They hadn't spoken again, but they were writing every day.

Because of Ceylan *abla*'s wedding, Fiona only had three weeks at home before leaving again for university, several hundred kilometres away. And those weeks were a whirlwind of spending time with her parents, seeing friends, and packing for school. When she did see her friends, they seemed very different, and all Fiona could talk about was how much she missed her life in İstanbul. She even found Turkish filler words like *şey* and *yani* had crept into her English. Her father laughed the first time she asked him to open the light and she wondered when she'd started saying that.

A week after arriving home, she got her first letter from Metin. Her hands trembled as she opened the envelope.

Sevgili Fiona,

I've just returned from the airport where I had to say goodbye to you. It was one of the hardest things I've ever done. I miss you already, sevgilim. I miss the feel of your arm in mine when we walk down the street. I miss your eyes gazing at me, and I miss the feel of your lips on mine.

I know you looked back. I didn't want you to see me cry, but I'm glad you did. It gave me one more chance to see your beautiful eyes. Seni çok seviyorum.

I hope your journey home was smooth. I know I will speak with you before you get this letter but I need to write it. The next few months will be hard for us both. I hope we can find a way to see each other soon but I think it will take a miracle. But miracles can happen and I believe we will get ours.

I can't wait to hear your voice. Until then, say hello to your mother and father and know that I love you.

Metin

Even though she'd mailed a letter just the day before, Fiona wrote back at once

Sevgili Metin,

Thank you for your letter. Every day here seems strange. The food seems strange, the customs seem strange, the sounds and the views are odd. I imagine you felt the same way when you returned to İstanbul a year ago. I just wasn't expecting the differences to be so big and to matter so much.

I so much want to get on a bus and come to you. For us to walk to the seaside in Göztepe and sit at our little çay bahçe and talk for hours.

The lake here is beautiful and peaceful. At night the loons call to each other. I wish I could show it to you. Remember that song I sang to you? The one that says that the moon and the stars are the same ones we each see? Let's remember that and make our wishes for miracles on those stars together.

Please give my love to all your family and kisses especially for your anne.

Seni seviyorum,
Fiona

Before she knew it, Fiona was in the back seat of the family car early one morning in the first week of September. Her possessions, some old familiar ones, some Turkish souvenirs, and some brand new were packed all around her, with her mum and dad driving to her university in Ottawa. She was the first of the four roommates to arrive. New residences had been built the year before, so Fiona was lucky. Unlike most new first-year students, she had a private bedroom that shared a living room and a kitchen with three other girls. They were like mini apartments, but on campus.

With help from her parents, they lugged her boxes into her room and got her settled. In short order her bed was made, her clothes put away, her books and typewriter were set up on her desk, and her pots and pans were in the kitchen. Nobody else had arrived yet, so the trio went for a walk along the canal and had a quick bite to eat before making a trip to the local grocery store to stock Fiona's kitchen. With that accomplished, George and Grace reluctantly said goodbye again to their daughter, wishing her the best of luck and insisting she write and call home frequently.

Fiona looked around her apartment. It was basic, but they'd make it home. Her room was bigger than the ones she'd had in İstanbul, she thought, a stab of homesickness setting in again. She shook it off, hoping her roommates would arrive soon. Because being at her home with her mum and dad had felt so strange, she was glad to be having a new adventure again so soon. She hoped she'd acclimatize to it quickly.

She met lots of new people at a mixer, including some in her program. Fiona wrote to Metin the next day.

Sevgili Metin,

Well, I've moved in. I'm away from my parents again and starting a new adventure. It's exciting, but please don't think I'm forgetting you. My new roommates seem nice, but it's you I want to tell everything to. When I came home from the mixer last night, I desperately wanted to laugh with you about the funny people, and ask your opinion about some of the interesting ones.

This is just a short letter to remind you to write to this address now so your letters will come directly. At home I looked every day in the mailbox hoping for something from you. I will do the same here.

I hope your first days at university are going well. If you run into Yeşim, please kiss her for me.

Dreaming of the day we meet again.
Your Fiona

Fiona threw herself into university to dull the pain of their separation. Her roommates were nice, but she missed Metin terribly and was desperate to hear his voice again. Overseas calls were expensive, but not too much so, so she'd asked if there was a way that they could schedule a regular time when he could be at his aunt's house to receive a call. Fortunately, new friends and new academic adventures helped dull the pain.

Like Fiona, Metin was pouring his own heartache into his schoolwork on the other side of the world. He continued to live at home while taking classes in computer engineering, and was starting to get interested in social activism. They wrote to each at least twice a week, sharing their experiences and their grief at the distance between them.

Sevgili Fiona,

Like you, I wait for your letters every day. Sometimes a few days go by without one and I am crushed, thinking you've forgotten me or that your new adventure is taking you away. But then the postacı will bring two or three together and my faith is restored.

University is great! I'm so glad to be back at school and learning again. My professors are good lecturers and the material is really interesting. I've met some really interesting people who want to make the world a better place. I had çay with Mehmet and Yeşim yesterday. They both say to say hello (so do Safiye and my mom) and Yeşim sends kisses. She will write soon. We three will go to a classical concert soon, but I will be sad, missing you beside me. I miss you all the time and want to feel your hand in mine, and our lips together.

Tamer is back from military service. He is glad it is finished and is looking for a job. I am not looking forward to my time. But that is many years away still so we won't think about it.

Seni öperim,
Metin

Fiona loved her classes. Her professors — all former and current professionals — were engaging and witty and happy to spend time telling stories of their careers. This program brought together some very determined students from across the country and Fiona was sure many of them would go on to be very successful.

She quickly became close with two of her classmates. Lysiane, often at the top of the class, and Jessica, a bubbly, friendly girl. If there was a party, Jess knew where it was. The three of them were as different from one another as possible, but together, they had a lot of fun and when they worked together on assignments, did very well.

Fiona auditioned and was accepted into the university chamber choir. Singing in a group was probably the one thing she had missed in İstanbul. Voices joined together in perfect harmony made her spirit soar. The weekly rehearsals were challenging and she was learning a lot. Her fellow choristers welcomed her and she enjoyed their company. They often went out for a drink after the rehearsals to socialize.

A few weeks into school, Fiona finally had time to write to everyone else with her new address and to let them know how she was settling in.

Hayley was the quickest to respond.

Merhaba, Fiona!

So glad to hear from you. Home is so weird, isn't it?! When I first got back, I missed lots of things, but I'm having a great time at college and am making tons of new friends. No more uniforms — yay!! And I have to admit, being able to understand everyone around me is nice. I never did learn Turkish the way you did.

My classes are challenging so I'm studying a lot, but I'm making time to pledge a sorority! And there are so many cute guys here. You say you're still in love with Metin, but make sure you look around you. I bet there are cute guys there too.

Anyway, I must run. My roommate and I are going clubbing tonight and I need to get ready. Write back soon!!

With love,
Hayley

When letters arrived from her Turkish friends, she realized it was going to be harder than she thought to stay close. Her written Turkish was abysmal, and their written English was a little more stilted and less fluid than she had expected, given their oral fluency.

Sevgili Fiona,

How are you? I hope your üniversite is good. I am just started studying at İstanbul Üniversitesi and I am liking very much. My classes are good and I am studying very much at home. Last week I saw Metin with Yeşim and Mehmet at AKM. I was at a concert and they were there too. He missed you a lot.

There is bad news for Ozan and me. We are not together any more. I was sad at first but now I am OK.

I miss seeing you all the time and talking about all the things. Today the weather is very cold. They are saying us that much snow will come this winter. Can you believe? Maybe we will be like Kanada!

Loves,
Nazlı

Merhaba, Fiona'cığım,

Hello from Ankara! I was very happy to get your letter. I recognized your writing on the envelope but my roommate asked me about the strange stamp. She was impressed someone in Kanada is writing to me. My classes are very difficult so I study all the time. But they are interesting too, so I like this.

I hope you are not missing Metin too much. I think it is very difficult for both of you now. But I think your love is strong and I am sure you will come back to Turkey soon.

I am missing you and Hayley, and Nazlı, and Yeşim. We were good friends for a long time and I wish we can be together again soon. But for now, we can write letters and study hard. I hope you will write again soon. I will answer quickly if I can.

Loves,
Aylin

Dear Fiona,

I was so happy to open your letter. When I read you are doing well, I am very happy. As you know, Metin and I are at the same school. My studies are going well. I finally choose chemistry. I think you know the classes are mostly in English, and you helped mine get better last year. So I say thank you.

I see Metin sometimes on campus and also with Mehmet. He is sad, Fiona. I know he is liking his classes, but he missed you a lot. He is my friend too and I am sad when he is sad. But I think you miss him the same so I am sad for you too. I promise that I will watch for him (does that make sense?) for you and I will write to you about him. Boys don't share their emotions very well, I think, so I can be your eyes here.

I am writing this letter on the bus, so please I am sorry for my handwriting. It is a long journey every day to the üniversite, but I am happy to do it because the lessons are very good. My stop is coming soon so I must go.

Loves,
Yeşim

Through their letters, Fiona and Metin had at last managed to organize a time to speak to each other during her visit home on Thanksgiving weekend. They hadn't spoken since that first conversation when she came home. Fiona dragged the long telephone cord into her room for some privacy. She dialled the number and listened to the strange overseas phone signal. Someone picked up the phone.

"*Efendim, buyurun.*"

"*Merhaba. Ben Fiona. Metin orada mı?*" She was surprised that the simple words of introduction and asking for Metin didn't trip off her tongue as easily as they had just two months ago.

"*Evet, evet. Burada. Bir dakika, kızım,*" said the kind voice on the other end of the phone. "He's here. Just a minute, my dear."

Fiona held her breath. Her heart was pounding with excitement. She heard a bit of noise in the background and suddenly Metin was with her.

"Fiona?"

"Metin. Oh, my God, it's so good to hear your voice. I've missed you so much."

"Me too. Tell me everything."

They talked for half an hour, sharing stories of their first weeks at university. They had two months of news to catch up on. Fiona told him about her room at school and he told her about his commute. He told her how stimulating his classes were and she told him about her courses. She asked about his family, who he said were doing well, and Metin asked what it was like being home. He remembered that it was difficult when he first returned to İstanbul. Fiona admitted it had been strange and she was glad to have gone to university so quickly.

"Just don't go find a new exchange student to talk to and teach a sport," he teased her, thinking back to the football game a year ago.

She laughed and then clicked her tongue. "*Asla yapmayacaktım!* I'd never do that!" she replied. Talking was so much better than letters. Finally, after declaring their love to each other, they said their goodbyes. Fiona sat quietly and wiped the tears from her cheeks before going back downstairs for Thanksgiving dinner.

When she arrived back at school, there was another letter from Metin. She read it again and again before adding it to a growing stack of letters in a shoebox.

Always an early bird, Fiona began filling her lonely mornings before others were up by running. Almost every morning before seven o'clock, she could be found with her ponytail swaying as she ran along the Rideau Canal in black leggings and her favourite teal vest. She found the rhythm of her feet hitting the pavement almost meditative and she was in her own world when she ran, not noticing anyone else around her. Fiona had always been slim, and running, coupled with a yoga class she'd started taking once a week to deal with school stress, had helped define her muscles.

The semester flew by and soon Fiona was heading home for Christmas holidays. During exams, she'd sent Christmas cards to the girls — New Year's cards really — and a small package to Metin. Of course, she knew he didn't celebrate Christmas, but he'd had one in the US and one with her, so she thought it was still appropriate. He'd told her he'd sent a small package for her birthday and Christmas combined, but she was still surprised to see it had arrived in time. Her mother handed it to her with a smile and Fiona took it upstairs to open by herself, and found a tiny package of *lokum* and a book of paintings from an exhibit they'd been to. She sat there for a few minutes collecting herself.

Fiona had told Metin she would call his neighbour around four o'clock — their tea time. So at nine in the morning, she picked up the phone and dialled the long international number. They chatted for a long time about everything and nothing. Fiona was disappointed that Metin hadn't received his package yet, but he assured her it would be there soon.

Fiona was happy to get back to school in January. She'd enjoyed the time with her family, but she'd been gone for essentially eighteen months now, and she was a different person than when she left. It was nice to visit, but she was starting to think of her parent's house as a nice place to visit, as opposed to "going home."

The trans-Atlantic letters continued at a fast pace throughout the winter and the young lovers managed another call for Metin's birthday in April. He was going out with friends to celebrate that night and Fiona told him to drink a glass of *rakı*, for her.

Jess and Lysiane had become great friends for Fiona. The only bone of contention was romance. Both Jess and Lysiane had found boyfriends soon after arriving at university and they didn't understand why she was hanging on to this long-distance love. They'd seen pictures of Metin, and agreed he was very handsome, but there were good-looking men in Ottawa, and he was a million miles away. They tried their best to be supportive, but they were always trying to introduce Fiona to handsome men. It irked her and her grey eyes flashed with frustration sometimes, but she knew they had good intentions.

They threesome decided to room together in second year and found a perfect apartment near the canal above a restaurant. They furnished it with futons, garage sale tables, and flea market finds. Jessica had a car, so they were able to bring things home with ease.

Every Sunday night they liked to have dinner together. During the week, everyone's schedules were crazy and they sometimes went different ways on the weekends, but Sunday was roommate time. Fiona loved to cook and they quickly settled on a routine that had her cooking and them washing up. She alternated between some old favourites and experimenting with new recipes, and often current boyfriends would join them. Her roommates occasionally teased her that they'd all gain weight because of her Sunday dinners.

After working hard for their first set of mid-term exams, they threw the first of what would become legendary beach parties, complete with a kiddie pool full of sand, pink flamingos, and leis. Their guests wore Hawaiian shirts and in the wee small hours of the morning, limbo competitions in the living room were fuelled by fuzzy navels and beer.

Fiona wrote to Metin about the party. She lay on her bed and tried to put into words how much fun it was. And then she felt guilty that she was enjoying herself so much without him. She was trying to write to her Turkish girlfriends every few months still and they wrote regularly too. Nazlı had found a new boyfriend, and this one her parents knew about, so she was more at ease. Yeşim and Mehmet were still together and Aylin had her head buried in her books. Fiona heard from Hayley less frequently, but knew she was having the time of her life at university.

By the beginning of third year, Fiona and Metin were still sending letters regularly, but not quite as frequently. Lysiane and Jessica were happy that Fiona was spending a little more time in the present day, but still looking for ways to encourage her to look at the local boys. They'd even taken her to a local salon for a make-over just before classes began, where they cut several inches off her long hair. She took a photo and sent it to Metin, wondering what he'd think of her now just above the shoulder waves.

The weekend after the salon visit, they introduced her to Sam Rickford at a party Lysiane's new boyfriend had thrown. She was more than happy to try and play matchmaker.

Sam noticed Fiona as soon as he arrived at the party. Quite apart from the fact that he thought she was the most beautiful woman in the room, he recognized her as the petite redhead he saw along the canal on his morning run. They laughed when they realized they'd been in the same place at the same time almost every day for months now.

Sam was a year older than Fiona. He was a very serious young man with golden-brown hair and intense but sad brown eyes. He was taking a double major of economics and business, and was planning a career in the investment industry on Bay Street. Sam had tragically lost both his parents in a car accident just over eighteen months ago — it was just him and his older brother now and they'd become very close through their grief, navigating all the arrangements for the funeral and the estate. Fortunately, their parents had invested wisely, so the young men didn't have to worry about money. Still, Sam lost a year of school after their death and it had made the already mature young man seem older than his years. His course load was heavy in his third year of university and he wasn't really interested in socializing. His roommate had dragged him to this party, but having met Fiona, Sam was glad of it now. They hit it off and spent most of the night talking together.

Soon, they were spending many friendly afternoons debating world issues and the environment over coffee. Sam had a car, so they went hiking in the Gatineau Hills in Quebec that fall. They'd tried running together but it wasn't a great fit. Sam was a full nine inches taller than Fiona and she had a hard time keeping up with his long stride. So, although he liked spending time with her, Sam wasn't offended when she suggested they run separately. They were great study partners, though, and they often kept each other company despite their completely different programs.

Despite her explanations about Metin, Sam found himself developing feelings for Fiona. He kept them to himself because she had become a good friend and he didn't want to risk that. Sam could talk to Fiona about anything — about his struggles, about the pressures of school, about the life he was planning after graduation, and even about his parents. With most people, it was awkward and they didn't know what to say so he found it easier to just not bring them up. It was different with Fiona. She directed conversation with smart questions that helped him understand himself better and see the details of his future more clearly. It was like the fog through which he'd been looking at the world for the past year and a half was clearing, and he started to really feel like himself again.

When he visited his brother at Thanksgiving, he couldn't stop talking about her. Ben, who was five years older, and a young environmental lawyer at a well-known Toronto firm, teased his brother about it, but he noticed a light in Sam's eyes and couldn't have been happier for him. Ben was testing the waters in a new relationship himself, but was keeping his love life under wraps for now.

Sam was a guest at the second annual beach party Fiona and her roommates threw after mid-terms. He arrived with a bottle of Jamaican rum, and was impressed with the sand-filled kiddie pool complete this year with pink flamingos. "You girls go all out, don't you?"

"Just you wait until midnight," Jessica warned. "That's when the limbo stick comes out."

Soon the stereo was blasting with Caribbean music and the apartment was full of university students shaking off the stress of exam week. Sam and Fiona clinked beer bottles and danced along with the others until late into the night.

Fiona wrote to tell Metin all about it the next day.

Sevgili Metin'ciğim,

How are you? I miss you so much. This is a quick letter before I go out for a run.

I've just finished mid-terms (are you writing exams now too?) and we had a huge party last night at our place.

Remember the beach party we had last year? It was such a success we did it again. Hawaiian shirts, leis, and flamingos. Even the limbo competition. You'd think I'd be good at that, because I'm so short, but my friend Sam won this year. I wasn't even close!

Next weekend a bunch of us are going to go hiking in the Gatineau Hills. It's so pretty there. It reminds me a little bit of Belgrad Forest.

Yeşim tells me she sees you at school sometimes. She says you look sad. Please try and see the beauty around you. You live in a magical city, that I still miss terribly. I would feel awful if you can't see that anymore. Promise me you'll try and smile more, canım. Go up to Çamlıca Hill and look over the city. Or go to Yıldız Park to walk in the trees. Or maybe look for some dolphins for me the next time you're on a feribot. But be happy, my love.

I hope your classes are going well. We're singing some really great music this year with the choir. I wish you could hear it.

Give my love to Safiye and kiss your anne for me. I miss you soooooo much. I'll write again soon . . .

All my love,
Fiona

As fall gave way to winter, Sam and Fiona continued to spend time together, and often went skating on the canal when they weren't studying. They never ran out of things to talk about and Fiona kept teasing Sam, threatening to set him up with one of her choirmates one of these days.

Taking a break from studying one afternoon, Fiona wrote to Nazlı.

Sevgili Nazlı'cığım,

Hello from Canada! I hope your studies are going well. It's cold in Canada now and we've brought our ice skates out. Sam and I rented snowshoes last weekend and went for a long hike. We took sunflower seeds with us and fed the birds. It was so neat when they landed on my hand and took a seed away. They must be Turkish — they love sunflower seeds!

How is life in İstanbul? Tell me more about your new boy-friend. I miss Metin so much. I can't wait until I can see all of you again. Maybe at spring break next year I can convince my mum and dad to let me come.

You asked me about Sam. He's just a friend. He's very smart and I guess he's handsome too. He'll make some girl very happy one day. But for now, he's focussed on finishing school and starting his career. We study together often, and we talk a lot about everything.

With love,
Fiona

She also wrote to Yeşim who sometimes saw Metin, and asked how he was. Fiona wasn't sure if he was telling her everything and she wanted to make sure he was okay. Yeşim knew that Metin was still missing Fiona terribly. But she didn't want to put that pressure on her friend so she was careful with what she shared when she wrote back. It was becoming obvious to her that as much as they still wished it, it was almost impossible for them. And Yeşim knew it would be difficult for both of them when they finally admitted it to each other.

My dear Fiona,

Thank you for your letter. I am always happy when I see an envelope with a Canadian stamp in my mailbox. Mehmet sends his hellos.

Let me answer your questions about Metin. I don't see him as much, but he and Mehmet are still close. I know he has made many new friends at üniversite and I know he likes his classes and his causes. But when we are together, he talks about you and I know he still loves you.

I am a little bit jealous of you and your roommates. Your beach parties sound amazing. I am still living at home, of course, and so it is different for me. Your friend Sam sounds nice. I'm glad you have a good friend to talk to. Does he know about Metin?

We all miss you and hope you can come and visit soon.

Loves,
Yeşim

Fiona realized with a sad heart that it had been ages since she'd heard from Aylin. Their once-whispered promises to stay friends forever was hanging by a thread so she scribbled a quick note to her in between study sessions.

Sevgili Aylin'ciğim,

It's been a long time since I've heard from you. You must be studying very hard. I'm very frustrated. I was hoping to come to İstanbul during my school break. I thought I could even come to Ankara to see you, but my father has said no. I was very angry at him today, and sad that I won't see you girls or Metin when I really wanted to.

I talked to my friend Sam and he reminded me that my dad just wants me to stay focussed on my studies. More like you, I guess! But it is still very disappointing.

Are you starting to think about a job after university? I know there is another year of school left, but I'm starting to think about how to get a good job at the end of next year.

Sending you my love,
Fiona

In February, Fiona and Sam found themselves at another party together. Walking home from the evening, with soft snow falling, they talked about how they imagined their futures. Fiona wanted a marketing career, of course, but she wanted a family too, and it was important for her to stay home with her children when they were young. And of course, she wanted all of this with Metin. Sam surprised her by saying he wanted the same kind of thing. She already knew about his Bay Street ambitions, but for the first time Sam shared with her that what he really wanted was a big family with a partner who wanted to raise children, volunteer in school, and be a real part of the community. He was frustrated that he couldn't find someone who wanted that. Fiona assured him that he'd find her eventually. She couldn't be the only girl with those dreams.

Sam's feelings for Fiona had continued to grow. She was this tiny little dynamo and she didn't seem to realize how she lit up every room she walked into. It wasn't just that red hair. Despite her diminutive stature, everyone somehow knew when Fiona had arrived. Sam had long since stopped thinking of her as just a friend, but he knew Fiona was still chasing a fantasy of a guy halfway around the world. She didn't share much of that with him, but he'd heard about it from Jess and Lysiane. That was a tough thing to compete with, so he was biding his time, but was beginning to wonder if he'd ever get his chance.

He'd continued to talk to Ben about her, all the things he liked about her and his growing feelings. His brother encouraged him to hang in there. Fiona sounded like a great girl and he knew Sam needed someone in his life that he could hold onto, and dream of a future with. From all that Sam had told him, Ben thought Fiona could be that girl — at least for now, but maybe even forever. His own relationship was flourishing, giving him the same hope for the future, and he hoped to share it with his brother soon.

Chapter 9

Just before reading week began, Fiona found herself rubbing her temples and wincing. She put the headache down to her continued anger with her father about the return visit to Turkey she had wanted to make, plus the stress from all the studying she'd been doing. She was really looking forward to a week off school. Fiona continued to ignore the signs when her throat started to hurt on the last day of classes, but on the weekend, she woke up with an annoying tickle in her nose and sneezed several times before she even really opened her eyes. Groaning, she sat up and realized her head was completely congested as well. Not fair, she thought. A nasty cold, on top of not being able to be with Metin, was more than she could bear. Leaving the warmth of her bed, Fiona bent down to retrieve the newspaper from outside the door and her head nearly exploded from the pressure. She tried to read the headlines but the words swam in front of her eyes. It wasn't long before Fiona realized that all she'd be doing that day was sitting on the couch in her living room pretending to watch whatever talk show or sitcom rerun was on television.

At least it was quiet. Her roommates had both gone home on Friday, so Fiona was alone when Sam came by early that afternoon to suggest they go to a movie matinee. Shivering, she buzzed him up and unlocked the door, so he could come straight in after he walked up the stairs. He found her curled up the couch in her comfortable powder-blue flannel pajamas with white snowflakes and wrapped in an afghan her mother had crocheted. Her cheeks were flushed, her nose was red, and the enormous pile of tissues surrounding her told him everything he needed to know. The movie was instantly forgotten as he became overwhelmed by a sudden need to take care of his sick friend.

"You should just go home," she croaked, her eyes watering and nose streaming. "I feel miserable."

"Don't be ridiculous. You shouldn't be alone when you're sick."

Fiona wanted to protest, but a sudden sneeze stopped her before she could get any words out. Sam sat down and put his hand on her forehead. She was burning up. "That's it," he said, "Chicken soup and rest for you, my dear. And I'm staying to make sure you do what I say."

While Fiona napped, Sam ran home quickly to get a change of clothes, his books, and a couple of movies. He had a feeling he was going to be there a while, and he was right. It was several days before Fiona was feeling herself again. During that time, Sam made sure she ate, brought her tea with honey, and stuffed her full of decongestants. He sat on the couch with her for hours with his arm around her, her head resting on his shoulder while they watched movies. He made sure she had a continuous supply of tissues for her tender nose. He stroked her hair when her body radiated feverish heat and rubbed her back when a cough set in. Sam bundled her off to bed each night, while he slept on the couch in case she needed anything. She was a bit embarrassed that he stayed, but if she was honest with herself, she was glad. It had made her feel better to be taken care of.

"You know what?" Fiona announced on the Thursday of reading week, gingerly dabbing at her very tender nose. "I'm hungry. Let me make us something to eat — after I have a shower."

"Well, that's a good sign. Glad you've got your appetite, and some energy back."

Fiona took a long steamy shower, washing away the worst of the illness. Sam spent the time thinking about his strong feelings for Fiona. It was getting harder to keep them to himself. This week, he'd been really concerned about her. But he still didn't know if she felt anything for him.

Coming back into the living room wearing jeans and a comfortable oversized university sweatshirt, Fiona thanked Sam for staying so long. "I ruined your reading week," she said apologetically. "I can't remember when I've been this sick before, so thank you so much for being here."

Fiona cracked open some eggs and whipped up some omelettes for a light lunch, chopping up some tomatoes and crumbling in feta cheese along with thyme and tarragon. She pan-fried some potatoes for Sam and cut up some oranges, apples, and grapes for a simple fruit salad for dessert.

"This is amazing, Fiona," he complimented her on the meal. "If this is how you cook when you've been sick for the better part of a week, then I can't wait to taste your cooking when you're one hundred percent." They laughed and then washed the dishes together before Fiona sent him home. "Really," she said, still coughing a little, "you've been so great. But you should go. I'll take it easy for another day, but I'm fine."

"As long as you're sure," Sam said, gathering up his things. "But call me if that cough gets worse again, okay?" He smoothed Fiona's hair with his hand and kissed her cheek. "Thanks for lunch. It was really good. I'll talk to you tomorrow."

After he left, Fiona sat at the table with a steaming mug of tea, staring out the window and thinking about how incredibly kind

Sam had been to her the last few days. She touched her cheek where Sam had kissed her. What had that meant, she wondered?

When Lysiane and Jessica came back from reading week on the weekend, Fiona filled them in and they were both sorry to hear she'd been so sick over the holiday, but they were glad Sam had been around. She was still confused about the kiss, but her roommates were not. That night, they put their heads together to come up with ways to help Fiona see what was right in front of her. It was obvious to anyone who saw them together that Sam was head over heels in love with her. She just needed to have her eyes opened. She deserved a romance with someone in the same time zone. The time for fairy-tale overseas relationships was over.

Fiona and Metin had set up a phone call a few days after Fiona's reading week. It didn't make up for the missed trip, but it was better than a letter. They had been ignoring the fact that their phone calls were getting more stilted. Their lives were moving in separate directions the longer they were apart and they were slipping away from each other as they had new experiences and new friendships. They were miserable without each other, and they were trying desperately to hold onto each other, but it was hard. Somewhere deep inside, they both knew that they were in an impossible situation but neither was ready to acknowledge it just yet. Metin told her about his new tutoring job and she volunteered that her choir was competing in a few weeks. She was still coughing occasionally and Metin asked if she was sick. She downplayed it but mentioned that Sam had been there when her roommates were away. Metin went into overprotective mode. He was upset and told her he thought she was spending too much time with Sam. Fiona was hurt that he didn't trust her and told him as much. The phone call didn't end well.

When they hung up, they both realized they had some serious thinking to do. It was just a small spat, but it finally opened their eyes to the reality of their situation. They still wanted to make things work, but it wasn't the first call that had left them both unsettled. Fiona sat on her bed, contemplating the situation. She loved Metin and she wanted to be with him. But the separation, now close to three years, was hard. Halfway around the world, Metin was troubled. He still loved Fiona deeply, but he was beginning to feel hopeless.

Over the next few weeks, separately, and very reluctantly, Metin and Fiona came to the same conclusion. They had hoped they would be able to spend summers together, but it hadn't happened. And it wouldn't this year either. Their idealistic dreams of a future together were fading quickly.

Whether by coincidence or fate, they both penned a letter to the other on the same early March day, suggesting that they shouldn't hold onto the other any longer. That it would be fairer to let go with love and allow each other to move on. And that if it were meant to be, they'd find their way back together.

When Metin opened Fiona's letter, he could see where her tears had marked the pages she'd written, and he knew it had been just as hard for her as it had been for him to write those words. But he knew it would be even harder to let her go for real.

Fiona opened Metin's letter with trepidation. It was too soon for this to be a response to her tear-stained goodbye. Her eyes filled as she noted the date and read the words he had written to her. It wasn't lost on her that they had both struggled with this separately, but at the same time and that they had written to each other on the same day. Metin wished her well as she had done him. This was not going to be easy, but at least they had come to the decision together.

She folded his letter, put it back into its envelope, and added it to the box — she had kept every letter he had ever sent her. Drying her cheeks, she tied the box with a blue ribbon, to which she added a *nazar* — the evil eye — out of sentimentality and put it on the top shelf of her closet. She wrote to her friends to let them know.

To Yeşim, she added a special plea to watch out for Metin and to help him as much as he would let her.

The next few weeks were difficult for Fiona. She kept wanting to talk to Metin. She found herself scribbling notes to herself to remind her to add something to her next letter and she was constantly on the verge of tears. Lysiane and Jess could hear her crying in her room at night and were starting to worry about her. They were doing their best to keep her busy, while reminding her that life would go on.

A few weeks later, on the last day of March, it was Sam's birthday. Fiona had remembered Sam's jest about her cooking, so she pulled herself together and made a special, if simple, meal as both a proper thanks for his help when she was ill. Sam had once told her his favourite comfort food was shepherd's pie and apple crumble, and that his mother used to make it every time he'd come home from school. She'd tucked that piece of information away and was going to serve the meal tonight as a surprise.

Fiona had always loved spending time in the kitchen. She had been asking for kitchen gadgets for every birthday since she turned twelve. She pored over cooking magazines and experimented regularly. Jess and Lysiane were always happy to be guinea pigs for her, and the results of her experimentation were almost always great. Fiona even cooked up some Turkish treats from time to time.

Sam could smell the shepherd's pie before he even came in the door. It brought back vivid memories of his mum's. He cleared his throat and took a deep breath to steady himself before going in.

"Happy birthday, Sam!" said Fiona, giving him a friendly peck on the cheek. "I hope you'll like the menu tonight."

"If it tastes anything as good as it smells, I can't be disappointed. I can't believe you remembered that I like . . ." He trailed off, seeing the apple crumble on the table too. "Oh, Fiona."

She watched his face, as he struggled between sadness for what he'd lost, and the excitement over what she'd created. "Good surprise?" she asked tentatively, putting his hand on his arm.

Excitement won. "The best!" Sam exclaimed. He picked her up and whirled her around before putting her back down and kissing her cheek. "You have no idea."

"Well everything's ready, so let's dig in."

It wasn't quite his mother's shepherd's pie, but it was pretty darn close and he had to admit that her apple crumble might have been even better than what was in his memory. Sam couldn't believe Fiona had remembered the long-ago conversation about this meal and couldn't stop talking about how good it was as they walked over to his place for a bigger party for his birthday that Kevin was throwing. Jess and Lysiane shared a glance when they watched the two come in from the cold laughing. They thought that maybe something was finally happening between them, even if Fiona didn't realize it yet.

Fiona had mentioned to her mother that she was spending a lot of time with Sam, but she was still surprised when Grace asked her daughter if there was a romance starting. "Don't be silly, Mum, we're just friends. I'm sure Sam doesn't think of me that way," she said, still oblivious to what everyone else could see. "And anyway, since Metin, I'm just not looking for anything right now." Grace wondered if her daughter just needed to open her eyes.

One evening, at the end of a rare run together after final exams were over, Fiona and Sam stopped to catch their breath. They rested on a park bench and Sam casually put his arm around Fiona's shoulder. She looked at him with a question in her eyes, but he left it there. And then, as she relaxed into it, Sam felt a small thrill. He knew Fiona had broken up with her Turkish boyfriend a couple of months ago and hoped that maybe she was finally ready to start something new. They sat there for a while talking about their plans for the summer — both of them had jobs in Ottawa, so were staying behind when their roommates went home. When they got up to walk the rest of the way back to Fiona's place, Sam took her hand. Fiona was surprised at how nice it felt so she left her hand in his and squeezed it back.

They reached her apartment, still holding hands. Neither one of them wanted to break the spell, so rather than go in right away, they stood outside the door, still talking. Emboldened by his earlier small successes, Sam took a chance and leaned over and kissed Fiona. She responded and suddenly they were in each other's arms. Sam ran his hands through her hair, and pulled her toward him. Fiona slid her arms around his waist and he kissed her again with a passion she hadn't known he felt.

She closed the apartment door behind her, and walked to the kitchen table, sitting down with a stunned look on her face. Lysiane saw her first. "Are you all right?" she asked.

"He kissed me." She sounded confused. "Out of nowhere. Sam kissed me. And I kissed him back, Lysiane! I haven't kissed anyone since Metin. But I kissed him back."

Lysiane grinned. "Fiona, Sam's been in love with you since the day he met you. He's been waiting for you to be free. I'm glad he finally made a move. It was good for you, yes?"

Fiona touched her lips. "Yes," she whispered, realizing how good it had been. "Very good. But how did I never see it coming?"

Sam and Fiona spent every spare moment together as they started their summer jobs. It was Fiona's turn to feel as if she was coming back to life as Sam showered her with the affection he'd been holding back for months. While her breakup with Metin was recent, it had been three years since she'd had the physical affection of a boyfriend, and she was enjoying it very much. Sam was ecstatic that his dreams were finally coming true. He'd bided his time with Fiona and it had paid off. She loved the way he made her feel cherished, and she blossomed as her feelings for him grew. He shared all of this with Ben, who was overjoyed for his brother.

On a warm Saturday in early June, the couple spent the afternoon at the farmer's market, picking up ingredients for dinner at Sam's place. Kevin would be at his girlfriend's apartment for the night so they'd have the place to themselves.

Fiona started putting the groceries away. Sam had been unable to take his eyes off her all day. Fiona looked spectacular in a simple sleeveless blue print dress that turned her grey eyes blue. Its floaty skirt grazed her thighs just shy of her knees with every step she took. She'd been wearing it with a jean jacket and tennis shoes, but both had come off when they got to his place.

Fiona stood on her tiptoes, arm stretched as high as she could, struggling to put a can of peaches on the top shelf making the skirt raise higher. Sam came up behind her, took the can from her hand, and easily put it away. He suddenly spun her around and brought his lips down on hers, with a fierceness that matched his feelings for her in that moment.

"Oh, Sam," she murmured when she could speak again.

"Fiona, I love you. You're so beautiful. Let me make love to you."

Fiona looked in his eyes and under his intense gaze, she melted. She couldn't find her voice so she just nodded. Sam took her by the hand and led her upstairs.

Dinner was very late that night. Fiona and Sam ate by candlelight, glowing in the aftermath of their first time together.

Things moved very quickly after that and although they maintained separate apartments, most nights they stayed together. Fiona felt so protected when they lay tangled together after they made love and Sam revelled in that role. He was enjoying the lingerie collection Fiona had. He had no idea that under her everyday clothes she wore such beautiful things, and was hungry every day to find out what was hiding under her work clothes, or plain T-shirts and shorts. Years ago, Fiona's mother had taught her how pretty underthings could make her feel good even on a bad day, and she loved adding new pieces in satin, silk, or lace to her collection. Sam's reaction certainly added to her joy.

Ben and his boyfriend, Max, came to Ottawa to visit for Canada Day. Ben had finally told his brother about his not-so-new-any-more romance. Sam and Ben were very clearly siblings, both tall and thin with the same dark eyes, light brown hair, and serious disposition, but Ben was more than four inches taller than Sam at a little over six feet tall. And Max was even bigger. A full six foot four inches, and as broad as a linebacker, Max was a huge hulk of a man with an infectious laugh. He had sparkling hazel eyes, dark brown hair, and a full beard that glinted red in the sun. A master craftsman who owned a small bespoke workshop that specialized in custom fine furniture, he hit it off immediately with Sam and Fiona despite the decade difference in age. They spent all after-noon enjoying the festivities on Parliament Hill before coming back to Sam's place, where Fiona treated them to a simple holiday feast of oven-roasted chicken, green beans, and potato salad. She'd made meringue with strawberries as a tribute to the red and white of the day.

Ben entertained them with tales of his latest legal cases and Max showed them photos of some of his latest pieces, which featured his fine woodworking skills. Fiona was awed by his original designs. They went back to the Parliament Buildings at dusk for a concert and fireworks. As they headed to bed for the night, Ben said to Sam, "You were right, Sam. She's the real deal. Don't let her get away."

Ben and Max took them out for breakfast the next morning to repay Fiona and Sam for their hospitality before they headed back home, and they had a little announcement. Over pancakes and sausages, eggs and coffee, Ben told them Max was moving in with him. Ben had bought a tiny little wartime bungalow in the same north Toronto neighbourhood the brothers had grown up in, with the inheritance from their parents, and he and Max were going to do a small renovation to make it just a bit bigger for the two of them. While surprised, Sam was genuinely pleased. Ben deserved someone special in his life and Max seemed like a great guy. They said their goodbyes at the car. With one last hug, Sam whispered in his brother's ear, "I'm happy for you, Ben. You deserve this. Looks like things are coming together for the Rickford boys."

Sam was ready to take the next step with Fiona too. They would soon be starting their last year of school and he wanted her to know where they were headed. At the beginning of August, he went to his bank to get into his safe deposit box. He knew it was fast, but he knew with absolute certainty that he wanted to spend the rest of his life with Fiona. He knew she was his destiny and he wanted to have his mother's engagement ring at the ready when he decided to ask her.

Fiona decided it was time that her parents met Sam. She took him home on a late summer weekend, when the lake was warm and the skies were blue. Grace and George were impressed by Fiona's young man and he felt very at home with them too. They could see that Sam treated their daughter well and that they were a good match. Fiona and Sam took out a pair of kayaks to explore the lake and spent one afternoon waterskiing. They walked with her parents on the local trails, and dined on Fiona's mother's amazing meals. Sam could see where Fiona had inherited her love of cooking. He had a quiet conversation with George before they went back to Ottawa.

"I love your daughter, sir. Very much," he started. George smiled, knowing where this was going. "We may be young, but I'd like to ask her soon to marry me. I don't have much family left, so I'm anxious to start mine. I hope I have your blessing."

George clapped him on the back. His daughter had told him the tragic story of Sam's parents. "Grace and I like you very much, son," he said. "When you're ready to ask Fiona, we are one hundred percent behind you."

Sam breathed a sigh of relief. "Thank you, sir. I'll spend my life making her happy."

It didn't take him long. Sam was completely and hopelessly in love with Fiona and his mother's ring was burning a hole in his pocket. He took her out to dinner at a little restaurant they liked that overlooked the canal where they sat outside on the terrace enjoying the Labour Day weekend weather, the food and the company. The waiter slipped away, after bringing dessert, and Sam saw his chance. He pulled the ring box out of his pocket. "Fiona," he began. "You are the best thing to ever happen to me. I have loved you since I first saw you — when you hardly knew who I was." She opened her mouth to respond. "No, let me finish. I know this is fast, but I can't imagine my life without you. You are my future." Sam got down on his knees. "Fiona O'Reilly, will you marry me?"

For just a millisecond, Fiona flashed back to Metin's proposal on the Bosphorus. But that was her past. Sam was her future. "Yes, oh yes," she answered, and they kissed, as the other restaurant patrons clapped, enjoying the scene that had played out before them.

Chapter 10

If Jessica and Lysiane were surprised at the speed with which Sam and Fiona were moving, they were thrilled to learn their well-intentioned meddling had paid off when Fiona showed them her beautiful diamond ring when they returned to school that fall for their final year.

"I feel so safe and secure with him," Fiona explained when people asked. "Sam loves me so much. I know we're still young but we're just so comfortable together. We just fit."

She was excited to write to her friends about her plans to marry Sam. The girls all quickly wrote back their congratulations. Hayley's letter arrived first.

Dear Fiona,

You're engaged?! Congratulations! I'm so excited for you. Your Sam sounds like a great guy.

How long will your engagement be? Does it take a long time to plan a wedding in Canada? Here, people can be engaged for a year or more, just so they can get the venue they want. Tell me all about your plans!

I'm nowhere near that, I'm afraid. I'm dating, but there's nobody special. My turn will come. I wish I could give you a couple of Turkish cheek kisses to congratulate you.

Must run — I have two papers due already!

With love,
Hayley

Fiona particularly appreciated Yeşim's response, a week later.

My dear Fiona,

Congratulations, canım! When you started writing about Sam, I wondered if it would get serious. He sounds like a wonderful man. It is very good that you have found love again and I wish you so much happiness.

Of course, you know I still see Metin. He is doing well, but he hasn't found a new girlfriend yet. I don't usually talk to him about you but I think I will share him this news. I know he still misses you, but it will be good for him, I think, to know you are getting married, so he can find love again.

Are engagements long or short in Canada? When will you be married? How does it go in Canada?

I must go to class now.

Loves,
Yeşim

Yeşim and Mehmet met Metin for *çay* after classes soon afterwards. She'd been careful not to mention in her letters to Fiona how hard he had taken their breakup. It was a mutual decision, she knew from them both, but Yeşim was worried about him, and thought this news might shake some sense into him. She hated seeing him hurt.

"*Arkadaşım*," she began gently, "I have news from Fiona."

"How is she?" he asked, a fleeting smile showing he was thinking of old memories. He knew they wrote to each other, but Yeşim didn't share much from those letters. Probably for the best, he thought, as a wave of loneliness threatened to engulf him.

"She's engaged." Metin's face fell and she kept going. "To Sam, a guy she's been seeing since spring. I thought you should know. She seems really happy." Yeşim held her breath and watched different emotions flit over Metin's face.

He took a deep breath, and put his game face on. "Good for her. Please . . . please give her my congratulations."

"Of course. How are . . ."

"Hey, my friend," interjected Mehmet, saving Metin from having to talk about his feelings. "Time for you to get back on the horse. For real. We all like Fiona, but you've been pining for her for too long."

"I know, I know."

"Listen, my classmate has a sister that you should meet. Her name is Sibel."

Mehmet arranged for Sibel and Metin to meet on a double date with him and Yeşim. The two got along well and started spending time together. Yeşim was happy to see that Metin was trying to move on.

Sam was a rock. Solid. Stable. He had a plan, he had ambition and the work ethic to be successful. Fiona sometimes wondered if he would ever regret not travelling before settling down. She'd had a taste of adventure, but he hadn't. He'd had to grow up too fast. When she voiced that concern, Sam laughed. There'd be time for that later. And then they could travel in style.

In October, Fiona's mother was diagnosed with cancer. A fast-spreading cancer. She had less than a year. As Fiona and her father reeled from the news, Sam had an idea.

"We should get married at Christmas," he suggested one morning while they lay in bed together. "You want your mum to see you married, and you want her to feel well enough to enjoy it when you do. So why not speed this up for her."

Fiona's heart burst at that moment, and she started to cry. She nestled in under Sam's arm and buried her face in his chest. "You think of everything," she whispered.

With that decision, a small, simple, and intimate wedding was quickly planned for Christmas break, in the tiny church in Fiona's hometown, followed by a beautifully catered dinner at her parent's lakeside home. They kept the guest list absolutely minimal, to make sure there was no stress on Grace. Just her parents and her two roommates. Sam would have his roommate Kevin and of course Ben and Max.

December came quickly and with it, Fiona's birthday. With all the wedding preparations, it almost went by unnoticed. But Sam had a tradition he wanted to start. He bought Fiona a beautiful Christmas ornament and they hung it together on the little Charlie Brown tree they had bought and put up at his apartment.

The night before the wedding was cold and there was a roaring fire in the hearth at Fiona's childhood home. She kissed Sam good night and he headed to a nearby hotel with the guys. The girls had already bedded down in the guest room and Fiona knew it was time. She opened the closet in her childhood room and took the shoebox down from the top shelf, into the living room. Opening it, she took out the stack of ribbon-wrapped envelopes. With a sad smile, she fed the letters, one by one into the fire, bidding a final goodbye to Metin.

Wedding day dawned bright and crisp. It had snowed over-night and fresh fluffy flakes hung in the boughs of the evergreen trees. The sun made the snow sparkle like the diamonds in Fiona's engagement ring.

Fiona woke early with the biggest smile on her face. Today she would marry the most caring man on earth. He loved her and would make sure she knew it every day for the rest of her life. They shared values and their vision of the future was aligned. She couldn't be happier.

Her wedding dress — a simple floor-length ivory chiffon A-line gown — was hanging where she could see it, and the lacy veil that her mother, and her grandmother before, had worn trailed down beside it. Fiona was going to be a beautiful bride.

Within an hour, Lysiane and Jess joined Fiona at breakfast. They were all still in pajamas, but the girls would soon put on beautiful velvet dresses — one wine coloured and one forest green — to match a sophisticated Christmas theme. She wondered if Sam and the guys were up yet.

Fiona had planned her something old, new, borrowed, and blue. There was the ivory veil, she had new pearl earrings, she borrowed a necklace from Lysiane, and she had pinned a little blue *nazar* into the bodice of her dress. It was her way of making sure her Turkish friends and Hayley were with her on this special day.

As the limo took her and her father the short distance to the church, Fiona looked out the window. A tiny wedding party in a tiny church in a tiny town. Every detail was perfect.

Fiona stood at the back of the church, fighting the butterflies in her stomach. Marrying Sam seemed like a dream, and she knew he would take care of her forever. She was so happy that her mother would see this day. Grace was already seated up on the chancel where the groomsmen were. When Fiona looked at her father, she saw a myriad of emotions on his face.

"I can't believe you're getting married," George said. "Sam is a good man and I'm so happy for you. But I'm losing my little girl at the same time as I'm losing . . ." His voice broke and he was unable to continue. Pulling himself back together he thanked her for doing this while her mother was still able to enjoy it.

Fiona stood on her tiptoes and kissed her father's cheek. "Daddy, you're not losing me," she said softly. "Sam will be part of our family now."

The sanctuary was a fairyland with tiny white lights twinkling throughout. Because it was just the attendants and Fiona's parents, they all joined together on the chancel and watched as Fiona and Sam vowed to love each other for better or for worse, for richer or poorer, and in sickness and health. Fiona had asked Lysiane to play "Jesu, Joy of Man's Desiring" on her guitar — it was one of her mother's favourites — and Ben read from First Corinthians, beginning with the familiar words "Love is patient, love is kind." Sam slipped a wedding band encircled with sapphires and diamonds on her finger. Like her engagement ring, it had been his mother's, and she knew what it meant that he was giving it to her. When the minister declared them husband and wife, and the happy couple kissed, there wasn't a dry eye in the house.

Thanking the minister, the small wedding party gathered their coats and prepared to leave the church. Jess helped Fiona drape a white velvet cape over her dress and tied the sky-blue ribbon in front to close it. George helped his wife into her coat and put his arm around her waist to steady her. Grace's cancer was spreading quickly. Sam threw open the double doors, and holding hands, he and Fiona stepped out into the world as man and wife.

George and Grace watched from the big picture window as the photographer took photos of the young couple and their attendants out on the dock, the young people's smiles as bright as the glittering snow. They would make stunning pictures. A few photos were staged inside the warmth of the house and then the whole party sat down to an amazing dinner from a local caterer. They had decorated Grace's dining table with fine linens and crystal and the two hired servers were making the meal very special.

After dinner and the many toasts that followed, Fiona's mother excused herself. It had been a long day for her and she was tired, but so happy she had seen her daughter married. Sam and Fiona hugged her as she left and a tear made its way down Fiona's cheek. Sam wiped it away with his thumb and kissed his bride.

Fiona's father rejoined the wedding party in front of the fireplace shortly after, where the young people were relaxing, having opened another bottle of wine. Fiona slipped her hand in her father's and gave it a squeeze. He squeezed it back and gave her a kiss on the cheek before taking the glass Sam offered. He listened to the excited chatter of the young people. Eventually, Ben, Max, and Kevin headed back to their hotel and Jess and Lysiane to the guest room. The newlyweds took the stairs up to the guest suite above the garage, which the girls had decorated for them, and celebrated their first night as husband and wife.

After breakfast the next morning, they headed off on a short honeymoon in Toronto at a lovely boutique hotel on the shore. Each had surprised the other with expensive top-tier tickets to incredible shows. They loved *Les Misérables* and *Phantom of the Opera*, and spent New Year's Eve watching fireworks, but they spent much of their honeymoon in bed, enjoying the view of the lake, the fantastic room service, and each other.

"You're going to make me fat," Sam said when they were back in Ottawa, as he stabbed another waffle from the serving plate and started adding fruit and whipped cream to it. Fiona had started cooking big Sunday brunches after they got married, replacing the Sunday dinners she'd cooked for her roommates, and Sam was loving every minute of it. Often, they'd have friends over as well, giving Fiona a chance to try new recipes and whip up different breakfast treats. She loved doing it and they loved to volunteer as taste testers.

"I could stop," she volunteered.

"Don't you dare," said Sam, grabbing her hand across the table and giving it a squeeze.

Winter slowly gave way to spring, and Fiona grinned when she found a letter from Nazlı in the mailbox one morning.

My dear Fiona,

I hope you are well. I am excited to be finishing üniversite soon. I have interviewed for a job and I hope I will win it.

You asked about Aylin. She doesn't write often, but she will be home in the summer, I think. It will be nice to have the "Three Musketeers" together again. But we will miss you and Hayley.

My new boyfriend Önder is coming soon and we will go to AKM for a classical concert. We will meet with his friends there.

Do you have a job yet for after school? Please don't forget to give me your address if you move.

Loves,
Nazlı

Yeşim had written recently as well, with news that she had applied for a master's program and that she had her fingers crossed she would get in. She casually mentioned that Metin was dating. Fiona was surprised as Yeşim usually didn't write much about him in her letters, but she was happy for him. Their romance might have ended, but she still thought of him fondly.

The last weeks of the semester passed by faster than any Fiona could remember. Four years of hard studying culminated in one final batch of exams. Fiona and Sam were excited, because it meant that their life together as grown-ups could *really* begin. They both had great jobs lined up in Toronto, he with an investment firm on Bay Street and she to work in marketing for a pharmaceutical company. That excitement was only slightly dimmed when Fiona felt unwell during the final days of exams and the lead up to moving day. They both remembered how ill she'd been the year before and didn't want a repeat of that, so Sam made sure she got plenty of rest. He was relieved when it didn't turn into anything serious.

Fiona finally heard from Aylin just before the big move to Toronto. She was writing her final exams in engineering but was staying in Ankara to do her master's. Two more years of school, and still no boys in the picture for her. Fiona wrote back, giving Aylin her new address and telling her how excited she was about her new job. Life was beginning and everything was good.

In early May, Sam and Fiona loaded up a trailer and handed their keys back to their landlord. Fiona had had one last brunch that morning with Lysiane and Jessica and now they'd sent her on her way. Lysiane had a job in Ottawa and Jess was still job-hunting.

"Here we go," said Sam, as he put the keys in the ignition of his car. "We're really moving, Mrs. Rickford!"

"Ms. O'Reilly." Fiona gently reminded him she had kept her name. "But yes, we are."

They hit the road, and Fiona was lulled to sleep by the monotonous sound of car travel. Sam glanced over at her, still absolutely amazed that this smart and beautiful woman had agreed to be his wife. He shook her shoulder as they reached the outskirts of Toronto, so she could wake up properly before they reached their new place.

They had found their new home in the city's north end, not far from Ben and Max. They had rented the second floor of an old stately home that had been converted into small one-bedroom apartments. With leaded glass windows, wide plank hardwood floors, and a huge clawfoot bathtub, they were sold as soon as they saw it. Now that the huge maple tree in the front yard was in full leaf, their living room and the balcony leading from it felt like a tree fort. The kitchen was tiny, but Fiona felt it was a small price to pay for the location and the original features.

Ben and Max showed up soon after they arrived to help take all their furniture in and up the stairs. "You'll stay for dinner, won't you?" Fiona asked as she unpacked linens for the bedroom. "We're just going to order in, but you've been such a huge help." The men demurred, wanting to let Sam and Fiona have their first night together in their new place.

The pizza arrived as dusk was falling. Fiona laid out a picnic blanket in the middle of the living room floor and opened a bottle of wine she'd kept safe in her purse during the journey. Sam sat down beside her and she kissed him. "We're home, Sam." It wasn't long before the pizza was forgotten and they were in each other's arms.

Three days later, with their new home in good shape, and the cupboards filled, Fiona's new job began. Sam had one more day before he started, so when she was in the shower, he made coffee and breakfast. Kissing her well, he sent her out the door in her new suit and high heels, briefcase in hand.

Fiona was excited and nervous. She arrived at the offices of the pharmaceutical firm she'd been hired to write for. Smoothing her skirt, she took a deep breath and asked for her new boss at the reception desk.

"Fiona, good to see you," he said as he came out to get her. "Can't wait to get you started." The morning flew by, with onboarding and paperwork. Her team took her out to lunch and they got to know each other. That afternoon, she got her first assignments and got straight to work.

Sam rode the subway downtown with Fiona the next day. She kissed him goodbye as she got off two stops before him and headed up to her cubicle. Sam continued further downtown and met with his new boss. He was equally excited about his new job and when he got home that night, Fiona heard all about the world of high finance.

Finally, it was June, and graduation day. Sam and Fiona splurged and booked a fancy hotel room close to the university. They were looking forward to seeing their school friends for a big celebration. Just as they were locking the front door to make the drive to Ottawa, the phone rang. Fiona ran back in to pick it up. She'd quietly made a doctor's appointment a few days before, because although she'd hidden it from Sam so he didn't worry, the upset stomach she'd felt during exams had never quite gone away and after a couple of months, she was a bit concerned.

Hanging up the phone, Fiona joined Sam for the long drive. She spent the next few hours on the road coming to grips with what the doctor had said. Fiona had a big surprise to share with Sam when graduation was over. She was pregnant — and already eleven weeks along. They'd been so busy with exams, moving, and starting new jobs that she hadn't noticed her missed periods. Other than the annoying mild queasiness, she had no other symptoms, and her body hadn't started to change in any real way yet. But she was going to be a mother.

It was difficult, but she managed to keep the news to herself for the whole weekend. She hadn't wanted to take the spotlight off graduation for everyone else. They'd had dinner Saturday night with all the old gang. Fortunately, nobody thought it odd when she only drank soda water at dinner. Everyone had jobs in their field so there was much to celebrate.

By the time they got home early Sunday evening, Fiona was bursting with excitement. She scrutinized her shape in the full-length mirror in their bedroom, but she looked exactly the same. When Fiona told Sam over dessert, he was as surprised as she was. But excitement quickly overtook the surprise. They were going to be parents in December. He came home the next day from work with a child's baseball glove and Fiona laughed. It would be a long time before this baby — girl or boy — would be throwing around a baseball.

It was a more delicate conversation at work. By early July, Fiona was almost four months along and although the nausea had passed, she couldn't hide the pregnancy any longer. She was thickening through the middle and none of her new work clothes fit anymore. She was a bundle of nerves when she had to tell her boss. She had only been working a couple of months and felt guilty about how much effort he and the firm had undergone to train her, only to be about to lose her a few months later.

Fiona loved being pregnant, and she absolutely glowed. Soon she began to feel the baby kick, and one Saturday afternoon, she called out to Sam. "Come quickly. Put your hand here," she said, guiding his hand to the top right side of her baby bump. "Now wait."

Sam did as she said and in a minute was rewarded with a tiny flutter under his fingers. "Was that . . . was that our baby?"

Fiona nodded and they kissed to mark this new stage. After that, whenever they were sitting together, Sam liked to rest his hand on her stomach to feel the life growing inside her.

Not that there was much sitting. Sam and Fiona had been house hunting. Sam had been left a significant inheritance when his parents died, and like Ben had, he'd earmarked it for a house. Although they loved their little apartment, with a baby on the way they needed more room sooner rather than later. They had spent much of the summer looking, but not finding, the right house. But now, a semi-detached house in their neighbourhood was up for sale.

The house was almost perfect. It had a lovely master suite on the third floor, with four small bedrooms on the floor below. The open concept main floor had been renovated to provide natural light throughout. The previous owners had kept the beautiful wooden floors and some of the leaded glass windows that they had loved in their apartment. A garage in back and a parking space were the icing on the cake. They put in an offer and celebrated when it was accepted. Taking Ben's advice, and with the help of Max's construction contacts, they did some renovations before they moved in, adding an extra few square feet on the third floor to allow for a small light-filled study and a walkout deck. Thinking long term, they also finished the basement with a guest suite and laundry room. A chute from the upper floors would make the chore of getting dirty laundry down to the basement. This was going to be a great place to raise their family.

They checked on the renovations regularly and just after Hallowe'en, the young couple moved into their new house. They met many of their neighbours and Fiona was pleased to see a few other pregnant women nearby, even if they appeared a few years older than her. Rachael and her husband lived almost directly across the street and she was pregnant with her first child as well. In fact, their due dates were within weeks of each other and the women bonded immediately over pregnancy stories.

Just days later, Fiona's mother quietly slipped away one night. It was almost like she'd been waiting until Fiona was properly settled.

Fiona was almost eight months pregnant at the funeral. As the soloist sang her mother's favourite hymns, the baby responded to the music and began kicking. As she cried for her mother and rubbed her stomach, Sam put one arm around her shoulder and his hand over hers. The baby settled under their loving touch.

They held the reception at the lake house. Her mother had been very popular in the town, and all afternoon there was a steady stream of visitors paying their respects. Fiona and her father found comfort in their words, but the day was exhausting for both of them.

Holly Grace arrived just before Christmas, in between Fiona's birthday and their first anniversary, weighing just five pounds six ounces. She was tiny but perfect. With her blue eyes and a sprinkling of strawberry-blonde hair, she favoured Fiona more than Sam. He was in love with her at first sight.

They brought Holly home on Christmas Eve, and spent their first Christmas Day as husband and wife — and as parents — in a little bubble of their own, paying no attention to the outside world. They snuggled together in bed watching movies, reading, and sleeping, with little Holly nestled between them, or nursing hungrily in Fiona's arms.

Fiona's father drove down on Boxing Day and with some help from Max and Ben, who had celebrated with friends the day before, they all sat down to a proper dinner of turkey and all the trimmings. Despite his still-fresh grief over losing Grace, George had arrived with a trunk full of gifts for them all and was tickled pink by his new little granddaughter.

Chapter 11

Sam started back to work just after New Year's Day and Fiona learned to manage on her own. As other families in the neighbourhood returned to normal schedules, Fiona started looking for connections with other mothers.

She and Rachael were already getting together a couple of mornings a week. Her little Emily had been born two weeks before Holly. They liked to bundle the babies up and walk, and then come back to one of their houses for coffee. Fortunately, Holly was an easy baby and quite content to nap in her stroller.

They joined a local new mums' group run by a community health nurse at the local church and quickly made friends with Hyun, whose son Zane was about the same age as Emily and Holly. It was a great place to meet other new mothers and get some guidance. With no mother of her own to ask questions of, Fiona found it a great source of support. The three women became very close over the following months, as their babies grew. They often spent mornings together, either walking, or in each other's living rooms, and as the weather warmed up, in their back gardens.

Fiona's boss had been very understanding of losing his new employee so quickly, but had encouraged her to enjoy every moment of her maternity leave. When she brought Holly into the office to show her off, he was at the front of the line to hold her and marvel at her tiny hands and button nose.

Fiona was shocked when, despite breastfeeding, she discovered just six months after Holly's arrival that she was pregnant again. "We're good at making babies, I guess," she joked with Sam. He was thrilled that their little family was growing again. He and Ben were five years apart and he was happy his children would be closer. Fiona was a little more practical, concerned about the difficulties this would cause for her at work.

She left Holly with Rachael one morning to go into the office to have a serious conversation with her boss. If she took the whole twelve months she was entitled to with Holly, she would be back for just three months before leaving again, which didn't seem fair to the company. She wasn't ready to give up her career, but it was important to her to be there for her children. Together they developed a plan that worked for everyone. Instead of coming back after a year, Fiona would start working part time soon, in a freelance capacity, working just a few mornings a week. After the new baby, she'd take at least six months and then start freelancing again. Fiona hired a sitter who came in Monday, Wednesday, and Thursday mornings. Thankful to Ben and Max for the renovation idea, she set up her desk in the little study off the master bedroom and started working three mornings a week, and occasionally in the afternoon, with a baby monitor beside her when little Holly napped.

One night, Sam came home with a bottle of sparkling cider. He had a huge grin on his face. It was late, and Fiona had put Holly to bed already. "What's that for?" she asked curiously.

"I have big news," he said. "Really big news."

"Tell me," begged Fiona. "Don't make me guess, just tell me!"

Sam got out the champagne flutes, poured the cider, and proceeded to tell Fiona about a big promotion he'd got at work that day.

"Oh, I'm so proud of you," she exclaimed, throwing her arms around his neck. Sam's career dreams were coming true.

Sam's promotion meant longer hours, but he did his best to be home to read bedtime stories to Holly and entertained her as much as he could on weekends to give Fiona a bit of a break.

Suddenly it was December, and they celebrated Fiona's birthday and then Holly's before going to the lake to have Christmas with George. Soon it was back to the city and Fiona got a babysitter so they could celebrate their second wedding anniversary with a quiet dinner out.

"Ouch," she gasped and rubbed her expanding belly, where she'd just been jabbed. "This little one is going to be a boxer, I think." She'd been able to feel this baby moving for some time, but recently she and Sam could see her entire belly undulating as the baby rolled around kicking and punching.

James Richard was born in the middle of a raging snowstorm in mid-March, just fifteen months after Holly. He was a strapping eight pounds eleven ounces. It had been a long, hard labour, and the doctor had wondered more than once if they'd have to do a caesarian section, but it had worked out in the end.

Jamie, as they called him, had Sam's dark brown eyes and brown hair, but he had a temperament that matched the storm he was born in. He was a fussy baby and nothing seemed to settle him. He cried constantly and unlike Holly who had napped contentedly in her car seat or stroller, he would only sleep at home, seriously curtailing Fiona's social life with the other mothers. Whenever he could, Sam took over walking the floors with his son, but nothing helped. They were at the end of their wits when suddenly, the crying stopped. Colic, Grandpa George had said. Fiona wasn't sure what it was, but she was glad it was over.

Holly and Jamie kept Fiona very busy and she seemed to be in perpetual motion. Sam had maintained his laser-like focus on his career to ensure his family was cared for, and he was rising quickly, but the extra assignments meant he rarely saw the children on weeknights. On weekends, however, he was fully present for them all, and they enjoyed family time together.

While the kids were napping, Fiona slipped out to the mailbox and pulled out a huge stack of mail. As she walked back to the house, without a coat for the first time this spring, she leafed through the envelopes. Bills, bills, junk mail, and — she smiled — foreign stamps. She had letters from both Yeşim and Nazlı. Fiona sat down in a sunny corner of their living room to read the latest news from her friends.

Sevgili Fiona'cığım,

Congratulations on your little boy. I can't believe you have two children already! My work is going very well. I love designing bridges and I can't imagine doing anything else. I have a new flat. My parents aren't happy, but it's important for me to be independent. I will give you the address at the end of this letter.

I have started doing yoga at a studio near my new home. I love it. You should try. I had lunch with Yeşim recently, and also with Funda. Do you remember her? They both send kisses.

Next weekend, Önder and I will go to the Black Sea. It is so pretty there. You would like it.

Hepiniz öperim,
Nazlı

My dear Fiona,

A little boy — how wonderful. Congratulations, my dear. I'm sure they keep you very busy. I have exciting news too. We are engaged and I will marry with Mehmet later this year.

I am finally finished my master's degree and have a job starting in the fall as a lecturer at Boğaziçi University. I'm excited to begin life as an adult. Mehmet is still loving his job at the insurance company and is travelling in Europe often. Maybe when we are married, we will travel together. And maybe we could even come to Canada one day.

Please give your children kisses from their Turkish teyze.

With my loves,
Yeşim

A few months after Jamie was born, Sam noticed that Fiona was more tired than he thought she should be, and he was concerned. She wasn't eating properly either, just picking at her food these days. When he asked, she said she was just tired.

She had mentioned this at her mum's group and they sympathized with her. She was young, but without much in the way of family support, in many ways, she was almost raising Holly and Jamie on her own.

Sam took a week off just before summer began and they spent it up at the lake with George relaxing by the water. His eyes lit up when he saw his grandchildren and he was happy to help Sam entertain them while Fiona napped. She felt like she couldn't get enough sleep, and she was sorry when they had to go back home and Sam had to go back to work.

One Saturday morning shortly after their vacation, Fiona ran to the bathroom with her hand over her mouth. Worried, Sam packed her off to bed for the day to rest, while he took over all kid duties, taking baby Jamie to her when he was hungry. Grateful,

Fiona took a long bath, and slept and read most of the day. By evening, Sam had a better appreciation of her days with the kids. They had worn him out, and it was only one day! But Fiona told Sam she was feeling a little better and that made it worth it to him.

The next morning, though, Sam thought Fiona looked pale again under her freckles as she made her usual big Sunday brunch. He hoped she wasn't getting the flu and he tried to keep the kids occupied again for large chunks of the day, when he wasn't answering phone calls from his boss. They both went to bed early that evening.

Fiona was sick again on Monday after Sam had gone to work, and then again on Tuesday. By now, she had a pretty good idea what was going on, and a home pregnancy test that day confirmed it, if the ongoing nausea wasn't enough of a clue. She booked a doctor's appointment to be doubly sure and when that test came back positive, she wasn't sure whether to be happy about it or to cry. Three children in thirty months would be a challenge. But it would also mean that they would be in school sooner and that would mean she could get her career back on track sooner. That evening, after the children were in bed, she shared the news with Sam, with a bit of fear and trepidation.

Sam had no such fears and was excited to know his family was growing again. They both wanted a big family, but admittedly it was all happening very fast. This baby was due in March — close to Jamie's first birthday.

When Sam got over his initial excitement, he admitted to his brother over a beer on Ben's patio that he was a little concerned for Fiona. Three pregnancies this close together would be hard on her, and she would soon have three children to look after. He wasn't sure she'd thought through the reality that her freelancing would probably have to stop, or at least slow down. Sam had received another promotion recently that came with huge bonus potential, but also had him travelling more on top of the already long hours he put in, so she would be largely on her own. He wondered if they'd need a full-time nanny and was glad they'd finished the basement when they'd bought the house. Sam was twenty-six years old and had worries that many men ten or fifteen years older than him were only just starting to deal with.

This pregnancy was very different from the first. While Fiona had only been very slightly queasy in the early months with Holly and Jamie, this time, she was living on saltine crackers and ginger ale, trying desperately to keep her stomach settled. The nausea was intense. And while she knew that women with third pregnancies showed very early, she was astounded by how quickly her normal clothes stopped fitting even though the combination of morning sickness and running after both a toddler and a baby was preventing her from gaining weight.

Sam noticed it too, and remembering her last labour, worried that this was going to be another big baby. But in contrast to her quickly expanding stomach, Sam thought she looked gaunt and noticed the dark circles that had formed under her eyes. He doubled his efforts to get home early at least a few nights to help when he wasn't travelling.

As fall rolled around, Fiona started working again, and they hired a nanny to come in two full days a week. Marta was a godsend. She even cooked dinner the days she was there, giving Fiona two full days to take meetings, and do her work. She was branching out a little and had taken on two small clients in addition to her continuing to write marketing materials for her pharma company.

Much to Fiona's dismay, the constant nausea lasted well into her second trimester. Life was very busy, and she put off a routine doctor's visit and her first ultrasound for a couple of extra weeks, figuring it wouldn't matter much. She was eighteen weeks along and feeling okay finally. She understood pregnancy well already. The only thing that concerned her was how big her stomach was, considering she hadn't gained much weight in the rough first few months she'd had.

She left the kids with Rachael on the day of her doctor's appointment and prepared to listen to him chastise her. But the doctor had some unexpected news after the ultrasound, and now Fiona finally understood why this pregnancy was different.

She drove home in silence, trying to process the news. Sam was out of town on business, and wasn't expected home until the weekend, so she sat on the news until then. When she told him, over a stiff drink for him and a glass of sparkling water for her, his jaw dropped and he had no words. "Twins?" he finally asked, clearly stunned.

"Yes, twins," she said quietly. "Our family is getting bigger fast."

Then a big grin came over Sam's face. "Twins!" he shouted excitedly, and she exhaled the breath slowly. Sam cradled her face in his hands and kissed her fiercely. "Twins!" he whispered, and Fiona laughed with relief.

⌖

Sam put his foot down at work and stopped travelling at the end of January. Twins often came early, and he was starting to worry he wouldn't be home when Fiona went into labour. On nights when he could get home in time, he massaged her feet and rubbed lotion on her belly. But on many evenings, she was on her own, humming to the babies and watching her stomach roll and swell with the movement of two bodies fighting for space. They'd learned that the twins were fraternal. Another girl and another boy would be joining the family soon.

She was often sound asleep when Sam got home late in the evening. He would slip into bed when he got home and spoon with Fiona, wrapping his long arms around her ever-expanding stomach and whispering to his babies.

At last Jamie had finally settled. He had been standing since December, but in mid-January, exactly as he reached ten months of age, he took his first steps and his entire personality changed. Gone was the unhappy little baby and in his place was a rambunctious toddler, full of smiles and giggles. Holly was twenty-one months old and starting to chatter away.

By the beginning of March, Fiona thought she wouldn't be able to stand being pregnant any longer. But there were things to do, and so she gamely threw a very small party for Jamie on the weekend after his first birthday. A few friends from the mum's group came by with their children, and of course Ben and Max joined the festivities, spoiling their nephew. Holly was excited and helped Fiona make the cake that Jamie grabbed enthusiastically with his hands and decorated his face with.

She felt like a beached whale, her stomach was so big. When everyone had gone, she put on a video to occupy the children and sat down to rest. Fiona's back ached from being on her feet all day and her ankles were swollen. She felt grumpy and sometimes wondered what on earth her husband saw to love these days. Sam brought her a cup of tea, and set it down next to her with a kiss. He saw a glowing and vibrant, albeit tired, woman who was carrying his children. He joked with her that he could use her stomach as a table for the tea, but that the babies would kick it over. She rolled her eyes and threw a pillow at him.

But Sam was looking tired too, Fiona thought. Long hours at work and helping out at home were wearing on him too. She rubbed her belly, where the twins seemed to be tangled up with each other and elbowing each other — and her — to get untangled. She felt quite lucky she'd managed to keep them inside this long. But how would they all cope when these babies were born?

That night, she woke up and knew she was in labour. She shook Sam awake. "It's time," she said, grimacing as a contraction took hold. Sam sat bolt upright in bed. As Fiona got dressed, he called Ben, who raced to get there.

It wasn't long before Simon Thomas and Margarite Anne — quickly nicknamed Daisy — joined their family. Simon weighed five pounds six ounces and Daisy was four pounds eight ounces. The twins both had red hair and while Simon's eyes were grey like his mother, Daisy had Sam's brown eyes. She was a little on the small side, so all three were kept in the hospital an extra day before joining the rest of the family.

Not quite three years out of school, Fiona was suddenly the married mother of four children. Even though she wasn't working, they had Marta continue to come two days a week to help with the children. Sam tried to work from home on Wednesdays as well, taking over Fiona's office. This way, he had at least one dinner with the children during the week. They were so glad they'd bought their house when they did. Some people had thought it was too big for them, but they had filled all the bedrooms quickly.

Six months after the twins, Fiona had done everything she could to get her pre-pregnancy body back, but she realized she would never be the pencil-thin girl she had been when she met Sam. Looking at herself critically in the mirror, she actually thought she looked better now. She was still slender, but had a few more curves than when they first got married, with a slightly fuller chest and hips. She was happy with the changes that motherhood had brought. Sam felt the same. If anything, this slightly more womanly Fiona was even more appealing to him. But he knew he would love her whatever shape her body was. And the silver stretch marks across her stomach were just souvenirs of how much her body had accomplished while she had been growing their family inside her.

Sam encouraged Fiona to buy new lingerie to accentuate her new figure. She was a bit embarrassed but had to admit she loved it. She always felt better about herself when she wore matching bra and panty sets made from satin and lace, velvet and silk under her "mum clothes." Sam still loved the game of imagining what was under there as much as he loved the discovery when he pulled off her clothes to make love to her. They might have four children, but they were young and healthy and determined to make sure their sex life was passionate and spicy.

In the years of early motherhood, Fiona took every opportunity to get out of the house with the kids. She had lost touch with many of her university friends who were building their careers while she built her family. Her circle of friends was now women with children the same age as hers. She often found herself the youngest in a crowd, but that didn't bother her.

Hyun had another boy now and Rachael was pregnant with her second. They continued to spend a great deal of time in each other's homes and backyards. In between, the days were a whirlwind of diapers, playdates, tantrums, and laughter. Her children were her life and Fiona barely had energy for anything else. She sometimes felt guilty when Sam arrived home after another day in the office. He was a good provider and was doing well in his career. But that came with trade-offs of long hours and travel. If Fiona thought she had been tired with two children to chase after, she was exhausted after a full day with all four, even with Marta's help.

Chapter 12

Suddenly, it was time to think about sending Holly to junior kindergarten. Fiona was ready to go back to work again so Marta began coming three days a week.

When Fiona had started freelancing, she added a few personal touches to the study on the third floor. Over the years, she'd added more. An orchid graced the desk and an antique radio, a gift from Sam, sat on the bookshelf. She also added a huge oversized chair that was big enough for two, which quickly become the place that she or Sam could bring one child for some special one-on-one time when they needed some space away from the hubbub of their siblings.

On a bright September morning, Fiona experienced the same pang that all mothers feel when they send their children off to school. She left the younger ones with Marta and walked hand in hand with Holly to the local school. Holly looked tiny, with her big backpack over her shoulders, and Fiona knew she was nervous because she kept playing with the ends of her strawberry-blonde braids.

When they reached the playground, a little girl with long brown hair in a ponytail ran up to her with a big grin. "I'm Nikki. What's your name?" Instantly, Nikki and Holly became best friends.

Fiona chatted with her mother, Mila, as the girls ran off to play. Mila was a musician and photographer, who gave private piano and voice lessons, did small photography exhibitions, and had taken the post of music director at the beautiful old church down the road from Fiona and Sam's house the year before. They had been going to this church on Christmas Eve services for several years now. Mila and her husband, Jaris, lived on the street behind them with Nikki and her older brother.

When Mila learned that Fiona had sung in a chamber choir in university, she invited her to join her church choir for Christmas and Fiona was thinking about it. Maybe when the kids were a were a bit older, she might give it a try. She did miss choral singing.

Max's business was thriving and he wanted to reach a new audience. Fiona built him a simple website that could be expanded as the business grew. Over the course of several meetings, the two got closer and Fiona realized she sometimes spoke to Max more than her brother-in-law. The men had a bit of shocking news that fall. Max's mother passed away. He had been estranged from his parents for decades. A very conservative family from a small town, they hadn't dealt well with his coming out. His father had been especially hard on Max, kicking him out of the house and cutting all ties. Max's mother had quietly given Max some money while he was still in college, but it had been difficult for her as well. Max's father had passed away a long time ago, but she hadn't been able to welcome her son back to her life. For Max, this was an old story and he'd long since made peace with it. Cut off from his own family, he only had Ben now, and took his role as honorary uncle to Sam and Fiona's children very seriously. Still, he admitted to Fiona, it surprised him how sad the news about his mother made him.

Fiona experienced her own loss shortly afterwards and Max was a great support. Her father had collapsed during a curling game and hadn't recovered. When she delivered the eulogy, she smiled through her tears, reminding everyone that George died doing what he loved most. She inherited the house at the lake and they kept it, using it as a family cottage.

The years went careening by. Sam continued to be promoted at work, and became one of the youngest directors the firm had ever had. Fiona's little business grew to the point where she was starting to turn down work so she could keep working part-time hours. Jamie joined Holly at school, and although he didn't like it as much as she did, he also made a fast friend on the first day. Steve lived close by and they were soon as thick as thieves.

Fiona closed up shop for a month every summer and took the kids up to the lake, where Sam joined them on weekends. They had begun to renovate it, adding a bedroom, expanding the living space, and updating the kitchen. The kids slept in bunk beds, roasted marshmallows, chased fireflies and frogs, played on the beach, and paddled in the water. When Fiona put them to bed every night, they slept solidly, worn out by their adventures during the day.

Ben and Max borrowed the lake house often, and Fiona was happy to lend it to her friends as well, when they wanted a getaway.

Suddenly, it was time for Simon and Daisy to join their brother and sister at school. Jamie was in senior kindergarten so he planned to show the twins the ropes. And Holly, ever the oldest child, walked to school the first day holding their hands, three abreast on the sidewalk. Fiona kept Marta on one day a week. She wasn't quite ready to give up the security of another set of hands around the house.

The new millennium was upon them, with lots of change for Sam and Fiona. The twins started grade one in the fall, so the family said a sad goodbye to Marta, who fortunately found another family needing her help. Fiona spent some time volunteering in her children's classes, but also started to build her business. Her skills were in demand, with many of her clients worried about Y2K and what might happen at the stroke of midnight at the end of the year. There was more work than she could keep up with and she occasionally sent some on to other freelancers.

Sam had been put on a fast track at work and was named associate vice-president. There were starting to be murmurs of an international assignment, which excited and terrified them both at the same time. He was at the top of his game and loved every second of it. Fiona was immensely proud of him.

Max's website had been a success and he kept working professionally with Fiona. She had refreshed it this year and they were meeting for coffee soon to go over some promotional flyers she was drafting for him. Once he was happy with the content, she would bring in a graphic designer to do the artwork. Max was expanding to handle the corporate commissions he was starting to get and he'd hired on two new craftsmen to keep up with the work.

Ben was having his own success and had been named a partner in his firm. The two couples went out for dinner to celebrate. "Here's to all of us," Max toasted. "To Sam for his promotion and to Ben for his partnership. Well done, Rickford boys! And to your hangers-on for their own business success. Well done, Fee!"

"And well done to you too, Max," she replied, raising her glass with the others. "What a great way to start the new millennium."

For Christmas, Sam surprised Fiona with a two-night getaway to celebrate their tenth wedding anniversary. Max's shop and Ben's office were closed over the holidays so they stayed with the kids while Sam and Fiona snuck away like newlyweds to the hotel overlooking Niagara Falls. Getting ready for dinner, Fiona zipped up her short black dress and piled her hair up on her head. She spritzed on the perfume that Sam liked and had looked at herself in the mirror. At an age when many of their old friends were just starting to marry and have kids, they were old pros. It showed a bit, she thought, in the dark circles under her eyes that never seemed to go away, but overall, she was pleased with what she saw. Coming back into the main room of the hotel, she looked at Sam in his dark suit and he took her breath away. How had she got so lucky, she wondered?

After dinner, they returned to their room, where they watched the light show over the falls, sharing a bottle of champagne. "To you, Fiona," Sam toasted. "The love of my life, the mother of my children, and the only person I want to share my future with." Fiona blushed and returned the compliment in a toast of her own. Sam kissed her and suddenly the beauty of the falls was forgotten as they celebrated their anniversary together.

Chapter 13

Just days later, it was time to go back to work and school. January had opened with spectacular weather and Fiona was up early enough to share a cup of coffee with Sam. They shared a passionate kiss before he headed downtown for his first day back in the office after the Christmas break. They were still feeling the glow of their Niagara getaway. Fiona felt very lucky to have this great man and their wonderful family. Sometimes she needed to pinch herself to believe it.

"I love you, Sam."

"Love you too, Fiona."

They always made a point of making their parting words important. Through the loss of their parents, they both knew how life can change in an instant.

Fiona got the kids ready, brushing the girls' hair and making lunches. She walked with them to school and then headed home for a cup of coffee before going up to her office to start her working day. Y2K hadn't been the disaster so many had foretold, and business continued to be good. Fiona landed a new client and finished a major project. She even had time to fit in a midday yoga class. The year was starting well.

Snow had fallen lightly almost all day but the sun broke through mid-afternoon. Fiona walked to the school to pick up the kids. Bundled up in their snowsuits, the twins and their grade one friends poured out of the classroom to play in the snow. Holly and Jamie came running up to Fiona from different school doors at the same time, asking if they could play with friends after school. Steve lived just down the street, and so asking his mother to send him home by six, Fiona sent Jamie with them. Holly wanted Emily to play in her house, so with Rachael's agreement, she came home with them after Fiona gathered Daisy and Simon from making snow angels.

The crew at her house came in for a quick snack and then played outside until dinnertime. Fiona loved it when the weather was good enough for the kids to play outside in the winter.

Jamie came in the door, cheeks red and full of energy, just as she sent Emily home across the street. Fiona soon had dinner on the table for the children. Chicken fingers, homemade potato wedges, steamed broccoli, and salad, with peach crumble for dessert. It wasn't anything fancy, but at nine, seven, and six, the children still got hungry early and it was easier to feed them and at least have the twins bathed and ready for bed before Sam got home around seven o'clock.

Sam loved to spend half an hour with the children learning about their day. In the summers, they'd take a walk around the garden, Simon and Daisy each holding one of their father's hands, looking at what was new that day. But on wintry days, they would talk by the fire, catching their father up on the day's activities. After lights out for the twins, and with Holly and Jamie tucked into bed to read for another thirty minutes, it was only then that Sam would trade his suit and tie for more comfortable clothes and Fiona would sit down for their own dinner. Tonight she was planning a simple salad, stuffed peppers, and the same peach crumble the children had eaten. They would enjoy it with a nice red wine and, if she remembered to pull them out, candles to brighten the table. Fiona liked to go to the effort to make the table special for her hardworking husband.

But now, as he waved around a forkful of broccoli, Jamie was regaling everyone with the story of how he and Steve built the snow fort. Holly and Laurie had made a giant snowman in the front yard, complete with a hat and scarf, and the twins had made more snow angels in the back garden. And everyone was laughing.

Fiona was so grateful for this family of hers. She didn't regret having the kids so early and so close together; her heart was full for these four rambunctious little monkeys who kept her on her toes. She loved the business she was building and the clients she served. She loved her husband who respected her, loved her, supported her. She wished Sam could spend more moments like this with them, but she understood the demands of his job kept him away more than he liked. Overall, life was very, very good. Fiona put the kettle on for a cup of tea and was opening the cupboard to choose an herbal variety when the doorbell rang.

"Stay at the table, kids," she said walking to the front entry. Two police officers looked at her solemnly as she opened the door.

"Can I help you?" she asked.

"Mrs. Rickford?" one of them asked.

She smiled. "Well, it's Ms. O'Reilly, but I'm married to Sam Rickford. How can I help you, officers?"

"We have some bad news for you, Ms. O'Reilly," said the younger officer, looking uncomfortable as he took in the joyful hubbub of activity beyond them in the kitchen. The children were in fits of giggles as Jamie told jokes and he was about to shatter their lives. "Mr. Rickford collapsed on the subway platform tonight. He was taken to the hospital, but unfortunately there was nothing they could do. Your husband had a heart attack and passed away immediately."

"No. No. That's not possible," Fiona stammered. "You must have mixed something up. Sam is only thirty-three. He's healthy. He runs. He can't have had a heart attack. I'm expecting him home shortly." She started to close the door.

The older officer, who had kind eyes, put his hand on the door and spoke gently. "Ms. O'Reilly. May we come in? Is there someone we can call for you? Someone who can watch your children? We need to take you to the hospital now."

The world faded away, her ears buzzed, and Fiona felt dizzy. "I need to sit down," she whispered, dropping to the bench beside the door as the news started to sink in.

"Who can we call for you, Ms. O'Reilly?" he repeated.

Fiona moved in a haze. She called Hyun to come and stay with the children. When she arrived, the police officers told her what had happened and that she should prepare to be there for the night, while Fiona mechanically grabbed her coat, scarf, gloves, and purse. They helped her into their squad car and sped off to the hospital. In an instant, her whole world had changed. She had just turned thirty-two, and now she was suddenly a widow, totally alone in the world, with four children to raise, not quite one month after her tenth wedding anniversary.

The officers took Fiona into the hospital and left her in the care of a nurse in the emergency room, who gently reiterated what the police had told her. Fiona let the nurse guide her to the room where Sam was.

Fiona gasped, seeing her husband lying in front of her. Suddenly it was real, and tears started pouring down her face. As she tried to pull herself together, the doctor expressed his condolences. A man in his early thirties dropping dead of a heart attack was tragic. He explained that they'd discovered that Sam had had an undetected heart condition called hypertrophic cardiomyopathy that caused the walls of his heart to thicken. It disrupted his heart's electrical system, which caused his death.

"I'm so sorry for your loss. You can stay with your husband for as long as you like," he said, feeling incredibly sad for Fiona. She was young, like her husband and he imagined they had probably recently married and were beginning their lives together.

"Oh, my God, what will I tell the kids," she cried as the doctor closed the road behind him. The nurse looked up in surprise. Like the doctor, she had assumed this was a new couple just starting out.

"You have children?" she asked gently, realizing now that this tragedy was even worse than she thought.

Fiona sat in the hospital room for some time, holding Sam's hand, shoulders heaving with silent tears. Finally, she kissed him one last time, dried her eyes, squared her shoulders, and said goodbye to her husband and steeling herself for the phone call she needed to make.

She scrolled through her contacts until she found her brother-in-law's number. She took a deep breath and dialled.

"Hello."

"Ben, it's Fiona," she began, her voice cracking as the tears started again.

"Fiona, what's wrong?" Ben was on high alert, hearing the strain in her voice.

"It's Sam. He's . . . he's . . . Oh, Ben, Sam's dead," she sobbed.

"What? Fiona what happened? Where are you?"

Fiona managed to give him the hospital name and he said he'd be there in half an hour. Ben looked grey when he and Max arrived. Fiona rushed into his arms and then took him to Sam's room, explaining what the doctor had told her.

Ben didn't hear any of it. The words in his head were on autorepeat. "Not my brother too."

While Ben and Fiona were with Sam, Max made some inquiries at the nurse's station so he understood what needed to be done and how much of the burden he could take from Ben's grieving wife — no, widow — he corrected himself, and brother.

Back at Fiona's house, after Hyun had put all the kids to bed, she called Rachael and Mila and then the three of them called everyone they knew. Everyone was shocked at Sam's sudden passing and incredibly sorry for Fiona. She didn't deserve this. Nobody did. The network sprang into action and soon a schedule had been made for meals, for help with the children, and anything else Fiona needed for the next month. Together, they would all make sure that Fiona and the kids were well taken care of.

With Max and Ben guiding her, Fiona signed a mountain of paperwork at the hospital. It was just after midnight when they drove her home. It was snowing again, and the world was beautiful under the cover of the fresh layer of white. But she didn't see it. She was still shell-shocked, and Ben was no better.

Max talked softly with them both while the car idled in the driveway. When he was convinced that Fiona would be all right with Hyun, he walked her to the door and wrapped her in a big hug. Taking her tiny hands in his huge roughened ones, he looked in her eyes. "Stay strong, Fee. I'll take care of Ben tonight. And I'll call you in the morning." She nodded, not able to speak. Losing her husband was completely devastating, and she had no reserves to help Ben, who had just lost his little brother — the last of his blood relatives.

Hyun had heard them at the door. Opening it, she shared a meaningful glance with Max as he passed a very pale Fiona over to her care. He handed her his business card with his cell phone number and email address, along with a small bottle with some sleeping pills that the doctor had given him. He would be giving Ben the same medication when they got home.

Hyun put her arm around her friend and led her to the couch in the living room without a word. She pressed a snifter of brandy into Fiona's hand. They sat in silence for a few minutes and then

Fiona got up and started to look at all of the silver-framed family photos on the mantel above the fire Hyun had kept burning all night.

On the far right was their wedding picture that had been taken on the dock at the lake. She picked it up and came back to the couch, hugging it tight. She rocked forward and back as she cried in anguish. Hyun took Fiona in her arms and let her cry until she couldn't cry any more.

"Fiona, we're here for you. Whatever you need. All of us." She got her friend a glass of water and one of the pills Max had given her. "Take one of these. You need sleep. I'll stay in your guest room and we'll deal with everything else tomorrow, okay?"

Fiona swallowed the pill down with the help of a sip of water. She nodded, looking lost, and let Hyun led her up the stairs to her room.

Fiona woke up with a start at six o'clock. Her head was fuzzy from the medication, but the pain of the previous night cut through it like a sharp knife. She started to cry, wanting nothing more than to stay curled up in her bed that still smelled like Sam. But she had four children who would be up soon, and some devastating news to tell them. Their world would never be the same again.

Hyun had been up since five and was relieved to hear the shower. She hadn't wanted to call because it was early, so she had emailed Max. It turned out he was also awake, waiting for Ben. They quickly divvied up a task list. Hyun would call the school and talk to the principal and each of the teachers. Rachael had already agreed to call the clients Fiona had been working with. Max would call Ben's boss and the family lawyer. Fortunately, he and Sam had been using the same firm that had handled their parents' estate. Max left a voicemail for his workshop supervisor to tell him they would have to manage the shop without him for at least a week. He knew all their current jobs would be in good hands, and his place right now was with Ben, Fiona, and the kids.

Hyun had the coffee ready when Fiona came downstairs, hair damp, but dressed. She could see a steely grit in her friend's bloodshot eyes.

The kids were all downstairs by seven o'clock looking for breakfast before school. They were too young to understand the pain on their mother's face, but they were confused by Hyun's presence.

"Hi, Auntie Hyun. Why are you still here?" asked Holly, as she sat down at the table where Hyun was pouring orange juice.

Hyun looked over at Fiona, not sure what to tell them. Fiona was staring out the kitchen window, hands gripping her mug tightly.

"Mum, he's poking me! Make him stop!" Daisy's shrieking, as she ran into the kitchen chased by Simon, jolted Fiona back to reality.

"Come here, kids," she said gravely. "I have something to tell you." The kids heard the tone in their mother's voice and fell silent as they gathered round her. Fiona held them close and tried not to cry as she shared the news.

Fiona had met Sam's boss many times over the years at company social events. Still, she was touched when he called her that day to offer his condolences. "Such a shock," he said. "Everyone in the office is devastated and thinking about you. Fiona, please let me know what we can do to support you and the kids."

Max and Ben came by after lunch. Fiona took one look at Ben and burst into tears again. They sat together in the living room in silence while Mila, who had taken over for Hyun, whispered in the kitchen with Max.

"I'm worried about her," she said.

"Will you help her with the funeral?" he asked. He knew she was a church music director. "None of us are particularly religious, but I think they'd like a proper church service and a minister."

With no family who needed to travel for the funeral, it was arranged quickly. Fiona and Ben made the decisions together, supported by Max and Fiona's circle of friends. They sat with the minister at Mila's church and decided with Max that he would give the eulogy. Mila helped them choose music that represented Sam, and Fiona's friends planned lunch at the house to follow.

The church was full. All of the partners from Sam's firm came to the funeral, as did many of Fiona's clients. Ben's colleagues came to support him, and the whole neighbourhood turned up. Sam had been incredibly well-liked and everyone wanted to show their support for Fiona and her kids. Max delivered a poignant eulogy that had many in tears, but Fiona didn't hear a word of it and she sleepwalked through the reception after the funeral. She sat on the couch in her living room and from time to time one or another of the kids would come and sit with her, but for the most part, they went up to her room where they could watch television with their friends who came by with their parents.

The house was full of people who wanted to extend their condolences. Fiona knew she had spoken with people, but at the end of the day, she had no idea what any of the conversations had been about. Finally, the house was quiet, Max and Ben headed home, and her friends had tidied up. Rachael, Hyun, and Mila looked at their friend, who seemed even paler and tinier than ever. There were dark smudges under her eyes and her shoulders were slumped. "Are you going to be okay tonight?" Mila asked her. She'd sent her kids home with her husband hours ago. "We can stay, if you like." Rachael and Hyun nodded.

"No," Fiona said sadly. "I have to learn to do this myself. It will be like Sam's on an extended business trip."

Rachael pulled her into a hug. "Are you sure?" she murmured. Fiona nodded her head. "You call if you need anything. Anything at all, do you hear?" Fiona nodded again.

The days that followed were a blur. The kids went back to school and Fiona spoke with their doctor about a therapist for them. She delved into their finances and spoke with the lawyer. Fortunately, Sam had things impeccably organized. He had insisted that they take out life insurance and make wills as soon as Holly was born. Both had been updated after the twins were born and through her grief, Fiona was relieved to understand between this, the generous package he had through work, and his incredibly successful investments of both his inheritance and his bonuses from work, that the house would be paid for, the children's university educations would be covered, and that she had enough money that she didn't need to work right away. She could take some time to heal.

It was as if that knowledge finally gave Fiona permission to grieve. She disappeared into herself, her feelings were so overwhelming. She managed to get up every day and feed the kids and get them ready for school. One of her friends would come to the door and take them and bring them home. After the kids were gone, Fiona climbed back into bed and stayed there until it was time for them to come home. She sat quietly in the waiting room while they talked with the therapist, but spoke to nobody herself. She reheated the casseroles people had dropped off and pushed them around on her plate as the family sat in silence eating. There was no more laughter in the house. A heavy veil of grey had covered her whole world and Fiona felt lost behind it, with no way to escape. And she wasn't sure she wanted to. What was life without Sam?

One morning as she robotically made a cup of coffee before the kids left for school, Fiona looked at the calendar and realized it was March already. March. The month of birthdays. She realized she needed to pull herself together for her children at least. So that day, she dropped the children at school herself, came home, took a long hot shower, dried her hair, and put on makeup for the first time since the funeral. Pouring herself a second cup of coffee, Fiona sat down at the kitchen table and started planning birthday parties.

It took every ounce of strength she had, but Fiona held a small party for Jamie and then a week later another for Daisy and Simon. Hyun, Rachael, and Mila could tell it was important to Fiona that she do this. They helped as much as she would let them, knowing that Sam's birthday was also looming at the end of the month. Fiona was battling rising emotions as that day got closer.

Parents of the children at both parties tried not to whisper. While Fiona welcomed everyone with a smile on her face, once the children were occupied with the activities, the cracks showed, and the adults could see the still raw pain in her eyes behind the façade. Many of them had not seen Fiona since the funeral and she had become a ghost of her former self. She had lost weight she could not afford to lose — her clothes hung on her slight frame — and the dark circles under her eyes told a story. She was holding things together, but barely. Fiona was a woman still keenly griev-ing her husband.

Some days when Fiona woke, she really did think for a moment that Sam was away on a business trip and would be home soon. But reality came crashing down all too quickly, and many days she still sobbed in the shower, where the kids couldn't hear her. But today was different. When Fiona opened her eyes on Sam's birthday, it was like she had an anvil on her chest. He'd never been away on his birthday. Sam wasn't there and her pain made it hard to breathe. Tears trickled from her eyes and she wiped them with the corner of the bedsheet. The bed didn't smell like Sam anymore, and she could just barely feel his presence when she opened his closet and buried herself in his suits. She hadn't yet been able to part with them.

She'd had talked with the kids' therapist and decided not to make a fuss about their father's birthday as they were all so young. For them, it would be just another day. After she dropped them at school, she walked to Ben and Max's house.

Max answered the door and pulled her into his arms. "How are you doing, Fee?" he asked, when he released her. "I know this will be a tough day." She nodded, not trusting herself to speak. "I'm going to run to the shop for a few hours, but I'll be back here this afternoon. Call if you need anything."

Ben was waiting for her in the kitchen, his own red eyes and sombre expression matching hers. They shared a cup of coffee and then headed to the cemetery. They'd been leaning on each other, trying to get past their grief, but it was still fresh.

Slowly, as the warm sun of spring began to take the chill out of the air and new signs of growth began sprouting in the gardens, so too did Fiona begin to come back to life.

The dark circles under her eyes faded as she began to sleep better. Her appetite returned and her children's eyes lit up as they saw their mother's smile again. Fiona spent hours tending her garden, which helped repair her spirit. She began running again, for the first time since she had been pregnant with Holly. Dropping the kids at school in her leggings and racerback tops, she started with short distances and worked her way back up to eight to ten kilometres. She had forgotten the meditative feeling of the steady rhythm of her shoes on the pavement or running trail.

Fiona started calling clients again. They were thrilled to hear from her, as her work was exceptional and they always had opportunities for her magic touch. She took on small projects at first and was starting to take on more as the year came to a close.

It was a year of firsts. The first week at the lake without Sam. The first Canada Day. The first Thanksgiving. The first Christmas. Their anniversary. Fiona and her family battled through them all, and came out the other side as survivors. Still, they'd all been dreading the first anniversary of Sam's death. Fiona was on edge, Ben was distraught, and the older children could feel the tension.

Fiona kept them all home from school that day and they all went down to the cemetery together with Ben and Max. Max hung back in the parking lot, wanting to give them a bit of privacy. He expected he might need to pick up some pieces when they were done.

Walking down the hill to Sam's grave, Fiona started to cry. Shoulders shaking, she tried to keep it together for her kids, but the pain of her loss was too much and she sobbed into Ben's shoulder. He was crying openly too, and the kids were scared.

There was a bench close to the grave and Fiona collapsed onto it, almost hysterical. She'd made it through this nightmare of a year and it was as if every feeling she'd stuffed inside was coming out now. Panicked, Ben shouted to Max to join them. He couldn't deal with his own grief, console Fiona, and reassure four frightened children on his own.

Max quickly assessed the situation. "You help Fee, I'll talk with the kids," he said quietly. Ben nodded and sat down with Fiona, rubbing her back and murmuring soothing words to her, doing his best to keep his own emotions in check. Max crouched down and reached out to the kids and they took some solace in the strength of the arms that hugged them tight. He let go and looked at them solemnly.

"Your mum is strong for you guys every day, right?" They nodded. "Well, today is a hard day for her to be strong. Do you think you can help her by each one of you giving her a little bit of your own strength?"

"Uncle Max, will Mummy ever stop crying?" asked Simon timidly. "I don't like it when she cries."

Max pulled the seven-year-old in closer and gave him a kiss on the top of his head. "She will, Simon, she will. It'll just take a little more time." He noticed Jamie had moved away from the other three. "Are you okay, bud?" he asked.

Jamie turned around, tears in his eyes. "I just miss him so much, Uncle Max . . ." He trailed off.

Max cleared his throat. "We all do, Jamie. But your mum and Uncle Ben and I are all here for you guys. Whatever you need, just ask."

"For real?"

"For real."

"Well, Uncle Max, can you help me with my kub kar for Cubs? I have to build one for the kub kar rally and . . . well, Mum isn't any good at that kind of stuff."

"I'd be honoured," Max answered, ruffling Jamie's hair and clearing his throat again. Things were so simple with kids. He led them back to the bench where Ben and Fiona were now sitting quietly. Ben had wrapped his arm around her protectively and they were whispering to each other quietly.

Ten-year-old Holly approached them first. "Mum, are you all right now?" Daisy was standing quietly with her sister looking up at her mother.

Fiona took a long, ragged breath. "Yes, I'm fine now, kids. I just got really sad. I'm sorry."

"It's okay, Mummy," Daisy piped up, slipping her hand in her mother's. "Uncle Max said we could help by being a little bit strong for you."

Fiona looked up at Max. "Thank you," she mouthed.

Ben forced himself to say some kind words about Sam, and the emotionally exhausted family slowly started to make its way back to their cars. Fiona held the twins' hands and followed Holly and

Jamie up the hill. Max put his arm around Ben as they brought up the rear. "Well done," he whispered. "Well done."

Fiona put the kids in the car and turned to Ben. "I can't do that again. I'm so sorry. I just can't. There has to be a better way to pay our respects." She got into her car and drove away.

Fiona texted Max the next day.

Not sure what you said to the kids, but thank you. I'm embarrassed that I fell apart like that.

Don't be embarrassed, Fee. You've had a hell of a year. And I'm happy to help. You know that.

I do. But still . . .

Fee? Jamie asked me to help him make his kub kar. Not your forté apparently?

Definitely not. If it's not too much trouble, I think he'd really like that.

Never too much trouble. I can pick him up from school a few times and bring him to the shop.

You're the best.

And Fee? One more thing.

Oh?

Don't want to overstep, but are you talking to anyone? A professional?

Me? No. The kids are, but . . .

It might be time, my dear. Think about it.

I will. And thanks again.

Any time.

Fiona talked with the kids' therapist shortly afterwards and he recommended someone for her. One of the first things Fiona spoke with Dr. Lee about was a more positive way for her kids to remember their father, and together they developed a plan. She told them about it, apologizing again to them for breaking down.

"I have a better idea. Instead of visiting your dad on the day that he died — because that makes us all sad — how about we visit him on his birthday instead. We can take cake, remember all the good times we had with him, and tell him about what's new in our lives." She saw four small heads nod.

So in March, on Sam's birthday, they went back to the cemetery, this time in their party clothes. Fiona brought a thermos of hot chocolate and a box of cupcakes with sprinkles. Ben joined them with party hats. One by one, they told Sam some good things from the past few months. Daisy told her dad about a new friend she'd made. Simon explained the plot of a good book he was reading. Holly proudly talked about the praise she'd received for her latest art project. Jamie brought his kub kar and bragged about his third-place finish.

After everyone had shared, Fiona asked the kids if they wanted to take a few minutes to talk to their dad privately. Holly nodded, so the others backed away. Jamie took a minute after her and then Fiona held Simon and Daisy's hands while they told their dad they loved him. She put their hands in Ben's while she took a few minutes herself to tell him she was coping but that she missed him terribly.

"Your turn, Ben," she whispered, smiling as she wiped her tears. "Max is waiting at the top when you're ready." She squeezed his hand, and she and the kids turned and started up the hill.

He put his hand on Sam's gravestone. "I love you, little brother. Happy birthday," he started, before a sob escaped and he began to cry quietly.

Max was watching from the top of the hill, debating if he should go down. He and Fiona exchanged a look as she reached the parking lot. "Kids, go get in the car," she said quietly. She rejoined Max, and they looked down the hill together.

"What do you think, Fee?"

"He needs this time, Max. He'll be up soon. But you're going to need to be gentle with him for the rest of the day. I'm so glad he has you." She reached up and gave him a big hug. "We'll leave you guys now."

Ben emailed Fiona the next morning.

Hi Fiona,

Thanks for yesterday. You were right. A really good way to pay respect to Sam. Healthier for the kids, I think.

I'll still go in January, but if it's OK, can I join you and the kids next March for another birthday party. I'm in awe of your strength.

Oh — Max says not to worry. He put me back together again yesterday. I'm lucky to have him.

Love you and see you soon,
Ben

Fiona and the kids learned how to be on their own. Max had been right to point her to a therapist. She'd been so busy helping her kids cope that she hadn't realized she wasn't coping as well as she was letting everyone think she was. As time went on, they continued to have a lot of support from friends, and slowly, the grief receded into the background. It jumped out and bit them from time to time, but life continued and they were starting to develop new memories without Sam. Slowly, Fiona was able to do more and more and relied less and less on friends. She always knew they were there if she needed them, but she was able to manage. Ben and Max were always there to support her as well, and they loved to spend time with the family, often joining them for Sunday's big brunches.

Chapter 14

"Go and wash your hands for dinner, Jamie. And for heaven's sake, shut the door. It's cold out there," Fiona called to her son as she heard the door open and felt the winter wind blow through the kitchen. He was the last one home and she was dishing up an early dinner before they ran out the door to take Holly to ballet class. Her son was spending a lot of time at Steve's house these days and Fiona made a mental note to make sure they returned the hospitality soon.

Sam had been gone for a little over two years. Her friends had been fantastic and she had been so grateful for their help. She would never have made it through that first year if it weren't for them. But they had their own families to tend to, and she was determined to take care of hers without bothering them anymore. It wasn't easy. Life was a constant juggling act, and Fiona was exhausted from the moment her alarm jolted her awake each day until the moment she climbed back under the covers late at night worrying about the next day's commitments.

Jamie bounded into the kitchen wiping his nose with the back of his hand and sniffling. He'd been doing that a lot lately. "Take a tissue," Fiona reminded her nine-year-old. "Are you feeling all right?"

"Dunno, Mum," he said, blowing his nose loudly and sitting down at the table. "I feel okay, I guess."

She hoped he was right. It felt like one or another of the kids had been sick all winter long. She didn't have the energy to start this cycle again.

They ate dinner quickly and Fiona shuttled everyone out into the car. She was glad that the dance studio shared facilities with the local library. Multitasking was the name of the game for her these days, so while Holly danced, Fiona helped the twins choose new books for the week. She'd done the same thing with Holly and Jamie yesterday while Simon and Daisy were at their gymnastics lessons. Thankfully, Jamie's taekwondo class was already finished for the term, but swimming lessons for all four would begin in another few weeks. Fiona pined for the days when she had time to read books.

Back home, with bedtime routines finally done, Fiona checked her never-ending to-do list and groaned. She'd forgotten that in a moment of weakness, she had agreed to cat-sit for Steve's mother. Jacqueline and her husband had brought home a kitten a few weeks ago, but this weekend, Steve's older brother had his final "away" hockey tournament, and the whole family was tagging along. She had to pick up the kitten tomorrow.

Fiona had grown up with cats and dogs, but she and Sam had wanted to wait until the kids were a bit older before bringing an animal into their midst. And then after he passed away, Fiona hadn't had the energy to even consider it. This weekend's pet-sitting might be a good test. But she'd worry about that tomorrow. Tonight, she had to write a note to Simon's teacher. He had been complaining about one of his classmates and it sounded like he was being bullied. She wanted to nip it in the bud before it got worse. After that, she still needed to sign a consent form for Jamie's upcoming field trip, write a cheque for Holly's book order, pack four peanut-free lunches for tomorrow, and write a quick note to the PTA head to schedule some volunteer time before the end of the school year. She mustn't forget to check that she had the ingredients to make cupcakes for Monday's bake sale and make a grocery list. If she had any energy after that, there was laundry to fold. She had been hoping to proofread a brochure she was finalizing for a client, but that would have to wait until the morning.

The next morning, Fiona was trying to tame Daisy's curly hair into a ponytail at the breakfast table. As usual, the kitchen was chaotic and loud. Jamie was poking Holly, who was loudly protesting. "Ouch," Daisy jumped as Fiona hit tangles.

"Mum, Mum, Mum, Mum," Simon was trying to get her attention. He waved his agenda in front of her. "You forgot to sign my reading yesterday."

"Did you remember my field trip money?" Jamie asked.

"Can I practise my presentation one more time?" Holly begged at the same time.

Fiona took a deep breath, battling back tears. She finished Daisy's ponytail. "Kids," she said in a small voice. "I'm doing the best I can." There were weeks like these ones, where she felt overwhelmed and less than capable. But she pulled herself together and walked the kids to school, taking the long way home through the woods on her run, to relieve some of the stress she felt before heading upstairs to her study. There was still that brochure to review and another deliverable due by the end of the day. Thinking about how busy next week would be, Fiona called her doctor to push out her annual physical. She still had to schedule the kids' dentist appointments, and she was looking for an orthodontist to consult on Holly's crooked teeth. She looked at her watch. She was already running late.

Fiona and Jamie picked up Shadow, her litter box, and toys from Steve's house after school and wished the Montforts a good trip and successful tournament. Shadow, a rambunctious fluffy black kitten, would go home Monday morning.

"Aw, she's so cute," said Jamie, listening to the kitten's soft meows as they took off their boots and shaking the snow off their coats as they came in the door. "Can we get one of our own, Mum? Pleeeeeaaaaaaassee?"

"We'll see," she said absentmindedly, her mind already moving to the next task on the list. "Let's see how we feel about it after the weekend."

Jamie grabbed a tissue from the hall console. "Shadow can sleep with me, right?" he asked.

"Mmmmm. Just as long as she doesn't sleep with me," Fiona said.

After Fiona closed her bedroom door, they let Shadow out of her carrier. The kitten tentatively explored the house, room by room, trailed by Holly, James, and Simon, who all wanted to be her new best friend. Daisy stayed behind in the kitchen with Fiona, helping to make supper for their traditional Friday night pizza and movies. Tonight, the eight-year-old was adding her favourite toppings to the sauce-covered homemade pizza dough, while her mother diced peppers and tomatoes for the salad that would accompany it.

After supper, they piled into the family room to watch a movie together. This was one of Fiona's favourite parts of the week, and she smiled as Shadow settled on Holly's lap. Holly rocked back and forth in the old easy chair, gently scratching the kitten's ears and listening to her purr contentedly. Simon was on his stomach on the floor, feet waving in the air. Jamie and Daisy had curled up under a blanket on the couch. Jamie had the box of tissues beside him. He'd continued to sniffle through dinner. Fiona wrinkled her brow worriedly when she saw Daisy reach for a tissue too.

"Hey, Holly," Jamie said halfway through the movie, seeing his sister sitting so comfortably with the cat. "Don't forget Shadow is sleeping with me. She's Steve's cat after all so I get to take care of her." They all heard the congestion in his voice. He was definitely getting sick.

"Fine," his sister huffed. "I'm going to get my book anyway. I don't even like this movie." At eleven, she was developing a bit of an attitude and Fiona added another mental note to the list to talk with her daughter about it. Holly put the ball of fluff on the arm of the couch beside her sister. "Your turn, Daisy."

But Shadow was having none of it. She jumped down immediately and started winding around Simon's legs. He giggled, settling himself down in the beanbag chair closest to the television. A few minutes later, she jumped into his arms and stayed there for the rest of the movie, much to Daisy's dismay. "No fair," she said, nose buried in a tissue again.

"You can play with her tomorrow," Simon offered. He was nothing if not magnanimous.

When the credits rolled, Fiona stood up and stretched. "Okay, everyone, time for bed."

"Come here, Shadow. Here, kitty, kitty. You're sleeping with me," Jamie called, sniffling loudly.

"Hey, buddy, are you feeling worse?" asked Fiona, putting her hand on his forehead but not detecting any unusual warmth.

"Maybe a little, Mum," he admitted.

The next morning, Jamie sneezed loudly over his cornflakes. Holly looked at her brother in disgust as he wiped his nose with the sleeve of his sweatshirt. "Bless you, Jamie. But please use a tissue," Fiona said, more sharply than she intended. Would he ever learn?

Here we go, thought Fiona, as her mother's alert ears registered Daisy's constant sniffling this morning. She wondered who would be next as she double-checked their supply of tissues, fever reducers, and decongestants. Fiona washed her hands. Perpetually run down, she'd caught more than one of the colds in the house this winter and she could not afford to be sick again.

Fortunately, Shadow's antics were entertaining and turned Fiona's mind from what she thought of as impending doom. The kids took turns playing gently with her, throwing her catnip mouse or running with a little ball of aluminum foil on a string for her to chase. Holly took pictures on her phone and sent them to her friends. Despite two sick kids, there was no bickering for a solid hour, and Fiona had time to drink a whole cup of coffee while it was still hot, and start meal planning for the week. She threw a load of laundry in the washing machine; at least it made a small dent in the pile.

It was mid-morning when Fiona went out to shovel the driveway. She chatted with her neighbours about the surprise overnight snowfall. Rachael's husband, Mike, from across the road warned her more was expected before the end of the day. As she hung up her coat, Fiona heard Daisy sneeze several times in a row and then saw her rub her little red nose with the heel of her hand. "Tissue, Daisy," Fiona said exasperatedly, feeling like a broken record. "Are you sure you feel like playing with Elaine this afternoon?"

"I really want to. I'm okay," Daisy pleaded. The girls had been looking forward to this playdate all week.

"You're sure, Libby?" Fiona double-checked with Elaine's mother, as she dropped Daisy off after lunch. "But please send her home if she gets worse or you change your mind." Fiona knew she would say yes to other people's germy children in her house as well. It was just par for the course with kids this age.

"Stop it!" Holly yelled from her bedroom, hearing another set of explosive sneezes from her brother's room next door that afternoon. "I can't concentrate on my homework with you making so much disgusting noise all the time. You're so annoying!"

"Leave me alone. Mum's right. I have a cold," he yelled back, and blew his nose loudly.

Fiona washed her hands again and took a long drink of water. Those two were constantly bickering these days and the sound carried through the house. She rubbed her temples. It was going to be a long weekend. She texted Ben for virtual support.

Sigh. We have another round of colds.

Again? Already? Didn't they just get better?

Yep, but it doesn't seem to matter. Starting again.

You OK?

Exhausted. So much to do, and now this . . .

Want help? Need company? I can come.

Thanks. No. You've got lots to do too, I'm sure. Just needed to vent.

No problem. Any time. Hang in there.

Fiona put lasagna in the oven for dinner and went upstairs to check on everyone. Simon was splayed out on the floor, feet in the air again, playing his computer game, and Holly was upside down on her bed, hair hanging down, listening to music. So far so good.

"Hey, Jamie, how are you feeling?" she asked, leaning against his door frame.

"My nose is really stuffed up, Mum," he admitted, looking up from his book and suddenly sneezed again, as if to emphasize his point.

Fiona heard a noise of preteen exasperation from Holly's room. She felt Jamie's forehead for the second time that weekend. Still nothing. He sounded rough but it could be worse. She rummaged in the medicine cabinet for a kids' decongestant. "Take this, buddy," she said, giving him the tablet with a glass of water. "It might help a bit." After kissing him on the head and ruffling his dark hair, she headed back to the kitchen.

"Mmm, the lasagna smells really good, Mummy," Simon said as he helped her set the table a little later. Tonight it was his turn to help with dinner.

The doorbell rang. Libby was dropping Daisy off with her thanks for letting the girls play together. Picking up the coat Daisy had dropped on the floor at the door, Fiona saw that Mike had been right. She would have to shovel again soon. Jamie came down to the kitchen to get Shadow's dinner ready.

"Holly, dinnertime!" Fiona called her daughter to join them.

"I can't smell anything," Jamie complained. He sniffed hard, trying desperately to breathe air through his nose and catch the scent of dinner.

"Oh, you're so gross," said Holly, sliding her chair as far away from her brother as possible.

"Mum!" Jamie yelped.

"Holly!" Fiona snapped. "Apologize to your brother. Now. And be careful what you say. You might be the next one to catch this cold." She turned her attention to her younger daughter. "Bless you, Daisy," she said, feeling her forehead and handing her a tissue before putting the salad and garlic bread on the table. She started dishing up the steaming lasagna. "Dig in, gang." Simon, always hungry, was first to pick up his fork.

"Sorry, Jamie," huffed Holly, with a tone that all but erased the apology. At least, thought Fiona, she'd said the words.

Alongside the apple crumble for dessert, Fiona put a newly opened box of tissues in the middle of the table. Daisy and Jamie reached out immediately. Fiona mentally ticked through what was on her freelance plate and hoped nobody would need to stay home from school after the weekend. She had another important deadline Tuesday. Multiple sneezes during dessert from both children suggested she might need an extension.

Daisy sniffled as she helped clear the table. "Mummy, can I play with Shadow?" she asked as she buried her nose in a tissue again.

Fiona nodded. Her kids were treating Shadow well, and there'd been no fighting over her. She smiled, watching Daisy gently pet the little thing. She was not the only one falling in love with this cat and Fiona felt her resolve starting to break. Maybe it really was time for a family pet when everyone was well again. But did she really have the energy to take care of an animal on top of four children? She'd have to think seriously about this.

Fiona handed her daughter yet another tissue and washed her hands again for good measure before loading the dishwasher. She went back outside to shovel the driveway again. The snow was still falling when she came back in and she realized she might have to shovel once more before bed. Just a few minutes of peace, she thought, sipping her tea, that's all I want. She finally opened the morning paper but found it hard to concentrate, hearing the noises of sick children in the next room.

Jamie blew his nose several times as he sat on one end of the couch flipping through a catalogue of model airplanes, trying to decide which one to ask for as a birthday gift. Daisy, who had picked up a book and joined Jamie on the couch, was sneezing repeatedly, sounding far sicker now than her brother. Simon and Holly were in the dining room with a laser pen and laughing loudly as Shadow chased the light. So far, they had escaped, but tomorrow might be a different story. Fiona knew she might well have three or even four sick kids by morning.

Fiona abandoned the paper and went to sit with Daisy for a bit. "Good book?" she asked, as she put her arm around her daughter. Shadow had abandoned the laser light and jumped up beside them. Daisy nodded, and succumbed to a fit of sneezing. "Fifteen minutes until bath time, okay?" An early night would be good for her. Daisy nodded again, trying valiantly to read as the kitten settled in her lap. "Bless you," Fiona said worriedly and kissed the top of her head.

"Mummy," Daisy was terribly congested now. "My nose is all itchy. My eyes too." She scrubbed at them with her fist. She looked up and Fiona saw how irritated and weepy they were. And that's when she suddenly realized.

"Oh no," she said, retreating to the kitchen to think and already beating herself up about not recognizing earlier what was painfully obvious to her now. "No, no, no, no, no."

"What is it, Mum?" asked Holly, who had opened the fridge for a drink of milk.

"I don't think your brother and sister are sick. I think they're allergic to Shadow." She turned and looked at her oldest daughter. "You're feeling okay, right? No stuffy nose, no itchy eyes?"

"Nothing," replied Holly. "And Simon's fine too. But what are we going to do? Shadow is here until Monday."

"I don't quite know," said Fiona quietly, hearing the sneezing continuing from the family room. She snapped into problem-solving mode. "But first things first. Shadow goes up into my study until we're sure."

Fiona got Daisy into the tub first before stripping her bed and Jamie's. Shadow had been all over their house. "This should make you feel better," she said, brushing Daisy's freshly washed hair as she stood in the bathroom dressed in clean pajamas. She put new sheets on the beds and vacuumed their rooms. "Jamie, you next, please," she said. "Bath or shower — your choice. But I want you to wash your hair too. And tonight, let's keep Shadow out of your room."

"But, Mum," he whined, wiping his nose again.

"No 'but, Mum' tonight. I'm serious."

By the time all four baths had been taken, and Fiona had remade the remaining beds, and vacuumed the rest of the bedrooms, she was exhausted. But there was still lots to do, and so when everyone was asleep, she leapt into action. She carefully vacuumed the rest of the house — including the couch and chairs — and then dusted all the tables and washed the floors to get rid of any cat hair and dander, hoping to confine the allergens upstairs to her study. With that done, she collapsed into bed.

Fiona was up early the next morning to make her traditional big breakfast. Standing in the kitchen in her old flannel pajamas and a fluffy bathrobe, she had a stack of pancakes and sausages warming in the oven and was working on her second cup of coffee when Jamie arrived in his pajamas.

"Good morning, Mum. Guess what? I think my cold is gone," he announced. But Fiona knew better.

The others emerged one by one, drawn by the good smells emanating from the kitchen, and Fiona stacked pancakes on their plates and poured maple syrup on top. Sausages were next, followed by glasses of orange juice. Daisy was last down, still sniffling and congested, but significantly improved over the previous evening.

Breakfast finished and dishes stacked on the counter, Fiona gathered the kids in the family room and broke the bad news to her animal-loving foursome about Jamie and Daisy's allergies to their adorable fluffy houseguest. She told Jamie that was probably why he always seemed to need a tissue these days when he came home from Steve's house.

"Is that why my eyes are itchy too, Mummy?" Daisy asked, rubbing them again. Fiona nodded, giving her daughter's shoulder a sympathetic squeeze.

"No! I don't believe you," cried Jamie. "I love Shadow! You must be wrong. I never sneeze at Steve's house." He ran all the way up the stairs to her study and brought back the squirming ball of fluff in his arms. Jamie tried to prove his point, burying his head in her long black fur. He looked up. "See, no problem," he proclaimed defiantly. And then, with the kind of timing Fiona thought only happened in movies he continued, "I'm not aah-aah-aller-ahh-ahhh-aahhhh-haachooo!" The first explosive sneeze was quickly followed by two more. He dropped Shadow and her fur went flying as she scrambled away. Jamie looked at his mother dejectedly. He sneezed again. "Or maybe I am."

Fiona put out her arms. "Come here, buddy," she said, consoling her son.

Jamie's eyes darted to his sister. "Bless you, Daisy," he said sympathetically as he wiped his nose. "And again. You're lucky, Simon. You too, Holly. This sucks."

"Simon, can you take Shadow back to my study?" Fiona asked as Daisy sneezed a third time. As he headed upstairs, Daisy and Jamie sniffled in unison. "Tissues, guys!" Fiona said, throwing her hands up.

She put Simon in charge of Shadow for the rest of the day. He and Holly spent almost all day in her study, loving their cat-sitting duties. Fiona gave out antihistamines, which helped Jamie tremendously, but only slightly dampened Daisy's symptoms. Fiona felt bad, as her youngest continued to suffer throughout the day. "That cursed cat is going home first thing in the morning," she muttered under her breath.

At the end of the evening, after shovelling one last time, she sat exhausted on the couch, and texted Ben.

Epic mum fail today.

You? Never. What happened?

Not colds. Allergies.

Oh no. To what? And who?

Steve's kitten. Here since Friday. Daisy AND Jamie. Took me until today to figure it out.

Ah. Genetic, I guess.

Really? I don't remember Sam having allergies.

Not Sam. Me. Everything from hamsters to horses. Anything
with fur. So no pets. He hated me for it. You didn't know?
Good thing I didn't come over yesterday. I'd have been a
mess. Better get them tested.

Already on the list. What a weekend. 1 grown-up. 4 kids. 1
little kitten. 2 allergic. Chaos. Damn, this single mum thing
is HARD.

Let me know how Max & I can help. Seriously. But after the
cat is gone. My nose itches just thinking about it.

Thanks.

Any time. You know that. Take care.

Fiona looked at the clock. It was ten thirty. She scribbled a note
on her to-do list. She needed to find an allergist now, in addition to
the orthodontist. She gritted her teeth. Would she ever get ahead?
Slowly, she returned to the kitchen and pulled out the mixer. The
bake sale was tomorrow, and there were still cupcakes to make.

"Hey, Max." Ben put down his phone and nudged his partner,
who was reading in bed beside him. "Fiona sounds like she really
needs a break. What do you think about offering to take the kids
for a week this summer?"

The kids were thrilled to spend the first week of summer at a
cottage with their Uncle Ben and Uncle Max. They loved going to
the lake house with their mum, but this would be a new lake and
the uncles had promised to take them fishing and swimming and
canoeing. Fiona thought she'd also heard the promise of far too
many s'mores and even sparklers for Canada Day.

"Ben, I can't thank you enough for this," she said, as he buckled
the kids up in their big SUV.

"Got big plans?" he asked.

"Honestly? Sleep, reading, and maybe a bit of pampering," she admitted. "I can't remember the last time I had a whole forty-eight hours to myself, let alone a week. I've told my clients I'm out of the office, so I really am really on vacation. I just hope you two are ready for what you asked for," she said with a grin.

Max gave her shoulder a squeeze before he jumped into the driver's seat. "There are two of us," he said. "Piece of cake."

She threw him a thankful glance. Ben and Max were great influences in her children's lives and they were always there for her. She waved as they pulled out of the driveway. Fiona ate a quick lunch and sat down on the couch with a new novel and a cup of tea. She thought she'd indulge in an hour of afternoon reading before deciding what to do.

Fiona jolted awake. It was dark. She had slept the entire afternoon and into the evening. She sighed. Doubtful she'd sleep now, she nevertheless went upstairs, brushed her teeth, and got into bed, expecting to stare at the ceiling, but her eyelids fluttered closed again within minutes.

She woke next to the sounds of birds singing, feeling more rested than she had in — well, she didn't know how long. Probably years. In the bathroom mirror though, she saw a woman who wasn't taking care of herself and looked older than her thirty-four years. She'd been sleeping in an old shapeless T-shirt. Gone were the days of silky negligees. She hadn't been to the hairdresser since Sam died and her wavy hair had grown long again, but it was shapeless, full of split ends, and she'd gotten used to mindlessly tying it behind her without any thought. Getting dressed, she realized she was pulling on an old bra and stretched out panties that had seen better days. Fiona wasn't sure who she was anymore.

Fiona had a session with her therapist that day. She still saw Dr. Lee once a month. She talked with her about this sudden realization that she was losing herself.

"Why do you think that is?" Dr. Lee asked.

"I suppose I'm spending all my time looking after other people. Between the kids and my clients, I don't have much left over for me."

Dr. Lee encouraged Fiona to look for a creative outlet, and to carve out time especially for it. She also suggested to Fiona that it was time to start thinking of herself as a vital, beautiful woman again. They'd work on that more in the following months.

Taking Dr. Lee's words to heart, Fiona signed up for a sketching class. She didn't think she'd be any good at it, but it would be something new. She also made an appointment with a hairdresser, and afterwards treated herself to some new lingerie. She even picked up some new makeup and looked into a yoga class. When she got home, she made lunch dates with several friends. All of that, coupled with long afternoons of reading and full nights of sleep, meant that by the end of the week, Fiona was starting to feel like her old self.

The week had been good bonding time for the uncles and their nieces and nephews. They had spent most of the week on the water. At eleven, ten, and nine, the kids were old enough to enjoy playing around in canoes and kayaks, as well as splashing by the water's edge. Ben had lit a campfire each night and they'd roasted marshmallows. Max had told ghost stories and the kids had dissolved into shrieks of laughter and fright at his escapades. They walked into town most days for ice cream and to watch the boats go through the locks on the Trent-Severn Waterway. It was non-stop activity for a week.

Jamie bonded with Max over a duck. Max had brought up some of the old carving tools he had used with his father and was teaching Jamie how to make a duck decoy. He'd offered to teach the others, but only Jamie was interested, giving up ice cream time on many days to keep working on this project. He'd already asked

Max if he could come back to his workshop when they returned to the city. He had good memories of it from his kub kar days.

Finally, Max and Ben piled the kids back into their SUV and made the trek back to the city. All four of them were fast asleep within half an hour. Ben put his hand on Max's. "Finally, some quiet," he joked. "They're quite a handful. I have no idea how Fiona does this on her own."

Max shook his head. "Neither do I. We should probably give her a hand more often." Both men lapsed into silence as they drove the rest of the way home.

Fiona was there to greet them when they arrived. "I missed you guys!" she told the kids, giving them hugs as they tumbled out of the car and ran into the house.

"Hey, you look great," Ben said, giving Fiona a quick peck on the cheek after getting out and stretching his legs. "A bit of rest looks good on you." He and Max looked tired but happy.

"Thank you so much for taking them. I missed them terribly, of course, but I have to say, I really needed this. I think you guys knew it before I did."

Ben looked at Max, who nodded.

"Fiona, we'd love to have the kids more — help you out more with them. They're a handful, we know, but it takes a village, right? And we'd like to be a bigger part of that village."

Chapter 15

In the years that followed, Ben and Max mad good on their desire to help, picking up a chunk of the father role that Sam had left behind. They took them every summer for a week and had them once a month for Uncles Weekends, as they grew to be called. The kids grew close to their uncles and for Jamie and Simon especially, the men proved to be great role models and confidants. They often talked to them when it was something they thought their mum wouldn't understand.

Fiona cherished Uncles Weekends and usually reserved them for a bit of pampering. A night out with her girlfriends, or just a long bubble bath and a glass of wine. Sometimes she sketched. On the rare occasion, though, work borrowed a few hours of the time. It was on one of those occasions that Fiona was catching up on a week's worth of industry news that was delivered daily to her email inbox when she had the shock of her life. Once a week, the newsfeed featured a newly published book. This one, about the social implications of new technologies, had an author with a very familiar name. Metin Özdemir. It couldn't be, she thought.

But when she clicked for more information a short biography and picture appeared. Indeed it was. Metin. Her Metin. Well, not *her* Metin, but . . .

He had done well for himself, she discovered after a bit of googling. A university professor now, he taught sociology courses and seemed to specialize in where technology and society met. This was his second book, and he'd done the speaking circuit with his first. If the review was anything to go by, he'd be doing it again. Well done, she thought, allowing herself to think about the young man who had stolen her heart all those years ago. She looked at the photo again. He was still a very handsome man. On a whim, Fiona ordered the book. I wonder if he's married with children, she mused, as she made herself another cup of tea, feeling slightly downhearted that she'd lost touch with everyone. Friends forever hadn't been in the cards apparently. What a year that had been. She hoped he was happy.

Fiona's phone buzzed after she'd returned from walking the kids to school. It was Max.

Hey. You around today? Got time for coffee?

Sure. Quiet day in the office. Where should I meet you guys?

Not guys. Just me.

???

Something I want to talk to you about. I'll swing by your place at 10?

OK. See you soon.

Fiona heard Max pull up in the driveway in his huge SUV. She grabbed her sunglasses, her purse, and her keys and met him at the front door. "Let's walk," she said, leading him out to the main street. "We can get coffee and chat."

Fifteen minutes later, they stopped in at one of Fiona's favourite coffee houses. He seemed nervous, Fiona thought as he paid for the coffee. That was unlike him. They sat down at a table, shrugging off their winter jackets. Max had come straight from the workshop in his jeans and plaid flannel shirt and Fiona grinned when she noticed a little bit of sawdust on the gentle giant's shoulders.

She cupped her hands on the huge café au lait cup to warm them. "OK, Max, spill. What's up?"

"So," he began quietly, staring at his own coffee cup. "You know the laws changed last year."

Fiona looked at him quizzically.

"And despite, umm, my outward appearance, you know me well enough to know, well, I'm a bit soft inside."

Fiona furrowed her brow trying to understand what he was getting at.

"Well," Max cleared his throat, stumbling along. "You know that Ben and I have been together for, umm, fifteen years now. This is a bit, well, old-fashioned and all, but you are, umm, his family, and . . ." He looked up, slightly flushed, and the rest of the words tumbled out. "And I want to ask him to marry me, Fee, now that we can. And I'd like your blessing."

Fiona sat there stunned for a moment. Max's face started to fall, suddenly worried she didn't approve. "Fiona?" he asked tentatively.

She jumped up and threw her arms around him. "Oh, you wonderful man," she said huskily. "No wonder Ben loves you so much."

Max released the breath he didn't realize he was holding and hugged Fiona back with a huge grin on his face.

The wedding was a joyous affair, attended by Max and Ben's huge circle of friends. They included the children in the ceremony and Fiona gave a toast at the reception. She was so happy for them, and wished them a lifetime of joy. And she said a silent prayer that their time wouldn't be cut short.

"Okay, ladies," said Fiona, pouring large glasses of red wine to go with the charcuterie board she'd put out earlier. "It's time. Sell me!"

Rachael, Mila, and Hyun had joined Fiona, excited that their friend was finally ready to dip her toe back in the dating scene. It had been five years since she lost Sam and two since she'd taken off her wedding ring. Fiona was still a very attractive woman and at thirty-seven, she had some world experience behind her. It was time. She'd joked with them that she could sell all kinds of products for her clients, but that she couldn't seem to write words about herself that would intrigue a man.

"Let's see. 'Exhausted mother of four kids — all still at home — loves dozing off during movies. Interests include sleep, rest, yoga, and tickle fests with aforementioned munchkins.' I wouldn't date that person, would you?" she laughed. "Help me see me like others do."

As darkness fell over the back garden, and the garden lights came on one by one, the women sat together poring over a computer screen describing Fiona in glowing terms.

It didn't take long. But then again, none of them expected it would. Between the photos that Mila expertly arranged that night and the awesome person Rachael and Hyun accurately described in her profile, Fiona soon had a number of men interested in meeting her. She was very selective, but soon had a couple of dates set up.

Mila helped calm Fiona's nerves as she got ready to meet Ron at a local coffee shop. His profile said he was an advertising executive who liked to run. Fiona recognized him when she walked into the café, which she took as a good sign — he looked like his photos.

She'd heard nightmares of people who uploaded photos that were many years old. Ron had been watching the door. He returned her smile and stood up when she joined him at the table.

"Fiona? Pleased to meet you." He held out his hand.

"Pleased to meet you too," replied Fiona, shaking it firmly.

Ron ordered them coffee and they started talking. Conversation was stilted. Eventually, she admitted this was her first date since her husband died. Ron didn't know how to react to that, and spluttered and started.

"It's okay," Fiona said. "It's time for me to start dating again. I'm just relearning how, I guess."

The date ended quickly. Obviously, Ron was not interested in helping to teach her.

Her next date, with a firefighter, was more promising. Fiona still had her training wheels on, but she found it was easier the second time out. Trevor had been widowed two years earlier so they found lots of common ground. He was very handsome. She found it endearing that he kept pushing his thick but greying blond hair away from his bright blue eyes. It wasn't until their third date that Fiona realized all they talked about was Sam and Trevor's wife. While possibly therapeutic for Trevor, this wasn't the way she wanted to start her future. When he asked her for another date, she politely declined, and focussed on her work instead.

"I thought it was supposed to get easier as they got older," said Fiona one day to Rachael. "But now with Holly in grade eleven and thinking about universities, and Jamie getting into trouble at school, I'm at my wit's end. At least Simon and Daisy are still pretty carefree. And I'm an expert at grade eight by now," she finished with a tired smile.

Jamie had been given another detention, the fourth time since he'd started high school in September. Fiona was worried he'd be suspended next. As grade nine started, he'd snubbed his best friend Steve, declaring him uncool and had found new friends that Fiona didn't like. They didn't take school seriously, they smoked and cut classes, and she was worried they were doing drugs. She'd received several calls from teachers and even one from the principal, who warned that her son wasn't behaving like the boy she read about from his elementary school records.

And he wasn't behaving any better at home. Fiona didn't recognize this angry boy her son had become, who slammed the door every time he walked in the house. He stormed upstairs to his room, picked fights with his sisters and brother, and even with her. His language was appalling. Jamie had been taller than Fiona since he was eleven, and recently he'd shot up and was still growing. Currently five foot, eight inches tall, he was almost as tall as his father had been, towering over his mother and all his siblings. It was unnerving to see her young son the size of a grown man. Recently he'd come right up to her, looked down and said, "Make me," when she'd asked him to take out the garbage.

"Maybe he should start seeing the therapist again," suggested Rachael. "Because something is clearly bothering him. Jamie's growing up and his hormones are probably a mess too. There's Ben and Max, of course, but maybe he feels uncomfortable talking with them about his feelings."

Fiona supposed Rachael had a point. And she knew he hadn't liked it when she started dating either. She called Dr. Khalid and he agreed to see Jamie later that week.

Jamie hated high school. He didn't see the point. He wasn't smart like everyone else in his family or his old friends and he already knew he didn't want to work in an office and wear a suit. So what was the point in studying? In fact, why go at all? He'd rather have some fun. So he found some new friends who would show him a good time. Doug and Tony were cool, and Natasha was hot, showing off her legs in her short skirts and her cleavage in tight low-cut shirts. He felt comfortable with these people. They understood him.

Jamie didn't feel like he belonged in his family. He didn't remember much about his father, but he knew his work had kept him away from home a lot. He didn't want that. Jamie didn't look anything like his mother or his siblings. He was more like his Uncle Ben, and although he didn't have many memories, he knew from photos that he looked a lot like his dad. His mum and his sisters were all pretty, petite, graceful redheads; he felt like a clumsy, uncoordinated giant next to them. The girls did well in school. Simon was a little boy still, but he was really smart too and he had red hair just like them. At least Daisy had brown eyes like him. He'd always had a sweet spot for his little sister.

When he was younger, he felt more at home with Uncle Ben and Uncle Max. There, he wasn't the biggest, and he looked so much like Uncle Ben that sometimes people thought they were father and son. He'd sort of liked that, but it felt like betraying his dad to say so. Uncle Max was really cool, and ran his own work-shop. Jamie had really liked it when Uncle Max had let him come and visit. He loved the smell of the wood chips and he enjoyed making things with his hands. But recently he'd been feeling a little uncomfortable with his uncles. Uncles Weekends seemed dumb. It wasn't that he thought there was anything wrong with them, but he liked girls. Actually, one girl in particular. Just thinking about Natasha made him excited. He really wanted to kiss her. And maybe more. They couldn't help him with her, he figured, and he didn't want to talk about it with them. So their house became just one more place he didn't fit in.

Ben and Max came by one Saturday afternoon. Jamie was in a black mood, giving monosyllabic answers at best to questions and ignoring everyone as much as he could. As the afternoon turned into evening, Ben braved the chilly November weather to barbecue burgers for dinner. Feeling whimsical, Fiona made lemonade ice cream pie for dessert. It had been a go-to dessert for years, and one of Jamie's favourites. Until now apparently. When she brought it out, Jamie said the frozen dessert was just for babies, and stormed up the stairs to his room. They heard the door slam. Holly rolled her eyes, used to his outbursts, but the twins were bothered by their brother's behaviour. Ben cajoled them out of it and the dinner ended peacefully, but he could tell Fiona was upset.

After dinner, the rest of the kids watched television before bed while the grown-ups stayed in the dining room. Ben mentioned Jamie's outburst to his husband while Fiona was inside getting tea ready. "I'm worried about him, Max," he said. "Jamie seems to be going down the wrong path. I wonder if we ought to spend more time with him?"

"I was thinking the same thing," Max admitted. He continued delicately, "But I wonder if this one isn't more for me than you." Ben raised his eyebrows. "I don't want to overstep, but Jamie and I really connected at the shop back when he was in Cubs and helped him with his kub kars for a few years. I'd like to offer him a job sweeping up and doing some other jobs that would keep him busy after school. That would keep him away from his new friends and teach him the value of being productive. What do you think? Should I offer it to Fiona?"

"Offer what to Fiona?" she asked, bringing the tea tray in. Ben caught Max's eye and nodded.

Max carefully outlined his thoughts to Fiona. Three days a week after school — more if she wanted, or Jamie was interested — Max would pay Jamie a small hourly rate and he would be responsible for sweeping up the floors, emptying bins of sawdust, and providing general help to the carpenters. "He really liked being there when he was younger, Fee," Max said. "Maybe he would again."

"You're so generous to offer," said Fiona. "And I think it's a great idea."

Jamie wasn't so sure. He grumbled about it at home, complaining about having to do such menial work, and at school, his friends tried to convince him to bail, but there was still a core of responsibility in Jamie so he showed up three days a week at Max's shop. He'd forgotten how much he liked the smell of sawdust and how the wood could be manipulated with simple tools.

As Christmas rolled around, Fiona began to see some small changes in Jamie. She was optimistic they'd nipped this in the bud. Jamie was still a moody teenager, but he was less obnoxious. He'd never be a stellar student, but he was trying now, and being so busy at the shop meant he had less time for his new friends. As a result, they were losing interest in him, and he started to see that they weren't everything he had thought they were. Over Christmas dinner, Fiona noticed that Jamie was asking Max questions about upcoming projects that were on the books at the shop. Max, as always, was taking the time to answer them seriously.

Soon afterwards, Jamie asked Max if he could make something for his mum for Easter. From then on, he spent a fourth afternoon at the shop. Max asked one of his newest carpenters to help and mentor Jamie with his project. Jason had only been employed for a year and was keen to gain the trust of the company owner, so was happy to work with Jamie. And for his part, Jamie enjoyed working with the younger man.

With a growing client roster, Fiona developed relationships with other marketers and consultants to expand her offering. Combining forces, they could offer an impressive array of services. Luca Romano was one of the people she collaborated on regularly, and they were just finishing an engagement together. Luca ran a three-person business that specialized in polling and focus group research. They worked together often, him providing the data that she would build into marketing plans and strategies to help companies improve sales.

"Thanks again, Luca," said Fiona, bringing the lessons learned call to a close. "It's been really great working with you on this. I hope we can do it again soon."

"It's been a blast, as always. I'm actually sad this project is coming to an end," said Luca. "Actually, Fiona, I was wondering if we could extend things personally. Would you consider having dinner with me next week?"

Fiona was caught off guard. But Rachael had been needling her again about dating, and Luca was a great guy who always knew how to make her laugh, so she decided to take the chance. "That would be nice," she said. "I'd love to."

They met for dinner at a local hole-in-the-wall Italian restaurant. Fiona stomped the snow off her boots before entering. Luca knew the owner, so the service was phenomenal. Luca and Fiona got to know more about each other on a personal level. Luca knew about Sam and Fiona knew about Luca's divorce, but over caprese salad, she learned that he was a marathon runner and he learned about her yoga practice and shorter distances. Fiona was enjoying good wine, seafood pasta, and the good company even more than she expected. They talked about what they were reading, the places they wanted to travel, her trials with raising teenagers. So far, her dating history hadn't been great, but she felt very comfortable with Luca.

He walked her home and left her at her doorstep with a tender kiss. As she closed the door behind her, she realized that it had stirred feelings in her that she hadn't felt in a long time.

He texted her when he got home.

Fiona, thanks for an amazing evening. Would you be interested in doing it again?

Hi Luca. Thank YOU for dinner. I enjoyed it. And yes, I'd love
to see you again. My treat this time?

We can arm wrestle for the bill! Do you own skates?

Sure do. Grew up on a lake and have never been without
them. What are you thinking?

Queens Quay rink this weekend?

Super. It's a date! Goodnight, Luca, and thanks again.

After an afternoon of skating in the blustery weather, Fiona and
Luca retreated to a pub. Luca blew on her hands to warm them
while they waited for the Irish coffee to arrive. Again, Luca took
Fiona home and kissed her on her front doorstep. Fiona kissed
him back and as she did, he put his hand on her back to pull her
in closer. Fiona responded, surprised by the emotions it stirred up.

They had dinner together again the next week and she talked
to Luca about her feelings. "Luca, I really haven't dated since Sam,
and I married him so young. You're making me feel things I haven't
felt in a long time. I'm not quite sure what to do with them."

Luca was impressed with her candour and reassured her he
wasn't in a rush and that they'd take this at her speed. "It's okay,
Fiona," he assured her. "This is pretty new for me too. I'm happy
to go slow."

Fiona was relieved. "I'm really enjoying spending time with
you. I've just been a little cautious when it comes to my heart."

Luca and Fiona saw each other several more times before
they made plans to do a day trip the following weekend to try
their hands at snowshoeing. Fiona's kids were having an Uncles
Weekend, so it wouldn't matter if they were home late.

The couple strapped on their snowshoes and headed out on the country trails on Saturday. Fiona had brought a pocket full of sunflower seeds, and when they stopped for a break, they fed chickadees and nuthatches from their hands. Luca watched the sheer delight on her face when the little birds landed and chose a seed before flying off to enjoy it. Her cheeks were reddened from the cold, and her long hair flowed from under an ivory toque. He was smitten. For her part, as Fiona followed Luca out of the forest, she was taken by his form. He'd done this before. He kept looking behind him, his twinkling brown eyes checking up on her.

Snowshoeing was hard work and they were hungry. Stopping at a café on the way home, they ordered coffee and dove into a huge shared slice of Black Forest cake. Luca was taken by the way Fiona seemed to enjoy every second of life. She was quite a woman.

Closer to her house, Fiona tentatively asked Luca if he'd like to come in for dinner. "I don't have anything planned," she said, "but I'm sure I can whip up something simple for us." Luca was happy to agree.

She passed him a cold bottle of white wine from the fridge to open while she dug deeper to pull out butter, green onions, mushrooms, and a block of good Parmesan cheese. "Risotto?" she asked. "And salad to go along with it?"

"Sounds perfect," Luca said, as his stomach grumbled. "How can I help?"

The couple contentedly worked together in Fiona's cheery kitchen. At one point she bumped her hip against him to get him to move, and later he put his hands on her hips to keep her in place as he passed by behind her. Their hands touched as they both reached for the wine bottle to replenish their glasses and their eyes met, but Fiona looked away quickly. She was nervous and didn't know what to do with the butterflies that started fluttering every time Luca looked at her.

After dinner, they sat on the couch with mugs of tea. Luca took Fiona's mug from her hands and put it on the table. He took her hands in his and leaned in to kiss her. Fiona felt the spark again and responded. Soon, they were kissing with a kind of desire that Fiona had forgotten, and Luca's hands were soon reaching under her sweater, making her gasp. Her own fingers tentatively followed as if they had a mind of their own.

Finally, Luca pulled away. "Fiona, I won't be able to stop if I don't stop now." His voice was ragged. "Are you sure you're ready for this?"

"Yes," she whispered, bringing her hand to Luca's face. She kissed him and he groaned with pleasure. Somehow Fiona got to her feet, took his hand and led him upstairs.

Fiona and Luca continued to date, but something kept her from introducing him to her kids. She talked about it with her friends and Mila told her that she shouldn't force it. If it didn't feel right, she should hold off. So she went on frequent dates with the handsome Italian and they slept together from time to time, but rarely stayed the night. Eventually, Fiona realized that the relationship wasn't going anywhere. He deserved more, but she wasn't ready to let him all the way into her life. She liked him a lot, but she wasn't ready to share her family with him. When she explained it that way to him, he understood. They parted ways as lovers, but stayed good friends and colleagues.

Fiona was thrilled with her Easter present from Jamie. He'd spent hours in Max's shop building her a wine rack and there were tears in her eyes when she opened it. The walnut wood gleamed from polishing and she knew the hard work he'd put into it.

"Thank you," she said, giving her son a huge hug. He returned it, which was a real turning point. Jamie was back. In fact, he'd given up on his new friends and was trying to apologize for his behaviour to Steve. Natasha was long forgotten, and the shop was Jamie's new love.

Fiona took Max out for coffee to say thank you. He had been instrumental in turning around her wayward son. He was happy to have done so, and he wanted to talk to Fiona about Jamie's future.

"Have you ever thought about a different career for him?" Max asked gently.

"He's studying again," Fiona said to him. "School is a struggle for him, but at least he's trying."

"Seriously, Fee. Not everyone is meant to go to university. I didn't." She looked up from her coffee curiously. "I've seen Jamie at the shop," he continued. "He loves it there. And I trust Jason when he tells me Jamie has some talent. There's a college program that I think would be perfect for him. It's three years, and he'd graduate with a diploma in craft and design. I hire kids with that diploma and I know tons of other shops that do the same. I think you know as well as I do that Jamie would chafe under the restrictions of office work. The thought of wearing a tie every day like Ben does makes me shudder and I know it's the same for your son."

Chapter 16

The more she thought about it, the more Max's suggestion made sense for Jamie. It was funny, she mused, that despite the same genes, and the same upbringing, that Jamie was the most different from the rest of them. It wasn't a case of better or worse. He simply had different talents and interests, and Fiona was determined to help him be successful at whatever he chose to do. She started making a point of talking to him about what he wanted to do after high school, and listened well, when he told her all about his afternoons in the shop.

She may not have understood his love of the shop specifically, but she did understand passion. Fiona was still passionate about helping her clients, and loved being part of the cutting-edge work they did. She still did work in the pharma industry, but more and more, she was working with high-tech clients, and had become an early adopter of new applications. So when Facebook was launched to the public in late 2006, she was among the first people who played around with it. Many of her colleagues were on the platform too, but it wasn't until her friends started to join that she found it very useful. But it had been the same way with texting. It took people having a phone that was easy to type on for it to catch on. She'd had a BlackBerry for a couple of years, and was very proud of the Canadian technology's success, but these days she texted everyone from her iPhone.

The kids laughed some days that it was weird to be introduced to technology by their mother, given how "old" she was. Some days she felt every day of her forty years. Other days, she felt as young as the girl who had taken the leap of faith and moved halfway around the world for a year.

One frigid January evening, Fiona pulled out an old photo album from the eighties and took a trip down memory lane. She'd heard a story about İstanbul on the news that day and realized it had been years now since she'd heard from any of her friends there, or from Hayley. She had been so caught up in the craziness of raising her children that she hadn't even noticed those friendships go quiet. It was a shame, really, she thought. Those girls had been such good friends during a life-changing year and they really had thought they'd be in each other's lives forever.

Savouring a glass of wine, she leafed through the pages, stopping to smile at pictures that brought back memories: a birthday party, a picnic in Belgrad Forest, vistas from Çamlıca Hill, a gaggle of uniformed girls at the back of the schoolyard, a concert, her host sisters, the Bosphorus ferries. She wished there were more photos. Today, her brand-new phone could hold hundreds and hundreds, but film and processing had been expensive back then, so everyone took fewer photos. Still, each one evoked fond remembrances of the time she'd spent with Nazlı, Aylin, and Yeşim. She wondered what they were doing now.

She stopped for a moment when she came across one of her few photos of Metin. He was on a boat and she remembered a day trip they'd taken up the Bosphorus Strait just before she'd come home. Good memories. He'd published a third book recently, and when

Fiona read a review of it, she ordered a copy and was impressed with his observations. Metin had been an important part of that year and she hoped that he had found happiness.

Turning the page, she found pictures of the five girlfriends in front of tulip gardens and then of Ceylan *abla*'s engagement, her *kına gecesi*, and the wedding. That had been a really special time and Fiona was still very glad she'd stayed the extra few weeks to be part of it.

Scrolling through Facebook later that evening, she was suddenly inspired to start searching for her lost friends. Why hadn't she hadn't done it before, she wondered. First, she tried Aylin and then Nazlı. No luck. But when she searched for Yeşim, she hit gold. Quickly hitting the "Add friend" button, she then sent a quick note in Messenger.

> *Merhaba,* Yeşim! Hello from Canada. I hope you are well. I would love to reconnect with you and the others. With much love, Fiona.

When Fiona woke up in the morning, she was delighted to see that Yeşim had replied already.

> *Merhaba* Fiona'cığım, I am so happy to hear from you. I was sad when we lost touch. I will try and connect you with Nazlı and Aylin too. We have many years to catch up on!

Before the end of the day, Fiona found a friend request from Nazlı.

> Fiona, *canım arkadaşım!* I am so happy to find you. I missed you. Please tell me all your news and I will share mine. *Öperim!* Kisses!

Over the next few months, she caught up on her friends' lives. Nazlı had a great career:

> I think you will remember I studied Engineering. Since then, I worked for several engineering firms, designing bridges. Last year, I won a promotion to manage the whole team. I love my job, even when it is stressful. I do yoga too and meditation and I live in Çukurcuma. Do you remember where that is? I didn't marry with anyone, but my boyfriend is an engineer too. His name is Berk.

Yeşim was no slouch either.

> I'm an assistant chemistry professor now and love every second of it. Mehmet and I adopted two children after trying for too many years to have our own. Melek is seven already and Kaan is nine. We are living in Beşiktaş. Mehmet is a consultant for a global insurance company and he travels in Europe a lot. We take the kids when we can. Melek loves languages and she is already learning some English, French, and Italian! Kaan doesn't care. He is more interested in the language of mathematics.

Aylin was married, they told Fiona, as their messages flew back and forth across time zones, and she was still in Australia. She'd drifted away many years ago and they didn't hear from her often, but they did know her parents had sadly passed away several years ago in the terrible earthquake of 1999, and she hadn't come back to İstanbul since. Fiona was disappointed, but understood too well how life could overwhelm you to the point of not being able to keep up old friendships. She was thrilled when Aylin accepted her friend request six months later.

> Hello, Fiona, from down under! Great to hear from you. Yeşim and Aylin told me about your husband passing — I know it

was a long time ago now, but I'm still so sorry to hear that. Hope life is treating you well now. I'm very busy with a business my husband, Oliver, and I run, plus my day job, but I'm happy. Not on Facebook very often but so glad to reconnect with you. *Öperim!* (Hope you remember some Turkish!)

It wasn't long before Fiona found Hayley as well. She had her work cut out for her because Jones was such a common surname and she couldn't remember where Hayley had gone to college or what her husband's surname was. But putting her research skills to work, she found the right woman.

Hayley! Greetings from Canada. I can't believe I've found you after all these years. I'd love to reconnect. Tell me everything! Husband? Kids? Job?

Fiona! Is it really you? Wow! It's been how many years? Better we don't count, I think! Brad and I have we have two beautiful boys. Tom is 7 and Jack is 10 already! We moved to Arizona (so hello from the sunny south!) many years ago for Brad's job. I'm a stereotypical "happy housewife" now, taking care of my guys. And I truly am very happy. Tell me all about your life! Your kids must be so big now. How are you and Sam? Are you working or at home? I'm full of questions! Write back soon!!!

Fiona wrote back to Hayley quickly.

Hi Hayley. So glad to hear your news. Two boys, eh? Busy household! Yes, my crew is getting older. I have — gulp — 4 teenagers. Holly is 17 and looking at universities. Jamie just turned 15 and the twins are 14. My business is doing really well and I'm really happy with my client portfolio. I get to help really good businesses tell their stories to their customers. I do have some sad news to share, though. Sam passed away

seven years ago. A sudden heart attack — he had an under-
lying heart condition nobody knew about. It was crushing
at the time, but we survived, thanks to the help of a lot of
friends and some amazing support from Sam's brother, Ben,
and his husband, Max. And life's been good generally. Have
you been back to İstanbul ever? I can connect you with Nazlı
and Yeşim. Aylin too, but she's in Australia and hardly ever
on Facebook.

Sitting in her kitchen, sipping her morning coffee, Hayley was
stunned to read Fiona's news. She couldn't imagine losing her
husband and raising her boys on her own. It took her a while to
compose a message back to her old friend.

OMG. Fiona, so sorry to hear about Sam. I had no idea. Can't
imagine how hard that must have been. And with four kids!!!
I can hardly manage two.

No, I haven't been back to İstanbul. Such a fun year, wasn't
it? Nice memory from a long time ago. Would love to reconnect with our 3 musketeers.

Brad travels a fair amount for business. If he gets up to
Toronto — or even Chicago or New York — in coming
months, I'll message you. Maybe we could reconnect
in person!

On the twins' sixteenth birthday, Fiona took stock of her family.

Holly had started in a nursing program in the fall and was just
about to head into final exams. Fiona had found it difficult to let
her daughter go, but she knew Holly was doing well. She was still
dancing. Like her mother, she was petite — shorter than most of
the dancers, in fact, at just five feet, two inches. She'd given up

hoping for another inch or two several years ago. She often wore her long hair pulled back in a dancer's bun. Her brilliant smile was one of her best features — the crooked teeth had long since been straightened. She and Jamie still fought like cats and dogs, but these days it was all in jest.

Jamie towered above them. He looked so much like Sam, but Fiona reminded him on occasion that he was taller now than his father had been, matching his Uncle Ben inch for inch. He loved spending time in the shop and couldn't wait to be done with high school so he could go to college in another year and focus on what he really wanted to do. Fiona had received several lovely pieces he had made for Christmases and birthdays. She was so proud of him. For his part, Jamie didn't love that his mother dated occasionally. Especially now Holly was away, he had taken on the role of protector.

Fiona had always thought that Simon's curly ginger hair, grey eyes, and ruddy complexion made him look like an imp, but in fact, he had always been her quiet, sensitive one. Where Jamie resembled Sam physically, Simon's personality reminded her of him. Wildly book smart and serious, Fiona thought he might go on to study economics like Sam had or perhaps go to law school like his uncle. He'd never be a tall man, but at five foot, nine inches like his dad, he wasn't short either. Simon was wiry and strong with a brilliant smile. He played a mean soccer game.

Daisy was the one who had both her mother and father in her, Fiona thought. She wore her red curly hair long, and with brown eyes, alabaster skin, and a sprinkling of freckles, looked like she had stepped off the pages of an advertisement for Ireland. Daisy was only five foot one — an inch more than her mother — with a slender frame. People tended to treat her as if she were a china doll. Once they got to know her, though, they saw her quiet determined strength and bright mind. Daisy was her artistic one, painting beautiful pictures with watercolours and oils.

Fiona decided to make another attempt at dating. Mila had been wanting to set her up with a divorced father who sang in her choir for some time. His name was Andries, Mila told her, and he had two children of his own who he parented full time. And he was late. Fiona tapped her fingers impatiently on the coffee shop table. After five minutes she got herself some café au lait and pulled out a book to read. Another five minutes passed and she heard the bell on the door tinkle as a handsome man walked in. He was blond, with blue eyes and a slightly greying beard. This must be the guy. She closed her book and put a smile on her face.

"Fiona?" She nodded. "I'm Andries Janssen." Mila hadn't mentioned that Andries was from Holland. Fiona smiled at the slight accent.

"Pleased to meet you, Andries. I'm afraid I started without you," she said, lifting her cup.

"I am so sorry I'm late," he apologized. "Let me get a coffee and then I'll explain. Do you want anything else? More coffee? Pastry?" Fiona shook her head, but kept her gaze on the handsome man as he quickly ordered his drink.

"Let me apologize again, Fiona," Andries said as he sat down. "It's been quite a day!" Fiona smiled, mildly amused, knowing that she'd had plenty of those days too. He explained that his children, aged ten and twelve, had chosen today to try and make bread. "I'm just starting to leave them alone for a couple of hours at a time, but the kitchen was a disaster, with flour everywhere. I needed to get it cleaned up and make sure they knew the dough had to rise — not be baked — while I was out. And so now I'm here, meeting a beautiful, composed woman, while I am a complete mess. And now," he said dejectedly, "I'm talking too much."

Fiona laughed. "Don't worry, Andries. I know a few things about chaos at home. I have four of my own. They're a little older than yours, but I have certainly been there!"

He suddenly looked at ease. "Okay, can we start again then?" She smiled and nodded. He took a breath and held out his hand. "Hello, Fiona, I'm Andries. Pleased to meet you."

"Likewise," she said, playing along.

"So how do you know Mila?" he asked, and she explained the story of their daughters introducing them on the kindergarten playground.

"And you?" she asked. "You sing in her choir, right? Tenor or bass?"

Andries cleared his throat and pitched his voice low. "Bass, my dear. I'm most definitely a bass. Do you sing?"

"Only in the shower these days, I'm afraid. Mila has been trying to get me to sing with her for years. Maybe it's time. I did sing second soprano in my university's chamber choir."

Fiona and Andries chatted for an hour in the coffee shop and then he asked if she'd like to walk for a bit. "I'd love that," Fiona said enthusiastically. She was really enjoying Andries' company.

"Do you like old movies?" he asked her.

"Love them, why?"

"There's a retrospective series playing at the independent theatre. I wondered if you'd like to go with me on Saturday. We could have dinner afterwards to discuss." He looked at his watch and shook his head. "Unfortunately, I need to head back home to deal with the bread dough. Kids!"

She met him on Saturday at the theatre. "How was the bread?" she asked, giving him a quick kiss on the cheek.

"Surprisingly good," he answered, impressed that she'd remembered. He bought two tickets to today's feature. *Breakfast at Tiffany's* was one of Fiona's favourite films, and she loved to see it on the big screen. Over dinner, they discussed Audrey Hepburn's performance and other films she'd gone on to do. Conversation flowed easily and it wasn't long before they were the only couple left in the restaurant.

Andries drove Fiona home and walked her to her door. "I had a lovely time, Andries," Fiona said as she unlocked the front door. She turned back to face him and Andries gave her a gentle kiss.

They went on several more dates, but Fiona just didn't feel a spark and gently let him down as they finished another lovely evening. "I'm sorry, Andries. You're a lovely man, but I think we're better off as friends."

The smile slid off his face. "I can't say I'm not disappointed, but I respect your decision. Maybe I'll see you again if you ever join Mila's choir." Andries gave her a kiss on the cheek. "Goodbye, Fiona."

Chapter 17

Fiona had been trading messages and emails with Yeşim and Nazlı for two years and recently had been thinking a lot about her exchange. She could tell when she reread her journals from the time, that she had romantic idealized memories of the city. The notebooks she'd written in reminded her of some of the more difficult moments she'd had, but also some of the highlights she'd completely forgotten. She was curious. What would the city be like this many years later? And when she realized she would have the summer alone — the first in twenty years — with all her kids working at the sleep-away camp they'd attended as campers, she decided to indulge that curiosity.

"Are you sure, Mum?" asked Jamie. The kids were surprised, but curious about the trip she was planning.

"Is it safe there?" Simon was clearly concerned as well. Fiona had never really talked about her year in İstanbul, but they did know she'd reconnected with some women she'd been close to in recent years. She assured him it was, and conversation turned back to their camp preparations.

Excitedly, Fiona messaged Nazlı and Yeşim who were both thrilled to hear she was coming to visit. They both wanted her to stay with them, but she gently turned their invitations down, preferring to be on her own, although she told them both she expected to see lots of them. After much online searching, Fiona settled on a little boutique hotel in Sultanahmet, the historic peninsula. She did that partly because she wanted to spend some time visiting the sites with adult eyes and partly because she knew that she could make do with English there if her Turkish turned out to be completely gone. She'd had nobody to practise with for close to twenty-five years.

Reserving the first couple of days for exploring on her own, Fiona found today's İstanbul very different from the one she remembered. They had built a huge infrastructure of trams, trains, and somehow, even subways in her absence. There was a second bridge now across the Bosphorus and a third being built. They were even building a tunnel under the strait. All this while Toronto had been arguing non-stop about whether to build a subway extension or a light rail line. It was amazing. Fiona had taken a quick trip on the ferry to see if she remembered Kadıköy any better, but it too, had changed immensely and she had trouble even finding her school.

Nazlı was busy at work during the weekdays, but Yeşim wasn't teaching in the summer, so they made plans first. As Fiona crossed the Bosphorus again on her third day, she turned her face up to the warm summer sun and closed her eyes. İstanbul sounded the same to her. It even smelled the same. But when she opened her eyes, she hardly recognized it. At least the ferry hadn't changed.

Yeşim was waiting at the ferry terminal, after visiting her mother who still lived in Kadıköy, and the two women hugged fiercely. "*Hoş geldin, canım!*" Yeşim said in welcome when they finally pulled apart. She kissed Fiona's cheeks. "I can't believe you are here."

"*Hoş bulduk*, Yeşim." Fiona smiled as the reply to the welcome came easily on her tongue. "I can't believe it either." The women hooked arms and walked up the street to a *çay bahçe* with a spectacular view of the water, and fell into the easy conversation of old friends. Fiona almost asked about Metin but decided against it. Yeşim didn't bring up his name either.

Fiona met with Nazlı the next day in the busy Zincirlikuyu area and she was amazed at the outstanding success her old seatmate was enjoying in her career. "But I am not sure I love it anymore," Nazlı admitted to Fiona. "I am thinking about a big change." Fiona was intrigued, but Nazlı wasn't sharing just yet.

While Fiona walked down memory lane for the week she was in the city, her friends planned a great night out, that would include both Mehmet and Nazlı's newest boyfriend.

On her last evening, they gathered for *rakı-balık* at a well-known eatery in Ortaköy. The waiter put ice into their glasses, and then poured in the *rakı*, a licorice-flavoured drink that served Turkey's national liquor. Finally, he added the cold water and Fiona watched it turn white. She remembered that some people called it lion's milk. There was hearty debate about their fish order — the *balık* part of the equation. Fiona relied heavily on her friends and they did not steer her wrong with their recommendations.

It was a magnificent evening with old friends. She was embarrassed that the evening had to be mostly in English for her, but all of them used the language in their work, and so were even more fluent than they had been when they were teenagers. She had debated asking Mehmet about Metin, but this evening was about today, so she decided to leave the past in the past.

Flying home the following afternoon, laden with boxes of baklava and *lokum* that had been pressed on her the night before, Fiona was surprised to find herself musing about when she could go back again. Despite its changes, İstanbul was still a magical city to her and the idea of spending more time near the Bosphorus was appealing. She had done a little bit of work while she was away and there seemed to be no reason why she couldn't rent a small place for a time and work while she was there. It was an intriguing thought.

She mentioned it to Rachael, Mila, and Hyun when she had them over to help her eat the baklava. Fiona even made them Turkish coffee to go with it. She'd brought home a pretty hammered brass *cezve* to make it in, just like her *abla* had on her engagement night.

"This is so good," exclaimed Rachael, popping another piece of *lokum* into her mouth. "If this is what Turkey is about, I'm in!" she joked.

Mila was a little more skeptical, peppering her with questions about whether she'd be able to work if she spent more time there, and what her children would think. Hyun, always able to bridge both sides, brought up some pros and cons. She thought spending time in a city Fiona clearly loved could be really interesting. "We might just have to come and visit," she laughed.

"Well," sighed Fiona, "it's just a dream. It will probably never happen." She turned her attention back to the baklava. "And besides, if I had this in front of me every day, I'd turn into a blimp!"

Fiona quickly got swept away by work and family obligations, including getting both Holly and Jamie off to college and university and the twins to their last year of high school, but she stayed in touch with Nazlı and Yeşim. They had rekindled old friendships in the brief time with them and Fiona was determined to keep them alive this time. She heard from Aylin occasionally, and had told her about her trip. She couldn't understand why Aylin hadn't been home to visit.

There was exciting news from Holly late in the year. She had been madly in love for some time now with a young doctor who she had met during her nursing placement. Greg was a great young man and Fiona had been impressed with how he treated her eldest daughter when they had met. Greg had proposed over the Christmas holidays and they were considering a small wedding in a year's time, a few months before she graduated. Fiona could hardly complain. She and Sam had been married at the same time of their university years.

Six months after she came home, Nazlı shared the changes she was making.

Merhaba Fiona'cığım,

Remember that big change I talked about? I am finally ready to say. I am opening a little yoga studio in Cihangir neighbourhood. I am very excited. I have just rented the space. There are some changes to make, but I hope by this summer that I can open Nefes Yoga for customers. If it is successful, in January, I will leave my job and do this full time.

Fiona wrote back quickly, congratulating Nazlı for the bold move and wishing her luck. She liked the idea of spending enough time back in İstanbul to have a regular yoga practice. But she put the thought out of her head quickly, and dived back into the latest white paper she was helping her client write.

Simon and Daisy were off to university in the fall. Simon was studying pre-law and Daisy had chosen fine arts. Fiona was officially an empty nester.

There was a magical wintery wedding in December. Fiona found herself dabbing at her eyes as her Holly and Greg recited their wedding vows, and she thought about her own winter wedding, so long ago. She and Sam would have been married for more than twenty years if he hadn't died so young.

Holly graduated from nursing school the next spring. Fiona sat in the audience beside Greg and they cheered her as she crossed the stage. The following week, she would start work at the same Toronto hospital Greg worked at. How young she seemed, and yet, Fiona realized that Holly's timeline so far was a repeat of hers. She met her husband at university, and married before school was done.

Fiona had just booked a second trip to İstanbul early in the fall. Nazlı helped her find a tiny flat in hilly Cihangir, quite close to her new yoga studio. The flat itself wasn't glamorous, but the entire front was windows and she would be able to see up and down the Bosphorus for miles. The plan was to pack her laptop, her yoga mat, and her leftover Turkish lira, and spend two glorious weeks in the city. She had just finished booking the plane ticket when her phone buzzed with a message from Holly.

Mum, got a minute to chat?

Sure, what's up?

Fiona's phone rang. "Hi, Holly."

"Hi, Mum. Are you sitting down?" Holly kept on going, not waiting for an answer. "I have news to share. Greg and I have kind of, umm, done what you and Dad did. I'm pregnant!"

There was silence while Fiona processed and Holly held her breath, but Fiona was excited for her. "Congratulations, Holly, that's wonderful! I imagine it's earlier than you expected, but I've never been sorry I had you kids when I was young."

Holly exhaled with relief. "Oh, I'm so glad you aren't angry. Greg's parents may not be quite so understanding, but we're excited. I'm due early in January."

"Don't worry about his parents. I'm sure they'll come around. They're reasonable people. More importantly, how are you feeling?"

"Pretty rough, actually. The morning sickness has been wicked. What were your pregnancies like, Mum? I don't remember ever hearing you talk about them."

"Actually, I had really easy pregnancies with you and Jamie. I didn't have bad morning sickness until the twins. Holly, you don't suppose . . ."

Sure enough, when Holly had her first ultrasound, it showed she was carrying twins and her due date was revised to mid-December.

Fiona almost cancelled her trip, but she realized September was a safe time for her to be away. Although she wanted to be there every step of the way for her daughter, missing two weeks at that stage of Holly's pregnancy wouldn't be the end of the world.

Nazlı had found her the perfect flat, Fiona decided. The view was as spectacular as promised and provided a nice respite for her feet when she'd overdone it, walking too far some days. When that happened, she made a glass of tea, picked up her sketch pad, and tried to recreate on paper the magic she saw in front of her. Most of the time, though, Fiona spent rediscovering the neighbourhoods further up the Bosphorus where the views were just as spectacular, but more authentic. With more time, she also took a ferry for a day trip out to the Princes Islands. There was still no motor traffic allowed and it was a relaxing way to spend the day. Fiona spent hours wandering around and enjoying the old wooden houses and the quiet roads to walk on.

Of course, Fiona had to check out Nazlı's yoga studio, and she was hooked, coming back several times during her stay. One evening, after a class, they sat together at the little café beside her studio. It was a little shabby, but the food was good and the elderly owners were lovely. "You've done such a great job with the studio," Fiona gushed. "I love the atmosphere, and your teachers are great, just like you. The little shop in the lobby was a stroke of genius," she added, referring to the small corner where Nazlı was selling yoga mats, singing bowls, crystals, and other items.

"I'm very proud," she admitted. "Even if I have no boyfriend now, the studio is doing well. I just wish I could reach the foreigners that live near here or who come for a few months to stay. I think there's an opportunity there but . . ." Nazlı trailed off.

"Oh, I bet you're right. Let me think on it for you," Fiona offered. "I'm your target customer. I might have some ideas." She loved the idea of helping Nazlı, whose eyes had lit up with Fiona's suggestion.

Fiona met Yeşim's children. Now teenagers, Melek and Kaan were very polite and eagerly accepted the gifts of maple sugar candy that she had brought with her. Kaan, unsure of his English was quiet, but Melek talked with Fiona for a long time about Canada.

On the plane ride home, after she'd typed up her marketing ideas for Nazlı, Fiona spent a long time thinking about how her friend had changed her life and how maybe it was time for her to shake things up herself.

Back in Toronto, she regaled her friends and family with stories of her trip while introducing them to the licorice flavour of *rakı*, which she served with melon and prosciutto. She showed them photo after photo of the city, and her walk down memory lane.

"You really love it there, don't you?" mused Hyun.

"I do. It's hard to explain, but it's like the city has a grasp on me and keeps whispering in my ear."

Christmas was magical that year. Holly and Greg's babies proved impatient and Jenna and Jonathan arrived early in the month, making Fiona a grandmother two weeks before her forty-fifth birthday.

"I have an announcement to make," Fiona said as she brought cups of coffee and tea to the table on Christmas Day. They'd all stuffed themselves, and thankfully the twins were sleeping. "I've decided to sell the house."

"What?!" The noise level rose as all four of her children started to question her.

"I've been thinking about it for a while. You guys are all grown up now. Holly's married and Jamie will be finished school next year. Simon and Daisy, you two are both away at school and you'll be done soon too. This place is too big for me on my own. I'm rattling around in here."

"But where will you go, Mum?" Daisy worried.

"I'm going to renovate the lake house. Hold on, hold on," she said, seeing the looks of incredulity on their faces. "I've always loved it up there and the views are inspiring. With internet connections being what they are these days, I can work from there easily. And before you all get concerned you'll never see me, I'm going to buy a condo in the city too and spend a good part of my time there. I'll need to come in for work — and for fun — and it will be there for you guys when you need it too."

"Wow, Mum, that's a huge change," Simon said. "You're sure?"

She was. She'd done a lot of thinking about this over the past six months, and had already drawn up plans for the renovations with a local contractor. They were starting right away in January.

"Good for you. We're behind you all the way, right, Jamie?" Holly kicked her brother under the table. He yelped, but added his agreement.

The Toronto real estate market always moved fast, and the house sold quickly. Fiona put much of her furniture into storage and moved into a condo in March, while she waited for the renovations at the lake to be finished.

She had a local contractor replace a piece of moulding that she'd measured her kids' growth on. She was planning to install it at the lake. There were tearful goodbyes in the neighbourhood. She'd miss having Rachael right across the street and Hyun around the corner, but they'd promised to get together often.

Fiona found that she loved her new little nest, high above the city. She had found a real jewel with windows on two sides, overlooking both Lake Ontario to the south and the Rouge Valley, the largest urban park in North America, to the east. The front room had a gas fireplace and room for a dining table. It had a small, but well-appointed kitchen where Fiona could putter and cook. Two large bedrooms meant she could have guests. She turned the third smaller bedroom with a view into her study.

The renovations were finished at the lake just in time for summer. She had expanded her childhood home wisely, so there was room for everyone. There were four big bedrooms upstairs and a sitting area with a huge window overlooking the lake. Fiona installed a tiny breakfast nook upstairs as well, with a bar fridge and sink, a coffee maker and a microwave, with an eye to the future. She lived on the open concept main floor, where she'd designed her dream kitchen, complete with a farmhouse sink, painted cabinets, and walk-in pantry. The massive living room with the original stone fireplace had a new wall of windows out to the lake and a cozy corner for reading or playing checkers. Beside her bedroom, she had tucked a small study where she worked.

The garage was rebuilt to hold all the lake toys and her car when she was there. Fiona added space above the garage for a self-contained suite. She'd originally been thinking about Ben and Max, when she'd asked for it, but it now seemed perfect for Holly, Greg, and the babies.

She moved up the furniture she had put in storage and had everything in order just in time to host a family gathering to celebrate Jamie's graduation. He'd followed the talent and passion that Max had recognized in him and had proudly joined him at his workshop as soon as school had finished. Fiona felt she owed such a debt of gratitude to Max, for having helped Jamie through the tough years.

Fiona and Hayley continued to chat over Facebook, and they managed a quick whirlwind visit just as Fiona started to feel the pull of İstanbul again. Fiona had client commitments, but couldn't resist going to Chicago for the day when Hayley messaged to say she was going with her husband on a business trip. Fiona hopped on a plane and met her old friend in the lobby at her hotel on the Magnificent Mile. The two women took each other in.

Hayley's hair was a shorter now, but still blonde — blonder, perhaps — thanks to a great stylist. Artfully applied blush, eye shadow, and lipstick gave her face a young look, but so many years in sunny Arizona showed in the beginnings of dark spots on her hands, betraying her true age. Like many women approaching fifty, Hayley was a bit thicker through the middle, but was fashionably dressed in dark chinos, a bright peach blouse, and jean jacket well cut to make the best of her figure. Fiona noticed her Louis Vuitton bag, straight from the pages of *Vogue*. Hayley's husband did well for himself.

Hayley looked at Fiona's wavy copper-coloured hair with some degree of envy. It hadn't faded in all these years. Fiona wore just a little makeup, but there were a few laugh lines that showed a life well lived. She was still tiny, but with a few more curves than Hayley remembered. They suited her, and she thought Fiona looked fantastic in flats, a denim skirt, warm tights, and a simple blue and green top, under her winter coat.

They shared news of their families while they walked up and down Fisherman's Wharf on the shore of Lake Michigan. When Tom and Jack weren't eating her out of house and home — teenaged boys ate a lot, she had learned — Hayley worked with a number of community organizations, raising money for disadvantaged youth. She envied Fiona's business success and Fiona thought her friend's volunteer work was commendable. When they stopped for lunch, they pulled out their phones and shared photos. Hayley still couldn't believe Fiona was a grandmother already. They led very different lives, but the bond of their exchange year drew them together again. The day was over too quickly and Fiona had a plane to catch so she could support her client's product launch just two days later. But they promised to try and get together again soon, and Fiona said she would send photos of herself, Nazlı, and Yeşim among İstanbul's spring tulips. She was headed back to Turkey in just two months' time.

Fiona wanted a different experience this time, so she rented a small flat in Beşiktaş not too far from where Yeşim and Mehmet lived. She did her exploring in the mornings, returning to the flat to work in the afternoons. Some evenings she would go to Nazlı's yoga studio. Fiona took a few cooking classes, trying to improve her skills at Turkish eggplant dishes with names as strange as "the imam fainted" and "the Sultan liked it" as well as sweets like "women's navels." As always, she spent hours walking along the Bosphorus and exploring tiny side streets. Despite the insanity of the big city, she found herself intoxicated by its excitement.

It was sobering, though, when she ventured up to Taksim one afternoon. Gezi Park had been the home to a major protest that had been big enough to make the news even in Canada. Angered about an urban development that would see a mosque built on the site of one of the city's green spaces, citizens protested with sit-ins at the park, which were met by the police with tear gas and water cannons.

Fiona had tentatively asked questions about it when she had her friends for dinner one evening. Yeşim volunteered that she had been one of the people who had helped organize a library for the protesters. Nazlı had been part of it too, bringing food and water. They had both felt it was important to stand up for what they believed in. They were proud to have been there, but both were angry with the level of violence they saw from the police. Fiona was reminded that she was very lucky to live in a "boring" country.

Just before Fiona returned to Canada, Yeşim told her she had been talked into being on their class reunion organizing committee. "Can you believe it's been almost thirty years?" she asked.

"*İnanamıyorum*. I don't believe it," Fiona replied. In some ways, high school felt like a million years ago and yet in others, it was just yesterday. "Will it be a big event?" she asked.

"Oh yes. We're already starting to make plans, and we're trying to track everyone down. It's going to be a lot of work, but I think it will be fun too."

"Well if anyone can make a huge success of it, it's you, my friend," Fiona said. She'd learned a bit about Yeşim's organizational skills over the years. "I'm sure you'll all have a great time. You'll have to say hello to so many people for me."

❦

Simon and Daisy graduated the following summer and the family celebrated at the lake. Simon was heading to law school in the fall. He figured this would be the last weekend he would have in a very long time, and he'd warned his girlfriend not to expect to see him much. Leah was taking it well, he thought. Daisy had shown some of her watercolours at a small gallery with some success. She knew her art wouldn't pay the bills, at least not right away, so she had wisely taken a graphic artist job for an acclaimed Toronto creative firm that Fiona knew. She was happy to have all of her children closer at hand.

Jamie still thought working at Max's shop was the best job ever. He'd recently bought a Portuguese water dog, a hypoallergenic breed, who loved splashing around in the lake. Rocky had introduced him to Cooper, a Welsh terrier and his pretty owner, Lauren, at the dog park. The dogs had hit it off and so had their owners. Jamie hadn't brought Lauren around to meet the family yet, but was beginning to think she might be the one. Holly and Greg's twins were in their terrible twos and Fiona thought she looked a bit ragged. Holly had gone back to work part time and as a doctor, Greg kept long hours. Fiona thought she might gently suggest they get some help. She remembered the days when Marta had been the only thing that had kept her going.

As summer faded into fall, Fiona had a bit of a lull in client work. It happened occasionally and didn't worry her. She used the time to catch up with friends and give Holly some much needed support by taking the twins for a few hours now and then. She messaged Yeşim and Nazlı from time to time as well, to keep up with their news. Yeşim was deep into reunion planning, and an idea was starting to take hold in Fiona's head. One afternoon, she messaged Hayley.

> Remember I told you Yeşim is on the organizing committee for the school reunion? I think we should go. What do you think? A fun trip down memory lane? Don't answer right away. Give it some thought. Could be loads of fun.

When Hayley hadn't answered by the next day, she added:

> Hey! No pressure. I think I'm going to go regardless. But I'd love it if you came too.

Hayley took another two days to reply. When she did, Fiona almost shrieked with excitement.

> Sorry for the delay. I thought about it a lot — then talked with Brad. Let's do it. Can only be away from him and the boys for a week, but I'm excited.

Fiona got Hayley set up with the little hotel she'd stayed at a few years before. It had been a perfect place to be reintroduced to the city. She booked her own flight a week ahead of Hayley and promised to meet her the evening she arrived. She shared the news with Yeşim and Nazlı and learned that Aylin was coming too. The whole gang would be back together.

Part 3

Chapter 18

Fiona shut the yellow taxi door firmly as she stepped out onto the curb at Hayley's hotel after lunch. As she walked up the marble steps, she saw her old friend was in the lobby, ready to go.

"*Canım*," she exclaimed, taking Hayley's hands and kissing her cheeks. "I can't wait to show you the city. You won't believe how much it's changed!"

They linked arms as they walked down the steep hill from the tourist attractions of the old city down to Eminönü, where they would catch a ferry back the other side.

"Does anything look familiar yet?" Fiona helped steer Hayley away from the tram, which was hurtling down the road.

"Absolutely nothing," admitted Hayley. "The city sounds the same, but everything has changed!"

A few minutes later, they walked by the gates to Gülhane Park. "Let's pop in here for a bit," suggested Fiona, even though it was busy on a Saturday afternoon. "Do you remember sitting on the park benches with Nazlı, Aylin, and Yeşim? We came here a few times when we did some of the tourist things."

Wandering through the gardens, Hayley did find fragments of memories coming back, but it wasn't until they finally reached the bottom of the hill and she saw Yeni Camii and the ferry docks that she finally started to feel her "İstanbul feet" back under her.

Fiona passed her *İstanbulkart* over the card reader and hearing it beep to indicate the ferry fare had been debited from her card, she passed through the turnstile. She handed the card to Hayley, who did the same, and before they knew it, the women were sitting on the upper deck of the ferryboat, headed across the Bosphorus to Kadıköy.

"*Çay?*" asked Fiona.

Hayley laughed. "I'd almost forgotten the constant tea. Yes, please."

Fiona left Hayley to gaze out over the sea while she went in search of the hot drink. Returning with two steaming paper cups, she handed one to her friend. "Oh, they don't do it in glasses anymore?" Hayley asked sadly.

"Sometimes," Fiona said, "but not always. I haven't figured it out yet. But it's not quite the same, is it?"

Fiona had a surprise for Hayley. She'd told her they would meander down old streets and stop in at some of their old haunts. What she hadn't said was that she'd arranged for Yeşim to meet them in front of their school. Because Yeşim was on the reunion organizing committee, she had special access to the grounds and she was going to take them to their classroom for a pre-reunion tour. She was also using it as her final visit before the event the next day. Once she made sure everything was set, she'd meet Hayley and Fiona and show them around.

Fiona was actually relieved to be getting this preview. She'd become more emotional as she'd aged, and she expected the reunion would bring back a rush of memories that she wouldn't be able to process fast enough. The last thing anyone needed was an almost fifty-year-old foreigner blubbering about an exchange year in the middle of their reunion.

Hayley and Fiona finished their tea, chatting about their children. As the ferry passed by the old Haydarpaşa train station, Fiona knew they were getting close to their destination, so she grabbed Hayley's empty cup. "Be right back," she said, popping around the corner to put the paper cups in the garbage but also to text Yeşim about their arrival time.

Jumping off the ferry, Fiona led Hayley up the hill. "I can't believe how much has changed here too," Hayley said. "Nothing looks the same."

Fiona remembered feeling the same when she first started returning. But she knew Hayley would recognize something soon. They walked to Altıyol, and there, right in the middle, was a big bronze statue of a bull. It had changed locations since they were schoolgirls, but Fiona knew Hayley would remember it, and she did, taking photos of it to send back to her husband and boys.

Checking her watch, Fiona directed Hayley up one of the six roads up the hill for the ten-minute walk up to school. Yeşim saw them coming up the street and popped out from the front gates as they arrived. "*Sürpriz!*" she shouted. With an excited shriek, Hayley gave Yeşim a huge hug. Finally releasing her, Yeşim kissed Hayley on both cheeks. "It is so good to see you again," she said, and she led them into the school yard and up the steps into the school.

Memories flooded back for both Hayley and Fiona. Memories of that first nervous day walking through the halls following the clicking of Ayşe *hanım*'s heels. Memories of carving watermelons at Hallowe'en and singing carols at lunchtime in December. Memories of school uniforms. But especially memories of the friendships they'd made during that year.

Yeşim also thought back to her years at the school. As idealistic teenagers, they were sure they'd all be in each other's lives forever. That hadn't even lasted through university. She and Nazlı still saw each other occasionally, but they both led busy lives and Aylin was halfway around the world, making anything more than superficial messaging difficult. Their lives had gone in different directions.

But everyone was excited about this reunion and she was so pleased that she had reconnected with Hayley and Fiona on Facebook a few years ago and that they had made the trip back for this special occasion. She took them to their classroom, to the canteen, and down to the end of the garden.

"They filled in the sea a few years ago," she explained, as Hayley stood open-jawed, looking at the busy bicycle and walking path down at the level of the water that hadn't been there before. "As you can see it is very popular on weekends."

Hayley leaned on the wall, remembering how she'd held court back there, flirting with the boys. She'd had so much fun that year.

Leaving Yeşim to her final preparations, they headed back to the European side of the city where they climbed the Galata Tower and walked up İstiklal Caddesi to Taksim Square. The avenue had been pedestrianized in the early 1990s and now had a historic tram running its length.

They had dinner together at a little fish restaurant Fiona had discovered, and walked back up the hill to Hayley's hotel, stopping halfway up for a quick dessert and tea. Hayley enjoyed baklava with pistachios and Fiona, looking for something a little different, ordered *kabak tatlısı*, a candied pumpkin dessert.

"I'd forgotten how hilly İstanbul is," Hayley said. "I expect my calf muscles will be screaming by tomorrow. But at least it lets me eat this." She popped the last bite of baklava into her mouth.

Chapter 19

The day of the reunion, Hayley was jolted awake early by the sound of the local *müezzin* and his call to prayer. Despite her best efforts to go back to sleep, her excitement to see her old classmates again meant she was soon up and looking for breakfast. She wondered who she'd recognize and what the boys would be like. Hayley was very much in love with Brad, but this was a chance to have a bit of harmless fun. She was glad Fiona had encouraged her to come. This morning, she was planning some sightseeing and a shopping trip to Mısır Çarşı. She remembered that the Egyptian Bazaar across the road from the ferry docks, and the tiny crowded streets behind it, had always been a cacophony of sights and smells.

Yeşim was up early as well. She kissed Mehmet goodbye and was at the school at ten o'clock, a full three hours before the main event. He would join them later, but for now, there were final decorations to hang, a sound system to check, a last-minute rehearsal for the formal presentations, and displays to set up in the lobby. It was going to be a long day. A lot of fun, but a long day.

Nazlı rolled up her yoga mat. She'd taken the day off from the studio, but still liked to do her morning practice. She showered and dressed before running some errands and dropping some donations she'd collected at the studio for Syrian refugees. There had been a huge influx in the last five years. Nazlı felt so blessed to have had a good engineering career and then to have built her yoga studio into a successful business. She liked to find ways to give back, and this filled that desire.

Aylin paced the living room of her rented flat in Caddebostan, close to, but not in, her old neighbourhood. There were too many sad memories there. Aylin was a bundle of nerves and was beginning to wonder why she'd come. Through carefully curated Facebook posts and messages, it had been easy to gloss over the hard parts of life. Nobody here — not even Nazlı and Yeşim — knew how difficult her last few years had been. Everyone at the reunion was going to ask her about her life in Australia and she would have to tell them something. She didn't have many hours left to figure out what that would be.

For Fiona, the day started a little later, which was unusual for her. She'd had a moment of inspiration the night before and had stayed up late working. She'd partnered with this particular client for several years and always enjoyed it when they collaborated. This project particularly appealed to her because it let her use her marketing skills in a storytelling capacity. It was her favourite kind of work. But today, work could wait, because it was reunion day. She was excited about seeing some of her former classmates, but especially Aylin. Fiona couldn't wait to see her again. Padding around her flat in a pretty dressing gown and bare feet, Fiona filled the bottom of her *çaydanlık* with water to make tea.

☙

Hayley looked for Fiona as she got off the ferry and they walked up to their old *lise* together. There were already people at the school gates when they arrived, so they joined the lineup to get their name tags and sign in. They waved to Yeşim, who was overseeing the volunteers, while she waited for them. She quickly ushered them in.

"Quick, before it gets too busy, we have to take a photo. Aylin and Nazlı are just over there," she said, pointing to a section of tables to the left. Hayley ran over to give Nazlı a huge hug, while Fiona and Aylin kissed.

"Aylin'*çiğim*," she said, taking in her friend. "Look at you. You look fantastic. And I love your hair!"

Aylin ran a self-conscious hand through her short curly hair, now silver and glittering in the sun. "Fiona. My dear, dear Fiona. It is so good to see you." She reached out her hand to squeeze Hayley's. "And you too, Hayley." Her English had become coloured with a faint Australian accent, making Fiona and Hayley smile.

They gathered together, arms around each other, as a volunteer took their photo.

"Yeşim, back to work," Nazlı said. "I'll take care of our *misafirler*."

"Guests?" Fiona raised an eyebrow. "Nazlı, we're hardly guests." But she was cut off as another old classmate came running up to Aylin and pulled her aside.

What a great day this has been, Fiona thought. Yeşim and the organizing committee had done a super job and it had gone off without a hitch. From decorations to food and from displays to presentations, everything had been wonderful. And it had been so good to connect with some other classmates as well. Nazlı had played host to them as promised and she made sure that people knew they were there. Just like slipping into old skins, Hayley and Fiona became the girls they had been way back when.

Aylin had faced her fears and had enjoyed the afternoon. It hadn't been as humiliating as she'd feared. She wasn't the only one with a failed marriage, and she'd found empathy with old classmates who also had seen some business difficulties. She hadn't heard this much Turkish in years and she found it surprisingly comforting as the familiar melody of the language washed over her. She moved in and out of conversations with ease and reconnected with many of her classmates.

Metin had arrived a little late, slipping into the school grounds after the presentations had already begun. He'd been at his sister's flat for lunch and afterwards lost track of time playing backgammon with his nephew Yusuf, generously letting the eleven-year-old boy win. Although Metin hadn't technically been part of the graduating class, these were the friends with whom he would have finished his high school years, if he hadn't done an exchange. Halfway through the afternoon, he saw Yeşim, with clipboard in hand.

"*Tebrik ederim!*" he said, congratulating her on a successful event as he kissed her on both cheeks in greeting. They still saw each other from time to time, working at the same university, and Metin and her husband had remained friends.

"Thank you," she replied proudly. "It was a lot of work, but it was worth it. Did you see everyone you wanted to? I had several people ask if you were here. We don't see enough of you these days, my friend."

"I did, thanks. It was great to see some people who've moved away, and it's always nice to catch up with the local crowd. You're right, I've been a bit of a hermit recently, but it's always that way when I'm researching," he said a bit apologetically. "But you know that. By the way, I'm still looking for Mehmet. I wanted to ask him about lunch sometime soon. Where is that husband of yours, anyway?"

"He's around somewhere," Yeşim said. "I haven't seen him in a while. Nazlı's here of course. But did you see Aylin? I'm so pleased she came home from Australia for this — for the first time in forever."

"I'll make sure I look out for her. I'd like to say hello." He turned to leave.

"Metin?" Yeşim hesitated, not sure if she should tell him or not. "I really don't know if I should tell you, but Fiona is here too. She and Hayley both came back — the first exchange students I know of to come to a reunion."

Metin nodded, taking in the news and she couldn't read his expression. They hadn't spoken about Fiona since she married. Congratulating Yeşim again, he headed out into the crowd again. Metin enjoyed another hour reminiscing with old classmates. He found Mehmet, and they made plans. A few minutes later, he saw Aylin and they chatted about her life in Australia. But Fiona was an enigma and he didn't see her among the hundreds of students. Maybe she'd changed a lot over the years — many of them had — and he just hadn't recognized her. It would have been nice to say hello, he thought, but that was ancient history.

As he'd told Yeşim, Metin was deep in research for his next book and had a long drive planned the next day for an interview that he still had to prepare for, so he decided to head home. On his way out, he stopped in the lobby and browsed through the photo displays, smiling at the memories of their high school years together that they evoked. They had grown up a lot in the years they spent there. He even spotted some photos from that first American football game he had organized after he'd come back from Charlotte. That had been a fun day with Mehmet and everyone. He looked up, and a flash of red hair caught his eye. Suddenly, he found himself taking long strides to try and catch the woman it belonged to.

Fiona had enjoyed looking at the photos, but was now ready to take a short break from the bustling reunion. She'd kept up reasonably well in Turkish, but it took a lot of concentration in the noise and she needed a break from the hubbub, so she headed across the lobby and back out into the courtyard. She squinted in the sudden bright light. She rubbed her suddenly twitchy nose and sneezed. A second sneeze followed quickly. And then a third.

"*Çok yaşa,*" she heard from behind her.

"*Sen de gör,*" she responded, reflex kicking in, while she dug in her bag for her sunglasses.

"You know," the deep voice continued in English, with amusement, "this reminds me of the day I finally got up the courage to talk to you."

She knew that voice. It hadn't changed at all. She spun around and came face to face with its owner. Metin was a bit more solid than she remembered, time having filled out the lanky teenage frame she remembered, but he was still trim. Unlike some of their classmates, he still had a full head of hair, although the unruly curls she had loved to run her fingers through were now trimmed a little shorter and were threaded with grey. He sported laugh lines like all of them, and like many he now wore glasses. But behind them, his green eyes still sparkled and he was just as handsome as she remembered.

"Oh." Her breath caught in her throat and for a moment, the world stood still as she was transported back in time. "Metin, *nasılsın*? How have you been?"

Metin hardly heard the question. As Fiona turned around, he saw the same girl he'd known at eighteen. Time had hardly touched her. He shook his head to bring himself back to the present.

"Yeşim told me you were here, but with so many people, I didn't see you until just now," Metin explained. "I couldn't let you leave without at least saying hello."

"I'm not really leaving. I just needed a minute of quiet. But I'm glad you found me. I admit, I wasn't sure if I would see you here. So many people have come."

"It's been a fun afternoon. What made you come back? And I hear Hayley's here too?"

"She is!" Fiona wondered how much to tell him, but decided to plow ahead. "I've actually been back to İstanbul a few times after Facebook helped reconnect me with Yeşim and Nazlı. I found Hayley the same way, and convinced her to come over for this. She's only here for a week, but I'm staying a bit longer. The reunion felt like an important milestone for some reason, so we came!"

"You've been back before?" Her words caught Metin by surprise. Yeşim and Mehmet had never mentioned it. He found himself asking her out to dinner. "It would be good to catch up. It's been a lot of years."

Fiona was suddenly nervous, as waves of memories of thirty years ago came flooding back. She took a deep breath. "That would be lovely," she answered, adding, "I'm in İstanbul for a couple of months, though, so there's lots of time."

"*Gerçekten mi*? Really?" His research trip tomorrow was suddenly forgotten. "Still, I have no plans this evening — do you? You can tell me about your other visits."

Fiona hesitated. But she didn't have plans either and maybe this was exactly the right way to end reunion day. "I'd like that," she said, her own tiredness quickly put aside.

"Where are you staying?"

"Right here," Fiona said with a smile. "I have a flat right here in Moda. And you? Where do you live now?"

"Kuzguncuk," he said, mentioning a picturesque neighbourhood in Üsküdar, about twenty-five minutes away. "Hey, do you still like to walk?"

"I do, why?"

"I'm thinking about where to go for dinner. How about a little trip down memory lane? We could walk for about an hour first — stretch our legs a bit."

"Sure. I just need to say goodbye to a few people first. Can I meet you at the front gate in, say, half an hour?"

Fiona plunged back into the crowd and found Nazlı, Aylin, and Yeşim, who appeared to be making their own plans.

"*Kızlar*," she called out, walking toward them. "I just ran into Metin. He's asked me to dinner. But can we get together tomorrow while Hayley's still here? All of us."

Three sets of eyebrows shot up.

"Dinner?" Nazlı questioned, protective of her old seatmate. "Be careful — Metin may be different from what you remember."

Yeşim chimed in. "I saw him earlier — I told him you were here. I'm sure you two have lots to talk about. And we will want to know all about it tomorrow."

"*Kahve.* Three o'clock tomorrow," said Aylin emphatically, slipping into her old role as group leader and setting the plan. It felt strange after so many years. "*İyi eğlenceler*, Fiona. Have fun," she whispered as the women kissed goodbye.

Fiona looked for Hayley next. Nothing changes, she thought, finding her old friend perched on the low wall under the trees, laughing with three or four of the boys — no, men, she corrected herself — just outside the canteen. Quickly inserting herself into the conversation, she updated Hayley on her plans.

"You're okay for tonight?" she asked. "I can do this another time, if you'd rather."

"Are you kidding?" Hayley demanded. "I'm having the time of my life, right here. Besides, you two had something special back then. Go and have fun. Just text me when you know the details about tomorrow."

Fiona threw her a grateful look as she headed back to wait for Metin. She leaned up against the fence outside the school, checking her watch and breathing deeply to calm her nerves. There were a few minutes left until Metin would return. She wondered if he ever thought of her. Of course, she knew about his writing success, but was he married? Did he have children? Was he happy in his career? She suddenly had so many questions and she realized Yeşim had been stingy in passing on news of him over the years. And what had Nazlı meant by her comment?

"Hazır mısın?"

Fiona was jolted out of her reverie by Metin's question. She hadn't heard him coming. *"Evet, hazırım,"* she responded with a smile. And she was. Ready to see what Metin had planned.

"This way then," Metin said, flashing a grin and guiding her up the street.

Side by side they walked by Yoğurtçu Park and along the sea in Kalamış. This had been the way she'd walked home from school. They tentatively asked each other questions about the past thirty years, and they gave polite formal answers as they danced through the highlights of the decades.

Metin filled in the blanks for Fiona. He had finished his undergraduate degree in computer engineering, but with a growing interest in how progression in technology was affecting society, had gone on to do a master's degree in sociology. After that, he'd gone on to a two-year fellowship in London, becoming an expert in his field, widely recognized for his liberal leanings and topical insights. The Gezi Park protest of 2013 had proven to be good fodder for his last book and he was often called on to speak on panels at conferences when he wasn't lecturing at the same university where Yeşim taught.

As they reached the Kalamış marina, Metin looked at his watch. "We're a bit early for dinner. Are you up for a longer walk?"

"Sure," Fiona said, shifting her bag to her other shoulder. She could imagine where they might go next on the promised trip down memory lane.

Indeed, she was right, and as they walked up the residential streets past Metin's childhood home and the apartment she'd lived in, they continued to talk. He had married, she learned, but had divorced after seven years.

"My *baba* died about the same time and I inherited our family's old stone house in Datça. I probably never told you about it." Fiona shook her head. "Nobody had lived there since I was a child. It was a wreck, so I recovered from my broken marriage by fixing the house whenever I wasn't working." Instead of building a family he'd thrown himself into his work, writing books, and speaking across Europe and Asia.

"Do you ever regret not having children?" No matter how hard it had been sometimes, Fiona couldn't imagine not having her family.

"No, not really. I'm free to go where I want, when I want, with whom I want. It keeps me busy. Safiye and her husband, Kerem, have a son who I get to play the doting uncle when I can, like I did with Tamer's daughters when they were little. That's actually where I was earlier today. Yusuf was beating me at *tavla*!"

The wind had shifted now and a cool breeze from the sea was blowing. Metin and Fiona turned back toward Kalamış. His mother was well, she was happy to learn. Tamer ran a small export company. He too was divorced and his two girls lived in Germany with their mother. Safiye worked in marketing and Fiona found it amusing that they shared the same profession.

"Maybe I'll work with her one day," she joked.

Over dinner, Fiona told Metin about her marriage to Sam and their children. She talked about the satisfaction of building her freelance business and explained that working for herself was why she could stay in İstanbul for longer than a usual tourist trip.

"I've actually read your books," she admitted shyly. "They were very good. I have a number of high-tech clients and they turned up in my weekly industry newsletter," she explained, when Metin asked how she'd learned of them.

As the wine flowed, they became more relaxed in each other's company. Fiona told Metin how tough it had been for her right after Sam died. Metin talked more about the Datça house, where he often spent time these days. Now fully restored, it was his retreat from the madness of İstanbul whenever he needed it and one of his favourite places to write.

Fiona pulled out her blue Lucite reading glasses to see the pictures on his phone. "It looks amazing," she said, admiring the restoration.

Metin teased her about the glasses. "Finally, I see something that acknowledges the years have caught up with you. Otherwise, you haven't changed at all, you know."

"Hardly," Fiona laughed. "But thank you for the compliment."

Fiona told Metin about the summers she and the kids had spent at her lake house, surrounded by rocky land and pine trees. "Kind of like you," she said, "I spend some of my time there now and some of it in Toronto. I love the city, but there's nothing like looking at the water for inspiration. That's why I spoil myself when I come to İstanbul with a Bosphorus view flat."

The waiter came by then to ask if they wanted anything else. Making a quick decision to get tea on the way back to Moda, Metin asked for the bill. Fiona tried to pay for part of it.

"Do you remember nothing about Turkey?" he teased. "You are my guest."

Fiona graciously admitted defeat. This was a game she'd rarely been able to win with Turkish friends. And never with Metin.

Close to her flat, Metin and Fiona sat on a little patio pleasantly passing the time with several steaming glasses of *çay*. They talked about technology for a while, each enjoying the easy conversation.

What Metin didn't volunteer was his surprise that Fiona hadn't looked him up when she'd been in İstanbul before. What Fiona didn't volunteer was that she'd considered it each time, but always chickened out.

Metin walked Fiona up the four floors to the door of her flat at the end of the evening. "This was really nice," he said, as she fished around in her bag for her keys. "I'm so glad I caught you at the reunion."

Fiona agreed. "It was. I knew you were writing, but I'd always wondered about your life." And then she added boldly, looking up at him through her copper eyelashes, "If you have time, I'd love to learn more."

Metin smiled, surprised to realize how pleased he was that the conversation of the evening might continue. And then he remembered. "Damn. I'm out of town the next two days," he said. "But how about Wednesday?"

Date set, Metin kissed her on both cheeks and slipped into the night as Fiona pulled the door closed behind her.

Chapter 20

"*Anlatsana!*" Aylin demanded. The women were all eager to know how dinner had gone and wanted details.

"It was a bit strange at first," Fiona admitted as their tiny cups of Turkish coffee arrived. "We didn't quite know how to talk to each other at the beginning. But we walked for a while and then we had dinner and eventually it got easier. And by the end of the evening we were really comfortable together." Then she remembered. "What did you mean yesterday, Nazlı, about him not being what I remember?"

"He told you about his divorce? Well, Metin worked very hard after Büşra. He is very successful, you know. But I do not think he has found love since her. For a long time we saw pictures of him in newspapers at gallery openings and so on. And there were gossips. These days we don't see him so much. I don't know — he just maybe is not what you have in your memories."

"We've all grown up, Nazlı," chastised Aylin, popping the little piece of *lokum* from her saucer in her mouth. "We've all had different experiences and changed. I think Fiona understands we're all different than we were then. God knows I am. And so are you. Engineer turned yogi? Quite a difference."

"Haklısın." Nazlı nodded in agreement. "And my change is very good. I am much more happy with my studio than when I designed bridges."

Yeşim laughed. "I guess I'm the one who has changed the least. Chemistry student, chemistry professor. Married to my high school sweetheart. But I'm very content."

They'd met today for coffee on the shore in Bebek, near the university where Yeşim still taught. "Maybe my future will be different," she mused, thinking about her possible retirement when she turned fifty in two years.

"You love your life like it is," teased Nazlı.

"You're right."

"I haven't had a lot of change either," admitted Hayley. "University, marriage, children, my garden. I love my husband, and my kids but there's not a lot of excitement in my life these days. Maybe that's why I came. Hey, Nazlı," she said suddenly, an old memory popping up. "Will you tell fortunes today?"

When Nazlı nodded, Hayley put the saucer on top of her little coffee cup and flipped it over. When it was cool, Nazlı would see what futures she could see.

"Nazlı, will you do mine too?" asked Fiona.

"Remember, this is just for fun," Nazlı cautioned. "But yes, I will do them all."

Catching each other's eyes, the remaining women flipped over their cups at the same time.

Nazlı looked at the cups one by one.

"Hayley, you will travel soon. I see long life. I see flower. And I see prize. Maybe you will take a gardening prize?" Hayley laughed. It was unlikely that her skills would go that far.

"Fiona, for you, I see great love. I see water — a ferry ride maybe? I see pen. You will be writing more, I think. And I see star. That means you will have good luck.

"Dear Yeşim, I see for you a key. You will be happy at home. Are you retiring soon maybe, *canım*? I see someone leaving you soon. I guess that is Melek most probably. Does she still want to study in London? Ah, and I see you are well loved."

"Well that's not a surprise," said Hayley. "I think it's adorable that you married Mehmet and that you're both still so happy together."

Yeşim blushed. "Enough about me. Read Aylin's cup."

Nazlı's brow furrowed and then cleared again. "Aylin, for you I see dark clouds. But they are behind you. This is good. The bad times are over, I think — look at all the coffee grounds that fell out. And I see friendship — friends are . . . *şey* . . ." she searched for a word. "*Destek olmak?*" she asked.

"Support," Yeşim offered.

"Yes, support. Your friends are supporting you."

Yeşim reached for Aylin's hand and gave it a squeeze. But Nazlı wasn't done.

"There is more. I see coffee cup. I have not seen that before. I do not know what this means."

"I've stumped you, I guess," Aylin said with a sigh. "But I have to say being home feels good. Better than expected, in fact. I've missed you all so much." She reached out her other hand to Nazlı.

Thanking Nazlı, they laughed over their fortunes, and made plans for dinner at Fiona's flat before Hayley went back to America.

Chapter 21

Aylin had been facing her demons since arriving in İstanbul. Reunion day had been quite stressful for her. Always the one "most likely to," she felt like she'd disappointed everyone, with no children, a failed business, and a failed marriage to her name. No longer the free-spirited girl with big dreams, Aylin was a broken woman.

She'd come back to İstanbul, not certain if it would be the beginning of a new chapter, or just a respite from her life in Australia, but she had to admit being back in the city, despite all its changes, felt like slipping on an old cozy sweater — comfortable, familiar, and soothing.

Yeşim had been busy at the reunion, but Nazlı had noticed the pain in Aylin's eyes and had kept an eye on her even while helping Hayley and Fiona. Aylin had always been the strong one, the one with the ideas that everyone else followed. Yeşim had been the practical one. Nazlı had been the sensitive, empathetic one. It wasn't by chance that she had seen friends supporting Aylin in her coffee cup. She sensed that her old friend needed a soft place to land right now.

Before they parted after coffee, she had suggested that Aylin come and try out her yoga studio, on the pretense of comparing it to what was offered in Australia. But really, she wanted to keep her close.

Aylin loved yoga. She practised frequently in Australia, and credited it with helping her mental health — which admittedly felt a little precarious again these days. So she agreed to join Nazlı for an ashtanga class. Aylin found the routine of ashtanga freeing, her body following along with the familiar moves, stretching, twisting, and bending. And savasana at the end always calmed her frazzled nerves.

Afterwards, she sat with Nazlı on the terrace of the tiny café beside the studio sipping glasses of hot tea. Nazlı hoped the little business would survive. She'd been talking to the owners, who were ready to retire and she had her fingers crossed that someone would buy it, spruce it up, and make it a going concern.

"Thanks so much for suggesting both the yoga and tea," Aylin said quietly, after they finished their first glass, and a second had appeared. "I really needed it. Your studio is fantastic. You must be so proud."

"I am actually. Getting it started was an uphill battle, but I've loved every minute of it. My staff, the clients — everything has gone well. And being an entrepreneur is so much more fulfilling than being an engineer. But Aylin'*ciğim*, I'm worried about you. There's such sadness in your eyes. How can I help you?"

"Oh, it's nothing," Aylin started, trying to brush it off as she usually did with her Australian friends. But seeing Nazlı's sincere concern, and after the emotional release that yoga had brought, her defenses suddenly crumbled. She began to cry. Aylin opened her mouth to speak, but no words came out, and the tears kept falling.

Nazlı reached around and gathered Aylin in her arms. "You're home now," she whispered. "Everything will be all right."

When Aylin pulled herself together, her story spilled out, punctuated from time to time by tears falling from her brown almond-shaped eyes.

She told Nazlı how her marriage had fallen apart years ago and how her husband had blamed her for the multiple miscarriages she'd suffered in her thirties. He'd made her feel worthless. It had affected her self-confidence, which had in turn affected their business, and started an ongoing cycle of self-loathing.

"That's why I stopped writing to you so many years ago. I believed the things he told me about myself." There had been no physical abuse, but Aylin had slowly been cut off from her friends both in İstanbul and in Australia. It had taken her years to muster the courage to leave him.

"But, Aylin, why didn't you tell me before? I had no idea you'd gone through all this. We used to be like sisters. All I want is for you to be happy."

"I'm just so embarrassed. There were so many expectations of me when we graduated. And today? I'm such a failure." She dissolved into tears again. "Why can't I can't stop crying, Nazlı? I can't turn it off."

"Yoga will do that," Nazlı gently reminded her. "You've allowed pathways to open to your feelings. And now you're feeling things you've been hiding away. But, *canım*, you're not a failure. There is a bright future for you. I know."

Drying her eyes, Aylin took a couple of deep steadying breaths, straightened her shoulders and stood up. "Thank you, Nazlı. For the class, for the shoulder, and for the kind words. I'll be okay now. I'll let you get back to your studio. But . . . do you mind if I come again tomorrow?"

"I wouldn't have it any other way."

Nazlı called Yeşim right away.

"*Özer dilerim*," Yeşim apologized. "I was too busy on reunion day, and the past couple of days have been a whirlwind of catching up at work. But let me talk to her. If you're worried, I'm worried too."

When Aylin checked her phone later that day, she realized Nazlı must have talked to Yeşim already. She had missed several calls and there were text messages too. With a sinking heart, she knew she had to face her too. And Yeşim would expect proper answers.

Chapter 22

Metin and Fiona met at the Kadıköy ferry pier wearing sturdy walking shoes, ready to spend a few hours walking on what had started as an unusually cool morning.

"You're sure this is what you want to do?" Metin asked, as Fiona offered him a choice between the *acma* and *simit* she had picked up at the bakery beside her flat.

After several text messages while he'd been away — they'd traded numbers at dinner — Metin and Fiona settled on Wednesday's plan. Fiona wanted to walk along the old city walls.

"Mm-hmm," she confirmed, boarding the ferry with him while taking a bite of her pastry. "I've wanted to do this for a long time, but I haven't wanted to do it alone."

The seagulls followed the ferry across the Bosphorus, knowing they'd get bits of food from the passengers. Up on the top deck, Fiona's hair was whipping around in the wind and he could just see the few fine lines around the edges of her sunglasses as she gleefully tossed bits of her *acma* to the seabirds. Despite those lines, Metin thought she seemed younger than her years, enthusiastically approaching life just as she had as a teenager. Just as his body had changed, he noticed she had some new curves. Her hair hadn't changed, though, still long and fiery in colour. Throwing the last piece of his *simit* to the birds he suddenly remembered how good that hair had smelled. Wondering where that thought had come from, Metin continued watching Fiona as she stretched as far as she possibly could, toward the birds.

When the last of the bits of bread were gone, they leaned on the boat's railing. Fiona gathered her hair into a ponytail to stop it blowing around and gazed out over the Bosphorus.

"I just love riding the ferries," she sighed. "I never get tired of this view." She suddenly pointed. "Oh, Metin, look — dolphins! *Yunuslar*, right?" she asked, searching her memory for the word.

Metin nodded his head. "I admit, the ferry ride is my favourite part of my commute. I love watching the dolphins play too."

The boat docked in Eminönü and the pair made their way up the Golden Horn where they would start their walk properly. They spent a few hours walking along the old stone walls of the city. Built in the fifth century, the walls had protected Constantinople, as the city was then called, from all manner of intruders before it was finally conquered by the Ottomans in 1453. In some places the walls were gone, nature, or more recently bulldozers, reclaiming the land. In others, crumbling bits of rock and stone remained, and in still others, whole sections were still intact, and could be scrambled up to get amazing views of the city. Fiona was glad she'd brought her camera in her bag, and took lots of photos along the way.

They stopped for lunch at a small *lokanta*, a cafeteria-style restaurant where the food was delicious, cheap, and plentiful. Fiona was hungry, but choosing from the many different dishes lined up in steam trays was difficult. She finally settled on *karnı yarık*, eggplant stuffed with ground beef and Metin chose *kuru fasulye*, a white bean dish. They sat at a tiny table on the sidewalk and washed it all down with *ayran*, a refreshing yogurt drink.

"Ready for some more?" asked Metin, as he stood up. The day had become warm, and he pulled off his sweater, revealing a blue shirt.

Fiona was also taking off a layer, removing a zippered moss-green fleece and pushing the sleeves of her matching scoop-neck shirt up her arms a bit. "Absolutely," she replied, stuffing the jacket into her bag and offering to take Metin's too.

They walked for a couple more hours, peeking through gates and climbing up walls until they reached a point where there were essentially no walls left. Along the way, Metin opened up about his marriage.

"I met Büşra when I came back from my fellowship in London. She was a nice girl and she loved me. We had a comfortable relationship. After a couple of years, I think people just assumed we would get married. I was twenty-nine and she was twenty-five," he explained. "It seemed like the next logical step and I thought we were aligned on our values. But after a few years, Büşra desperately wanted a baby and I still couldn't imagine being a father — ever. She knew that, but I guess she thought she could change me. We fought. A lot. After seven years we finally called it quits." He stopped for a minute and then added quietly, "I disappointed a lot of people."

"Metin, you can't take all the blame. It takes two to make a marriage work."

"Still," he said. "It was a hard time for both our families. But Büşra remarried quickly and has two kids of her own now. She and her husband live in İzmir. I tried dating a little after that, but I was jaded and it just seemed so pointless. It was easier to focus on work. And Datça."

Stopping for a glass of *çay*, they rested their feet.

"Thank you for this," said Fiona. "I know it was an odd request. But I've had a lot of fun, and it's been nice to get to know you again too."

"My pleasure. It's always good to be reminded of the city's history, and even better with someone who appreciates it so much." He caught the attention of the waiter, who swapped out their glasses with fresh *çay* and also brought a plate of assorted *tuzlu kurabiye*.

Fiona crunched into one of the savory biscuits. "So good," she said. "I'll have to be careful, though, or I'll gain ten pounds. My metabolism is not quite what it used to be! Although I'm still looking for the perfect Turkish breakfast."

"I might be able to fix that," Metin offered on a whim, as he chose his own biscuit, covered in sesame seeds.

If someone had asked at that moment, neither Fiona nor Metin could have put their finger on it exactly, but something was starting to happen and it felt like the years were melting away. The very polite conversation of their first dinner had disappeared and the banter that they'd shared as eighteen-year-olds had returned, this time as the repartee of two mature adults with full lives, comfortable in their own skins, but who shared common interests and a rediscovered bond.

In fact, Metin had spent far more time over the past two days that he'd been away thinking about Fiona than he liked to admit. They'd only spent an evening — and now a day — together, and yet it seemed they had picked up just where they'd left off. When he'd caught up with her at the reunion, he felt the same instant attraction as when he had first seen her in the classroom all those years ago. Just five feet tall, she somehow lit up every space she was in. You couldn't miss Fiona — then or now. It was ridiculous after all these years, but he'd had a rush of feelings and he realized he wanted to explore them. But that would have to wait, he realized as he checked his phone, which had been buzzing repeatedly since they sat down.

"Fiona, do you mind terribly if I leave you at the ferry?" he asked apologetically. "I need to run into the university to deal with a small problem. I feel really bad asking, but there's no reason for you to get bogged down in academic politics."

"You've already been generous enough with your time. I can't thank you enough for today," she said, with a small pang of disappointment. "But you can leave me here. No sense in you coming back to the ferry. You can get there faster from here, can't you?"

Metin smiled, recognizing that she had a better command of the city's much expanded transportation system than he'd given her credit for. He reached for the sweater she was already taking out of her bag. "As long as you're sure. But I was serious about breakfast. I know a great place in Kuzguncuk. Can I tempt you for tomorrow morning?"

Fiona hummed to herself as she made dinner in her flat that night, thinking about the great day she'd had with Metin exploring the walls. She was experiencing new but familiar feelings for him, she realized. She felt herself letting down metaphorical walls, letting him in where few had been. And she was looking forward to breakfast more than she probably should.

Aylin had been right. When she and Yeşim met late that afternoon for *çay* following another yoga session at Nazlı's studio, there were many questions. Aylin was determined not to cry this time. Slowly, patiently, Yeşim drew out the whole story at the little café next door.

Aylin had finished her undergraduate degree in computer science, and as some of her friends started marrying, she doubled down on academics and pursued a master's degree. One of the only women in her class, she experienced a lot of harassment. To combat that, she limited her social interactions in her undergraduate years, studied every spare moment and kept to herself.

In the two years it took her to complete her masters, Aylin kept up her intense studying schedule and by then, she'd all but cut herself off from old friends and focussed solely on her work.

She wrote to Yeşim and Nazlı a couple of times a year, and she'd recently received another birth announcement from Canada. She couldn't believe that Fiona had just had twins, adding to her family so quickly. Their lives had gone very different ways.

Despite her seeming aloofness, Aylin was ambitious, and wanted to see the world. So she got a job offer from an Australian firm, including a relocation package, she jumped at it.

Life in Melbourne was exciting. Australia had a large Turkish diaspora, but Aylin had come for a new experience so she stayed away. Her job paid well, so she could afford an apartment on her own. She loved exploring the city. She took cooking classes to perfect the local cuisine and shoved all her Turkish recipes in a drawer. She took up surfing and learned how to follow cricket.

Like many Turks abroad, she found her new colleagues anglicized her name, and she quickly got used to being called Eileen. It was close, she supposed, and she was grateful she didn't have any unique Turkish letters in her name to trip people up.

Aylin's ambition fuelled her. Just as she had poured all her energy into her studies at school, in Melbourne, she poured it all into her job. She progressed quickly, rising to a management position. But she had little life outside of her job.

She met Oliver at an industry event. Four years into her career, Aylin was participating on a scholarly panel, sharing her expertise and opinions as a young professional woman in the industry. The man in the front row caught her attention when he asked a really good question. His suit, a rarity in the IT world, fit him well and his blond hair and handsome tanned face didn't hurt any either.

Oliver hung around after the panel so he could meet the beautiful woman who'd given him such an insightful answer and immediately asked her to dinner. He treated her very well, something she wasn't used to from men in the industry, and Aylin was flattered by the attention. Soon they were seeing each other regularly.

At thirty-five, Oliver was seven years older than Aylin, but they clicked. When he kissed her, it sent shivers up and down Aylin's spine. She didn't have a lot of experience with men, but everything about Oliver made her feel wonderful.

They dated for several years, and on her thirtieth birthday, he got down on one knee and proposed. The wedding was an intimate affair at city hall, just them and their closest friends. They celebrated afterwards in a small restaurant owned by Aylin's best friend, Zoe.

Oliver was her source of strength when her parents were killed. They had been visiting Aylin's aunt in İzmit when a terrible earthquake rocked northwestern Turkey. Aylin had returned home to deal with the estate, and while Oliver hadn't been able to make the trip, he helped her through the grief that followed. They agreed to wait a few years before having children and instead continued focussing on their careers and the successful side business they had started. They were a very successful couple.

When Aylin was thirty-four, it was time. They were very excited when she got pregnant just a few months later and told all their friends. Zoe helped her plan the nursery and Oliver bought a crib and rocking chair. Life was good.

When Aylin began cramping one night at eleven weeks, Oliver rushed his almost hysterical wife to the hospital. But it was too late. They lost the baby and Aylin felt as if she had lost a piece of herself along with it.

Oliver went straight back to work, but Aylin took some time to recover from the loss. She was inconsolable, spending the first few days rocking in the nursery in her dressing gown and crying. Zoe came by several times, but Aylin hardly noticed she was there. After a week, Oliver started to get frustrated with her. When she was still depressed a month after the miscarriage, he told her to grow up, and that they'd just try again. Aylin was hurt by his cold-ness, but she pulled herself together and went back to work.

It took two years for Aylin to get pregnant again — during which Oliver meticulously monitored her cycles looking for her fertile times. He became very controlling and Aylin felt claustrophobic in their relationship, but told herself he just wanted the best. Aylin was nervous this time and insisted on keeping the news to them-selves through to the end of the first trimester. Oliver thought she was being ridiculous, but he humoured her and only told his friends at the gym where he worked out three times a week.

Aylin finally felt herself starting to breathe normally again as she passed the eleven-week mark. At thirteen weeks, Aylin told her very small circle of girlfriends and colleagues at work. Everyone was thrilled for her and Oliver. Zoe's children were start-ing school now, and she started itemizing all the baby things she could pass along.

Two weeks later, Aylin woke up in the middle of the night and when she got up to go to the bathroom, saw blood running down her leg, and the dreaded familiar feeling of cramping began.

Aylin felt broken, and retreated from the world. Oliver had no patience for it. He yelled at her frequently telling her she must be doing something wrong to have had two miscarriages in a row and that she'd better get it right next time. He berated her for not being able to get out of bed and told her to be stronger.

After two months, Aylin finally emerged, but something had changed. She stopped seeing friends as it was difficult to see them with their families, and she closed herself off from colleagues, talking only about work. Even Zoe found herself on the outside. Aylin couldn't bear to see her friend or hear about her children.

Aylin dragged herself back to work and managed to stay afloat, but her efforts on their side business were affected. Oliver was never happy with her anymore, which made her feel even worse. He was always telling her how incompetent she was — at work, in the kitchen, and in the bedroom — and Aylin slipped further away. He became even more controlling, insisting that he know where she was at all times. He managed their money, giving her only enough cash every week to buy the groceries. She saw fewer of their side business clients and did more of the backroom work, by herself.

By now, she was desperate to get pregnant, hoping a child would fix what was wrong with their marriage. But despite her hopes, there were two more miscarriages in the next four years. Aylin was now forty and her doctor told her she shouldn't try again. She was crushed. She would never be a mother. And she'd failed her husband again.

Oliver was irate. He'd married her ten years ago and she couldn't even give him a child. Aylin was useless to him, he said. No children, she worked too much, she cried all the time when she was home, and she couldn't keep a house or cook a decent meal. He told her she was useless with clients and that she made more work for him because he had to double-check her work to make sure she hadn't made mistakes.

One afternoon, Aylin checked Facebook, something she rarely did because it was another source of pain, with so many people sharing happy family photos. Tears threatened to spill from her eyes as she stopped at a post from Zoe sharing photos of her two beautiful children on the beach at Christmas. She quickly scrolled by. Checking her messages, she found several from Yeşim, including one about having reconnected with Fiona, and another making sure she knew that Fiona's husband had passed away. She noticed a friend request from Fiona and accepted it, writing an upbeat message that belied her reality.

Oliver continued to rise at his company, and was now a senior director. He was smooth as silk at work, and when Aylin had to accompany him to events, he was all smiles. But when they got home, it was a barrage of all the things she'd done wrong, how she'd embarrassed him with what she'd said, what she'd done, what she'd worn. It seemed there was nothing she could do that was good enough. She had heard Oliver's cutting words for so many years that she believed them, and her self-confidence was at an all-time low. He never hit her, but he used her as a verbal punching bag, knocking her down again and again. The wounds weren't visible, but they were just as damaging. It began to show at work, and her boss had gone from encouraging counselling to all but demanding it as a condition of employment.

Somehow, Aylin held it together for five more years, walking on eggshells around her husband every day. But in 2012, drawing strength from Nazlı, who had just made a huge change in her life by opening her yoga studio, Aylin filed for divorce. Oliver fought her all the way, racking up huge lawyer's bills. But two years later, she was finally free.

Aylin had managed to keep the business. As Oliver achieved more success at work — he was a vice-president now — he had spent less time on it. Fortunately, their customers returned time and time again, so Aylin had slowly taken on more and more of the work as his distraction increased. It was clear that despite what he said, Aylin was the backbone of the company. The clients loved her and thought her work was great. But keeping the business came at a high price. Aylin had to give up her share of their house, and a summer house they had bought many years ago. But it was a price she was willing to pay because she knew the business would keep her afloat.

She messaged her friends, telling them she and Oliver had divorced, without going into the details and saw their notes of sympathy a few months later. She was free. Or so she thought.

But for the first time ever, clients began to fade away. Oliver was well-known in the industry and Aylin was sure he was bad-mouthing her and her work. She scrambled, but it proved almost impossible to get new clients to replace the old ones. Even after the divorce, Oliver was still controlling her life. By Christmas of 2015, she made the difficult decision to close the doors.

And then just three months ago, Aylin was let go from her company. There was a handsome severance package, but it was a huge shock after almost twenty-five years. Her boss was apologetic, and explained it had nothing to do with her work, which had improved significantly after the divorce. He knew something of what she'd been through and was not happy giving her this news. But business was business, and downsizing was not uncommon.

"So that's where I am," Aylin said softly, looking up from her tea, wiping a stray tear away. "Almost fifty with no job, no business, no family. A colossal failure."

Yeşim reached out to give her friend a hug. She couldn't believe the story Aylin had told her. She needed good friends around her now and Yeşim was glad Aylin had come home. She needed a new start.

Chapter 23

"*Gün aydın*," said Fiona, standing on tiptoes to kiss Metin on both cheeks when she met him for breakfast in Kuzguncuk.

"Good morning to you too. They do a great breakfast here. You're in for a treat." He pointed to the paper he'd been reading. "Did you hear the news today? The latest Silicon Valley announcement?"

"I did. I thought it was quite insightful." Fiona's eyes twinkled. "One of my clients was part of the research, and I worked with them on the white paper that was launched as part of the announcement. We put it to bed just before I came to İstanbul."

Metin was impressed. He didn't realize Fiona was working with clients of that calibre.

Fiona looked at the spread that had been put in front of them. The table groaned with the sheer abundance of different plates. "I'll weigh a ton after all of this," she laughed, picking up her glass of *çay*. "Did you get your academic politics all worked out yesterday?"

"I did. It turned out to be nothing much, but I needed to be there to solve it." Metin explained about the scholarship and bursary program he oversaw and the changes that were being proposed. "At the end of the day, I think everyone's satisfied," he said, as he stirred sugar into his glass.

The pair slowly worked their way through cucumber slices, tomato wedges, fresh bread, different types of cheeses, jams, olives, and the classic *sucuklu yumurta*, an egg dish with spicy sausage. They washed it all down with *çay* until they were stuffed. Still not ready to end their leisurely morning, Fiona and Metin walked along the seaside for about forty minutes, and then stopped for Turkish coffee in front of the Maiden's Tower chatting about everything and nothing until, having dragged the morning out as long as they reasonably could, they reluctantly said goodbye to each other, going on with their day, each still wondering exactly what was happening between them.

Fiona loved shopping at Turkish markets and today she was in heaven. She was having her friends over for dinner before Hayley headed home. There was such a variety of fresh produce and the banter back and forth between the vendors trying to get her attention was entertaining. She walked the length of the local *pazar* making menu plans in her head based on what she saw.

Making her way back, she asked one of the vendors if he had raspberries.

"*Maalesef, efendim.* Unfortunately not, ma'am," came the reply. "*Ama taze çilek var.*"

Fiona decided his fresh strawberries would work well with the pavlova she planned for dessert. She also bought arugula for salad and some tomatoes and peppers to add to the spread. Fresh green peas were an afterthought, and demanded an extra lemon to grate over them. She picked up some herbs and headed back to her flat, stopping at the butcher for a whole chicken. The night was looking good.

With the groceries packed away in the fridge, Fiona whipped the eggs and sugar into a stiff meringue and put it in the oven on low heat. Then she whipped the cream until it too was stiff and put it back into the fridge to chill. The rest could wait until closer to dinner.

She took her laptop out to the balcony and checked her email before moving on to editing an editorial she was working on. There were messages from two clients wanting her to work on new projects, a positive response from another on the proposal she'd sent on Saturday night, and a personal note from Rachael demanding details after the reunion.

As she gazed out across the water, Fiona reflected on what she'd built. She was proud of her business, and pleased at the freedom it offered her. She remembered then what Metin had said about Safiye and wondered if they ever would work together. Laughing at the absurdity of that idea, she closed her email and got to work, making a mental note to reply to Rachael the following day.

Fiona put the chicken in the oven to roast late in the afternoon and then wandered down to the ferry dock. Hayley was coming a bit earlier than the others and she'd agreed to meet her there. Fiona waved to her when she saw her coming off the boat. She was looking forward to some time alone with her before the others came.

"*İyi akşamlar*, Dilek *abla*," she greeted her neighbour, as they passed her on the stairs up to her door. Fiona had always been able to strike up conversations with new people and she and Dilek had got to know each other in the almost three weeks Fiona had been there.

"So," she said, pouring wine after she'd given Hayley the grand tour. "You know I love it here, but how has your week here been? Is it everything you remember?"

Hayley sighed. "In some ways, yes. In lots of other ways, it's so different. I'm glad I came, though. Thank you so much for suggesting it. It's been wonderful seeing you again, and the others of course." She giggled. "And I can't deny it was really fun to flirt with the boys again at the reunion. It made me feel young again and it's been a great escape. I'm glad I stayed in Sultanahmet so I could be a tourist, but it's time for me to go back to real life. I really miss Brad and my boys. What about you? What are your plans."

Fiona took a sip of wine. "Well, I have this flat for just over another month, and I might sneak down to the Mediterranean coast for a bit before I go home."

The birdlike tweet of the doorbell brought an abrupt end to the conversation. Fiona slipped away to let their friends in. "*Hoş geldiniz!*" she greeted them.

"*Hoş bulduk,*" said three voices in unison. In they came, slipping off their shoes at the entrance.

"*Buyurun, buyurun,* please come in. I don't have *terlik*, I'm afraid." Fiona apologized away the lack of slippers for her guests as she ushered them in.

"*Boş ver.* Don't worry about it," Nazlı said. "Now, if you lived here . . ."

Everyone laughed. No one would dare enter a Turkish home without taking their shoes off at the threshold and slipping on the proffered footwear.

"Fiona, something smells really good," called Aylin appreciatively as Fiona rummaged into the kitchen for more wine glasses. Laughter continued as stories from the past were shared. The five women spent a very enjoyable evening together drinking wine and reminiscing about those simpler days. They sang songs from their youth and savoured every last bite of Fiona's meal.

Yeşim helped Fiona clear the table. Together in the kitchen, waiting for the tea to brew, Fiona had a chance to ask her the question that had been bothering her for days now.

"Yeşim, you didn't tell me anything about Metin all these years. He says you didn't tell him anything about me either. You and Mehmet are the common link between us. Do you mind me asking why?"

Yeşim looked embarrassed. "It's hard to explain. At first, you were both so hurt that it seemed kinder not to talk about it. And then later, I guess it just became a habit. Why do you ask?"

"I'm not sure," Fiona admitted. "We've been having a lot of fun the last few days catching up on all the years. I guess I just wondered."

Yeşim looked at her seriously. "Be careful, Fiona. I care about you both very much."

Fiona brushed off her concern, slightly annoyed, and remembering back to that year when Yeşim said the same words, cautioning her about the future of any possible relationship with Metin. She put the tea glasses on a tray. "Let's go back and join the others."

Fiona joined Hayley at her hotel in Sultanahmet the next morning for one last cup of coffee before she headed back to America. Hayley was excited to be getting back to her family, but so happy to have had this short trip into the past.

She was explaining all of this to Fiona and talking about her plans for the summer with the kids when Metin joined them, a quick planned stop on the way to meet a colleague just up the road at İstanbul University. They made small talk for some time, before Metin had to leave for his meeting, leaving Hayley and Fiona to have a few final minutes together.

Hayley took Fiona's hand. "I saw the looks between you two when Metin left. You're only in İstanbul for another month, Fiona. Keep your wits about you."

"What do you mean?"

"Just be careful."

"Don't be silly. It's just friendship. Old friends with a past, enjoying each other."

Hayley shook her head. "Whatever you say . . ."

With a giant hug, Fiona assured her she was reading too much into it. She put Hayley into a taxi, wishing her safe travels, and promising to keep in touch when they were both home.

Waving goodbye, Fiona thought about what her friend had said. She too would have to go back to real life soon. But for now, she thought, as she took a detour through the tiny shopping streets between the Covered Bazaar and the Egyptian Bazaar, she planned to enjoy everything İstanbul had to offer.

Chapter 24

Metin arrived at Fiona's flat for dinner, with tulips in hand.

"*Ne güzel laleler!*" she exclaimed when he arrived. "What beautiful flowers. I can't believe you remembered they're my favourites."

Over the week, they'd slipped back into a form of Turklish — English and Turkish mixed together — with more and more coming back to Fiona day by day. She was trying hard and Metin, just as she remembered, was a kind teacher, gently correcting her and supporting her efforts.

For this evening, Fiona had slipped on one of her favourite spring dresses — a chiffon floral print with a slim-fitting bodice and a full floaty skirt that reached her calves and moved gracefully in the breeze. She'd left her hair free, so the waves cascaded down her back.

After he admired how she looked in the dress, Metin turned his gaze to the sunset over the Bosphorus Strait from her balcony while Fiona put the pink and purple buds in a vase.

"Nice place you've got here," he said as she brought out two wine glasses, a bottle of shiraz and a corkscrew.

"Will you do the honours?" she asked as she joined him on the balcony.

"*Tabii ki, canım,*" he answered and she looked at him suddenly. He'd called her "dear," common between good friends, but also something he had called her all the time when they were young. She wondered if it meant anything, but let it go until he handed a glass of the dark, spicy red wine to her. Their hands touched for just a second and she felt a spark. She wondered if he felt it too.

"What shall we toast to?" he asked, smiling and looking into her eyes. Tonight, they seemed to be glowing in evening light. He remembered how easily he used to get lost in her eyes.

"To old friends."

"To old friends. *Şerefe.*" They clinked glasses.

"It is a lovely view," Fiona admitted, returning to the pre-toast conversation. "I know I'm really spoiling myself with this place."

"And why shouldn't you. You've worked hard, you've raised four children on your own. You deserve to treat yourself."

Fiona popped back into the kitchen to check on dinner. Tonight there would be a simple meal of salad, chicken pot pie, and roasted asparagus. Fiona had tinkered with some Turkish recipes at home but certainly hadn't wanted to try them tonight. Except for one thing. Just as he'd remembered her favourite flower, she remembered that Metin's favourite dessert was *aşure*. This was going to be tricky, as everyone's *aşure* was made differently. Often described in English as Noah's Pudding, the story went that it had been made to celebrate Noah's Ark finding solid ground on Mount Ararat with whatever was left in the ark.

As Fiona stirred in the grains, legumes, dried fruit, and nuts, she crossed her fingers. Whether she had been able to conjure up one that was close to the one that Özlem *teyze* made, was debatable. But she'd had fun trying to live up to his mother's *aşure*.

"*Sofra hazır,*" Fiona called Metin to the dinner table. She had put out the dishes and brought the bottle of wine to the table.

Metin refilled their glasses. "*Afiyet olsun*," she said as they helped themselves. She was pleased when Metin came back for seconds. "Save some room for dessert," she said. "I have a bit of a surprise."

Fiona cleared the main course dishes. "So," she started, suddenly nervous, as she came back holding a big glass bowl. "I thought I'd try something new, and I remember this was your favourite," she said. "No promises, but I think it's okay."

"You made *aşure*?" Metin suddenly remembered his mother teasing Fiona she would have to learn to make it if she was going to be part of the family. How long ago that was.

Metin picked up his spoon and dug in. "Mmm. *Eline sağlık*," he said, offering her his appreciation for the pudding.

"*Afiyet olsun,*" she replied.

After dinner, Fiona sent Metin back to the balcony while she lit the gas stove and set the *çaydanlık* on the burner. She wanted to make proper Turkish tea tonight. Joining him a few minutes later, she found him sitting pensively looking out over the water. Fiona joined him in companionable silence, leaning on the balcony railing and watching the ferryboat head across the Bosphorus. She could never tire of this view, and reluctantly headed in when she thought she heard the water boiling.

"A penny for your thoughts," she said when she returned with glasses of *çay* on a tray. Metin stirred sugar into his and sipped it slowly. He put it down on the side table, got up to join her at the railing and gently put his hands on her shoulders.

"Fiona," he began. She looked up as his long fingers stroked her cheek. She brought hers up to gently cover his. An old, familiar, yet still electrifying, jolt shot through her again as their hands touched. They both felt it and locked eyes.

"Metin?" She was losing herself in those green eyes.

"I . . . I'm having trouble finding my words tonight," he admitted quietly, feeling the heat between them rising. "I don't understand, but it feels so . . . so right spending time with you. It's been so long and I didn't know that I had missed you. *Ama . . . ama seni çok özledim."* Metin broke off.

Fiona felt butterflies in her stomach. "I know what you mean. This is so sudden and unexpected, but so familiar and so comfortable at the same time. *Ben de özledim seni.* I've missed you too."

They stood there, scared to break the moment. Then Metin leaned his head down to brush his lips gently against hers and a featherlight kiss melted away the years.

The next morning, Fiona woke early. Dressing quickly in black leggings and a teal tunic, she draped a shawl around her shoulders and curled up in the comfortable living room chair, her mind returning to the previous evening.

Despite her assurances to Hayley just a couple of days ago, Fiona was surprised at how quickly her feelings for Metin were returning. It seemed they had rekindled old passions with that first gentle kiss, as if they'd both flown through time to their youth. But in the ones that followed they charted new territory. They were adults now, who had lived lots of life. The intensity befitted two mature adults, confident in their histories.

When they had finally pulled apart, Fiona had sent him home before it went any further. They both needed time to think about what was happening. When he'd pulled her close and run his hands through her hair, it had sent shivers down her spine. She hadn't felt this way in a very long time. Maybe a walk along the seaside would help clear her head. Tea finished, she washed her cup, grabbed her wallet, and headed down the stairs. On the way she ran into her neighbour.

"*Gün aydın,* Dilek *abla,*" she greeted her. "*Nasılsın?*"

"*İyiyim,* Fiona. *Sen nasılsın?*"

"I'm well too. *Abla,* can I ask you a question?"

Dilek had welcomed Fiona when she first arrived three weeks ago. She had been pleased to know that the flat had been rented for longer than usual. She liked getting to know new people, but when they stayed only a few days it was hard. Since then, they'd had *çay* most days. Dilek was ten years older than Fiona, and was a widow herself. She had spent more than twenty years living in England, but had returned after her husband passed away. Despite their very different lives, they'd found common ground.

Sitting in Dilek's front room, Fiona told her about Metin. How much they'd been in love as teenagers, how distance and time had separated them, and how surprising it had been to feel what she was feeling after just a few days with him.

"*Ah, canim, yeniden aşık oldun!*" Dilek exclaimed.

"Fallen in love again? Oh, I don't think so, *abla*. It was a long time ago. And surely I'm too old."

"Darling, you're not old. And sometimes first love is better the second time around," Dilek winked knowingly. "Enjoy it while you're here!"

Laughing, Fiona left Dilek for her walk. Her mind lingered on the conversation. Perhaps her new friend was right. Maybe she should just enjoy the moment.

That same morning, Metin had breakfast with Tamer. "*Ne haber, kardeşim?* What's new?" he asked as he joined Metin at the restaurant.

Kissing each other on both cheeks they sat down, Metin began absentmindedly stirring sugar into his *çay*, the tiny teaspoon clinking as it went around and around in the glass.

"Hello, anyone home?" Tamer teased.

"Sorry, *abi*. I'm a million miles away. I've had a strange week and I'm still trying to make sense of it."

"Oh? What do you mean, strange?"

"You know it was my high school reunion recently, right?" Tamer nodded. "Remember, I was dating an exchange student that year, after I came back from Charlotte? Fiona. She came back for the reunion!"

"What I remember is that you thought you were head over heels in love with her back then. You wrote me letter after letter after letter about her while I was away doing military service!"

"Well, she was there and I took her out to dinner afterwards."

"Metin," Tamer said abruptly, suspicious of where this was headed. "Don't forget how hard it was for you when you broke up after she went home. And then Sibel. That was a disaster. And then Büşra turned out to want things you didn't. You've had bad luck in love, little brother." Tamer had always hoped that Metin would settle down, but it hadn't happened. He thought for a minute. "I'm surprised to hear she came back for a reunion here, though."

"She's been back a couple of times before, apparently. She's here now for a couple of months."

Tamer raised his eyebrows.

"We've spent a lot of time together this week," Metin admitted sheepishly. "Last night she cooked dinner for me. And I kissed her. I know it's ridiculous, but I think . . . I think I have real feelings for her again."

"Metin, *saçmalama*. Don't be ridiculous. She's someone from another lifetime and another world." Tamer thought it was important to counsel his brother bluntly. "You'll get hurt. She'll get hurt. Have your fun, but don't get carried away, *kardeşim*. For both your sakes."

Metin had to admit Tamer had a rational argument. But his head and his heart weren't talking to each other. Leaving his *abi*, Metin went to the university and tried to concentrate on his latest research. But his focus kept being drawn back to a certain red-headed beauty who had kissed him back last night with an intensity that had matched his own.

Fiona had been thinking about it all day too, and she decided they needed to talk about the kiss. Well, kisses. They both had lives that would be terribly disrupted if they let it get out of hand. She texted Metin that evening.

> Hope you had a good day. I'm a bit confused after last night. Wonder if you are too. Can we talk?

The phone was in Metin's hands when it buzzed. He was about to make the same suggestion. It was amazing how in sync they were. He texted back immediately.

> Good idea. Tomorrow morning? Walk?

Tamer was right. He needed to nip this in the bud and make sure Fiona knew this couldn't go anywhere. He didn't want to hurt her again, and he also needed to protect his own heart.

> Sure. Where?

> Caddebostan Beach? 10 am?

> Beautiful spot. *Yarın görüşürüz.* See you tomorrow.

> *İyi geceler.* Good night.

Chapter 25

The next day was grey and gloomy, threatening rain. Fiona popped her striped Hudson's Bay umbrella in her purse before catching a *dolmuş* up to Caddebostan. She liked to travel with this umbrella. It marked her as Canadian to those who recognized the red, yellow, green, and blue stripes, but was unobtrusive enough not to scream her nationality to those who didn't. Fiona had pulled her long hair back into a thick French braid today, and in her violet tunic top and black pants, she made a pretty picture.

As usual, she arrived early. Finding an empty bench, she started to make notes for a magazine article she was pitching to a national magazine on solo travel. Fiona wrote mainstream media pieces from time to time to keep things fresh. Her friends laughed at her, but she still took notes longhand in an old-fashioned way in a battered leather notebook the way she had since she was a kid, dreaming up her first stories. Looking up, she saw Metin coming toward her in jeans and a green button down shirt that she knew would make his eyes pop. A huge smile lit up her face and she felt her stomach do flips.

Metin had actually been watching Fiona from a distance for a few minutes. She tapped her pen against her lips as she thought, and as she bent her head down to write, her braid fell over her shoulder. He couldn't believe she still had a notebook, and he made a note to buy her one as a gift.

A gift? What was he thinking? He started walking again, and as he got close, she lifted her head. Her dazzling smile made his stomach lurch. And he smiled back, green eyes glittering with the excitement she made him feel. Kissing each other's cheeks in greeting, they began to walk up the coast. Fiona shoved her notebook into her bag.

"I can't believe you're still writing in a notebook with a pen," Metin teased as they started up the road. "You, a high-tech marketing expert!"

"I know it makes me look a bit like a luddite, but it's always felt like a nice counterpoint to my iPhone, computers, and everything digital."

Fiona slipped her arm into Metin's. He looked at her quizzically; she shrugged.

"Old habits," she said. But she left her arm there, and he didn't object.

"Metin," she began, a few minutes later. "I need to say something. I'm not entirely sure what we're doing, but I do know I'm really enjoying your company."

"So am I," he said. "And the other night when I kissed you, it felt so right. It reminded me of old times. I felt young again."

"I know what you mean. It was like the years flew away and we were eighteen again. I haven't been kissed like that in a long time. But, Metin, I'm only here for a little while."

"I know, *canım*. We have lives halfway around the world from each other. And I don't want to make things complicated for either of us."

Fiona smiled. "So can we agree that we'll just enjoy this one day at a time — no strings attached, no commitments — knowing that it has an expiry date."

Metin nodded, looking relieved. "Okay then. *Anlaştık*. We have a deal."

With that seemingly resolved, Fiona and Metin continued to walk along the shore for a pleasant hour before leaving each other. The rain had held off, but Fiona felt the first sprinkles as she arrived home. She spent the afternoon trying to work as the raindrops slid down the windows in her flat.

They saw each other a few times over the next couple of weeks, scheduled around their commitments. Metin took her to a great jazz club in Beyoğlu one evening, and Fiona surprised him with concert tickets at Aya İrini, an eastern orthodox church with great acoustics in the courtyard of Topkapı Palace. They met for lunch one day and took in an art exhibition on another afternoon. They were purposely staying in public spaces.

In between, Metin continued his research and Fiona kept busy with client work. She spent some time with her girlfriends as well, and although she didn't mention how much time she was spending with him to them, she did let it slip in a message to Rachael.

> Having the best time! Would love to show this amazing city to you and the girls one day. Will send some pix soon. Oh, and remember I told you about an old boyfriend who's an author now? We've been spending some time together. Metin is as handsome as he ever was, and I'm really enjoying it.
>
> Don't leave me hanging — what do you mean? A fling??
>
> I'm not sure I'd call it that, but he has kissed me. I think it scared us a bit. No future obviously. But felt so good . . .!
>
> Have fun!!

Fiona was video-chatting with Holly when her phone buzzed. After she said goodbye to her daughter, she checked her messages. Metin wanted to take her to one of his favourite restaurants in Kuzguncuk the next evening. Fiona was free, so she texted to agree.

Fiona dressed for dinner choosing a simple sleeveless navy polka-dot silk wrap dress that showed off her figure. She wore her favourite necklace which incorporated her children's birthstones, added big hoop earrings, and put her hair up in a messy bun to show them off. She draped a short-sleeved cardigan over her handbag, in case it got cool later.

Metin arrived at her door at seven o'clock sharp. When she came to the door, his breath was taken away. Fiona looked elegant and beautiful. He took her to the little fish restaurant by the shore.

"It's not just the view," he told her as they took their seats. "The food is just as good." He was right. By the end of the evening, Fiona was stuffed. The sea bream had been delectable, the wine Metin had selected was perfect, and they'd shared a huge slice of the most decadent chocolate cake for dessert. When his hand brushed hers as they put their dessert forks down, Fiona felt the jolt.

"We're right around the corner from my place," Metin said casually, as he dealt with the bill. He still wasn't letting Fiona pay. "Would you like to come up for a look? It has a decent view."

Metin's flat was in one of the colourful old buildings Kuzguncuk was famous for. The ground floor flat had flowers at the window, which gave off a lovely fragrance as they passed by. Fiona gave the cat on the doorstep a quick ear scratch and then they climbed three flights of stairs up to the top floor. Metin turned the key in the lock, and pushed the door open.

Fiona went through, leaving her shoes, purse, and cardigan at the door and stepping into the *terlik* he pulled out for her after putting on his own. Following Metin through the narrow hallway and into the front room, Fiona suddenly stood stock-still.

"My God, Metin, it's stunning." An oriel jutted out in the centre of the room with enormous windows on all sides, offering a full 180-degree view of the Bosphorus. Metin called it a *cumba* and it was a common feature of old Ottoman houses — a part of the building that protruded from the main wall, but didn't go down to the ground.

"I'm glad you like it. I got very lucky," he said as he threw open the windows to the sounds of the evening, making the *cumba* seem almost like a balcony.

"I'll say you did," Fiona agreed. "I thought the flat I've rented was amazing, but this is spectacular. I can only imagine what it's like in the afternoons, with the sun streaming in."

"When I first saw this place about eight years ago, it was a complete wreck," Metin explained. "So the price was right. I figured I'd learned enough from restoring Datça to take this on. The building was sturdy, but the flat needed a lot of work. Safiye and Tamer thought I was crazy. But I've put in a lot of sweat equity to make it what it is today."

Fiona tore her gaze away from the view. The finishes inside and the art on the wall hadn't even registered with her yet.

"I know you did the restoration of your family house. You did this too?"

"I've gotten remarkably handy with a hammer," he admitted sheepishly. "I've taken a lot of pride in restoring these two old beauties." He headed into the kitchen while Fiona continued looking around.

Metin returned, holding a bottle of wine. "*İçer misin?*" he asked, holding it up.

Even though she knew she probably shouldn't have another glass, after the bottle they'd shared over dinner, Fiona nodded her head. Metin removed the cork and generously poured the crisp white wine into the large stemmed glasses.

They stood in the *cumba*, taking in the view and listening to the sounds of the sea for a long time, enjoying the wine. Fiona shivered as the night breeze suddenly began to blow cool over her bare shoulders and Metin closed the enormous panes of glass that he'd opened when they first arrived. He stood behind Fiona, gently rubbing her upper arms to warm her. He kissed the top of her head and then her cheek, and the nape of her neck, drinking in her scent. His warm lips tasted her shoulders and Fiona let out a little sigh. She put her wine glass on the window ledge, slowly turned around. Standing on her tiptoes, she reached her arms up and around Metin's neck. Metin kissed the hollow of her throat and she ran her fingers through his hair. He brought his mouth to hers and they kissed passionately. Fiona gently guided him to the chair and leaned over him. She pulled the pin out of her hair and her long wavy locks tumbled down around his face. The scent of her lavender shampoo brought back memories.

Suddenly Metin's hands were on her waist, pulling her closer, as she kissed him.

"This feels so good," she whispered as her kisses tickled his ear.

Metin groaned in response to her touch. "Don't stop," he whispered, hungrily guiding her lips back to his.

Fiona's fingers found the placket on Metin's shirt, and she kissed him with each button that she set free. His hands left her waist and explored her curves.

Metin reached up to tug at the bow at her waist that held her wrap dress in place.

"Metin." She put her hand over his, stopping him for a moment, suddenly nervous. "It's been a long time for me. And I've had four children," she said more softly. "It won't be what you remember."

"It's been a long time for me too," Metin said softly, his green eyes finding her grey ones. "Besides, we're both older," he reassured her. "You haven't been put off by the grey in my hair and some wrinkles."

She leaned in to touch his curls lovingly.

"Nothing about you could disappoint me, Fiona." He kissed her again, and as he slowly pulled the bow, her dress fell open. He stood up and as he gently slid the silky fabric from her shoulders, it slid into a puddle on the floor behind her. "You are exquisite, maybe even more beautiful than before. *Çok güzelsin, sevgilim,*" he whispered, taking in the beautiful woman standing in front of him, a lacy black silk slip skimming her tantalizing figure in all the right places.

Fiona pushed Metin's shirt off his broad shoulders and was rewarded when it also dropped to the floor. He was very handsome in the moonlight. Metin's torso was toned and tanned, and Fiona felt shock waves go through her as she ran her fingers over it. Metin shuddered at the light touch.

It took all he had to pull away, but he needed to be sure. "Fiona, *emin misin*?" he asked, looking her directly in the eyes.

"*Eminim.* It's not just the wine. I'm sure," she said huskily, looking back at him.

Metin slowly took off his glasses and lay them on the table, his eyes never leaving Fiona's. He scooped her up in his arms and took her to his bedroom where they discovered each other all over again.

Later, as Metin's fingers lazily traced patterns with the freckles on Fiona's shoulders, he asked her to stay the night.

"I shouldn't."

"Why do you need to leave? Please don't go."

Unable to come up with a compelling reason, Fiona rolled over and kissed him with renewed ardour instead. He responded and melted under her spell.

When Fiona awoke the next morning, they were spooned together, Metin's body forming a protective shell around her. He was sound asleep. She slipped out from under his arm and found one of his shirts to wear. She glanced back one last time before she quietly closed the bedroom door.

In the daylight, his flat was even more spectacular. She wandered into the kitchen and found a French press in the compact but very well-appointed space. Metin hadn't spared any detail in restoring this flat, she realized taking in the stone backsplash, the tall baseboards, and the gleaming original herringbone floorboards.

She found a hand grinder and coffee beans. Soon she added the ground beans to the French press and as she waited for the kettle to boil, she touched her lips, reflecting on the night before. She hadn't felt loved like this in a very long time. She was planning to enjoy it for however long it lasted. She poured the brewed coffee and carried the steaming mug into the front room, admiring some of the artwork she'd noticed the night before. The pieces perfectly suited the space and she made a note to ask him about them. Then she noticed the bookshelf that spanned an entire wall in his dining room.

She was curled up in one of the chairs in the *cumba*, with a second cup of coffee, thinking through the complexities last night had brought while being spellbound by the Bosphorus view when she heard him come up behind her. Metin nuzzled her neck.

"*Gün aydın, sevgilim.*"

"Good morning to you too. Did you sleep well?"

"Better than I have in a long time, to be honest. Something about the woman sleeping next to me, I think."

Fiona blushed and let him lead her back to the bedroom. Complexities be damned.

♄

Metin and Fiona were soon seeing each other almost every day. They fell into a comfortable routine, working in the mornings and then spending most afternoons or evenings together. Metin's book research continued and Fiona's clients didn't seem to be taking the summer off this year. It was a busy time for both of them professionally, so they often spent the afternoons working as well. Fiona had grown fond of taking her laptop to Metin's flat and working opposite him at his dining room table or from the comfortable chairs in the *cumba*. Sometimes she sketched from those same chairs. Metin noticed that she tended to hum when she sketched. It made him smile. He liked to read on Fiona's terrace, enjoying the fresh breeze off the water. They visited Belgrad Forest and Çamlıca, and made day trips to Şile on the Black Sea and Yalova on the Sea of Marmara, getting further out of the city and enjoying the variety that was offered as spring turned into summer.

When they weren't together, they texted often. Fiona always smiled now when her phone buzzed.

> Good morning, *sevgilim*. Talked to my *anne* this morning — *Çay* tomorrow morning, OK? My brother and sister will be there too. Too much family at once?

> Of course not. Would love to see your *anne* again. I'm honoured by the invitation. Will make something to bring.

Fiona was nervous as she made coffee cake that evening. She wondered what Metin had told Özlem *teyze* about them, and what she'd be walking into. She put the cake in the oven, having sprinkled cinnamon and sugar over the batter, and thought about how much she'd learned in Özlem *teyze*'s kitchen. Almost all of her Turkish cooking skills came from this woman.

The next day, Metin greeted Fiona at the door with a kiss. "For courage," he teased. "Seriously, *sevgilim*, they're excited to see you."

"Tell me a bit more about Tamer," she asked, as they got in a taxi for the short distance. Özlem *teyze* lived in the same apartment block that Metin grew up in, but a smaller unit now that it was just her.

"Ah, Tamer. Tamer is a bit direct," Metin admitted. "He's actually really caring, but he doesn't trust easily. You might find him a bit difficult at first, but my *abi* is a really good guy underneath, when you get to know him." This did nothing to settle her nerves.

Safiye was watching out the window for the taxi, excited to see Fiona again.

"*Geldiler, anne!* They're here!" she called when she saw them arrive. When Özlem *teyze* opened the door, there were kisses all around as the three women reconnected. When Tamer arrived fifteen minutes later, Fiona was determined to make a good impression, so she greeted him in her best Turkish.

"*Merhaba, Tamer. Memnun oldum.*"

"*Ben de memnun oldum,*" he replied, although his expression suggested he wasn't actually terribly pleased to meet her at all. Safiye glared daggers at him.

She helped her mother bring out a tray of *çay*, and some small plates and forks so Fiona could serve her coffee cake. As she cut it, displaying the red ribbon running through it, she explained that the cake actually had no coffee in it, but some fruit, which she agreed, made little sense. At home, Fiona made this cake with cranberries to balance the sweetness. Here, she had substituted sour cherries. Regardless, Fiona was pleased to see that everyone seemed to like it. With some help from Metin, she answered questions and they shared memories from twenty-five years ago.

"Remember when *anne* taught you how to make *mantı*," Safiye laughed. "You had such a hard time making them so small."

Metin noticed that Tamer was quiet. Clearly, he was holding back approval. Metin wasn't surprised, but he was disappointed.

Even if it had only been a short time, Fiona was very important to him again, and he wanted his family to appreciate that.

"We were so sad when you went home," Safiye said. She glanced at her brother. "Especially Metin. I know he missed you a lot back then."

"We both missed each other," Fiona said. "I'm so glad we found each other again. The last few weeks have been very special." She squeezed Metin's hand. "Now, Safiye, tell me about your work." She wanted to know more about marketing in Turkey.

Soon it was time to go. Fiona tried to help Özlem *teyze* and Safiye take the dishes to the kitchen but they wouldn't let her. She was a guest again. Metin's phone rang and he stepped into the hall to take the call, which gave Tamer and Fiona a few moments alone.

"Fiona, please think what you are doing," he began in his halting and accented English. "You will go home soon. What will happen with Metin then? You will leave him, no? I don't want my brother be hurt."

Fiona opened her mouth to answer him, but Metin came back into the salon, his phone call finished. It was clear where she stood in Tamer's opinion, and she didn't think she'd be able to change his mind.

"Metin *ciğim*, what are we doing?" she asked as they walked back to her flat in Moda. Tamer had her questioning everything again. "It was lovely to see your family again, but it makes me wonder if we're being smart."

"I don't know. All I know is that I'm very, very happy like this." He had seen Tamer's face and he knew where her question had come from. "I don't want anything — or anyone — to spoil it." He squeezed her hand.

"Neither do I," Fiona replied, releasing his hand to open the door of her building. "Spending time with you feels so right. But . . . I'm just trying to figure out what happens when I have to go home. It's coming so fast."

They started up the stairs.

"So don't go."

"What?"

"Let's go inside, and then you can hear me out."

Metin let Fiona open the door and then he followed her in. "*Sevgilim*, the past few weeks have been the best I've had in a very long time. I think it's the same for you." Fiona nodded. "I'm not ready for it to end yet. Do you really need to go back to Canada right away? You said it yourself. You can work from anywhere. Why not see if your landlord can extend your time in this flat and then you could stay another month, or even two."

Fiona was quiet. She hadn't considered this as a possibility, but suddenly her mind was suddenly whirring with the possibility. Metin watched, hoping she'd agree.

"I suppose there's nothing pressing workwise that I need to take care of in person," she started. "I'd have to check, but maybe I could stay a bit. I'd have to explain to my kids, but at least we can video-chat these days."

Metin wrapped his arms around her. "Please stay," he whispered in her ear, kissing it playfully. Fiona sighed and brought her lips to his.

Fortunately, the flat was not booked and her landlord was happy for her to stay on. Fiona let her family know she was staying in İstanbul for a few more weeks. Her kids were surprisingly at ease with it, but she thought it might have more to do with the fact that the lake house was available to them for summer weekends and short vacations if they wanted to go. Jamie had already asked if he could go up with his new girlfriend and the dogs. Max and Ben were surprised, but supportive. Fiona emailed the lawn care people and asked them to continue cutting the grass and taking care of her gardens. Her Toronto condo would be fine. She sent one quick group message to Aylin, Yeşim, and Nazlı and another to her friends back home. She messaged Rachael separately to tell her things were going well with Metin.

Fiona's Turkish girlfriends were thrilled she was staying, but Yeşim had some concerns that she and Metin were falling into an old pattern that would end up with at least one of them getting hurt. She shared her thoughts with Mehmet that night.

"I love them both," she said to her husband as they got ready for bed. "They were special together then, and I can see it again now. I just don't know how it can work."

"It's *kismet*," Mehmet said. "If I didn't think so then, I certainly do now." Mehmet and Metin had met for lunch a couple of times recently and he knew his friend was falling in love again. "Don't worry. They'll find a way." He kissed his wife and they turned out the light.

Evenings were Fiona's favourite time. Even when she and Metin didn't spend the night together, it was in the evenings that they shared quiet confidences. They told each other stories of the last thirty years until they felt like they'd known each other forever. Fiona sensed she was being swept away by something deep and powerful. She didn't have words for what she was experiencing. And so when Metin found some, she found she couldn't disagree.

"Fiona, I know we said we'd take this one day at a time," he said, as they lay in each other's arms one night, "but you've been in my bed almost every night this week, and I can't *not* say this anymore. I am head over heels in love with you again. *Seni seviyorum.* And I'm not sure what to do about it."

Fiona gasped. She hadn't expected to hear those words. But she felt it too. "I love you too, Metin."

Chapter 26

With summer properly upon them, and children's school finished for the year, İstanbullus started heading to the sea for holidays.

Yeşim invited Fiona to spend a few days with the family at their summer home on the coast, and then she joined Aylin for a girl's long weekend in the holiday town of Kalkan, enjoying the fun atmosphere and the sun.

"So what are your plans now? Will you go back to Australia?" Fiona asked her friend, as they walked along a narrow flower-filled street after dinner. The smell of bougainvillea filled the air.

"I think I'm going to stay. Actually, I know I'm going to stay. Wow. That's the first time I've said that out loud. It's the right time in my life for a new start."

"Good for you." Fiona grabbed Aylin's hand and squeezed it. "Do you know what you'll do?"

"Not yet. I'm thinking of some kind of small business, but something completely different from what I did in Australia. I have a bit of time before I need to know exactly what it is."

"Are you nervous?"

"Surprisingly not. It kind of feels like things are settling into place."

"Well, let's celebrate that then!" Fiona dragged Aylin into a small bar and they toasted her new start.

"I've missed you," Metin said when she arrived at his flat after her Mediterranean getaway with Aylin. It was a hot July evening and Fiona had picked up the makings of a cold dinner and was headed into the kitchen to put the bags down. "Seriously, Fiona, I've really missed you," Metin reiterated.

She put the bags down and put her arms around his neck. "I missed you too, *hayatım*." She tested out the term of endearment.

Metin felt a warmth spread all through him. "I like hearing that." Fiona was rewarded with a smile and a kiss.

"I like saying it." She gave him a quick kiss before turning her attention back to dinner.

Metin joined her in the *cumba* the next morning bringing two steaming glasses of tea.

"*Sevgilim*," he began. "I was thinking while I watched you sleep last night. Why are we pretending? We're spending more nights together than apart. Why not give up your flat and move in here? I want to take you to Datça soon anyway, and it would give you some more flexibility on your return date. So why not stay with me?"

There was silence for a moment as Fiona processed what he'd just said. "Metin, it's a very kind offer," she started. "But . . ." she trailed off. This was suddenly moving very fast. She took a deep breath and started again more confidently. "I'd like that very much."

They settled into an easy routine. Fiona was an early riser, and liked to work in the morning — she was most creative then, so she was often at her computer by six thirty or seven o'clock. On days when she didn't need to work, she still woke early, but she enjoyed a few extra minutes in bed. Snuggling into Metin's warmth, she loved these peaceful moments before she pulled out her yoga mat or her sketch pad.

Metin was a night owl by nature. He liked to roll out of bed around eight or even nine, as he wasn't lecturing over the summer. He would pop out to the local *fırın* to get bread and the *bakkal* for a newspaper and then come back to slice up cheese, peppers, and tomatoes. Fiona was ready for a break by then so they would eat breakfast together and read the paper.

Metin was then ready to get to work, so Fiona made more *çay* and tidied the kitchen. She would often head out to run errands, meet friends, or just explore the city, giving Metin some time and space to work alone in the middle of the day. Sometimes he had to go into the university, but mostly worked from home in the summer semester. Fiona tried to catch a yoga class at Nazlı's studio once or twice a week. She returned to take meetings with clients back home in the late afternoon as Metin was winding down. On weekends, when they weren't out exploring or meeting with friends, they loved to just sit together on the couch, feet tangled in the middle, reading books or newspapers. Metin teased Fiona as she was forever misplacing her reading glasses.

They walked together most evenings, catching the cool breeze from the water, sometimes meeting friends. Fiona had met Safiye's husband, Kerem, and their son, Yusuf, who was eager to practise his English. No matter where they were, if they were out, every evening ended with a final glass of *çay* by the side of the Bosphorus before they headed home and tumbled into bed.

It was almost embarrassing, Fiona mused. They couldn't get enough of each other. At their age. It was almost as if they were making up for lost time. The young Metin of her memories was an earnest young man with a wicked sense of humour, curly hair that called out to be touched, and sparkling green eyes that took in the whole world. He had drive and a thirst for knowledge. She'd had no doubt then that he would be successful. And the love they had for each other then had been rooted in something special. Letting him go had been one of the hardest things she'd done in her young life.

Now, many years and many harder things later, they were both older but it was like two lost gloves being returned to make a pair. Sure, he needed glasses now, and the curls she still loved running her fingers through were turning grey. But Metin's mind was as sharp as his zest for life and it was complemented by a world view and a relentless optimism that she found at least as attractive as the package it was wrapped in.

Metin was having similar thoughts. He remembered making love to Fiona as a teenager in Bodrum, her lean narrow body making him lust for her. But now, all these years later, her new curves had captivated him completely. They would lie in bed together and he would wrap himself around her and forget the outside world. When she leaned over to kiss him, her long hair tickled his cheeks as her lips took his, and he couldn't get enough of her. But it wasn't just about sex. It was her mind, her quick-wittedness, her kindness, her work ethic, her cheery outlook on life, and even her fierce protection of her family. When he saw her in the kitchen, on the couch with her reading glasses perched on her nose, talking with her kids on the phone, or even meeting her in the street after a time apart, he lit up inside. He was determined to make best use of this second chance life had handed them.

Metin had learned that this adult Fiona didn't have the expensive tastes in shoes or handbags that many other women he had known did. He loved discovering what she was wearing under her clothes as she disrobed each evening. It was like unwrapping a special present every day. In bed, he would run his hands over both the delicate fabrics of her negligees and her soft skin, sighing with contentment that she was in his bed. Metin lay with Fiona each night watching her as her breathing slowed and she fell asleep.

She looked so tranquil, and he envied the peace she found in slumber. Metin had suffered from insomnia for years, and in the past, he had often been awake late into the night. He still sometimes got up after Fiona had fallen asleep to read for another hour or two. He loved slipping back into bed with her when he was finally ready to try again to sleep, enjoying her warmth. But the longer they were together, the more peace he found with her, and the better he was sleeping. More often than not, he now found himself sound asleep within minutes of her.

July turned into August and Fiona had once again told her family she was extending her stay. By now they knew that she was living with Metin, but they also knew she had to come home at some point.

Fiona was torn. Her grandchildren would be four this winter, and while they video-chatted at least once every two weeks, it wasn't the same as being there to hug and kiss and cuddle them. She did miss her friends, but they texted from time to time and she'd stayed up really late a few times to have an "early" video drink with Hyun, Rachael, and Mila. It had been midnight for her, five o'clock for them. They had laughed together, and Fiona had given them a quick tour of Metin's flat, including the view.

But despite all of that, Fiona also found she was building a new life in İstanbul as well. The owner of the *bakkal* where she picked up groceries knew her name now, as did several other local shopkeepers. Delighted with her improving Turkish, they showed her local delicacies, and the fishmonger was very good about giving her suggestions on how to cook his catch of the day. Fiona had met several of Metin's friends and colleagues, and she had regular plans with her own friends. Her clients had no issues with her being abroad, and thanks to Safiye, she'd even taken on some simple editing work from a couple of local companies looking for assistance from a native English speaker.

She knew she'd have to go home eventually, but today was not the day. Today, they were packing bags for a week-long getaway. Fiona was finally going to get to see Metin's Datça home.

Chapter 27

It was a long drive, so they did it over two days, stopping in the port city of İzmir for the night. The following day, they drove through to Bodrum and caught a ferry across the water to Datça. Metin kept a Vespa in Datça, and usually flew down to the coast. This time, though, he had rented a car so he could show more of his country to Fiona.

The first night, they dined at a table right on the beach in Datça Town, with the sea lapping at their feet. They enjoyed a glass of *rakı* as they gorged themselves on fresh seafood. Hand in hand, they strolled along the harbour, browsing at artisan stalls that dotted the walkways, stopping at one of the shops for ice cream before continuing on. As the sun set, Fiona gawked at the size of the yachts anchored out in the deeper water. They walked among groups of holidaymakers, many from the city, but Fiona heard other languages around her as well. The beauty of this spot, where the Mediterranean Sea met the Aegean Sea, was clearly understood by more than just Turks.

Right on the edge of Eski Datça, high enough to take advantage of the cooling breeze, Metin's old stone house was a complete counterpoint to the hustle and bustle of İstanbul, and Fiona understood why Metin liked to write there. She had her own version of his two worlds with her condo in Toronto and her lake house, but here, she felt the disparity was heightened.

Fiona felt the temperature begin to drop as they opened the metal garden gate and walked through the small walled garden. Olive and almond trees provided shade, and a convenient place to hang a hammock for lazy afternoons. A wooden table and chairs on a stone patio beckoned, and she already knew they would eat most of their meals in this garden set high in the hills.

As they crossed the threshold into the tiny house, its stone walls provided a real respite from the summer heat. Inside of house, the furnishings were simple and spartan. It had originally been just one room until Metin partitioned off the bedroom and the bathroom for privacy. He had built a bookshelf all along that wall, and had been working on filling it for years. He had restored the original wood-beamed ceilings and had helped to modernize the electrical, which ran in conduits attached to the stone walls. An old whitewashed wrought iron bed sat at the back, with a brightly coloured duvet on top. A couch and two chairs sat opposite an adobe fireplace that provided most of the heat for the house in the winter. Metin had put in modern plumbing, so there was water in both the bathroom and the kitchen. A friend had handcrafted the kitchen cabinetry and an old farmhouse sink added to the rustic feeling. A long slab of live-edge wood served as both dining table and workspace.

Eski Datça was charming. Fiona loved to just wander through the narrow hilly streets while Metin worked. The house was just close enough to the action that it was easy to pop into a restaurant for a meal or an evening drink, but far enough away that it was quiet and serene.

The day before they had to leave, they took the Vespa into Datça Town for lunch. Metin took her into a jewellery store.

"*Kolay gelsin*," he greeted the jeweller, who looked up from his table with delight, welcoming his customers.

"*Hoş geldin, Metin bey*. And who is this lovely lady?"

Metin introduced Fiona. She browsed while the two men chatted for several minutes. Fiona briefly considered treating herself to something pretty when Metin called her over. The jeweller had laid a necklace out on a velvet tray. She came closer and saw a gold chain and pendant. It was two seagulls flying together, both set with diamonds. She ran her fingers over the pendant.

"*Muhteşem*," she whispered. "It's gorgeous."

"I'm glad you like it," Metin said. "It's yours. It's time I replaced the one I bought you in Marmaris." He picked the necklace up, opened the clasp, and put it around Fiona's neck.

"I still have that one," she whispered, pulling her hair out of the way. "It's tucked in my jewellery box at home. But this," she continued, looking in the mirror. "*Hayatım*, this is too much."

"It looks perfect on you, *sevgilim*. I want you to have it. No argument."

The jeweller watched the couple with a smile. He had known Metin's father and grandfather and he knew they would be pleased with this match.

Chapter 28

Back in İstanbul, Metin and Fiona were having a lazy Sunday. The weekend newspapers in English and Turkish were strewn around them. Metin had just gone into the kitchen to get more *çay* when his phone started buzzing. Fiona glanced at it and called out to him.

"Metin'*ciğim*, Tamer *arıyor*." His brother was calling.

Metin came back in and grabbed the phone. *"Buyurun, abi."*

As Fiona looked up from her book, she saw the blood drain from Metin's face and he sat down heavily on the couch beside her.

"Annem. It's my mum," he whispered, covering the phone before returning to his conversation. "Okay, Tamer. I'm coming. Right now. You'll call Safiye? Okay, see you soon."

"What's wrong?" she asked worriedly when he hung up the phone, looking as if the world had just ended.

"Öldü . . . annem öldü," he whispered, his voice cracking. Tamer had just told him that their mother had passed away overnight.

"Oh, Metin. *Başınız sağolsun*," Fiona said, extending her condolences and reaching for his shoulder. Even though it had been many years, she knew what it was to lose a parent.

He shook off her hand, standing up quickly. "I have to go. I have to help Tamer. There are things to do."

"Metin, how can I help?"

"There's nothing. Just stay here." He grabbed his wallet and his phone.

"Metin," Fiona said gently but firmly. "What do you need?"

"Just be here when I get back. Please."

"All right. But please give my condolences and my love to Tamer and Safiye." She kissed him as he started out the door, distracted by the devastating news.

After Metin left, Fiona texted Nazlı. All she knew about Turkish funeral traditions was that it happened very quickly after death. She needed a crash course, and she needed it now. Nazlı called right away.

"What do I do, Nazlı?" Fiona asked. "Please help me do the right thing."

"Well, the funeral will be tomorrow, I think," Nazlı said. "You will need a scarf for your head. I can lend you one. Yeşim and I will come with you to the funeral. Yeşim will want to go anyway, and Aylin probably will too. We will help you to help Metin."

Nazlı snapped into an organizational role. "Now, do you know where the reception will be? I guess it will be at Metin's or at Tamer's. Who has the largest flat?"

"I'm not sure, but probably Metin."

"Okay, so text him when we are finished talking. Tell him we will help you do everything. He knows you don't know what to do but they will have a problem. Tamer's daughters are abroad and he is divorced. Safiye can't do it, she will be overwhelmed. They don't have other relatives, so we will do everything.

"I'll call Yeşim and Aylin now and get another teacher to cover for me this evening. We will start the cooking. And we should make *helva*. Yeşim is really good at that. You start cleaning the flat now and I will be there soon."

Thanking her friend for her help, Fiona texted Metin about the reception and the help her friends had promised. His response came a few minutes later. He'd had to convince Tamer this was really the only solution.

Are you absolutely sure, Fiona'*çığım*?

I'm sure. Anything for you and your family. I love you.

Çok teşekkür ederim.

Metin was incredibly thankful and relieved that this was one thing he and his siblings didn't need to worry about. He trusted Fiona's friends and he knew she would want to do this.

Fiona let her friends direct the next few hours. The four women crowded into the kitchen and cooked up a storm. As the sun went down, Yeşim started the *irmik helvası*, explaining its importance to Fiona as she went along. She melted the butter and stirred in the semolina and pine nuts, browning them slowly before she added the milk. They all took turns stirring in the sugar before leaving the dish to stand. The sweet dessert would be served to all the guests tomorrow to help counter the bitterness of loss. Before they left, Yeşim told Fiona that she should offer Metin and his siblings an opportunity to stir it before it was served.

Metin came home late that evening and found Fiona had already pulled a suit out of his wardrobe to air and had ironed a shirt. She'd even shined his shoes. It was just one more way she was quietly helping him through this. That night, she stroked his hair as he tried in vain to sleep. He left again the next morning after giving her directions to the cemetery.

Fiona dressed carefully for the funeral, making sure that her arms were covered. She put her hair up and covered it loosely with the scarf that Nazlı lent her. Her friends had told her what to expect but it still felt strange. Everyone was dressed respectfully, but not necessarily in dark colours. Women and men didn't stand together. The body was buried in a shroud, not a coffin, and many people pinned photos of Özlem *teyze* on their clothes.

Safiye was surrounded by her friends so Fiona stood with Nazlı, Aylin, and Yeşim at the back of the women's side. Tamer and Metin stood at the front of the men's side and Yusuf stood solemnly with his father just behind his uncles. When the prayer was finished, the brothers lovingly lowered their mother's body into the earth and placed ceremonial shovelfuls of loose dirt into the grave. They were stoic, keeping their emotions inside, while Safiye, watching this ceremony, cried quietly for her mother.

That afternoon, a steady stream of people came by the flat to pay their respects. Fiona answered the door solemnly, welcomed people graciously and waved them toward the three mourning siblings. Her friends helped to make sure that everyone was fed and that the *çay* was always fresh.

When the final mourner departed, Fiona stood with her friends in the tiny kitchen, she thanked them profusely for everything. They had done so much to help her help the grieving family. She could never repay them. Quietly, they slipped away so as not to disturb Metin and his siblings.

Fiona poured two glasses of piping hot tea and joined Tamer on the couch, where he was sitting pensively after the long day. Safiye and Metin were sitting in the *cumba*, quietly sharing memories of their mother with each other.

"*İyi misin*?" she asked, checking in and inquiring if he was alright. "Can I get you anything?"

He looked at her seriously and began, in his halting English, "Fiona, I want to say to you something."

"*Tamer abi, Türkçede söyleyebilirsin*," she replied gently with a soft smile. "You can say it in Turkish."

"No, no. This very important. I want to say in English so you know how much. For today, Fiona, I want to say thank you."

"You're very welcome, Tamer. I'm happy to do what I can for your family while you grieve. And I had a lot of help," she said, appreciating the significance of not just the words he spoke to her but that he had wanted to say it in English. This was a turning point for them.

They sat in silence for a minute, and then Fiona began again quietly in Turkish. "*Abi, merak etme,* don't worry. I love your brother. I would do anything for him — and for his family."

Tamer took another sip of his tea. In English again, he said, "Fiona, I make mistake about you. You are good woman. Metin is very lucky man."

Draining his glass, he called to Safiye. Kerem had left a couple of hours ago with Yusuf. "*Kardeşim*, it's time for us to go. Let me take you home."

Safiye joined him and they thanked Fiona again and said good-night to Metin, hugging him one last time. Fiona saw them out, and just before they disappeared down the stairs, Safiye whispered in her ear, "*Abla,* please take care of my brother." Fiona nodded her understanding, tears in her eyes at Safiye's use of the "sister." She told her not to worry and closed the door behind them.

Metin was still standing in the *cumba* looking out the window when she returned. She took his hand and led him to the couch.

"*Metin'çiğim*, it's your turn now," she said gently. "Everyone's gone and you don't need to be strong anymore."

He took one deep ragged breath in and another out, and pressed his lips together. As he began to sob, Fiona took him in her arms and let him feel everything he'd been holding in since the day before. When he was finally spent, she took him to bed. She slowly and tenderly made love to him and then held him tight and stroked his hair until he finally drifted off in the wee small hours of the morning.

As usual, Fiona woke early the next morning. She slipped out of bed quietly, hoping that he would sleep late after the intensity the past two days. After a light breakfast, she cleaned up from the day before and put the flat back to its normal state. She had just begun to catch up on her business email when Metin emerged and folded her into a giant hug.

"Thank you for everything yesterday. *İyi ki varsın,* Fiona*'çığım.* I'm so glad you're here. You were perfect, it was perfect. I couldn't have asked for anything more."

Chapter 29

On a glorious early September morning, Fiona checked her email and then left her laptop to spend the day with Aylin. She wanted to catch up with her friend to see how she was doing and how she was getting on with reinventing her life here in İstanbul.

"I'm almost ready to talk about it," Aylin said, as they linked arms and walked along the main shopping street in Kadıköy. "I will tell you that I'm moving soon. I've found a flat near Nazlı in Çukurcuma. And there will be more to share in a day or two," she teased. "No more for now. Let's talk about you. You must need to go home soon. How does that feel?"

"I'm avoiding thinking about it," Fiona admitted. "I miss my kids and my grandchildren are growing so quickly. Video-chatting is only so good. I really can't stay much longer, but the more time I'm here, the harder it is to think about leaving. Maybe the end of this month. Or October."

"So things are good with Metin? University is back in, so his routine must have changed. You maybe don't see as much of him."

Fiona laughed. "I think it was harder on him, having to get up earlier, than it has been for me. Don't tell him, but I'm actually getting more work done this way! But you're right, it has been a transition."

"I'm going to miss you when you go," Aylin said. She looked at Fiona seriously. "But more importantly, what will the two of you do when you do go home?"

That question weighed heavily on Fiona's mind. "I honestly don't know, Aylin." They sat down on a café terrace and ordered *çay*. "I'm not ready to give up what I've found again with Metin. But an overseas romance? I wasn't very successful at that the first time. I know, there's technology now, and I could come back every year for a few months, but it's going to be really difficult. I can't live here full time and I can't ask him to leave Turkey. I really don't know." She took a sip from her glass. "Let's talk about something more positive."

Later that afternoon, Fiona headed to the university to meet up with Metin. She was joining him after his last lecture of the day to walk along the shore in Bebek and stop for *çay* somewhere along the way.

"Knock knock," she said playfully, as she came upon her handsome man, looking every inch a professor, in khakis and a tweed blazer. Fiona hadn't seen Metin's office yet, and was suitably impressed at the vast library he had there, complementing the wall of books at both his flat and at Datça. Metin looked up from his desk and grinned.

"You've been shopping."

"Guilty as charged! Aylin and I spent some time indulging ourselves today. Do you like it?" She spun around for him, modelling her new belted shirtdress. The little diamonds in the seagull necklace she never took off glittered on her neck. "New shoes too," she added, showing off the low wedges.

Coming out from behind his desk, Metin gave her a kiss. "Just as lovely as the woman wearing them," he said. "Shall we go?"

They walked down the winding street to the shore, sharing events of their days and taking shortcuts on the stairs. They were just about at the bottom, when Fiona turned her ankle on an uneven step, and tumbled to the ground with a cry. Metin was at her side immediately, concerned. "Are you all right?" he asked.

"I'm not sure," she said shakily as the world spun. She took some deep breaths and after a minute, she gamely put out her hands for Metin to help her up. When she tried to put weight on her left ankle, though, she cried out again in pain. "Ow, that really hurts," she exclaimed. "I need to sit for a bit."

They sat on the curb as Fiona tried to will her ankle better. But it was quickly obvious that she wasn't going to be walking on the shore that evening.

"Fiona, let me take you to the hospital," Metin suggested.

"I'm sure I can get home," she said, not quite ready to admit total defeat. But her ankle was already starting to swell. And when she tried to stand up again, she gasped and the blood drained from her face.

"That's it. Stop being so stubborn." Metin picked her up and carried her down the rest of the hill, where he flagged a taxi and bundled her off to the nearest *hastane*.

An hour and a half later, Fiona left the hospital with a tightly bandaged ankle, some painkillers to hold her over until they could fill a prescription, and instructions to keep off her feet for at least three or four days. The doctor had ordered an x-ray just to be sure, and it confirmed a mid-grade sprain. But rest was required for it to heal properly. After that, she could use a cane to get around until she could walk properly. She would have to do strengthening exercises and the doctor warned her it might take several weeks to heal completely.

"What are my kids going to say," she groaned, as they headed home in a taxi, her head slightly fuzzy from the pills the doctor had given her in the hospital.

"They're going to say how lucky it is that you have me to take care of you," Metin joked, kissing her gently on the cheek.

Fiona smiled and leaned into Metin, but she was a little concerned about breaking this news to her children so far away.

Paying the taxi driver and handing Fiona his house keys, Metin picked her up again and carried her up the stairs to his flat.

"It's a good job you're tiny," he joked as he got to the third-floor landing.

In his arms, Fiona unlocked the door and pushed it open with the cane that the doctor had given her. Metin settled her on the couch with a bag of ice wrapped in a towel on her ankle and went to start the tea. Fiona was sound asleep when he returned.

The next morning, Fiona texted Nazlı and Aylin and Yeşim to let them know what had happened. She'd unwrapped her ankle to have a look and instantly wished she hadn't. Not only was it swollen, it was now black and blue — and very tender to the touch. That was all the encouragement she needed to stay on the couch and keep icing it. Metin took the day off work to ensure she stayed there.

All three texted back quickly offering food, company, and well wishes. They made plans to visit the next day.

After lunch, Metin slipped out to get some groceries and fill her prescription. Fiona picked up her phone again to start calling her kids.

"Are you okay, Mum?" Holly asked worriedly, her nursing instincts kicking in. "Should I come and bring you home?"

Fiona laughed. "Holly, I'm fine. The hospitals here are great and Metin is taking good care of me."

Holly's antenna went up. "He's taking care of you? What about the *teyzes*?" she asked, referring to her mother's Turkish girlfriends as the "aunties."

"They'll come by tomorrow, but for now, Metin's doing a great job."

Holly heard the warmth in Fiona's voice as she talked about him and was happy for her mum. It had been a long time since she'd had a relationship and Holly wanted her to be happy.

"I'd love to meet him one day, Mum," she said. "Ankle notwithstanding, you sound like you're having a lot of fun. You deserve it."

"I am, my dear, I am! And yes, I hope you'll meet him soon too."

Fiona repeated the same conversation with Holly and Simon and then called Jamie. He stepped out of the busy workshop to talk with her.

"Mother, you need to get on a plane and come home now," insisted her overprotective son. "This İstanbul business has gotten out of hand. I'm serious. Let us take care of you now."

Fiona sighed. She had known this conversation would be harder. "Jamie, I'm fine. I'm tucked in on a couch in a flat with the most spectacular view. Metin is taking very good care of me, and my girlfriends will be by tomorrow to keep me company. Besides, the doctor wants me to stay off my feet for a few days and after that I'll have to walk with a cane for a bit. I can't fly like that."

"I'm still not sure I like the idea of you shacking up with this guy," Jamie muttered.

"Jamie," replied a frustrated Fiona. "You are overreacting! Metin is a respected university professor, an internationally sought-after lecturer, an author and not that it's any of your business, we love each other. While I appreciate your concern, I'm plenty old enough to know what I'm doing."

"Fine," said her oldest boy, clearly exasperated by his mother. "But be careful, Mum."

They said their goodbyes and Fiona silenced her phone. She was looking forward to Metin arriving with her prescription. She closed her eyes. Between the pain and the phone calls, she was exhausted.

Metin found her sound asleep an hour later when he returned. Despite the injury, she looked peaceful and he quietly put the bags in the kitchen before sitting down beside her on the couch with his laptop. After reading the same sentence several times, he looked up and watched Fiona's chest rise and fall as she breathed in and out. Metin knew he was in trouble. He loved his woman deeply. And he knew she had to go home. They would have to find a way to make it work.

Fiona slept for another half hour, only rousing when Metin brought two glasses of tea. She stretched sleepily and told him about her children's reactions. Metin thought it was understandable that Jamie was concerned, but was pleased the other three seemed to accept that he would take good care of their mother.

"How are you feeling?" he asked. She still looked pale, and he saw her wince as she shifted her weight on the couch.

"I think it's time for another of those pills," she admitted.

The next morning, Aylin and Nazlı came by early. Metin opened the door and gestured to them to come in.

"*Ayyy, geçmiş olsun,*" cried Nazlı when she saw Fiona on the couch, with her bandaged ankle resting on a cushion. "Feel better soon."

Fiona shrugged. What else could she do? Aylin shooed Metin off to work and said they'd stay with her. Nazlı was already in the kitchen making fresh *çay*.

Fiona looked curiously at her friends when Nazlı returned. They shared a look, and Fiona could tell they were bursting with excitement. "*Ne haber?* What's up? Tell me!"

"Well," Aylin began. "Remember when I told you I was almost ready to share some news with you? It's official now. You know that place next door to Nazlı's yoga studio, right? And you know I've been looking for a small business. Nazlı told me the owners were ready to retire, so she made introductions and I wrote a business plan. I am now the proud owner of a little café that's seen better days!"

"Oh, Aylin, that's amazing!" The news perked Fiona up immediately. "What will you do with the place?"

"Well, it needs some serious love and attention, so at the beginning, I'll just do *çay* on the terrace while I fix things up inside. I'll need some help in the kitchen, so I'm reaching out to lots of people. Honestly, though? I've missed cooking Turkish food, and I'm excited to do some of it myself. My mind is exploding with menus!"

"And I'm so excited to have Aylin right next door," said Nazlı. "My students will like her café so much."

The friends chatted away the morning, covering Aylin's new adventure and Fiona gave them all the details about her accident. Nazlı fussed over her and brought more tea, and eventually she and Aylin put lunch together.

"Let me help you fix up the café before I go home," Fiona said to Nazlı. She gestured to her foot. "I mean, after I'm healed." They laughed. "But honestly, you can use me now too. Do you have a name yet? A marketing plan? I want to help you while I'm here."

"I'd love to bounce a few ideas off you," Aylin said. "Especially as I think I can appeal to tourists as well."

Fiona's phone rang, cutting the conversation short. Fiona hit the accept call button and her son's face showed up on her screen. "*Gün aydın, oğlum*," she greeted him, laughing. "Good morning, Simon. It's awfully early for you, isn't it?" Fiona had counted backwards and it was only six o'clock in the morning.

"What's with the Turkish, Mum?" Simon teased her. "I thought I'd call to see how you are before I head out to work. How's the ankle? Are you stuck inside? Do you have company?" The questions tumbled out.

"I'm fine, dear. My ankle is still pretty sore, but I have some good pain medication and my friends are keeping me company today." Aylin and Nazlı stood behind her and waved. "And it really doesn't matter that I'm inside. I've shown you the view from here. It's amazing. And we have the windows wide open so there's a wonderful breeze. It's almost as good as being outside."

With Simon's questions answered, they chatted for half an hour. He was doing well at work and had just been given an important client to manage.

Fiona noticed her friends talking quietly while she spoke to Simon. They kept throwing glances her way. Saying goodbye to her son, she turned her attention back to them.

"What are you two whispering about?" she asked. Her friends looked at each other again, neither speaking.

Finally, Nazlı started. "You said 'before I go home.' Are you starting to think about it?"

Fiona looked down at her hands. "I don't want to, but I have to go. My family is there." Her eyes filled with tears. "I just don't know how I'm going to leave Metin behind."

Building on their conversation a few days ago, Aylin jumped in to ask if they'd talked about it yet.

"No, not really," Fiona admitted. "Neither of us want to bring it up. It's hard enough just thinking about it. But I came in the spring and its autumn now. We're going to have to deal with it soon. I've missed half a year of my grandchildren's lives."

Fiona finally sent Nazlı and Aylin away in the middle of the afternoon. She was expecting Metin home by dinner, and she wanted to catch up on her email before he arrived.

It wasn't Metin, but Yeşim who opened the door close to six o'clock.

"*Sürpriz!*" she said, as she put Metin's keys down on the hall console. Fiona looked up at her with a quizzical look. "Metin stopped by my office at the university this afternoon," she explained. "He wanted to update me, and also ask me if I could stop in so he could go to a meeting that popped up."

"I'm so happy to see you," Fiona said, meaning it. "Come and sit down. I'd offer you *çay*, but I'm still not very mobile."

"I can't stay long, but I wanted to see you and make sure there was nothing you needed in the next couple of hours. Metin should be here by eight." Yeşim looked at her with concern, but Fiona brushed her off.

"It's getting better, but yes, it's still tender. I'll be fine," she said pre-emptively. "Now tell me what your kids are up to."

Yeşim said goodbye half an hour later, and left the door slightly ajar for Metin, who came home with *paket servis* — takeout from a local restaurant — for dinner, looking a little frazzled. His meeting had been full of university politics and he was still put out by the gentle questions Yeşim had asked earlier. He knew she meant well, but she was making him think about things he didn't want to think about yet.

"Everything okay?" Fiona asked as he leaned down to kiss her.

"Yeah, yeah," he answered absentmindedly. "Nothing to worry about."

Fiona wasn't so sure, but she let it go. Metin didn't look like he was in the mood to explain. If it was important, he'd tell her soon enough.

He was still distant when she sent him off to work the next day, but was relieved when she told him she could hop from the couch to the kitchen if needed. "And besides," she continued, "tomorrow I'm allowed up for real."

"As long as you're sure," he said, getting ready to go. "I love you, you know."

"I love you too."

By the weekend, Fiona was hobbling around the flat quite well with her cane, and was starting to get cabin fever. To help with that, but also to keep her close for one final day, Metin asked Safiye to stop by with Yusuf. He owed his nephew a backgammon game or two. Fiona was happy to catch up with Metin's sister in the *cumba* while the game happened behind them on the dining table. They were discussing Aylin's café and it dawned on Fiona that Safiye might be able to help with the promotion.

"I'd be happy to," Safiye agreed. "Why don't we meet for lunch in a couple of weeks with Aylin when your ankle is better. It would be fun to work on this project." She changed the subject, asking about Fiona's children and grandchildren. Fiona was happy to show her photos and talk about their accomplishments.

"Jenna and Jon are almost four years old now. They're growing so fast." Safiye noticed a touch of melancholy in Fiona's voice as she continued. "They're up at my lake house this weekend. They'll spend all day building sandcastles and splashing in the lake. If I were there, I'd take them for ice cream to give Holly and Greg a bit of a break."

"You miss them."

"I do." Fiona put on a smile. "But I love your *abi* too. If I were there, I'd be talking all about how if I were here, we'd be going to Moda for *dondurma*."

Seeing her son win the fourth game, Safiye decided it was time for them to go. Metin walked them down to the street.

"*Abi*, what are you going to do?" asked Safiye. "I know you love each other but I think Fiona will need to go home soon. She's missing her family."

Metin nodded. He had actually been thinking about this for a while. He hadn't told Fiona yet but he'd reached out to universities in the Toronto area inquiring about the possibility of guest lecturing for a semester. He was still waiting to hear back, and this was contributing to the distance he knew Fiona had sensed. He didn't want to say anything until there was something to consider. But Metin definitely wanted there to be something to consider.

Chapter 30

Fiona and Safiye met with Aylin to talk about possibilities for her café. Aylin had just taken possession and there was a lot of work to do. Nevertheless, the three women pulled wooden stools up to a rickety table and plowed through the discussion. Aylin felt bad. She didn't have electricity yet so she couldn't offer them anything.

"Fine way for a café discussion to start," she apologized.

"*Boş ver*," Fiona insisted. It wasn't a problem for either of them.

Aylin was impressed with the initial ideas that Safiye brought for the opening, and was ready to sign the paperwork for the short engagement. Fiona felt good knowing that her friend was in experienced hands. They discussed some clever ideas for names, but nothing felt quite right to Aylin. She was torn between wanting a name that felt meaningful to her and one that would be easy to remember. Fiona and Safiye said they'd go away and think about it a little more.

They walked slowly down the hill to the sea and decided to stop for a quick treat to celebrate a successful meeting and small contract for Safiye. A waiter brought them a few different types of baklava to share along with their glasses of tea.

"I've been thinking about what Aylin said," mused Fiona. "What do you think about Umut Kafe — Hope Café? It's easy, the project has filled her with hope, and if she plans to go after tourists, it's easy for foreigners to say."

"It's perfect!" Safiye exclaimed. "I don't know why I didn't think of it."

They talked it over a bit more as they finished their *çay*, but by the time they were ready to go their separate ways, they were sure they had it. Fiona suggested Safiye reach out to Aylin with the name when she got back to her office. She received text messages from them both within minutes of each other. They had a winner.

Fiona rode the ferry back to Kuzguncuk feeling conflicted. On one hand, she was elated that they had a name for Aylin's café. She felt very invested in her friend's success. But the pull of home was getting stronger and Metin continued to be withdrawn. Fiona knew he was working hard to finish the research for his book, teaching a full course load for the fall semester, but that didn't seem to be the issue. It just didn't ever seem to be the right time to discuss her departure and what came next for them.

So today, when she arrived back at the flat, she fired up her laptop, and reluctantly did what she knew she had to do.

As they cleared the table after dinner that night, she plucked up her courage. "Metin, we need to talk."

He put the dishes he was carrying down on the counter and took her hand. "I know, *sevgilim*. Let's go sit down."

They took their *çay* into the living room and sat next to each other. Fiona tucked her legs up under herself on the couch.

"Metin, I booked a ticket home today," she began quietly. "We have to talk about what that means for us and where we go from here." She could see disappointment and hurt on his face. "We always knew this time would come," she said gently.

Hurt gave way to anger and his green eyes sparked as the questions poured out. "*Ciddi misin*? Are you serious? You booked it already? Without even talking to me? When? When are you leaving?"

"In a month. At the end of October." A tear slid down Fiona's face. "This wasn't easy, *hayatım*. But I need to see my family, and my friends. We've had a wonderful, magical six months together." She kissed him gently. "I don't want to lose you, but please try to understand. I had to do this."

Metin was trying to process what Fiona had just told him. He was incensed that she had just decided this on her own. He would never have stopped her, but he had expected to be part of the discussion. He pulled away from her and stood up suddenly. And then he sat down again.

"I know you're right. I'm just going to miss you so damn much." His shoulders slumped. "I just need some time to get used to the idea." He stood up again and stormed into the kitchen. Bracing his arms on the counter, he took a couple of deep breaths before going back to the living room and grabbed his wallet and keys. "I'm going for a walk," he said brusquely. Fiona got up to join him. Metin put out his hand. "No. I need to be alone."

Fiona spent much of the week riding a roller coaster of emotions. She let everyone at home know when she was returning, which elicited a great outpouring of happiness and relief. She set up some lunches and other gatherings with Rachael, Hyun, and Mila among others. Max and Ben wanted to have her for dinner as soon as she got home, and the kids were all excited to know their mum was returning. On the other hand, as she told her Turkish friends, their responses were full of sadness as they began to count down the days. Aylin was especially disappointed that Fiona wouldn't be there for her café opening, but she understood.

As Fiona make plans, Metin watched her disappear into herself, mentally preparing to leave. He was not looking forward to that day, but he didn't know how to talk to her about it. So he pulled back further, simmering silently. He knew he was being irrational, but he didn't care. He was hurt and he was mad. It was so right between them and he didn't want it to end. And if he was honest with himself, he was starting to build a wall around his heart because he knew, he really did, that she had to leave. For her part, Fiona noticed Metin was spending longer days at the university and even when he was home, he was moody and short-tempered. It seemed their last few weeks together would not be easy.

Finally, the pot boiled over. Fiona had made plans to spend Sunday with Aylin, Yeşim, and Nazlı. They were going to go to a *hamam* to be scrubbed squeaky clean and then planned to spend the afternoon at İstanbul Modern, where a new art exhibit was opening. She was explaining this to Metin as they ate breakfast Saturday morning. She was looking forward to the day and she suggested to Metin it might be a good opportunity for him to spend some time with his brother.

It was the straw that broke the proverbial camel's back. He slammed his fork down on the table. "You are unbelievable. You just decide everything on your own, don't you?" He spat out the words. "You don't bother to talk about it, to ask my opinion, or think about me. You just do what's right for Fiona. And now you're deciding what I should do too. Honestly, Fiona, it's like I don't matter at all in this relationship." He pushed his chair back from the table.

Fiona sat with her mouth gaping open as the rant continued.

"Do you ever give any thought to what I want? We have so few weekends left. Maybe I want you to myself."

"Metin, it's not like that at all. You know I love you. But I have friends I love too. This is kind of our last big event together. Aylin's so busy getting the café ready and it's the only time that worked for everyone. Please understand."

"I don't understand at all." Metin's emotions were getting the better of him. "You're so selfish. You're not thinking about anyone but you. You, you, you! If it works for you, how it affects me doesn't matter to you at all. I can't believe I never knew this about you."

Fiona couldn't believe what she was hearing. "Metin, calm down. Let's talk about this. I love you."

But Metin couldn't stop. He needed to lash out and hurt her as much as he was hurting inside. "It's just as well you're leaving soon. This was clearly a mistake," he snarled. He turned away from her, moving to the *cumba*.

It was one step too far. Fiona felt as if he had stabbed her through the heart. But through the pain, she also felt angry and knew she needed to get out of there quickly before she said something she'd regret.

"*İnanamıyorum.* I cannot believe you. *Sen çok, çok . . .*" She threw up her hands, her Turkish having abandoned her. "I have to go." She grabbed her purse and slammed the door behind her, storming down the stairs.

Fiona wasn't quite sure what had just happened. Why were her final weeks with Metin turning so sour? How could she fix it? She sat down on a bench on the seaside and leaned forward so her hair covered her face as hot, salty tears began to fall. Didn't he understand? She didn't really want to go home but on the other hand, she did. She loved Metin and they had to find a way to make this work.

For his part, Metin stood in stunned silence in the *cumba*. He'd been almost shaking with anger and now he was almost shaking with fear. The instant the words had come out of his mouth, he had wanted to take them back. He didn't mean them. Surely she knew that. He just didn't know how to talk about his feelings yet. And yet they needed to as time was starting to run out. He kept hoping he'd hear back from the schools he'd been speaking with. He wanted to run after her, but he knew she needed time to cool off. Instead, he sent a group message to her friends.

> *Arkadaşlar.* Friends. We've had a fight. Fiona's really angry at me. If she comes to you, please take care of her until we can make up. I love her.

Fiona walked anonymously along the sea through the throngs of other İstanbullus enjoying the beautiful fall day until she calmed down a little. Fishermen lined the banks and those who had been up early showcased their success in the shallow buckets near their feet. Here and there, young men were setting up strings of balloons in hopes of enticing other young men to part with a few lira for target practice. She saw a *çiçekçi* setting up her big plastic buckets full of the flowers she would sell for a few lira and, of course, it wouldn't be İstanbul without a red *simit* wagon dotting the landscape.

Soon, Fiona found herself on a ferry over to the European side of the city, letting the sea air clear her head. Seagulls chased the boat, looking for odd bits of bread but she didn't have any this time. When the ferry docked, Fiona walked up one of the steep staircases of Cihangir and knocked on the window of a closed café. She could see Aylin inside, wearing overalls and a tank top, painting the walls a beautiful buttery yellow. Aylin turned at the sound. Fiona waved, looking forlorn.

"*Gel, gel.* Come in," Aylin said after she unlocked the door. "What's wrong, *canım.* You look like you could use a hug. I'd give you one but I'm covered in paint."

That elicited the beginning of a smile as Fiona noticed more than one smudge of paint on her friend's face. Aylin had seen Metin's message and she was angry at him for hurting her friend and worried for them both. But she thought it best for Fiona to explain.

"*Çay getireyim.* I'll get tea. And you can tell me everything." Aylin went into the kitchen to bring out the tulip-shaped glasses. She took a moment to message the group.

Merak etme. Don't worry. She's with me.

Fiona wasn't sure why she'd ended up in front of Aylin's new business. Maybe it was because Aylin had lived outside Turkey so long that she would understand both worlds. Maybe she could help her understand why Metin was behaving this way. Fiona poured her heart out to Aylin. How she had responsibilities in Canada. How she had to go home. How she didn't want to. How much she loved Metin. How she knew she had to just book the ticket or she'd never do it. He knew she had to. But he was so angry.

"*Ah, canım arkadaşım,*" Aylin began soothingly. "This is the Turkish way. You know our emotions run high. You have to remember that Metin is just like all other Turkish men, no matter how education he received in America and the UK."

Fiona looked at her quizzically. "What do you mean?"

"He's likes to be in charge. With his time abroad, he is maybe ready to make decisions together with you, but not so ready to let you make them all. But you've spent a lot of years on your own. You're a strong woman. An independent woman with her own business and a good life. You're used to making decisions and running with them."

Fiona realized with a start that Aylin had a point. She hadn't needed to consult anyone for a very long time, and she hadn't stopped to think about that.

"There's a part of him that will be frustrated with you, until he calms down and becomes rational again," Aylin continued. "But it will be okay, really. You two will talk, and he'll come around."

Fiona wasn't ready Metin let him off the hook just yet. "But Aylin, that doesn't mean he's allowed to be cruel. He chose words that he knew would hurt me."

"He's hurting too, *canım,* and he's anticipating a whole lot more hurt. Think about it. You're going home to something. But for him, you're just going. Remember, he lost you once a long time ago and it was really difficult for him. From his point of view, the same thing is happening again. But this time, you have a much more mature relationship. I know it will be hard for you, but don't forget his pain in all this. You will both need to compromise."

Fiona took a sip of her *çay* as she took that in. "Am I being selfish? He accused me of that."

"I don't think so. But I do think you're working hard to protect yourself. And that's what Metin is doing too. It's just in a different way. You two have a lot to talk about in the next few weeks to make sure neither of you is hurting. Make sure you always talk. Don't hold things in, and don't let him do it either."

They lapsed into silence for a few minutes and then Fiona said, "Well, this place won't paint itself. Will you let me help, Aylin, while I mull over what you said?"

"*Kesinlikle,*" her friend said with a smile. "Definitely. I'm always happy to have some help. Just as long as you don't mind the possibility of paint on your shirt." The two friends worked together and after a couple of hours, they finished the last wall of the café.

"Have you given any thought to your logo yet?" Fiona asked as they had a quick snack of *tost.* Aylin was starting to get the kitchen in shape and she could cook simple things there now. They'd pulled a couple of wooden stools out onto the terrace and were enjoying the sunshine.

"That's next," Aylin answered. "Safiye has promised me some design ideas tomorrow or the next day. She's amazing to work with."

Fiona nodded and popped the last of her toasted cheese sandwich in her mouth. "And now, I'd better go try and fix the mess I left this morning." She flung her arms around Aylin and gave her a long, tight squeeze. "Thank you for everything."

"*Elbette. Her zaman.* Of course. Any time. Friends forever, right?"

Metin was waiting when Fiona returned. He heard her key turn in the lock and he went to the door to greet her. As she opened the door, he pulled her into his arms. "I am so sorry," he whispered soberly in her ear. "I'm behaving like an ass. Can you forgive me?"

"I should be the one asking for forgiveness," said Fiona, looking up into his eyes. "I've been making decisions for me that affect you. And I haven't been talking to you about them. I've lived alone too long, I guess." She dropped her keys in the bowl by the door and led him to the couch. "Can we talk now? Aylin reminded me that we have to talk. I have loved every single second of the last six months, Metin. From the moment I heard your voice at the reunion and our first dinner, I knew I still had feelings for you. I couldn't believe it when you kissed me on my balcony. The intensity of my feelings scared me, but when I realized you felt the same it was like a second chance. It seemed impossible to me that we found each other again like this. I'm so lucky that my work allows me to be anywhere. I love it here and I love what we're sharing. But I have a whole other life I can't just give up either. I should have talked more with you and I should have told you how I was feeling. And for that, I'm sorry. I'll do better."

Metin started to speak. Fiona put her finger on his lips. "Please let me finish. I know we said we wouldn't put expectations on what we have. But I don't think either of us expected this to become what it is. And so we're going to need to find a way to be together a lot of the time, while still being apart for some of it. I have some ideas, but I'm not sure how practical they are. But if we don't talk about them, we'll never find out." Fiona's head dropped and Metin pulled her close.

"I have some ideas too," he said, as he stroked her hair. "And I've been just as bad as you. I've kept a lot bottled up and haven't talked with you. I've been thinking about this for a long time. I'm not ready to give you up again. I lost you once, but we're both older and wiser now. What would you think if I came and spent some time with you in Canada?"

Fiona sat up straight. "Can you do that? I didn't think that was even on the table. I thought we'd have to wait until I could come back here."

Metin laughed. "I guess this is why we need to talk!" He outlined his idea. With the research for his book just about finished, he had always been planning to take a semester-long sabbatical to write the first draft. Fiona couldn't believe he'd never mentioned it. "I'll have no classes to teach from January through April," he explained. "When I first planned it, I thought I would be in Datça for most of the time, but there's no reason why I can't spend at least some of it in Canada. That is, if you'll have me." Metin still had a small fear that Fiona had her two lives neatly divided into two.

"I didn't know you were ready to write," said Fiona, taking in what he'd said. "You'd really give up some of that special time in that beautiful spot to be with me?" A delighted grin slowly spread over her face. "Even in winter? And of course I'll have you. I can't wait for you to meet my family and friends, and there's so much there that I want to share with you. Oh, we have so many plans to make!"

Metin was still keeping the potential of lecturing in Toronto close to his chest, but this was a good start. Over the next few days, he and Fiona were more open with each other about their hopes and fears for their relationship. They finally decided that he would join her in Canada as soon as December exams were finished. They would spend some of their time in Toronto and some up at her lake house. Metin would probably stay until March and then go back to the warmth of Datça to finish his book. Fiona would likely join him a couple of months later for a time. They were cautiously optimistic that this would all work.

"Of course, you'll have to deal with my kids. Are you sure you're up for that?"

"Fiona, I would go anywhere and do anything for you."

Chapter 31

Metin insisted on taking Fiona to the airport on the day she flew home. Fiona protested, but in the end, Metin got his way. He helped her take her bags down the stairs and they climbed into the waiting taxi.

"I'm feeling a certain déjà vu," Fiona said wryly, thinking about the last time she headed to the airport with Metin in a taxi.

"At least this time we know that we only have a few weeks apart," Metin said. He had already had a ticket booked to join her in Toronto as soon as classes finished.

He saw her through to security and gave her one last kiss goodbye. And much like the last time she left him in an airport, Fiona clung to him, not wanting to go. Finally it was time, and she headed through security as she had so many years ago. She looked back just before she turned the corner and saw him, hands jammed in his pockets, with an incredibly sad look on his face. This time, though, they had technology, and not trusting her voice, she texted him when she got to her gate, and he replied quickly.

She texted him again as soon as she landed in Toronto

Just landed. I miss you already.

Ben de seni. Me too. I found your note. Love you.

Me too.

Fiona had left a letter on their bed when she left, trying to explain her jumbled up feelings. She had needed to make clear to him that no matter how confusing the tornado of real life was around them, she loved him and that she knew they'd find a way to make it work this time. Metin was touched. He felt exactly the same way. Together, they'd figure it out.

It was strange walking through the door to her condo. Fiona hadn't been there since early May. Holly had gone in the day before to give the place a quick clean, fill the fridge, and leave some fresh flowers, but she was so used to being in Kuzguncuk that it didn't feel like home at first. Fiona kicked off her shoes and laughed out loud when she realized she was looking for *terlik*. She gazed out over the valley for a few minutes before texting the kids to let them know she was home safely. Her phone pinged as they all welcomed her back. She'd connect with Ben and friends tomorrow.

Toronto seemed very orderly and organized to Fiona after living the chaos of İstanbul for six months. Drivers and pedestrians alike were more courteous and there was so much space. She planned to spend two weeks in the city before heading to the lake. Those weeks were a whirlwind of work, interspersed with lunches, dinners, coffee dates, and drinks with friends and with family. She filled her days and her evenings because the nights were lonely and her bed was cold and empty. Fiona's girlfriends were all incredibly interested in the tall, handsome Turkish man who had captured her heart. The story seemed incredibly romantic to them. Her kids were a bit skeptical, and were really happy to have their mother closer at hand. Fiona spent hours with Holly and Greg's kids, re-establishing her relationship with the twins. Even though she'd stayed in touch through video chats, they were a bit shy around her at first, but quickly came around.

She saved Max and Ben until the end. These two wonderful men had been at every important moment of her adult life and she gave them huge hugs when she arrived at their house for dinner, laden with gifts. They plied her with good wine and food, catching her up on everything she'd missed while she was away. Ben brought an amazing salted chocolate tart in from the kitchen and Max refilled their wine glasses before either of them asked.

"So," said Max gently. "Tell us. How are you doing? Missing Metin? Or is it a lovely dream that you're waking up from now that you're back?"

Fiona took a deep breath. "Gosh, I miss him so much. I don't know how to explain it. We've been texting every day and talking of course, but it's not the same."

"I'm happy — we're happy — that you've found someone, Fiona," Max said. "I hope you can make this work."

"I hope so too. But there's a lot to figure out." She shook her head. "Lots to figure out."

Fiona drove up to the lake the next morning. After filling her fridge with fresh fruits and vegetables, and stopping by the butcher for some chicken and beef, Fiona lit a fire in the stone fireplace. She stood in her front window watching the cold rain fall over the lake as heat from the crackling logs started to warm the room. She loved this view as much as she loved the view over the Bosphorus. Fiona was missing Metin fiercely today and was counting down the hours until she could call him.

They had developed a routine since she'd been home. If Metin got up just a bit earlier than usual, he could call her just before she fell asleep at night. They might text occasionally during her day and they would try to video-chat again, or at least chat by text around two or three o'clock in her afternoon before he went to bed. It wasn't great, but they were making do.

Fiona focussed on work, cleaning out several days of work email. The last couple of weeks in İstanbul and the first couple of weeks back in Toronto had been full of emotion and she'd channelled some of that into the beginnings of a proposal for a magazine article. But her regular clients wouldn't wait forever, so she rolled up her metaphorical sleeves and started making calls.

Umut Kafe opened to rave reviews. Fiona had sent a giant bouquet of Siberian irises and sunflowers and as an extra surprise, had Safiye order some bud vases with for even more irises for all the tables. Aylin teared up when she saw just how beautiful her new business looked.

She and Safiye had become quite close working together and had become friends. She had met Kerem and Yusuf and was touched when he brought his friends by after school.

The café was bustling all day long. Safiye had suggested an opening day discount for Nazlı's yoga students, and she wrote an advertisement for the alumni newsletter. Local business owners in the *mahalle* stopped by, curious about their new neighbour, and Safiye's publicity campaign had neighbourhood residents stopping by all day long.

Yeşim met her children there after school and stayed on to lend a hand when things got even busier in the evening. Mehmet was on another business trip and was missing the excitement.

Metin was astounded at the crowd when he arrived at eight o'clock. It was cool but even the terrace was busy. A young server took his order and he sat, sipping his tea, just watching. Aylin was like an orchestra conductor, keeping everything moving at the right pace, with a smile on her face the whole time. She smiled and waved when she saw him, but it was almost an hour later before she finally had time to catch her breath and say hello. He stayed, and when she finally closed the doors at ten, they video-chatted with a sleepy Fiona together.

People may have come on opening day out of curiosity, but they returned for the food and the conversation. To nobody's surprise, Aylin whipped up magic in her kitchen. She had hired several part-time cooks, but liked to go into the kitchen now and then and make a special dish. Over time, popping in to find out what "Aylin's special" was that day became part of many families' traditions. Umut Kafe served all the traditional favourites along with European desserts and pastries. Aylin had perfected pavlova living in Australia, so the sweet meringue dessert was often featured with varying fruit fillings.

After the first week, when opening kinks were worked out, Safiye moved into the second phase of her promotion plan. Umut Kafe employees had been chosen for their exceptional language skills, and because of that, the expat community in Cihangir flocked through her doors, knowing they could be served in just about any language. Safiye was sure the café could capitalize on tourist trade for exactly the same reason and Aylin was more than willing to try.

"The wi-fi is still terrible, *sevgilim*," Metin apologized, when their video chat turned into audio only, for the fifth day in a row. "I don't know what the problem is. I can hear you fine, but when I turn on my video, it all goes to hell."

"It's OK," she said with a sigh as she puttered in the kitchen getting a morning cup of coffee. "I still remember what you look like. Tell me about your day."

"It was pretty miserable, actually." Metin lay in bed and told her about it. Thursdays were his longest teaching day and his last class seemed to be full of first-year students who weren't interested in learning. December had started two days ago with unusually cold weather and tonight the wind was driving the rain against the window panes. "I wish you were here in my bed," he said softly.

"I miss you too," Fiona answered. "You'll be here soon. And we'll need each other to stay warm. It's snowing again today." The two chatted for a bit longer before Metin yawned. "You sound tired," Fiona said.

"Mmmmm. I'd better say good night. I'll call you in the morning."

Chapter 32

Fiona watched the arrivals board nervously. It was two weeks before Christmas and she'd driven back from the lake a few days ago. She was expecting Metin to come through the doors any second. It was a cold day and Fiona had worn her long wool coat over a green cashmere sweater, a black skirt, and tall heeled black boots. She played nervously with her seagull pendant.

The wait was excruciating. But she'd been patient for this long already, so she could wait a few more minutes. A sudden horrifying thought came over her. What if he hadn't got on the plane? What if he wasn't coming after all?

Finally the doors opened and Metin strode confidently out, pulling his roller bag behind him. Fiona's heart skipped a beat when she saw him, hardly believing he was here. Her eyes widened in surprise at the beard he was sporting. Metin's eyes scanned the crowd and when they landed on Fiona, he broke into a broad grin. She raced to meet him at the end of the ramp and he pulled her into his arms, picked her up, and whirled her around.

"*Hoş geldin, hayatım.*" She whispered the greeting in his ear and gave him a kiss. When he put her down, she reached up and touched the beginnings of the beard. "*Bu ne yaa?* What's this?" she teased him.

"Do you like?" he asked. "I thought it might be good for the cold weather." She giggled as he nuzzled into her neck to kiss her. The beard tickled, and it certainly explained why Metin's internet connection hadn't been "good enough" for a video connection for the last while.

An hour later, they arrived at Fiona's cozy condo. Fiona parked her car in the underground lot and they made their way up to the fourteenth floor. Night came early in the winter and it was already dark.

"It's not much, but it has great views in the daytime," she said, opening the door and welcoming him in. Metin stood in the doorway with a big grin on his face. "What is it?" she asked.

"Christmas," he whispered, taking in the holiday décor. "It reminds me of the Christmas of my exchange year."

"What do you mean?" Fiona knew he'd spent two Decembers in the UK as well.

"Your decorations. They look like family heirlooms — things that have been passed down with love rather than bought in the store. In Charlotte, my host mom's decorations were the same. But when I did my fellowship, anyone who had a tree had to buy new things. It wasn't the same."

Fiona smiled. In fact, he was right. The city apartment was home to her mother's delicate decorations — memories of her childhood — so it really was a throwback to an earlier time. All her newer ones, including the homemade decorations her children had given her, were on the big tree at the lake house. She also kept the ones that Sam had given her each year on her birthday there.

Metin yawned. The day of travel and change of time zone was catching up to him. Fiona put out a light dinner of salmon and roasted vegetables before they headed to bed, where they soon made up for the time apart and then fell asleep spooned together, Metin with his arm protectively over her.

The next morning, his body still not quite in the right time zone, Metin woke early. He stretched out his long body and ran a hand through his hair as he realized with a sleepy smile where he was. It was unusual for him to wake before Fiona, so he lay in bed for a while watching her sleep. His grumbling stomach finally betrayed him and he begrudgingly left her warmth in search of food. After pulling on jeans and a sweater, he put on his glasses and the world came into sharper focus. He put on the kettle for tea and looked in Fiona's fridge. He found bagels and cream cheese and cut up some tomato and cucumber. Taking his breakfast into the front room, he watched the sun rise.

Fiona woke with a start to an empty bed and for a moment she feared it had all been a dream. Maybe Metin wasn't here after all. She looked around the room and her eyes landed on his suitcase in the corner and realized he really was here, in Toronto, and in her condo, if not currently in her bed.

Smiling with the memory of the night before, Fiona pulled on a periwinkle silk peignoir that matched the lace on her negligee and padded out in her bare feet to find Metin.

"*Gün aydın*," she greeted him. Metin pulled her close and kissed her. "What do you think, now that you've seen it in daylight?"

"It's not the Bosphorus, *sevgilim*," he teased her, "but it's still a beautiful view."

Fiona had big plans for this week, but the first day would be just for them to enjoy each other and for Metin to recover from jet lag. Max and Ben were coming for dinner, but first, she wanted to show Metin around her little neighbourhood and get him acclimatized.

"Bundle up," she said to him an hour later as they pulled on their coats for a walk along Queen's Quay. "It's not that cold today, but it may be more than you're used to." Fiona had checked her weather app. It was minus eight degrees. There was just a little snow on the ground, but the wind was blowing off the lake which always made it feel colder.

Metin watched as she donned wool-lined leather gloves and pulled on a headband to cover her ears. She wrapped a sky-blue cashmere scarf around her neck, making her eyes appear bluer than they had before. He raised his eyebrows. He had bought a warmer coat, but it was possible he wasn't as prepared for a Canadian winter as he thought. His US experience had all been in the south and England hadn't been that cold either.

"*Sevgilim,*" he said sheepishly holding up his thin leather gloves. "We may have to do some shopping."

"We can do that," Fiona laughed, digging through the chest by her front door. "But for now, try these. I'm not sure if they're Jamie's or Simon's, but they'll do in a pinch." She handed him a dark grey knitted toque and scarf and followed with a pair of thick mittens with red maple leaves on the palms.

Even with the borrowed winter wear, Metin felt the chill of the biting wind. They didn't stay out for long, and Fiona made the hot chocolate her kids liked when they returned red-cheeked to her apartment.

"Go ahead and turn on the fireplace," she called to him. "I have gas here, but there's a proper wood-burning one at the lake." Metin was happy to warm his hands and his toes in front of the instant flame.

That afternoon, they went to one of her favourite independent menswear stores. She'd been shopping here for Ben and Max for years and had recently started picking up a few things for Jamie and Simon. They had a good selection of more corporate attire in his store, but also casual warm options. Metin picked up a warmer scarf, some thick wool-lined gloves, and a toque of his own, that would pull down over his ears.

She wouldn't let Metin pay. "You're in my country now, *beyefendi*," she teased him. "The least I can do is keep you warm. This is my treat." Fiona had noticed him eying a few other warm things and she made a note to call the store later and see if they would put them aside for her as Christmas gifts. One more stop for proper insulated winter boots and they were on their way to lunch. Inside the little restaurant on the quay, they watched skaters make their way around the rink in front of them.

"Have you ever ice-skated?" Fiona asked Metin after they ordered.

"Never," he admitted. "I roller-skated a few times during my exchange year though. You said you skate on the lake, right?" Fiona nodded. "Maybe you can teach me." He gave her hand a squeeze across the table.

After lunch, they rode the subway up to midtown and Fiona showed Metin the house she and Sam had bought and that she'd raised her family in. They stopped for coffee at her favourite coffee shop and she reminded him that Ben and Max were coming by for dinner that evening. They would be a gentle warmup, she hoped, to meeting the kids the following day.

Ben had wanted to host them to their place, but Max gently pointed out that meeting your lover's dead husband's brother and his husband at their house might be more than a little intimidating.

ᑌᕮᕼᗝ

"So this is the famous Metin," Ben said as Fiona introduced the three men that evening, wondering if the newcomer would notice the sarcasm in his voice.

Max was more gracious. "So good to meet you," he said. "It's nice to meet the guy who's put such a big smile on Fiona's face." She blushed as she wiped her hands on the apron she'd put on to cover her sweater and jeans. It was a casual dinner, so nobody had dressed up.

Metin took the bottle of wine that Ben offered and opened it, pouring everyone a glass.

Over dinner, as the men got to know each other better, Fiona felt the stress she didn't realize she was holding in her shoulders dissipate. Max and Metin talked about Metin's restoration work in Kuzguncuk and Datça. Both Ben and Max were impressed by the before and after photos, and Metin showed a lot of interest in Max's business. "It was good of you to find a place for Fiona's Jamie."

"He's a fine woodworker," said Max. "He deserves to be there on merit alone. But it's nice to have him too. Fee's done a great job with all those kids." Metin noted the nickname.

As Ben and Max got ready to leave Fiona's apartment, Max took Metin aside for a moment. "Don't worry about Ben," he said. "He thinks of Fee as his little sister. It may not be obvious to you yet, but he's warming up to you already. A word to the wise, though. Invest some energy in Jamie. He's a good kid, but he's very protective of his mother and the start may be a bit bumpy."

"Thanks for the warning. And I'd love to see your workshop sometime."

"Any time."

"I like him, Fiona," Ben said as he hugged her goodbye. "I almost didn't want to. But I do. I really hope it works out for the two of you."

"They seemed nice," Metin said as they got ready for bed. "But Max calls you Fee? Do other people call you that?"

"He's the only one," Fiona laughed. "Ben and Max are like brothers to me. They're the only family I have left, other than the kids. And I'm theirs. They really helped me after Sam died."

They slid under the covers and Fiona snuggled into Metin's shoulder.

"Max told me Jamie might not be too happy about us," he said pensively. "You've mentioned it too. Looks like I might have my work cut out for me. I'll have to pull out my charm tomorrow night," he teased, only slightly concerned.

"Jamie may give you a hard time, my love, but he'll come around in time. After all, his mother loves you."

By the second day, Metin's body clock had reset itself and he was sound asleep when Fiona woke. She had a busy day planned for them, including a drive down to Niagara Falls, so she slipped out of bed quickly to do the advance prep for dinner. Her heart did little flips when he emerged, stretching and yawning, his curls still slightly wild from sleep. She almost had to pinch herself to believe Metin was in her apartment.

They shared a quick breakfast and then were off. Fiona stopped in Niagara-on-the-Lake first and they walked a bit in the quaint village, popping into several of the little stores to browse. Then it was off to the falls themselves, which Metin declared magnificent. Fiona was enjoying his excitement, and wondered if that's what it was like for him, watching her visit new parts of İstanbul.

The spray from the falls had turned the ornate railings into ice curlicues, and they stopped to take pictures. Metin trained his phone on them both and clicked away, trying to get the prefect shot to send to Safiye and Tamer. They strolled, hand in hand, down the river for a while.

Fiona stopped and looked up at Metin. "Thank you for coming here," she said quietly. "This means so much . . ."

Metin stopped her, putting his gloved hands on her red cheeks and kissing her. "Didn't I tell you? I'd go anywhere for you."

Back at home, Fiona worked on the dinner preparations, while Metin uncorked a bottle of wine. Daisy was first to arrive, bringing flowers and a cake for dessert.

"It's really nice to meet you, Metin," she said. "Mum has told us so much about you." Fiona blushed. She noticed Metin had slipped into North American manners and didn't reach out to kiss her daughter on the cheeks, but instead held out his hand for introductions.

"It's nice to meet you too, Daisy. You're the youngest, right?"

"Only by two minutes, but Simon never lets me forget it," she laughed as the door opened. "Speak of the devil," she said, greeting her twin.

Simon gave his sister and his mother a kiss, depositing his contribution to dinner in the kitchen. The smell of the fresh rolls from a new bakery near his was tantalizing. He and Metin hit it off immediately, talking about high-tech start-ups.

The noise level went up several decibels as Holly and Greg arrived next, with Jenna and Jonathan. Simon and Daisy quickly took the twins off their hands and Metin introduced himself to the young parents. Holly quickly joined her mother in the kitchen to see if she could help and to pop her scalloped potatoes into the oven to keep warm.

"Mum, he's cute!" she exclaimed, approving wholeheartedly.

Metin looked at the happy gathering, almost complete as they crowded into her little living room. The three grown-up children who'd arrived so far looked very much like her. The girls were almost as tiny as she was and Simon wasn't tall for a man. The red hair, in various shades, clearly marked them as family and the easy banter as they interacted with each other showed that they all loved each other. It was a happy picture.

Jamie stood outside his mother's front door, carrying bottles of wine and some chocolate milk for the "littles" as he called his sister's twins. He was not inclined to like Metin, but he'd come along to dinner because his mother seemed to love this man. Jamie had talked with Holly and she seemed fine with it, but it was his job to protect his mother and he was going to make sure he did it. Determined, he opened the door and announced his arrival.

Metin had seen photos, of course, but he was still surprised at how different Jamie was from the others, with his dark hair and eyes and height. He was almost as tall as Metin, towering above the rest of his family and as the young man shook hands with him, Metin noticed the carpenter made sure he felt strength in their formal handshake.

As Metin pondered his cool welcome, Jamie warmly greeted his family with smiles, kisses for the women, and hugs and back-slaps for Simon and Greg. Jenna and Jon ran to him and wrapped their arms around his legs. Metin could see Uncle Jamie was clearly loved.

Dinner was a loud, raucous affair full of teasing and laughter. Fiona did her best to include Metin, explaining family stories and he jumped in, telling her kids about some of their adventures. Simon and the girls drew him in with curious questions of their own. Remembering Max's advice, Metin made a point of trying to engage with Jamie, but he could see it might be a long road. So far, Jamie had spoken to him with as few words as possible, and had sent a couple of hostile looks across the table.

After dinner, Fiona took her grandchildren to the spare room. They were tired, so she put on a video for them, and sat with them for a few minutes, while they drifted off to sleep after the excitement. The others sat in the living room with cups of coffee and tea that Holly and Daisy were serving. Metin was trying to make conversation with Jamie about his cabinet work.

"Well, the custom orders we do are a lot more complex than the simple carpentry work needed to fix up old houses," Jamie said, effectively suggesting Metin's exquisite restorations were just rudimentary work. Daisy glared at him.

"So, Metin," Jamie continued, after he drained his coffee cup. "You'll be in Canada until March, right?"

"Yes, that's the plan."

"And so what happens then?"

"Well, at the moment, I expect I will go to my house on the sea to polish up my book with my editor, and I'll teach again in the summer semester." He looked at the group and smiled. "I hope your mother will come and join me for a bit."

Jamie had other ideas. "That's ridiculous. She just spent six months there." Holly kicked him under the table, but he kept going. "My mother is a successful businesswoman. And she has a full life with friends and family here. She can't just be flying off to satisfy whatever needs you have."

"Jamie!" Holly hissed at him. Simon and Daisy looked at each other, embarrassed at Jamie's histrionics.

But Metin took it in stride and tried to reassure him. "Of course, she does, Jamie. I wouldn't dream of asking your mother to abandon any of that. But she and I have gotten very close and I think she also wants to have me in her life. I know I want her in mine. There's lots to figure out still, but I'm sure we will manage."

"Well, I think it's great," said Daisy. "Mum deserves some love in her life. And, Metin, you seem to make her very, very happy."

"Daisy!" Fiona had walked back into the room, having settled the twins and was embarrassed to hear them talking about her relationship with Metin.

"She was just coming to your rescue, Mum," said Simon. "Not that you need rescuing."

Fiona opened her mouth to speak, but couldn't find any words. She sat down and Holly passed her a cup of tea with a sympathetic look.

Metin tried valiantly to get the conversation rolling again. "Toronto seems like a beautiful city, although I had to buy some warmer clothes. I'm looking forward to seeing the lake house too."

Jamie harrumphed. "If you think it's cold here," he muttered.

"You'll love it there," said Simon, jumping in to cover his brother's rudeness. "It's a really nice contrast to the bustle of city life. I think Mum is most at home there." Everyone agreed, and the conversation was steered back to safer grounds.

Jamie left first, thanking his mother for dinner and coolly shaking Metin's hand. Holly and Greg, each carrying a sleeping twin, headed out next.

"Thanks for a wonderful night as always, Fiona," Greg said. "We'll see you at Christmas. And, Metin, it's been great to meet you. Don't mind Jamie. He'll come around — just give him some time. He didn't like me much at first either."

When Simon and Daisy left together, Daisy gave Metin a hug. "I think you're good for my mum," she whispered in his ear. Simon shook his hand heartily and said how much he'd enjoyed their conversation.

As they got ready for bed that night, Fiona apologized again. "Jamie behaved abominably. You didn't deserve that, Metin."

"It's fine, *sevgilim*. He's worried about you and I'm a complete stranger. I respect that, but I'll win him over. Because I love you." Metin saw she still looked sad. He put his hand under her chin, lifting it up. "*Bana bak*. Look at me, my love. We will be fine."

Fiona and Metin spent the rest of the week in the city, Fiona delighting in showing Metin her corner of the world. They usually walked in the mornings, and Metin was impressed with the trail system and the amount of green space inside the city. They would return to her apartment to warm up and often curled up together on the couch reading newspapers or current periodicals until lunchtime. Metin was enjoying the break from work, but knew Fiona still had one last deadline to meet. So he was happy to leave her in the afternoons and explore on his own. Fiona thought he was doing a bit of secret Christmas shopping, but in fact, on two of those afternoons, he had meetings with two local universities. He was very hopeful one would offer him a semester-long guest lecturer position soon.

Several of their evenings were taken up with dinners with Fiona's friends, who all wanted to meet the handsome man who'd won her heart. Metin grinned to himself when her phone buzzed repeatedly after those dinners, imagining what the women were gossiping about. The rest of the time, they hunkered down at Fiona's flat together, just enjoying each other's company again.

Finally, at the end of the week, Fiona sent the final report to her client. "And that's a wrap," she said, closing her laptop firmly. "Let Christmas begin!"

That night, they were going up to her old neighbourhood to hear Mila's choir's Christmas concert. "Are you okay with this?" she asked Metin. "There's a bit of a carol sing along with it." She knew he wasn't religious, and neither was she really, but other than one Christmas Eve twenty-five years ago, they hadn't spent a religious holiday of either faith together yet and she was sensitive that there were traditions they would have to navigate together. But Christmas wasn't Christmas to Fiona without singing the traditional carols.

"Don't worry about it," he said. "I've had Christmas in the UK and in America. I may not know all of the words, but I don't mind listening."

They bundled up after dinner and rode the subway up to the old church, which was, Fiona explained, just more than one hundred years old. "That's old here," she laughed. "You have to remember just how young Canada is. Even the US has a hundred years on us." She compared that to İstanbul's New Mosque, built in the 1600s.

The church was decorated beautifully for the holidays, with poinsettias and greenery everywhere and lights shining through the stained-glass windows. They held hands during the concert and stood to join the choir in several carols. Metin knew the tune of most of them, as he expected, but it was good to have the words projected on the screen at the front. He stopped singing occasionally to look at Fiona. Her eyes were gleaming and she looked so beautiful singing harmonies to songs that obviously meant a lot to her.

The final song of the concert was "Silent Night." Before it was sung, Mila stepped to the microphone to thank everyone who was part of the event. While she did that, young children passed candles out to everyone in attendance. Metin looked at Fiona quizzically. The organ started playing and the lights were brought down. As the audience began singing, the church's youth walked up the aisle on both sides lighting candles on the ends and then each person lit the candle of the person standing next to them until the entire church was filled with the soft glow of candlelight. Metin lit Fiona's candle as she continued singing, and she passed on the light to the woman sitting next to her. There was such peace in that song, sung by candlelight every year, and Metin could feel it too.

As they walked back to the subway, arm in arm, Metin thanked her for taking him to the concert.

"You liked it?" she asked.

"It was very special," he said. "I liked the music, but I liked hearing you sing even more. I love you very much."

"*Ben de seni seviyorum,*" she answered in Turkish, squeezing his hand. They'd been speaking more English here, she'd noticed and she wanted to make sure she kept working on her language skills.

The next afternoon they packed up and headed to the lake. Fiona's car was loaded up with suitcases and last-minute presents. The space under the tree at the lake house was already full, but Fiona couldn't resist picking up a few more things, and Metin had brought a few gifts with him from İstanbul.

They headed north on the busy highway for an hour before turning up a smaller country highway. Fiona had Christmas music playing all the way. Metin watched as the landscape changed the further they drove. Quickly leaving behind the city skyscrapers, they passed by cattle farms and then dipped into a valley that Fiona told him was some of the best vegetable farming in Ontario. Soon the vegetation changed again, moving from leafless deciduous trees to snow-laden conifers. They drove through several impressive rock cuts, pink granite glistening in the sun. Metin commented on the dynamiting that must have been necessary to build the road.

"Tell me again about your house on the lake," he prompted her as they got closer.

"I grew up there, and I inherited the house. The kids and I spent a lot of summers here, and then when I sold the city house a few years ago, I made a lot of changes," she explained. "I probably spend about three-quarters of my time up here now," she said. "Well, that is when I'm not spending six months of the year with you! It's my retreat from the craziness of the city. If you're lucky, we'll see deer and foxes while you're here."

"How did you change it?" Metin asked.

"I made it bigger, for sure, and more modern," she admitted. "It needed to be my house, not my parents'. I wanted to make sure there was room for the kids to all be here comfortably — they can't share bunk beds anymore. And I was thinking ahead to when they have partners and grandchildren. I expect Jon and Jenna will have cousins one day. And, of course, there had to be room for Max and Ben. I wanted this house to be where everyone comes together. So it's far bigger than I need just for me, but it's served us well so far."

In fact, the small three-bedroom bungalow Fiona grew up in had been more than doubled in size, making room for her whole family to make new memories there and she delighted in explaining it all to Metin.

Snow began to fall, heavy and thick. Fiona took a quick detour to show him the town and then they headed down Lakeview Road. As its name would suggest, Metin caught glimpses of the snow-covered lake and he admired the houses that dotted the lakeshore.

Finally, after close to three hours in the car, Fiona pulled into the driveway and arched her back. She turned and looked at Metin nervously. "Welcome to the lake. I hope you like it here as much as I do." Snow was falling heavily now so they quickly unloaded the car. Fiona put the kettle on and left Metin to light a fire. Soon they were snuggled together on the couch watching the snow fall over the lake and listening to the logs crackle.

Fiona was standing at the kitchen counter the next day writing a grocery list when she heard Metin come in from outside. He'd left his charger in the car and after talking with his brother and sister this morning, his phone needed a boost.

"You weren't kidding about it being colder up here," he said to her as he joined her, slipping his hands around her waist. He touched his cold cheek to the nape of her neck and she shrieked. "Care to warm me up, *sevgilim*?" he whispered in her ear. Fiona turned slowly around, and saw the desire in his eyes. Suddenly, his hands were lost in her long loose hair and his lips crushed hers.

Lying in bed afterwards, tangled up in the sheets and breathless, Fiona couldn't remember a time she'd been happier. She rolled over and kissed Metin's cheek.

"I hate to do this," she sighed. "But I have to get up. Everyone's coming up on Christmas Eve and there's a lot to do before they get here." Metin groaned and grabbed her wrist as she tried to slip away. He was rewarded with another kiss for the effort. But she was serious. Pulling on her clothes she glanced over and saw Metin looking jokingly forlorn. "Sorry, *hayatım*," she teased. "You have to share me here!"

When she returned from the supermarket, where she was pretty sure she'd bought out the store, she overheard the end of Metin's conversation on the phone.

"Thank you, sir. I really appreciate you calling before Christmas. It will be a wonderful surprise. I'll speak with you again in the new year." It took a moment for her to realize the conversation was in English and it piqued her curiosity. But she knew that the week before Christmas you never ask questions.

Metin was amazed at the whirlwind of productivity Fiona became that afternoon, baking and preparing for Christmas meals. He knew it would be a full house — eleven of them — and he knew her well enough to stay out of the way. Exploring a bit, he found the cord of firewood behind the garage and had started chopping it into smaller pieces for the fireplace. Stomping his feet to remove the snow, he came back into the house and found her still in the kitchen, hair piled on top of her head and flour on her cheeks.

"What are you making now?" he asked.

"Family secret," she teased and then seeing the quizzical look on his face, continued. "There are a couple of special recipes I only make at this time of year," she explained. "Like *güllaç* is for *Ramazan*, mince pies and shortbread are some of the things I only make for Christmas. And the kids love my chocolate bark. Want a taste?" She held up a plate with samples of five different sweets she'd baked up that afternoon.

"*Eline sağlık,*" Metin said with his mouth still full, praising her baking. He shook his head. "You really need a word for that in English. And you need a break from the kitchen." Metin held up two pairs of snowshoes he'd found in the garage. "Care to teach me about these?"

"*Afiyet olsun,*" Fiona murmured in reply to the compliment and then wiped her hands on her apron. "Snowshoeing, eh? Let's give it a whirl."

The house was in chaos. Well-oiled chaos, but chaos nonetheless. Ben and Max were joining them for Christmas this year, a welcome surprise. Ben had put on a Christmas classics playlist that Daisy and Simon were singing along to when they weren't teasing each other. Greg and Jamie were shouting excitedly at the hockey game they were watching. Holly was dealing with her overexcited children and Fiona was clanging pots and pans in the kitchen as she got dinner ready. Max looked around and saw Metin standing aside looking slightly dazed and trying to take it all in. He took pity on him and poured him a scotch.

"It's a lot, isn't it," he said, handing him the glass. "And fair warning. Tomorrow will be crazier. But Fee is in her element. She really is the heart of this family." He looked seriously at the newcomer. "I'm sure this Fiona is different from the Fiona you know from İstanbul. But you're going to have to love this version of Fee too, if you want a permanent place in her life."

Metin took a sip of the liquor. "I never had kids, you know," he said to Max. "Never thought I could do the family thing. But I love her so much." He knocked back the rest of his drink.

Max nodded. "Then you better find a way to fit in," he said quietly, and slipped back into the mayhem, grabbing a crying twin in each arm and twirling them around.

Christmas morning dawned cold and bright. The adults had a leisurely breakfast and watched the little ones play with the toys Santa had brought. They'd been allowed to open their stockings before the rest of the house was awake. Metin thought that Holly and Greg looked like they needed a nap already.

"All right, everyone," Fiona said finally, clapping her hands and breaking into his thoughts. "To the tree!"

Metin had added small gifts for everyone to the almost embarrassingly big pile under the tree and he was eager to see people's responses. For Fiona, he'd bought an exquisite silk scarf she could tie over her shoulders from Vakko, a luxury Turkish store. He also gave her a *cezve* and *çaydanlık*, so they could make proper *kahve* and *çay*. For her daughters there were brightly coloured ceramic bowls and for her sons and Greg, soft leather belts. For the children, he had bathrobes made from fine Turkish cotton and for Max and Ben, who he knew from Fiona were foodies, baklava, *lokum*, *sucuk*, and real Turkish saffron. At the last minute, he'd added a *tavla* set for the whole family. Backgammon would entertain them all and maybe help him build a few bridges.

Fiona's family were delighted with their gifts and he breathed a sigh of relief from his place on the couch. Max came up behind him and put his hand briefly on Metin's shoulder.

"You did good, man," he said quietly and Metin nodded in silent thanks. He noticed that the gifts the family shared with each other, and with him, weren't necessarily of great value; the act of giving was at least as important as what was given. He liked that spirit of generosity that Fiona had instilled in her children.

Finally, the gift-giving frenzy was finished. Simon threw another log on the fire and Jamie started gathering up all the discarded paper.

Jon came up to Metin shyly carrying one of his new books. He pulled on Metin's sleeve. "Read," he demanded. Jenna was right behind him and before Metin knew it, he had a lap full of small children and several new books to read.

Max came up behind Fiona, who was watching the scene unfold. He squeezed her shoulder. "Your guy is settling in nicely," he said gruffly, and they watched as Metin made his way through a book about a pig named Olivia and another about a box of crayons who had gone on strike.

Ben and Jamie pulled on their coats. The sun had disappeared shortly after breakfast and big fat snowflakes had been falling all morning. They wanted to shovel the driveway before they really needed the snow blower. Fiona was pretty sure they were going to talk about Metin as well.

They all sighed with relief as the house quieted in the afternoon. Greg and Holly had taken the twins back to the apartment over the garage for a nap and Metin saw his chance.

"Can I interest you in a game of backgammon, Jamie?" he asked the young man. Metin didn't know Jamie's skill at the game, so he played easy the first time through and let friendly competition ease them into conversation. "Okay, I'm rolling my sleeves up now," he joked, as they started a second game, in which he thrashed Jamie.

"Two out of three?" Jamie asked, wanting to settle the score. Metin agreed readily, pleased to continue, and the two men battled it out. In the end, he won, but only by a hair. "Good game," Jamie said, shaking Metin's hand. "Maybe we can play again later. But now," he continued, waving his arm at the nearly empty firewood box, "duty calls. I'd better go chop some wood."

"I'll give you a hand," Metin said, not willing to let the progress he'd made with Jamie stop.

No explanation was given, but when they came back in, Fiona's son and Metin had become friends.

Fiona collapsed into bed that night. "They'll all go home in the morning," she said quietly as she slid in beside Metin and nestled into his shoulder. "I know they're a lot to take." She kissed him gently. "Merry Christmas."

"It was a great day, Fiona," he assured her. "But I still have one more gift for you."

"What?" She sat up again. "Another one?"

"This is a gift for both of us. At least I hope it is. I've been talking with universities in Toronto for some time now. And just a couple of days ago, I got an offer to teach for the fall semester next year. If it goes well, it could become a yearly thing." Fiona stared at him and Metin could tell it wasn't sinking in. He took her hands. "Fiona, it means I'll be able to be here with you in Canada next fall. You do still want that, don't you?"

It finally clicked and Fiona flung her arms around his neck. "For real? I can't believe it. That's the best Christmas present ever."

Metin was beginning to think that the snow would never stop. It had snowed almost every day since Christmas. Fiona checked the weather report and told him that the second week of January, it would probably stop because it would be too cold to snow. That confused him, and frightened him a bit. It was too cold already!

But he was more confused when he found her later that day in the pantry, clutching a photo album and crying softly. She looked embarrassed, as if he'd caught her in the act of doing something wrong.

"Fiona, *canim, ağlama*, don't cry." He took her in his arms tenderly. "What's wrong?"

She put down the album and breathed raggedly in and out before looking at him.

"Sam," she said simply as another tear rolled down her cheek. "He died seventeen years ago today." She shook her head and used her thumb to flick away the tear. "I'm so sorry," she apologized. "I didn't mean for you to see me like this. It's not fair to you."

"*Gözlerime bak*. Look at me." He lifted her chin so he could see her eyes. "You're allowed to grieve. It's okay." He pulled her into his arms again kissing the top of her head. "He was an important part of your life. He's the father of your children. You don't need to hide it from me."

They stood there like that for a long time, Fiona gathering strength from Metin's strong arms around her. Finally she looked up. "He'd have liked you, you know." Metin kissed her tenderly.

Soon, just as they had in İstanbul, Fiona and Metin quickly settled into a routine now that the holidays were over. Fiona retreated to her study for the mornings, sometimes working, sometimes sketching, and Metin worked on his book in the spacious living room. They often walked or hiked or snowshoed after lunch and Fiona had even taken Metin cross-country skiing a few times. She introduced him around town, and they had a few nice dinners with some of her long-time friends. He shaved off his beard. It had been an interesting experiment, and it did keep his face warmer, but it itched, and he didn't like how it irritated Fiona's skin when he kissed her.

"Do you mind if we go into the city this week?" she asked after they'd spent several blissful weeks at the lake.

"Of course not," Metin said, looking up from his laptop and pushing his glasses up his nose. "I've been meaning to ask you what kind of cadence you keep between the two places."

He quickly realized that while Fiona cocooned at the lake, she was much more social in the city and he joked with her that it was much like his relationship with İstanbul and Datça. So he happily continued writing or exploring the city on his own while she took meetings and went to lunches. While they were in Toronto, he also met with the university and they nailed down the specifics of his semester lecturing. They went out to the theatre and concerts, had dinners with friends and family. Metin settled nicely into Fiona's life here, just as she did into his.

And so back and forth they went between the city and the lake through the winter. Metin sent a first draft of his book to Göçke, his editor, in February and she had sent it back full of notes for him to work through. Fiona was curious to see how this process would work, as Metin was writing in English. He explained that Gökçe had a British mother and a Turkish father. She had moved to London when she was fourteen and her degree was from Oxford. Fiona was impressed when she saw the notes. Gökçe was very thorough and her corrections were meticulous. Metin's book was in good hands.

It was an early spring, Fiona said, and by the second week of March, the snowdrops pushed their way through the frozen earth, the first flowers of spring. Metin still hadn't booked his flight home, but Fiona knew he would have to leave soon if he wanted any time in Datça before the summer semester began. When the tips of the crocuses came up the next week, they talked and decided together that he would go home in early April. It would shortchange him some time in Datça, but he was not ready to leave Fiona yet. She had promised to join him in İstanbul for a month in mid-June. They were going to make this work.

On the last day of March, Metin woke up at the lake to a quiet, empty house. He found a handwritten note propped up against the kettle in the kitchen.

> Metin'ciğim, I am so sorry. When I woke up, I suddenly knew I had to be in the city. I'll be back by tomorrow night, I promise. But today, I need to be with my kids and with Ben. Please understand.
>
> I love you, and I'll be back soon. Please forgive me.
> Fiona

He looked at his watch. It was only eight thirty. He wondered when Fiona had left. He knew about the family ritual on Sam's birthday, but she'd told him she wouldn't go this year. Something had changed. Metin made himself a cup of tea and some breakfast and sat down to read the newspaper, but first he picked up his phone.

Anladım, sevgilim. I understand. Nothing to forgive. I love you. Drive safe.

Fiona arrived in the city about an hour later. She'd texted Ben and the kids before she left the house to tell them she was coming and now she read their loving replies and then opened Metin's. Smiling, she sent him back a quick heart emoji, and opened her city closet looking for black trousers and a blouse. She tied her Christmas scarf over her shoulders, enjoying the splash of colour near her face.

Shortly after lunch, the whole family met at the cemetery in what had become a familiar ritual. Max had come with Ben, as he always did, and Fiona gave him a quick hug when she arrived. Max hung back in the parking lot as the group headed down the hill. It was Simon's turn to bring the cupcakes this year, and he carried the box down with them. Daisy had a thermos of hot chocolate.

Fiona followed her children down the hill, arm in arm with Ben. He was quiet. Over the years, this day had morphed from painful to bittersweet for her, as she remembered Sam's love for her and the children. But Sam had been the last of Ben's family, and she knew that this day continued to be harder for him.

At Sam's gravesite, they took turns telling him about the best parts of their past year and toasting their father's birthday with paper cups of hot chocolate. Ben was subdued, even more than usual, Fiona noticed. The children headed up the hill one by one after private conversations with their father, stopping to give their mum a hug and a kiss on their way up. Then it was Fiona's turn. She took a deep breath and put her hand on Sam's headstone.

"I've found someone, Sam," she told him quietly. "Well, re-found someone, I suppose. He makes me happy. I will never forget all that we had together, but I hope you can understand that it's time for me. Happy birthday, Sam. Be happy for me." A single tear rolled down her cheek as she stepped back. She brushed it away and gave Ben's hand a squeeze as she headed back to her car so he could have his moment.

She saw Jamie talking with Max at the top of the hill as she made her way back. Her son gave her a wave and a smile before getting into his truck and heading back to their workshop.

Max held out his arms when she got close, and gave her a big hug. He'd been waiting for Ben beside their SUV.

"How is he, Max?" she asked, with a glance down the hill. "He seems, I don't know, off, this year."

Max sighed. "You're right, Fee. I wasn't going to say anything, but since you asked, Ben's been really agitated recently, especially when you told us all you weren't coming. He was relieved to get your text this morning."

"Really?" She was surprised. Over the years he'd come to think of this ritual as something she did mostly for the kids.

"I know it's crazy, Fee, and so does he, when he thinks about it clearly, but he's really conflicted. He's happy you're in love again and God knows you deserve it, but he sees you as his last bond to his brother and he's scared of losing that."

Fiona was taken aback. "I hadn't realized that was the issue," she said after a moment. "Do you think it would help if the two of you came for dinner tonight and we could talk? I'm not going back to the lake until tomorrow."

Max nodded.

"Come by at six o'clock. And, Max, drag him if you must." She knew that Ben would probably spend the rest of the day in a bit of a funk. They looked down the hill and saw him starting to make his way back up. "I'm glad he has you, Max. Take care of him today," she said, giving his hand another squeeze before getting in her car.

As he waited for Ben, Max reflected that he'd known Fiona for almost as long as he'd know Ben. He remembered that trip to Ottawa where they'd sprung the news on Sam and his girlfriend that they were moving in together, not sure what the reaction would be. It hadn't been long before he thought of her as family.

Fiona popped into the local market to pick up some things for dinner. She spent the rest of the afternoon preparing Irish stew, biscuits, and apple crumble, humming in the kitchen. She was pleased that after all these years, she could now celebrate Sam's birthday, remembering the good times. She hoped Metin understood. She just wasn't quite ready to talk to him yet as she geared herself up for what would likely be an emotionally charged evening.

She had just pulled the biscuits out of the oven when the doorbell rang. She opened the door and Max caught her eye. He had, in fact, had to drag his husband to Fiona's that evening. And Ben was being petulant about it.

Max and Fiona made polite chit-chat through dinner, while Ben picked at his meal. Fiona thought she could almost see the grey storm cloud over his head, like a cartoon character.

After dinner, she and Ben moved to the living room with the remains of their wine while Max cleared the table to give them a few minutes alone. Ben sat grumpily on the couch and Fiona sat across from him.

She began bluntly. "Look, Ben, it's clear you're upset. Talk to me. What's going on?"

"My God, Fiona, how do you not see it? Are you that blind?" Ben exploded. "I miss my little brother. It's his birthday. Surely to God you feel it too." She was taken aback by the intensity of his outburst. She nodded, but Ben kept going, his emotions getting the best of him. "And I'm frustrated. I'm a grown-ass man and for some reason I can't explain, I'm missing my parents more than ever. And now, suddenly, I'm afraid of you leaving me too."

"But, Ben, I haven't gone anywhere."

Ben took a deep breath, trying to steady himself. Max, who'd been watching from the kitchen, quietly walked behind the couch and put his hand on Ben's shoulder for support.

"Fiona, you've got Metin now. Anyone with eyes can see how much in love you two are. But he lives halfway around the world." His voice was raw with emotion now, cracking as he continued. "You don't need Sam — or me — anymore. You were away a long time last year. You might decide to live there with him. And when you do, I'll lose my last link to my little brother. There's no one else who knew him like we did."

She opened her mouth to speak.

"Let me finish," he pleaded. "I'm the same age Dad was when they died. It's freaking me out. A lot. Maybe it's making me less rational. Maybe I'm not seeing clearly. I don't know. I have no road map for this. Nobody to look up to for guidance." His voice was raised again now. "All I know is I'm feeling a deep and profound sense of loss. And you haven't even goddamn *gone* yet."

Fiona started again to respond, but a glance from Max stopped her short. He knew there was more, and he kept his hand firmly on Ben's shoulder. Ben took a ragged breath, putting his hand on Max's and drawing strength from it.

"You were my brother's one true love. I've never told you this, but he clung to you, Fiona, for dear life. When you met him, you were the beacon that brought him back. Sure, he'd returned to school, but he was still sleepwalking through life. You showed him what life could be like. I couldn't do that. I was struggling with my own demons. But Sam found you and he loved you and you saved him. He loved you and the kids more than life itself. He'd be so proud of you for how you raised them and for the people they've become." Tears were streaming down Ben's face now and she leaned over to hold his hand. "You deserve happiness again, Fiona. You really do. But I don't know how to stay Sam's big brother without having you here. And then there's . . ." He broke off, wiping his eyes before trying again, softer this time. "You're like my little sister. You know that, right?"

There were tears in Fiona's eyes now as she nodded.

"I couldn't stand it if anything happened to you. I like Metin. He seems like a decent guy and I can see he loves you. But I'm still not sure how you two are going to make this work." The tension was rising in his voice again. "And if he hurts you . . . so help me God . . . I might . . . well . . . I might just have to fly to Turkey to deck him." With that absurd declaration, Ben drained his wine glass, and went to the table to get the bottle to fill it up again.

Fiona used the time to centre herself as Ben returned and Max sat down next to him.

"I'm not really sure I know where to start. Thank you for sharing all of that with me, Ben. I knew you were upset this afternoon, but I didn't realize everything behind it." She refilled her own glass and took a fortifying sip.

"I need you to hear me," she said, reaching for his hand. "Really hear me. I am not abandoning you. Whatever happens, or doesn't happen, with Metin, or where I am, I will always be here for you if you need me. Because it goes two ways, Ben. I may be your little sister, but that makes you my big brother. And I love you. You are never going to lose me no matter where in the world I am.

"And yes, I think maybe you are freaking out a little," she smiled gently, "but I also think that's pretty normal for everything that's going on in your head. I didn't realize about your dad. I wish I'd met him — and your mother — Sam told such great stories about them."

Fiona continued frankly. "You're right. It's possible I might not always be here to have cupcakes on Sam's birthday. But the kids will, Ben. You'll help each other keep that tradition alive. And if I'm here, I will come too. Just like I came today."

Ben started to speak, relieved at her reassurances.

"Wait," Fiona said, holding up her index finger as realization dawned on her. "My turn to finish. I have something important to say. And it's long overdue." She glanced quickly at Ben's husband. "I don't think you were fair to Max earlier. You have him too, and we all know just how much he loves you. I'm *not* your last tie to Sam, Ben. Max knew Sam too. And I think it's high time that he started having cupcakes and hot chocolate with us instead of staying in the parking lot and watching us have all the fun." She smiled at Max now, who was now struggling with his own emotions as Fiona opened the one door that he thought he'd never be able to enter. Fiona turned her attention back to Ben, watching him process what she'd just said. It was true, but like her, he hadn't realized it before. He turned and grabbed his husband's hands.

"Max, oh, my Max, I'm so sorry. I don't know why I never . . . Fiona's absolutely right."

Max and Ben embraced and Max whispered in his ear, "And I'm not going anywhere either."

After Ben and Max left, Fiona sat quietly, emotionally spent, watching the city lights. Her phone buzzed.

How are you, *sevgilim*?

Long day, and a longer evening, but I'm fine. Just tired. I'm sorry I left like that. I just had to be here.

It's OK.

Thanks for understanding.

Coming back tomorrow?

Of course. By lunchtime, I hope. Having breakfast with Ben first.

Miss you.

Me too. Will text before I leave.

Fiona met Ben for breakfast on her way out of the city. He apologized for the previous night's outburst.

"Don't be silly," she admonished him. "It's important to talk about how you're feeling, even when it gets messy. Metin and I have learned that the hard way."

"Max and I talked for a long time when we got home," Ben said, "And he's convinced me to get counselling. I probably should have done it years ago, but I think I really need it now."

"It was really helpful for the kids right after Sam died," Fiona said, adding quietly. "And for me later on."

"I didn't know."

"I didn't broadcast it. For years, I thought I had to handle everything on my own. And I nearly killed myself trying. Remember my total meltdown on the first anniversary of Sam's death? That's when I first realized I wasn't superwoman. Even then, it took me years to learn to accept help. Believe it or not, it was Max who encouraged me to talk with someone. And my therapist — I still see her sometimes — really helped me work through a lot of things. She's the one who convinced me I wasn't a failure when you and Max stepped in to help me more with the kids. And I've had a few conversations with her Metin. Anyway, I think it's great you're going to do it now."

Ben nodded. "I'm a little nervous, but Max keeps telling me it's a good thing." He shifted gears. "Thank you, Fiona, for last night. There was a lot I needed to tell you. And I guess there were some things I needed to hear from you. I really do like Metin and I'd like to get to know him better."

"I'm sure he'd like that. He's headed back soon, but he'll be in Canada in the fall. And you know you and Max are welcome at the lake any time. You two are my family and my relationship with Metin doesn't change any of that. If I didn't say it loudly enough before then that's my fault. You became my family when I married your brother. We've seen each other through a lot, you and I. Time and new romances don't erase that."

Chapter 33

They were counting down the days before Metin left for Turkey and this time, they both recognized the signs. Soon after Fiona returned to the lake, they put on their metaphorical armour, preparing themselves for the pain of being apart. They bickered about inconsequential things. Metin found Fiona crying softly in the pantry. Fiona found Metin thrashing out his emotions at the woodpile. But they'd learned from the days leading up to their last separation and this time they talked things through and made decisions together. It didn't make it easier, but at least they understood each other. They drove back to the city two days before his flight in sombre silence.

Suddenly they were at the airport, holding tightly to each other. Metin's bags were checked through to Dalaman, the closest airport to Datça, and there was nothing left to do but say goodbye before he headed through security.

"Don't cry, *sevgilim*," Metin pleaded as his own voice cracked. "Please don't cry. I don't think I can get on that plane if you do."

Fiona knew she had to be the strong one this time, and although tears glittered in her eyes, she wouldn't let them fall as she looked up at him. "*Bana bak, hayatım.* It's only a few weeks. I'll be there before you know it. *Seni çok seviyorum.*"

"*Ben de seni.* I love you too." Metin wiped the tears from his cheeks and held her so tight she thought she wouldn't be able to breathe. He was beginning to understand how hard it was for Fiona when she left. And then she gave him the gentlest of kisses.

"It's time," Fiona whispered. "Go finish that book in the warmth of the sun. Have a safe flight." She looked up at him with a smile. "And to quote a handsome man I happen to know, just promise me you won't look back."

As Fiona had done twice now, he squared his shoulders and joined the security line. Just before he turned the final corner, he looked back and his heart broke as he saw Fiona standing there alone, looking for all the world like she was about to fall to pieces. She lifted her hand and waved. He turned back and put his carry-on bag on the belt for the scanner. When he got through security, his phone dinged.

You looked.

⌒꙳ᴐ

Despite a heavy heart at leaving Canada, Metin was glad to be home. As the bus left the airport, and headed to Datça he smiled, taking in the scenery. He opened the house, and the Mediterranean sun warmed both his body and fed his soul. The trees were green, the flowers were blooming, and the daytime temperatures were regularly climbing above twenty degrees. Perfect weather. The Canadian winter had been a challenge for him and he was glad to be back where he didn't have to worry about hats and scarves and frostbite. Metin planned to spend the rest of April here and return to İstanbul at the beginning of May. He'd sent Gökçe a second draft of the book while he was still in Canada and they were working on final edits now. He would have it back in her hands within a week, ready for layout, just in time for Tamer to come and visit.

Fiona had taken on a big project to keep herself busy. She knew she would be lonely when Metin left and while she tried to keep things in perspective, she looked forward to their daily video date. Three o'clock in the afternoon for her, ten in the evening for him. Sometimes he called her in the morning too, just after she'd woken up, to start her day off with a smile.

Her project was going well. She hadn't worked extensively in the energy industry and she'd been courting this client for several months. This engagement was her first for them, but if she did it well, and they called her again, it would be a real feather in her cap. She'd enjoyed researching and interviewing experts to develop a report and white paper on sustainability, which would be launched with a series of thought leadership articles. Fiona had been in the city for much of April and May, spending time with all her children, as if she had to make up for being away the previous year.

"Don't get me wrong, Mum," Holly said to her as they sat together in her family room watching the twins play and drinking coffee. "We love having you here, but we know you have a life outside of us! Don't feel guilty about wanting to be with Metin." Fiona reached around and hugged her eldest daughter.

Fiona was jolted awake in the middle of the night when her phone rang. "Hello," she muttered sleepily.

"It's done! I just sent Gökçe the final file. Now Tamer and I can play." He grinned, and Fiona could imagine Metin almost bouncing with excitement.

"Oh, I'm so pleased for you." She yawned as she sat up in bed. "Tamer comes today, right? Or is it tomorrow?" She wasn't awake enough to remember. Her bedside clock said it was not quite four o'clock.

"Today. This afternoon. And Gökçe thinks it will do really well." He was back to the book. Metin's stomach grumbled. It was almost noon and he was hungry. Noon. In his excitement, he hadn't thought about the time difference. Fiona congratulated him again as lay down and yawned again. Apologizing profusely, he told her to go back to sleep. "I love you."

"Love you too," she murmured, already half asleep again.

Metin had already set a meeting with Gökçe to work through publishing dates and interview schedules. He'd already warned her that he would be in Canada for the fall semester, so there'd be no European tour for this book. He didn't know it, but Gökçe was already talking with her North American counterparts to see if they could do some publicity there.

Later that afternoon, Metin picked Tamer up. The two brothers clapped each other on the back and put their helmets and speeding off on the Vespa. They were both looking forward to spending the week together and the first order of business after the two-hour drive back to Datça was heading into the old town for a drink. Metin's phone rang as the *rakı* and *meze* were delivered to the table.

"*Abi*, I need to take this. My editor." Metin excused himself to go out on the street where it was quieter. "*Merhaba*, Gökçe. It's late. What can I do for you?"

"Metin, I won't keep you, but I just needed to say, it's brilliant!"

Metin smiled. Gökçe's enthusiasm was one of the reasons he liked working with her. It helped keep him on track when he had doubts about what he'd written. "I'm glad you think so. Can't wait to catch up with you when I'm back." They said their goodbyes and Metin went back to the table.

"Good news?" Tamer asked.

"She really likes the book. I'm really excited about this one and it'll be fun getting it over the finish line now." He picked up his *rakı* glass. "*Şerefe.*"

A week later, the brothers flew back to İstanbul, relaxed and refreshed. They'd spent a lot of time outside, and both had healthy tans.

"Thanks for this week," Tamer said, giving his brother a hug before they climbed into separate taxis to their homes. "It's been great to spend some time with you. No matter how often I go, I'm still amazed at all the work you did on that old house. We'll have to go again soon."

Metin gave Tamer a final wave as he gave the taxi driver directions. He started to think about the semester ahead. He had a full slate of courses to teach and he had some new ideas he wanted to incorporate. He looked at his watch. It was too early still to call Fiona, so he texted her instead, so she'd know he was home when she woke up. Tomorrow he was meeting Gökçe at the publishing house. She'd emailed him some ideas about cover art already, and there would be final layouts to look at too.

Metin opened the door to his flat, dropped his bags, and wandered into the living room. It had been ages since he'd been home and it felt good to look out over the Bosphorus again.

"*Hoş geldin*, Metin *bey!*" Gökçe's assistant welcomed him into their Beyoğlu office early the next morning. "*Çay, kahve istiyor musunuz?*" Declining the offer of either tea and coffee, Metin waited in a deep and comfortable chair for his editor to arrive. Five minutes later she swept into the office and he stood to greet her.

"Gökçe, you look marvelous," he said, kissing her warmly on both cheeks. Indeed, the tall young woman with her glossy coffee-coloured hair pulled up in a topknot looked very pretty. Metin had been working with Gökçe for ten years now. She'd been fresh out of Oxford, and full of amazing ideas at just twenty-five. She never ran out of them, and with her polishing, his last two books had been very successful.

Over the next couple of hours, they went over the galleys, marking them up here and there until they were both satisfied. Metin was pleased with all three of the cover art options and asked her opinion. Gökçe leaned across the table and pointed at the second one. "This one. Definitely." He nodded, and with that final decision made, their business was done.

Metin spent the rest of the week getting settled back into his office at the university and visiting with Safiye. He took his laptop with him and showed them all photos of his time in Canada. Safiye oohed and aahed over pictures of Holly's twins, and Yusuf asked when Fiona was coming back.

"Soon," Metin assured him. "But not soon enough." Safiye saw a touch of sadness in his eyes.

Metin popped round to Aylin's café one evening, hoping to catch both her and Nazlı there at the same time. He'd brought with him a big bottle of maple syrup for Aylin to see if she could do something with it at the café, and for Nazlı, had the same maple sugar candies he'd left with Yeşim.

The café was booming. The terrace was full, and inside was buzzing too. Metin sat at a table and drank *çay* until Aylin had a break. He heard Turkish, English, German, French, Japanese, and a couple of languages he couldn't place. She certainly was making a success out of Umut Kafe. Finally, as things quieted, she dropped into the seat across from him, with her own glass of tea.

"Your sister is a marketing genius," Aylin said, waving down one of her servers to freshen his glass after they'd greeted each other. "I'm so grateful to Fiona for introducing us."

Metin cocked his head curiously. He knew Safiye had worked with Aylin for the launch, but he had assumed that was more a favour to Fiona than anything.

"She's been using social media to really boost our visibility with tourists. Of course, the locals and expats have already found us, and Nazlı's studio has been a huge source of customers, but look around you." Aylin waved her arms giddily. "There are people here from everywhere!"

"I'm glad she's been helpful."

"Helpful? She's been the key to this. Honestly!"

Metin looked out the window to see a crowd of yoga students coming over to the café, mats in hand. "Do you need to . . ." Aylin shushed him, letting her staff assist them. Soon, he saw the lights go off at Nefes Yoga and Nazlı followed five minutes later. Metin noticed her smile and nod at a man sitting alone. He must be a regular, he thought and put it out of his head. Her smile broadened when she saw Metin.

"It's good to see you back here. How was Canada? Did you survive the winter?" Nazlı loved to tease him.

"Only just! It took a few weeks in Datça just to thaw me out. I just got back to İstanbul a couple of days ago. Here," he said, passing a small box to her. "A gift from Fiona and me."

Nazlı opened the box immediately. "Mmmm. Fiona knows how much I love these." The delicate maple sugar crumbled as she nibbled around the edges. "Thank you."

The three friends settled into easy conversation, catching up on the last months. They took a few selfies and Metin sent one to Fiona with the caption "one last day to play before school starts." He thought it would start her day off with a smile. He'd be in a lecture hall when she woke.

Checking her texts during breakfast, Fiona grinned and quickly sent back three heart emojis. She missed her girlfriends and it looked like they'd had a good time last night. In fact, her day was beginning with a quick meeting with Safiye. Metin's sister wanted to pick Fiona's brain about how to reach North American tourists for Umut Kafe. Safiye was having a blast working with

Aylin. The two women had hit it off, and Safiye was very glad for the introduction.

"Merhabalar!" Safiye's cheery voice came over loud and clear as Fiona's joined the video call. *"Nasılsın? İyi misin?"*

Fiona grinned and responded to the pleasantries. They took care of business quickly and before hanging up, she asked if Safiye had seen her brother recently.

"Just the other day," Safiye said. "He showed us a lot of photographs — your house is beautiful. My *abi* misses you very much. I can see it in his eyes."

"I miss him too."

"Will you come soon, *abla*?" Safiye asked with warmth. "We all miss you. Not just Metin."

"Six more weeks." There were tears glistening in Fiona's eyes and even over the video call, Safiye could tell it was very emotional for her. Fiona loved Metin as much as he loved her and they were getting through their separation one day at a time.

Chapter 34

Metin paced the floor in front of the arrivals area at Atatürk Airport. Fiona's flight had been delayed and he was anxious to see her. It had only been ten weeks but it felt like ten months. It was a new feeling, waiting for her to come, instead of seeing her off, or being sent off. Finally she came through the doors and he met her at the end of the ramp. She dropped her bags as he put his arm around her waist and bent her backwards with an intense and demanding kiss that melted her and had her gasping for air.

"Well, hello to you too," she said, when he pulled her back up and she could breathe again. Metin buried his face in her neck and breathed in the fresh lavender scent of her shampoo. He hoped she'd never change that. Fiona laughed. "I see you've missed me!"

She woke up alone the next morning with warm sunshine streaming in the window. Metin had an early class, and he'd left before her jet-lagged body had stirred. Fiona padded into the living room. She stood in the *cumba*, taking in the beauty. It fed her soul. She pulled out her sketch pad and began to make marks on a fresh sheet of thick creamy paper.

She had plans to meet up with Nazlı and Aylin for a late lunch, after the noon rush. It was a lovely surprise to find Yeşim there as well, and the women caught up over endless glasses of tea.

"I saw Metin this morning," Yeşim said. "You haven't even been here for twenty-four hours and he already looks lighter."

"It is definitely hard when we're apart," Fiona admitted.

"I can only imagine," sighed Nazlı. Fiona noticed that Aylin and Yeşim shared a meaningful glance.

"*Anlat bakalım!*" Fiona demanded. Something was going on and she wanted in on the secret.

Nazlı blushed. "His name is Yıldırım. He's an accountant."

"He does my books," laughed Aylin. "They met right here!"

"When did this happen?" asked Fiona

"Well, I met him when he was here setting up the accounts before Aylin opened — just after you left, actually — and we've been seeing each other for four months." Nazlı was beaming now. "He just swept me off my feet. I've never been this happy."

"I can't wait to meet him," said Fiona, giving Nazlı a huge hug. "I can't believe you didn't tell me."

"Well, I'm not the only one," Nazlı said slyly.

"Nazlı!" Aylin said sharply and Fiona looked at her in surprise. "It's too early, really."

"Never too early to share with girlfriends," Nazlı pushed gently. "I'll help you start. There's a certain gentleman who has been frequenting Umut Kafe ever since Aylin opened up. A few months ago he started coming more and more often. I think he gets lunch here every day now. And sometimes he's back at closing time. Right, Aylin?"

Aylin had turned beet red. "Yes, but . . ."

It was Yeşim's turn. "Wait. You mean . . ." Clearly she knew something but not everything. Nazlı nodded gleefully.

"Tell me!" Fiona hated being left out.

Aylin sighed in frustration. "Well, seeing as Nazlı has blabbed already, here goes. His name is İlker. He's a lawyer who works on freedom of expression cases. He's very smart and funny and he's very handsome." She smiled dreamily but then snapped back to reality. "But it's very new. I really wasn't planning on telling anyone about it yet." She glared at Nazlı.

"It's not that new," Nazlı returned. "You've been seeing him for close to three months already!"

"Oh, that's wonderful," Fiona exclaimed. Love was in the air this spring. "We must all get together for dinner." Aylin blanched. Fiona squeezed her hand. "We'll go gentle, Aylin, I promise."

"Hazır mısın?" Mehmet looked at his watch impatiently, a few evenings later. If Yeşim wasn't ready soon, they'd be late for this dinner to meet the new boyfriends. At least Metin would be there, so from his point of view, the evening wouldn't be a complete waste. Mehmet turned his thoughts to something happier, imagining his wife sitting at her dressing table fastening her necklace and dabbing perfume behind her ears. She was still beautiful after all of these years and Mehmet couldn't believe his luck having known her literally all his life and having her fall in love with him in *lise*. The children, now nineteen and seventeen were his pride and joy and he loved them fiercely. He was looking at photos of them on the wall when Yeşim joined him in the living room. She smiled and gave him a long passionate kiss. He still made her heart beat fast. "We still have five minutes," he murmured, putting his arms around her tightly and returning her kiss with one of his own.

Aylin was not happy about this dinner. Not one little bit. She was furious at Nazlı for sharing her secret. Nervous about men after her failed marriage, she hadn't wanted to introduce her friends to İlker for some time yet. But here she was, dressed for dinner and pacing the floor while she waited for him to pick her up. She looked in the mirror again. She'd tamed her wild silver hair into respectable curls tonight, and wore large gold hoops in her ears. A bit of red lipstick had given her face some colour. She supposed she was still a reasonably attractive woman. At least for fifty.

Nazlı, on the other hand, was excited. She and Yıldırım had started to talk about living together and she wanted this evening to go well. She'd told him all about her friends, including Fiona. He didn't use his high school English often, and he was a little nervous, but Nazlı assured him that Fiona's Turkish was very good. She looked every inch the yogi, in a bohemian dress and a long braid that she wore over her shoulder. A touch of mascara was all the makeup she wore and yet she glowed. She couldn't wait for Yıldırım to arrive.

Fiona and Metin lay next to each other in bed breathing heavily. "You've ruined my makeup," she joked. "But it was worth it."

He rolled up on his elbow and rested his cheek in his hand. "Do we have to go to this dinner?"

She swatted him playfully. "Of course we do! And besides, you promised Mehmet." She looked at the clock and bolted out of bed. "And if we don't hurry we're going to be late." Fiona pulled her dress back on and ran a brush through her hair before pinning it back casually. She looked at her reflection in the mirror and Metin joined her. He pulled her hair to one side and began nibbling on her neck. She giggled. "Don't start again!"

Dinner was a success. İlker and Yıldırım were interesting, intelligent men who got along well with Metin and Mehmet and each other. It was obvious by the way they treated the women that the matches were good. Fiona took photos of the group and sent them to Hayley, encouraging her to come for another visit.

Fiona was taken with the efforts Yıldırım went to in speaking English with her, even after he'd realized she really could manage very well in Turkish. In fact, everyone noticed that she'd improved, despite being away about eight months. Fiona had been working hard and had spent some time with an online tutor when she was in Canada and it had helped bring her to the next level. She had been proud when Metin told her he thought she could navigate Turkish bureaucracy on her own now, which would be quite an accomplishment. Everyone laughed when she recounted the story of her Christmas package and university applications. Fiona admitted to them that it still got harder in loud places and when she was tired, but generally she was pleased with her fluency.

İlker was a lovely man, and his humour had them laughing all night. Fiona liked him a lot and thought something real was happening there. It would be good for Aylin to have some romantic stability, she thought. Aylin kept stealing glances at him all evening, and at the end of the night, he put his arm around her protectively, as they walked up the street.

"You did really well tonight, *sevgilim*," Metin complimented Fiona on the way home as she lay her head on his shoulder in the taxi. "I think I'll leave my English to Canada and speak to you only in Turkish here."

She yawned. "Not yet, please. I really was starting to lose the thread of conversation by the end of the night even with the studying I've been doing." She snuggled deeper into him as the car crossed the bridge back to Kuzguncuk. "What did you think of the guys? In English, I'm sleepy."

Metin indulged her. "İlker seems perfect for Aylin. He grounds her. I hope he sticks around for a while. And Yıldırım is a good match for Nazlı too. I liked them both. You?"

"*Aynen*," she mumbled as her eyes fluttered closed. Metin chuckled and put his arm around her. They seemed to agree on most things.

In Beşiktaş, Yeşim sat on the side of the bed struggling with the clasp of her necklace. "How did Aylin seem to you," she asked Mehmet as he leaned over to help.

"What do you mean?" He kissed her neck and handed her the gold chain.

"She's been skittish ever since she's been back. More so than she used to be when we were kids. But she seemed different tonight. Calmer, happier. More content than I've seen her in a long time."

"I thought that was just nervous energy about the café, I guess. But you're right. Tonight she was more serene, less jumpy. İlker must bring out the best in her."

Yeşim joined her husband under the covers. "I hope so. If anyone deserves some happiness, it's Aylin. She's been through so much." She giggled as Mehmet's kisses tickled her collarbone. "If only I knew what I did to deserve you."

Metin and Fiona headed to Datça for the mid-semester break. Fiona loved how cool the stone house kept them in the heat and she looked forward to getting back there after they finished in the market. She had thrown on a linen shirt over her tank top and her usual floppy hat and sunglasses to protect her creamy freckled skin from the sun while they chose fresh fish and vegetables for dinner as well as some fruit and cheese.

Later that afternoon, she sat reading a novel on a chaise in the shade while Metin thumbed through the paper in the hammock.

"Okay, you win," she signed contentedly. He looked at her and shook his head, not understanding. "The lake may be beautiful, but the weather here is outstanding."

Metin laughed loudly. "Then I'm glad we have the best of all worlds." He slid out of the hammock to give her a kiss. "*Çok şanslıyız, sevgilim.* We are very lucky, my love."

Too soon, they were back at the airport. Jamie had proposed to Lauren in a canoe at the lake on the Canada Day holiday, and Fiona was anxious to get back to congratulate them properly.

Max and Ben had also spent a week at the lake house just before she returned. Fiona had promised Holly she'd take the twins for a week in early August, before they began junior kindergarten, and the whole family was planning to come up later in the month. Summer was too short and they had to squeeze in as much swimming and boating as they could.

She'd spent a long time working on the sketch she'd begun on her first day of this trip. It was small, but she liked it so she'd framed it and left it on their bed as a gift. Metin didn't know she was doing it, so she hoped he'd be pleasantly surprised. When he video-chatted with her, he showed her the prominent place it had in the bedroom. He wanted to wake up every morning seeing the beautiful sketch of the view out of the *cumba* windows that she had done.

The plans for the book launch were well in hand, after several more meetings with Gökçe. Metin couriered a copy to Fiona as soon as he had a press copy in his hands. And then the flurry of interviews and readings began as he finished up the semester. Gökçe had been right. This book was going to do well. She had worked with her colleagues in New York and Toronto and they developed a promotion plan that worked well with Metin's schedule.

Fiona and Metin video-chatted and texted up a storm, missing each other very much, but surprisingly, they were both beginning to see that these short times apart might actually be good for them. It gave them a chance to give their full attention to important projects without worrying about inconveniencing the other. Fiona used some of the time for long girls' evenings or to devote to her family and she imagined Metin did the same. And then, when they were together, they could be present for each other in a more focussed way. It didn't stop them longing for each other though. Video-chatting helped them keep their relationship alive when they were apart, but it couldn't replace the joy of touch. Metin knew he'd appreciate Fiona more than ever when he saw her next.

Chapter 35

Fiona slid her hand inside Metin's as they walked across the airport terminal in Toronto back to her car. He gave it a quick squeeze. They both felt the thrill of skin-to-skin contact. Fiona couldn't wait to get Metin home. As electrifying as holding hands was, nothing could replace that half-drunk feeling of Metin wrapped around her in bed, her head tucked under his chin and his arm draped over her almost possessively.

Metin met Gökçe's Toronto colleague and was excited. There were radio and newspaper interviews scheduled in the coming weeks and some speaking opportunities were taking shape that intrigued Metin a great deal.

In a week, he would start lecturing. He had classes scheduled Tuesdays through Thursday mornings and he planned office hours in the afternoons. That left Mondays and Fridays free for book promotion and to spend as many long weekends at the lake as they wanted. They loved to take the canoe out on the lake on autumn mornings to check on the progress of the fall colours, and they snuggled together in front of the fireplace on chilly evenings.

They hadn't been together in the spring for Metin's fiftieth birthday, but he wanted to do something special for Fiona's in December. Classes would be done, but they wouldn't be at the lake house just yet. Working secretly with Holly and Ben, they planned a party at Ben and Max's house. It was perfectly located so all her old friends could come by. And it would be natural for the guys to have them for dinner, so she'd never suspect. Metin asked their Turkish friends and his brother and sister to record birthday wishes. He was especially touched when Yusef sent a separate greeting. Metin even reached out to Hayley. And at the last minute, Holly had the twins, who would be with a sitter the evening of the party, sing "Happy Birthday" to their gran and she begged Metin to include it. He was happy to oblige.

"It's nice of them to have us for dinner," Fiona said as she pulled on a pair of cream wool pants. "But it does mean it's a busy weekend. We have the concert tomorrow too." It was the weekend before her birthday, and Christmas was only ten days away. She pulled a bright blue cashmere sweater over her head and reached behind her head to flip her hair out. "Do you mind?" she asked Metin.

"Of course not," he replied. "I like spending time with Ben and Max." All the final preparations had come into place and Fiona still had no idea. How they'd kept it a secret, he would never know.

They rang the doorbell and then walked in, as they usually did. Metin felt Fiona jump under his arm, as a living room crowded with her family and friends erupted with shouts of "Surprise!"

She brought her hands to her mouth and then dropped them again as the biggest smile came over her face. She turned to Metin. "Did you do . . ." She was cut off as someone pressed a glass of champagne into her hand and swept her away into the crowd of well-wishers.

When it came time for cake, Metin stood in front of the giant television in the family room. He clinked his glass with a fork several times before the room quieted.

"Thank you all for coming tonight. I know most of you by now, but for those I don't know yet, I am Metin, and I love this woman we are celebrating tonight." There were hoots and hollers from the crowd. "I met Fiona when we were just teenagers. Somehow, I was stupid enough to let her slip away from me then. I'm not that stupid anymore." Laughter filled the room. "I'm sure you have all had a chance to give her your birthday wishes, but there are friends of ours in Turkey who couldn't be here. I thought about having them call, but it's four o'clock in the morning there." More laughter. "We have a special way of saying happy birthday in Turkish. *İyi ki doğdun.* It literally means 'It's good that you were born.' And so, *iyi ki doğdun* Fiona*'cığım* and enjoy these birthday greetings from afar." Ben dimmed the lights and played the video.

There were tears in Fiona's eyes even before she saw Nazlı on the television. She told the story of how scared and nervous she was the day she first met Fiona. Yeşim talked about how much it meant that Fiona had rekindled their friendship. Aylin sent her thanks for her strength when she needed it. Fiona was surprised to see Hayley's face, and blushed when her friend said how inspiring she'd been even as a teenager and how thrilled she was to know her as an adult. She sobbed against Metin's chest when Tamer, in his halting English, said what a gift she was to his brother. Safiye told the story of how Fiona had helped them through their mother's death. Yusuf called her *abla* and his Turkish rendition of the "Happy Birthday" song made her smile and then when her grandchildren closed out the show dancing while they sang the English version, she joined the whole room in laughter.

Fiona clinked her champagne glass. "Thank you all for coming. And thank you to the mystery organizers." Pointing to Metin, she continued, "I'm sure this guy had help. But most of all, thank you, Metin." Fiona turned and faced him. "*Hayatım*, I love you more than you can know." The cheers from her friends and family seemed to disappear as she kissed him.

They had a week to themselves at the lake before the family arrived on Christmas Eve and the house erupted with chaos. One by one, Fiona's children trickled in and added to the craziness.

Jamie was first, wearing a Santa hat and carrying in armloads of gifts. Just as he brought in the last boxes, Daisy pulled in the driveway and he helped her in with her things. They joined Fiona and Metin for a cup of tea beside the fire, warming their toes near the flames.

Jon and Jenna had dozed off in the car on the way up and were almost vibrating with excitement when Holly and Greg unbuckled them from their booster seats and set them free. Tonight Santa would come, and their mum and dad had assured them he would know to find them at the lake. Refuelled from a quick snack, the twins raced outside with Greg and Jamie to build a giant snowman while Holly unpacked in the guest house. Metin took one last turn with a snow shovel on the ice so it would be clear if anyone wanted to skate. Fiona had tried to teach him, but he'd quickly decided this was a sport best left to younger people.

When the kids came running back in from snowman building, there was hot chocolate waiting.

"Thank you, Gran. Thank you, Auntie Daisy," they said politely as their aunt snuck extra marshmallows into their mugs.

"What about us?" Jamie asked, pointing to his and Greg's steaming mugs.

"I've got you covered," smiled Metin, pulling out a bottle of peppermint schnapps and pouring a generous shot into each.

Simon was last to arrive. His office hadn't closed until noon and then he'd had one last gift to get. Jenna heard the crunch of tires on snow first.

"Uncle Simon's here!" she shouted, running to the door to meet him.

"Hey there, munchkin," he greeted her, ruffling her hair. Jon was right behind her and he picked them both up in his arms, closing the door behind him with his foot.

Christmas morning finally came, and the twins fairly shrieked with excitement when they learned they would be able to help hand out the gifts this year, now that they were in school. They took their new responsibilities very seriously, delivering a big hug and kiss to the recipient of every package they doled out.

Ben and Max drove up early Boxing Day. They had spent Christmas morning quietly in the city as they preferred to. The men had acquired a ragtag group of friends over the years with no family for one reason or another, and in recent years, their Christmas dinner had become quite anticipated in their circle. But Boxing Day was always reserved for their nieces and nephews.

Shortly after lunch, Metin drove up to the train station at noon to pick up the rest of the guests. Jamie's fiancée Lauren — they still hadn't set a date — had organized for Simon's long-time girlfriend, Leah, and Daisy's new boyfriend, Rahim, to join her on the same train, to make collecting them easier. They would all go home with their respective partners tomorrow.

It would be a full house that night. They would fit, but barely. They would be fourteen around the Boxing Day dinner table so Fiona drafted some help to prepare the meal as their new guests got settled in.

Dinner was wildly successful. Lauren regaled them with stories from her classroom of seven-year-olds, and they could always count on Leah to share funny stories about her Quebecois upbringing with her thickly accented, but perfect English. She and Simon had made the trip to Montreal to celebrate Hanukkah with her family a week ago. Leah showed the twins how to spin a dreidel and told them that they lit candles and there were presents for all eight nights of the celebration. The middle child of nine, she'd seen her fair share of big family events. Daisy had been concerned that Rahim, who she'd only been seeing for two months, would be overwhelmed by her family, but he told stories about his extended Indian family that had everyone in stitches. He had three brothers and two sisters and was looking forward to sharing Diwali next year with Daisy and couldn't wait to see her in a sari. His youngest sister had a gorgeous teal one with gold accents that would look spectacular with Daisy's freckles and long red curls. He and Daisy were getting serious fast.

Metin was more comfortable with the mayhem this year, even with the extra guests, and he chimed in with his own stories of *Şeker Bayram*. He taught them how children kiss their grandparent's hands and then touch them to their foreheads to honour their elders. Jon and Jenna's eyes bugged out when they learned that when you did that, your grandparents gave you money. By the end of the evening, the twins were convinced that they were hard done by because Christmas was only one day long.

The adults packed the children off to bed and small groups started to form. Lauren draped her arm around Jamie's shoulder as he played *tavla* with Metin. Ben, Max, Simon, and Leah were deep in conversation about human rights. Holly lay her head on Greg's shoulder as they put their feet up for the first time all day and sighed with relief that their children were finally asleep. It was Rahim's first visit to the lake and Daisy was showing him some of the family treasures. He kept her close and it was obvious to anyone watching that they were very much in love.

Fiona took in the whole scene as she started to get evening cups of tea ready. She was a lucky woman indeed.

Holly and Greg stayed on for two more days after the others had left. Jon and Jenna hads the time of their lives tobogganing, building more snowmen, and skating on the patch of ice that Metin shovelled every morning after the previous night's snowfall.

In the afternoons, he played board games with children and read to them to give their parents time for a break. Greg and Holly snuck off to the guest house above the garage for an hour or two, where there was a cozy couch and second fireplace. They were grateful to Metin for this opportunity to unwind alone. With the kids, he was discovering English children's books for the first time. Roald Dahl's *Charlie and the Chocolate Factory* was a new favourite as was Dr. Seuss's *Fox in Sox*. Listening to him try to read its tongue twisters sent the twins into fits of giggles. Fiona, listening in from the kitchen, where she was often elbow deep in meal preparations, laughed along with them.

When she and Metin finally waved goodbye as Holly and her family headed out in their jam-packed minivan, they tidied up all the toys and books, and collapsed on the couch.

"I think *I* need a nap," said Fiona, putting her feet up on the coffee table. "I'd forgotten how exhausting young kids could be."

"*Haklısın*. You're right. Those two are great, and I've enjoyed having them here, but they're a handful. I think I was right to not have children, you know. I would have been a terrible father at Greg's age. No patience. It's easier to have grandchildren, I think. How on earth did you manage raising four of them?" Metin asked, putting his arm around her and pulling her close.

Chapter 36

Over the years, Fiona and Metin fell into a comfortable habit. He would teach the fall semester in Toronto, and they would split their time between the city and the lake, always spending Christmas with her whole family. He returned to İstanbul just after New Year's Day and they would spend the winter months working hard separately. Fiona flew to İstanbul in early April and they went to Datça in June. She returned to Canada in July. This left the lake house free for her family to enjoy in the early summer. Then she'd return to spend time with them at the lake before Metin flew in again in late August. He always liked to spend the last week at the lake before the cycle started all over again.

It was an unusual arrangement, and had its complications, but it worked for them.

Fiona and Metin took to leaving some of their things in each other's country, to make travelling easier. Fiona loved to open Metin's closet and drink in the smell of him whenever she missed him. He did the same, and fingered the fabric of the peignoirs she left in Turkey, sighing a little when he did. It didn't erase the ache of missing each other, but it held them over.

Suddenly, they had been living like this for five years. Metin was thinking about retiring. Yeşim and Mehmet already had. Ben was toying with the idea, and Max had sold the shop to Jason, who'd mentored Jamie so many years ago. Fiona wasn't ready to stop yet, but she had scaled back. Nazlı and Yıldırım had married quietly and without any fuss one glorious autumn afternoon. Fiona had finally forgiven her for doing it while she and Metin were in Canada. Aylin and İlker were madly in love and living together.

Jamie and Lauren had been married for three years now. They had a two-year-old boy they'd named Sam, who was his father's delight, and they wanted more. Rahim proposed to Daisy and they planned to get married in the fall and have babies right away. Daisy was thinking three or even four. Holly thought she was crazy. She and Greg had long ago decided the twins were enough for them. Jon and Jenna were almost ten now. Simon was working long associate's hours and was on track to becoming a full partner in a few years. Leah had moved with him and joked that if she hadn't she would never have seen him.

Yusuf was sixteen and thinking about universities. He asked Fiona a lot of questions about Canadian schools and Safiye was worried he might want to go there. Metin teased her and said if that's what it took to get her and Kerem to visit them, then he was behind Yusuf all the way.

Fiona had always wanted to show her children İstanbul and this year they were finally coming. The kids had decided to leave partners and children for a week and saved their money. The trip was already planned when Hayley made a surprise announcement that she was coming back with her family too. She'd finally convinced her husband and was excited to share the city with Tom and Jack, who were now several years older than she had been as an exchange student. Unfortunately, they hadn't managed to coordinate it for the same time, but still, it would be a magical summer.

Fiona was surprisingly nervous when they went to the airport to collect her kids. She and Metin spoke mostly English in Canada, and he slipped into North American customs. But equally, she knew she slipped into Turkish customs and she spoke almost exclusively Turkish now. She wondered how different she would seem to her children and what it would be like when her two worlds collided. Metin told her not to worry. Suddenly they came bursting out of the arrivals gate. Fiona saw them first and gave them a wave.

Fiona gave her girls kisses and then did the same with her boys. "This is how we do it here," she explained, seeing their surprised reactions. "You'll get used to it."

"*Haydi.* Come on," Metin said. "Let's get a couple of taxis, and get you settled into your hotel. You must be exhausted."

Fiona and Metin waited in the hotel restaurant drinking *çay* while the kids settled in their rooms in the historic peninsula. The Kuzguncuk flat was simply too small to host all of them. Metin was teaching most of the week, so Fiona played tour guide to her family, and he joined them later in the afternoons, feeling like a full member of her family.

Fiona showed them around some of the city's most famous historical sites including the Blue Mosque and Topkapı Palace. They spent some time shopping at the Grand Bazaar and Fiona took them up the Galata Tower. She also showed them some of more modern İstanbul and one day took them across to the Asian side of the city to show them the school she'd attended thirty years ago. That afternoon, they headed to Kuzguncuk so they could see where she and Metin lived together. When they saw the views, they understood why she loved it so much.

Another day, they took the long Bosphorus tour and climbed the hill to the castle at Anadolu Kavağı where they sat in a lovely fish restaurant that overlooked the Black Sea before taking the return trip home.

"What's that smile for, Mum?" asked Simon, seeing his mother drift off.

Fiona told them about when she and Metin had done this same trip when they were teenagers, when all they could afford was fish sandwiches.

They went out for dinner every night, sampling all kinds of Turkish cuisine. Metin and Fiona took them to a five-star seaside restaurant in Bebek where the stars dined, to their favourite place in Kuzguncuk near their flat, to a tradesman-style *lokanta,* and to a Syrian restaurant they had started going to occasionally. Fiona made sure they had some great Turkish breakfasts and they ate street food all day long. From *simit* to *lahmacun*, from *durum* to *döner*, from *kumpir* to *midye,* they were never hungry.

On their last full day, they had lunch at Aylin's Umut Kafe, where they could finally meet Fiona's friends. Aylin told stories about their mother, embarrassing Fiona. Yeşim arrived as they were finishing lunch, full of apologies and blaming her lateness on İstanbul traffic.

"Have you had your fortunes read yet?" she asked. When they said no, she asked Aylin for *kahve* for the young people. "I'll do it this time," she said to Nazlı, whose eyes had just lit up when Yıldırım walked through the door.

In Holly's cup, she saw dark lines. "This means you will reach your goals." In Jamie's cup, she saw babies. "Two more, I think. And coming soon." For Simon, she predicted a promotion from the ladder she saw. "And this square? It means you have peace in your life. This is very good." When it came to Daisy's cup, she smiled. "For you, I also see a fish. So you will have good luck in all things you pursue.

"It's just for fun, but fortunes have a way of coming true. Just look at your mum and Metin." Yeşim directed her next words to them. "I admit, I had my doubts at times — and I think I told them that more than once. But not anymore. Your love is so strong that you make it work. You two belong together." She smiled as they shared a kiss.

Fiona's phone buzzed as she and Metin were getting ready for bed. It was Nazlı.

What lovely children you have. You are very blessed.

Metin and Fiona offered to take everyone to a Turkish bath on their last day in the city. The boys weren't sure about that, so Metin went to Plan B and they split up. Fiona and the girls were scrubbed and massaged within an inch of their lives at one of the oldest bathhouses in the city late in the afternoon and had dinner on their own at a lovely rooftop restaurant near the hotel. The boys decided to go to Süleymaniye Mosque on their own and they wandered around the hilly streets behind the Grand Bazaar while Metin did a bit of work. When he was done he rushed to pick them up and they had a guys' night out. Metin took them to a *meyhane* in Nevizade Sokak, a tiny street filled with tables and chairs. They drank *rakı* and ate a whole selection of *meze* listening to live traditional Turkish music. After dinner, he took them to a jazz club and finally, very late in the evening, they walked down the hill from Taksim and feasted on *kokoreç* and *ıslak* hamburgers.

"Now you've had a proper Turkish night out," he told them.

Fiona's kids all gushed about İstanbul at breakfast the next day and how they wanted to come back with their partners in the next year or two. They were starting to understand why Fiona loved it so much. They all agreed their mother and Metin were different here. They couldn't explain why, and it wasn't that it was better or worse. They'd discussed it in the hotel and the conclusion was that they simply adapted to the culture of the country they were in. Hugs and kisses were exchanged, and suddenly, they were heading to the airport.

Metin put his arm around Fiona's shoulder. "Be strong, *canım*," he said, kissing the top of her head. She nodded, not trusting her voice. She'd see them again soon.

∽

A week later, Hayley flew into Atatürk airport, this time with Brad and her boys in tow. They spent several days being tourists, and now, they were having their own special reunion. After the lunch rush, Aylin had closed her café for this special event. İlker had his arm draped casually over her shoulder and she was laughing with Nazlı who had joined them. Yıldırım was parking the car.

Yeşim arrived next and she was expecting her children and husband shortly. Metin would be with them as soon as his lecture was over, to round out the party.

Brad and the boys had enjoyed their week, and were finally able to understand why Hayley continued to wax nostalgic about her exchange year and this amazing city.

Tom, was finishing up his undergraduate degree in oceanography and Jack, had just finished his final paper for his master's in Art History. He'd been blown away by everything he'd seen in the historical peninsula. He couldn't believe his mom had spent a year here, and he was already trying to figure out how he could stay longer to learn more about the history, but also to take in the eclectic modern art scene that he'd heard about from Aylin earlier in the week. Jack had learned a few words and phrases from his mom and also from Aylin, Fiona, and Nazlı, who he'd met earlier in the week. He was proudly using them whenever he could.

Yıldırım came through the door next. Nazlı brought her husband a glass of tea, and was rewarded with a kiss.

Fiona had been helping out at the café today, and was still behind the counter when Metin arrived. "*Hoş geldin, hayatım*," she greeted him. He leaned over the counter and returned the greeting with a kiss that almost knocked her off her feet. Five years on, their eclectic patchwork agreement continued to work for them, and he smiled when he saw that she was wearing her seagull pendant. Their passion for each other had continued to grow and their love was evident to anyone watching. They joined their friends at the table, bringing two more glasses of tea.

"*Abla, abla!*" Fiona turned her head to see Yusuf arriving with Safiye and Kerem just a few steps behind. Giving them all kisses, she introduced them to Hayley's family.

Finally, Mehmet arrived with his children. İlker stood up and brought *çay* to the family. No longer gangly teenagers, Melek and Kaan had grown into a pair of wonderful young people just starting their careers. Kaan had stayed in Turkey for university and recently had a promotion at the architectural firm he'd been with since graduation. Melek had gone to London to study fine arts and had joined İstanbul Modern, a well-respected art gallery in Beyoğlu a year ago.

"*Hoş geldiniz,*" Aylin welcomed them, and brought more *çay* for everyone with help from İlker, who slipped his arm around her waist. Jack was stirring sugar into his glass, the tiny spoon tinkling as it went around and around. But when Nazlı introduced the young people, his spoon stopped. She shared a meaningful glance with Fiona and the other ladies.

Jack had looked instantly smitten as he took in the raven-haired beauty in front of him. Melek was tall and willowy with long limbs, and long silky dark brown hair. She looked like she might blow away in the wind, until you looked in her brilliant blue eyes. There you saw a strong, determined woman. It was that combination of softness and strength that had Jack tongue-tied. She sipped her hot *çay* gracefully. Jack still hadn't figured out how to hold the rim of the glass so it didn't burn his fingers.

"M . . . M . . . *Merhaba,*" he managed finally.

Melek smiled. "*Sana da merhabalar*, Jack. Pleased to meet you. I do hope you're enjoying İstanbul," she said with a perfect English accent as she took in the tall blond former college football player in front of her who her mother had been raving about all week. He'd been having trouble with his tea, she noticed, but that didn't bother her. She flashed him a confident smile. "My mother tells me you're an art historian. Our antiquities are famous around the world of course, but I hope I can show you the modern side of art in our city as well," she offered. "And just wait until you see some of our incredible street art." She took another sip of her tea.

"I would love that," he stammered and her heart melted.

And over tea, another İstanbul romance had begun.

CPSIA information can be obtained
at www.ICGtesting.com
Printed in the USA
BVHW051551210622
640113BV00007B/6

9 781039 145603